Second Coming

George McCarthy

Mom + Larry
Hope you enjoy
the story!
Thanks
George
G McCarthy

First published by Dog Ear Publishing
4011 Vincennes Rd
Indianapolis, IN 46268
www.dogearpublishing.net

dog ear PUBLISHING

ISBN: 978-1-4575-3970-1

This book is printed on acid-free paper.

Printed in the United States of America

CHAPTER 1

At 12:30 am, Detective Sergeant Danny Warburton climbed into his Hyundai Santa Fe for the 25-minute drive home. It hadn't been a particularly busy shift, but he'd had a short delay getting out of the bureau because he'd gone over some late paperwork. He continually told his detectives to get their reports to him prior to 11, but on the rare occasion when they did get them in late, he didn't break balls. They were a good bunch. They might screw around sometimes, but when there was serious work to be done they never let him down.

Danny usually went to the department weight room after work, which was on the third floor of the building, but tonight he didn't feel up to it. The combination of the 30-minute delay to get off work and the five hours he'd spent mowing the lawn and doing other yard chores before his shift were cause enough to skip the workout.

At 5'9", 175 pounds, and 38 years old, he tried to keep himself in shape. His short, curly brown hair showed traces of grey at the temples and a patch on the right side over his forehead. He supposed that weight training and jogging every other day were his way of trying to hang onto his youth.

Danny looked over the cloth CD holder that slipped onto the visor and couldn't decide who he wanted to listen to. He had several choices from Fiona Apple, Sade, and Norah Jones: he was a sucker for a sultry voice. He narrowed it down to the smooth jazz saxophone of Mindi Abair or the sweet voice of Corinne Bailey Rae. Mindi's sax was what he usually needed after a long shift, but the last eight hours were not stressful. He popped in a Bailey Rae CD and began the short ride home.

The Santa Fe hit the Warburton driveway just before 1 am, and the operator headed for the dimly lit house. Danny was used to unlocking the door and easing in as quietly as possible. His wife of 13 years, Carmel, was asleep in the master bedroom. The girls, Kate and Sandy, shared a room on the second floor, and his son Jack, the youngest of the three, had his own room next to the girls. Danny looked in on Jack and then the girls.

Kate and Sandy were getting bigger and were cramped in one room. He looked at the posters and pictures of the current teen idols and boy bands that covered the walls and the clutter of furniture and thought for the tenth time that week that they needed a four-bedroom house. He could convert the basement into another bedroom, but Carmel was reluctant to have an 11-year-old on her own down there. He didn't understand his wife's argument, but he'd told Kate he would work on her mother. Maybe by the end of summer he could soften Carmel's stance and then have the fall and winter to work on that project.

Danny liked doing construction-type projects and was good with his hands. He had learned a lot from his grandfather and uncles, who had all been in the construction business for years. He thought of it as relaxing, and the orderliness of it all, the measuring, cutting, drilling, and hammering, also appealed to him. Sometimes it seemed to him that the carpentry was the exact opposite of what he did for a living. He liked police work too, but wearing the badge brought on the responsibility of others and being a supervisor added to that responsibility, which occasionally became heavy.

He poured himself a glass of merlot, unwrapped a Hav-A-Tampa, and stepped onto the back deck. He kept the drinking down to one or two glasses of wine when he did indulge, he was all too aware of his problem with the bottle during his army years. On the flip side, he was nowhere near ready to give up his nightly cigar. Danny lit the cigar and inhaled deeply, knowing, as do all smokers, that this wasn't good for him but enjoying it immensely. He settled into a deck chair and relished the early June night. The sky was clear, the half-moon was visible through the trees, and about a million stars were shining overhead.

He didn't like a lot of things about working the 4 to midnight shift, such as being away from dinner with his family; getting called back to work a serious crime after one or two hours of sleep; and then following leads for the next 20 hours, to name a few. But his wine, cigar, and the solitude of the early morning hours were some of the perks.

Before he was done with half of the cigar, Danny had drained the glass of wine and knew that this was a two-glass night. Balancing the cigar on the ash tray, he stood and went inside to pour himself another glass. He returned to his seat with his refill and stared out into the night. As the wine's warmth coursed through his body, he did what he did at least once a week during his time on the deck: he reflected on his life to this point.

He always thought that he'd had it pretty good. He was 38 years old and had been married to Carmel for 13 years. She was five years his junior and as hot as the day she said "I do." Carmel had blessed him with three children. Katherine, the oldest at eleven, and Sandra, at nine, were his two beautiful princesses. Jack, who wasn't planned, was six and the spitting image of his father.

He had been on the New Britain Police Department for 15 years, the last two in the Detective Bureau. He loved his assignment, and he had the greatest crew he could have hoped for. All in all, he was very happy with his life so far. Were there days that sucked? Sure there were, but they were nothing when you looked at the bigger picture.

He sat on his back deck with a wide grin on his face, as he always did when he thought of his family and his career. Then he noticed a bright spot in the sky that seemed to be right above his head. The flash of light was far away, and his attention was diverted to a movement in the back yard. A deer, perhaps? When he looked back toward the sky, he was surprised to see that the bright spot was a lot closer and was bright enough to make him squint. Danny stood in shock and watched as the light came even closer to his house. He felt like he couldn't move as the light came closer and slowed to a hover over the deck.

He was able to see some detail of a device that had an aura about it which he assumed accounted for the glow. It was metallic and about as big as a refrigerator but thinner. Two metal protrusions were at the top and the bottom, and Danny instantly thought they were antennae. He was sure he was seeing a UFO and took a step back as the object came to a stop about a foot from the deck and ten feet from him. Blue and red lights were on either side of the UFO, and he could do nothing but stare into the aura of the device.

His breath was shallow, and he felt an electricity surround his body. The UFO split down the middle, and a set of double doors opened up, as blinding light hit him in the face. He felt a presence envelope him, and the next thing he knew he was under the UFO in some kind of bubble that afforded him oxygen and he was rocketing up toward space at an incredible speed.

Danny struggled to remain conscious as he left the earth's atmosphere and headed toward the dark side of the moon. As he circled the moon, he saw a large object on the far side and mouthed the words that he would come to call the object in the following years: Mother Ship. Before he had another thought, the g-force became too much, and he passed out.

# # #

A low humming sound seemed to come from nearby and far away at the same time. This was the first thought that Danny had as he struggled to consciousness. At first he didn't know where he was and believed he was in his own bed and couldn't understand why he didn't feel Carmel next to him. As his eyes focused and he came out of his haze, three bright lights flicked on over his head. He remembered the ride below the UFO, and he bolted upright. Danny looked around and saw that he was in a small room with grey curved walls. The only fixture was the bench where he had been sleeping. His cop instincts kicked in, and he immediately looked for clues for a way out. He noticed that the walls looked smooth, and he saw no crease or break that indicated a doorway. The air that he breathed tasted fresh, but no vents or other openings were visible for air circulation.

He knew that he was inside a UFO, specifically the large ship he saw on the dark side of the moon: the Mother Ship. Some of his friends used to give him a hard time for believing other intelligent life existed in the universe and not believing in a supreme being, but for Danny, aliens were a matter of odds. If the scientists were to be believed and the universe was endless and also expanding, then the odds that humans were the only intelligent life was not only arrogant but illogical. But to believe in a "God" that watched over humanity just did not wash with him. He had seen too much of man's inhumanity to man as a cop, especially considering the state of the world today, what with starvation and oppression in third world countries, dictators who lived lavish lives as their people struggled to survive, and few cared when the elderly, infirm, and very young were victimized. No, if there were a being that cared for the people of the world, and he had the power to save the truly innocent, it would be only logical that he would intervene. But since no one has intervened, the only conclusion is that this Supreme Being does not exist. Danny was a diehard atheist, but given the circumstances he currently found himself, he hoped he was wrong, and whatever God was out there would save him from an alien anal probe.

As soon as he got up from the bench, it slid into the wall and disappeared. He watched the bench go into the wall, but as soon as it was gone, he saw no indication that it was ever there. He could see no seam where the bench was. He ran his hand over the space previously occupied by the bench but felt only the smooth wall. Danny felt his way around the room in hopes that he could determine the location of the door by touch, because his eyes saw nothing. The magic show that the bench put on dashed his hopes of locating the exit. Nonetheless, because he couldn't think of anything else to do, he went to the wall and work his way around the room feeling for any abnormality. He started to move to his left and was about ten feet from where he began, when he heard a whoosh from his right and turned to see a doorway open up as a portion of the wall moved from the floor into the ceiling.

Danny went for his off duty weapon on his right hip and then heard himself mutter "shit". He usually carried a Smith and Wesson 40 caliber in a pancake holster when he was off duty but it wasn't there now. Back for her last birthday he had bought Carmel a bistro set for the back deck. It was a nice little set with two wicker chairs on swivel bases and a glass top table. The first time after he had bought the set, he went out to the back deck for his after work wine and cigar. His Smith was strapped on, and when he sat in the bistro chair, the bottom of the holster jammed against the arm of the chair and drove the grip of the gun into his side. Since that day, Danny always put the Smith in the lock box before pouring his wine. He knew this when he reached for the side arm, but it was instinct to fill his hand when he felt threatened.

All he could do was stare at the opening in the wall. He felt a presence about to enter the room and didn't even realize that he was holding his breath.

CHAPTER 2

Danny began breathing again with a deep inhale that filled his lungs, and then he took shallow and rapid gulps of air as adrenalin coursed through his body. He could only stare in astonishment as two robed beings entered the room. From the time he awoke, he'd known he was in some kind of alien craft, but to be in the presence of other beings that were not human and whose intentions were unknown was unnerving.

His first observation was that the aliens were quite tall. He estimated that both were about eight feet in height. At 5′9″, he was used to being a little shorter than most males of his species, but he felt particularly dwarfed by this pair. The robes were dark green but at times shimmered as the beings moved, which gave them a metallic air. Their faces, if they had any, were not visible, as were any other parts of their bodies.

The aliens seemed to glide rather than walk to the center of the room, as Danny instinctively tried to put a wall to his back and moved to the farthest part of the room from the aliens. About the time he was assigned to the Detective Division, Danny was asked by the commander of the SWAT team, Captain Franti, to take over as supervisor of the Crisis Negotiating team. This was a dream come true for him, as being a crisis negotiator was one of the jobs he wanted since his first day on the department and relished in the intense training that ensued. It was this training that kicked in during the stress of the initial encounter with the aliens on the Mother Ship.

With no weapons, he thought his chances of overpowering the two aliens were thin at best. And besides, what would he do if he succeeded in escaping this room? Danny had no way of knowing how many more occupied the ship. Even if these were the only two, how would he get back to

Earth? He didn't think he'd find an instruction manual on how to drive this thing in the glove compartment. No, in this situation Danny believed that his best course of action would be to rely on his skills as a negotiator. Apparently Franti knew what he saw in the new Detective Sgt. as he excelled as a negotiator and was able to use that gift to talk people out of their current actions and believe that the alternative that he suggested was actually what was best for them, which was often the truth. He was good and had saved lives by using only words.

Danny began "Good evening. My name is Detective Sergeant Daniel Warburton, and I assume you wished to speak to me on some matter. I only deduce this based on the extravagant measures you have used in order to bring me here."

The aliens appeared to face each other, but this was a guess on Danny's part, as he could not see their faces. The negotiator gave it a few minutes, but no response seemed to be forthcoming from the space-bred Sequoias. He wondered if they didn't understand what he was saying. He knew a little Spanish from his days working patrol division in New Britain, and he'd picked up some German from two years when he was stationed there in the Army. But he was only fluent in English, so they'd have to adapt.

He continued, " Okay, you guys want something from me, and I want to go home and cuddle up with my naked wife and get some sleep before I have to go back to work at 4. But I have to tell you that I will not say anything about the Earth's defenses against an alien invasion, mostly because I don't know anything about that shit. I've been out of the military for 17 years. But even if I did know, I would rather die first than give you an advantage in a fight. And speaking of a fight, you two are in for a big one if you think you're putting any kind of probe up my ass. Those are the ground rules, everything else is negotiable."

Danny heard the response more in his head than through his ears as one of the aliens spoke. "Daniel, we do not believe you are in a position to negotiate. We have no desire to place anything in your rectum, and if we wanted to take over your planet, we would have done so thousands of years ago. But you are correct in your assessment that we want something from you. My partner and I are scientists on our planet and have traveled great distances to conduct an experiment on Earth. And you, Daniel, are the person we have chosen to take part in this experiment. But before we tell you any more, I must inform you that if this experiment produces negative results it may cause your planet to be isolated from the peaceful planets of this universe, which may mean extinction for your species."

His bravado was shaken by the alien's response. Foolishly he thought by taking the reins in the conversation he could gain some kind of advantage. But these two knew they held all the cards. They knew his name and probably knew all about his life, as they said he was "chosen" for their experiment, unless this choice was random, which he felt was not the case. This was the reason behind the hesitation in a response but he did gather his wits and said, "Ok, I admit that you seem to have the upper hand. But that doesn't necessarily mean that I have nothing to negotiate. You yourself said that you want something from me, that you are scientists conducting an experiment. It doesn't sound like you're talking about a rat-in-a-maze type of experiment. It sounds like you are going to ask if I want to participate in this thing."

"You are correct, Daniel, in assuming that we would like your cooperation in this endeavor. You are our first choice, but not our only choice. Time is short, if you wish to continue your defensive stance, we may have to reconsider our options here."

The aliens hesitated, and even though there were no words between them, Danny got the impression that they were kibitzing. After a short time, he heard the alien voice in his head again. "We apologize Daniel, this has started out as an adversarial conversation, and that is not what we wanted. Believe us when we tell you that we mean you no harm, and we want to work together in this experiment. For that to happen, and although you have no reason to as we have taken you from your home and family, we would like for you to trust us."

Danny used all his negotiating skills to assess what he had just heard. The aliens were giving indications that they were being truthful, but he based his observations on what his training taught him about reading humans, not some beings from space he knew nothing about. When it came right down to it, he always relied on his gut feeling. Finally he said, "Okay, we are all adults here, I think, anyway why don't you guys lay it out for me? And as you say, I will have the choice to participate or not."

"Thank you, Daniel," one of the aliens responded and for the first time Danny thought that he did not know which alien had spoken to him.

He said, "You two gentlemen know my name and who knows what else about me. So if we are to start again in an air of mutual cooperation, I would like to know your names and understand which of you is actually speaking to me at any given time."

"Daniel," one of the aliens responded, "as you may have guessed, we communicate with you through a form of telepathy, and therefore you have no indicators as to which one of us is speaking. I believe that we can create a brief aura around us as we speak so that you can see which of us has communicated with you."

"That sounds like it would work," Danny said. "And do you have names?" A soft blue light glowed around the alien on the right, and Danny heard in his head, "In our language, our names would be unpronounceable to you, and we know of no known words that would translate our names into English."

Danny said, "Ok, but it is my habit when I talk to people to use their first names. I find it breeds relaxation on both sides of the conversation, adds a sense of familiarity, and is just damned polite. So if you don't mind, I would like to pick names for each of you."

A green aura formed around the alien on his left, and Danny heard, "That would be acceptable."

He did not need any time to think about what he would call the aliens. He had been enamored with a comic strip some years back and was saddened when it was discontinued. He had several books of compilations from the strip and decided the two main characters would be his inspiration for the aliens' monikers.

"You on the right I will call Calvin and the one who glows green will be known as Hobbes." He sensed that neither of the aliens had ever seen that particular comic strip, which was probably a good thing.

Hobbes said, "Daniel, I believe that we have made good progress toward trusting each other in a very short time, but now we are at that point where we must discuss the reason we brought you onto our ship and present to you our proposal."

"Ok, but if we are to do that here could you bring back the bench so I'll have a place to sit down if I need to?"

Calvin said, "We will be going to a much more comfortable room. This room was only used for our initial contact. We did not know how you were going to react to this situation, and this room afforded little in the way to harm yourself."

"Well, how did I do?"

Calvin responded "As we expected, but Hobbes and I were pleased you did not have your weapon strapped to your side."

Danny chuckled as the door to the room opened rapidly into the ceiling and the three stepped out.

CHAPTER 3

As Danny walked with the two beings down the hall that led from the room he was in, he couldn't help but continue to think like a cop. He tried to get his bearings as to the size of the ship he was on and the location of the front and back. It wasn't that he was thinking about an escape just the opposite. Even though he had been on the ship for a very short time, he liked Calvin and Hobbes, he was curious as to the experiment they wanted him to participate in, and, oddly enough, he trusted them.

Calvin led the trio, with Danny following and Hobbes bringing up the rear. As they continued along the hall which he noticed it was slightly curved. He also recalled, as he was hurtling toward the ship in the transporter, the basic shape of the ship was an immense oblong. He estimated there were maybe 50 or 60 floors, and that was taking into account the size of the floors to accommodate the aliens' height. He thought it odd that they had been walking for over five minutes and had yet to encounter another alien. This may have been part of the experiment, but Danny did not think that was the case. Nothing concrete, it was just a feeling he had.

A short time later, Calvin turned to his right and another door slid into the ceiling. All three entered the new room, which was bigger and was furnished with chairs, tables, and a couch that looked to Danny like it would not disappear into the floor or walls.

Hobbes offered a seat to his guest and told him to make himself comfortable. Danny selected one that looked like a recliner, but when he sat down it seemed that the cushions enveloped him. He could feel all the stress of the situation ebb from his pores.

"Holy shit, this is by far the most comfortable chair I have ever sat in. Ok, if this experiment you have in mind doesn't work out the way you want it, could I take this chair home as a consolation prize?"

Calvin and Hobbes both thought to themselves that with each passing moment, they liked Danny more and more.

"Daniel, we must begin to explain what we have in mind for you," started Hobbes. "But we understand that the human body needs food and drink to sustain its energy levels. Therefore we have brought aboard water, wine, and what your people call Pepsi products."

Danny replied, "Well, you guys did interrupt my wine and cigar time, but I should keep my head clear. So I'll have a water, please."

A thin shelf came out of the wall to Danny's left and proceeded toward the center of the room. He observed that a bottle of water was on the end of the shelf. As it reached the center of the room it angled in his direction and then came to a stop directly in front of his chair. He plucked the bottle off the shelf, which then retreated the same way it had come and as it left the room, the wall appeared as it was.

Hobbes said, "Our processors have also replicated numerous types of your food. Later we can cease our discussions so that you may consume what you wish."

"As tasty as you made that sound, I think I'll stick with the water for now." Danny didn't know if the boys picked up on his sarcasm or not, but he decided to let it go for now.

Calvin began, "Daniel, it is time for us to, as your people say, lay our cards on the table. We want to start by telling you a short history of our race as a way of showing you our sincerity and so that you may further understand the motives for our actions. Our planet is millions of miles from Earth. Even with our advanced form of space travel, it still takes our ship over 1,000 of your years to reach Earth from our home. We evolved in somewhat the same way your people have, and still are. Early in our history, like the people of Earth, we battled among ourselves. But unlike Earthlings, we quickly learned that this was counter-productive and began working together for the advancement of every being on our planet. This allowed us to put our best minds to solving the problems we all faced and to use the technological advances to create ways to help instead of harm ourselves. Our space travel program took a giant leap forward, and soon we were contacting other intelligent beings throughout the universe. We found races in all different stages of evolution, and we decided to help those struggling to survive."

Danny interrupted, "Are human beings struggling?"

"Yes, you are," replied Calvin. "We believe that if your people continue on their current path, they will destroy themselves and, in the process, make this planet uninhabitable."

Danny was shocked. He knew that mankind was in trouble, as it seemed that hardly anyone could get along, and he couldn't remember a time when a war wasn't going on in some part of the world. But he always believed that human beings would rise up from their violent ways and work as one, similar to how Calvin had described his people. He didn't know what to say. He felt saddened and ashamed by this revelation.

Hobbes broke the silence by continuing where Calvin had left off. "We have traveled great distances in this universe helping those who we thought could be productive members of the coalition of planets that we had formed. This is why we are here, and the reason we have made contact with you, Daniel. But I must tell you now that if you fail in this experiment, there will not be a third chance. Calvin and I had to bring before the coalition council several months' worth of evidence that we believed showed your people could one day be an asset to our interplanetary community. The council was close to rejecting our bid to conduct this experiment, but at the eleventh hour we convinced several of the members to vote our way. So you can see that a positive outcome is essential to Earth. Failure would mean total isolation from the planets of the coalition, which would almost certainly result in the extinction of your people."

Again Danny was stunned into silence. His thoughts went directly to his family, specifically his children, as he tried to imagine the world that might exist for them and their children.

"We sense that our words have upset you and that this might be an appropriate time for you to be alone to gather your thoughts."

He didn't even know who had spoken to him, but looked up just in time to see the green aura around Hobbes fade away.

"No!" Danny nearly shouted, then more calmly, "No. I already have about a thousand questions, and a delay will only drive me crazy as I try to figure this thing out. Let's push on. Tell me what I have to do."

Calvin responded "It is not necessary for you to accept our proposal at this time. Listen to what we have to say. This is a vast undertaking, and you will, quite literally, carry the weight of the world on your shoulders."

"Ok, I will try not to interrupt again. Please continue with the story of your planet."

"In all our travels through the universe," Calvin said, "we did not encounter any race that was more technologically advanced than our own. Over the years, we developed a fatherly type of role to most of the races that we choose to assist. We are a peaceful race, but we will defend ourselves if attacked as was the case over 2,000 of your years ago. Our planet and several of the stronger coalition planets were set upon by a fleet of ships from a race that we had never encountered before. They were close to our equals, and we suffered many losses before we were able to repel their armada. They tried to flee, but our ships gave chase and the decision from the defense ministry was that there would be no prisoners, and there were not."

Hobbes continued, "Even in victory, we were not without casualties. To this day, we are unsure if our enemies introduced a chemical weapon into our atmosphere, or exposed us to a disease that was indigenous to their race. Either way, every being on our planet contracted a virus. This virus affected our outer shell, or what you would call skin. But our internal organs and our minds were unaffected. As you can imagine what would happen to your people if they were to lose their skin, it was similar with us. As many lives as we lost during the war, that number was doubled by the virus until our medical scientists were able to develop a synthetic covering for our bodies. This is the reason that we are wearing robes. The covering that was developed takes years to become symbiotic with the rest of our body. During that time, we cannot be exposed to any form of light. Calvin and I were not on our planet during the war. We were a thousand years away conducting another experiment. We were called home because of the crisis, but by the time we arrived, the enemy had already been vanquished. Despite our absence and late arrival, our atmosphere was still infected with the virus, and we also contracted the disease."

Calvin said, "As you may have guessed, over the many centuries that our people have existed, our minds have developed to the point where we can do a great many things just with our thoughts. This has been instrumental in the healing process of our bodies as it melds with the synthetic covering. Daniel, you have only witnessed the use of our minds as a communication avenue with yourself, but what you may not have noticed is the fact that we do not use our legs to propel us around the ship. With the use of our minds we can transport our bodies anywhere we please. In fact, the transport pod that we used to bring you to the ship was completely controlled by me. These are but a few of the things we can do just by thought. It would take us days to explain all of the ways that we use our minds, but that is not relevant at this time."

"Our people believe that, given the right circumstances and the chance to evolve naturally, most species can develop their minds as we have. You are aware that your people believe that you only use about 10 percent of your brains?" Calvin asked.

"Yes," said Daniel.

"Actually, we have found that in general most earthlings use about 7 percent of their brain's potential, you, Daniel, use 9 percent. But that is only part of the reason that you are here. All scientific experiments look to answer questions. Some are more general than others. The question that you would be attempting to answer, if you choose to participate, is this: is it possible for one man to convince an entire species to alter their self-destructive behavior as individuals and, on a philosophical level, how an entire species treats their own kind?"

Danny almost laughed. "If you expect me to be able to talk to every individual on Earth and get them to be civil to one another, then this endeavor is doomed before it even gets started. The simple logistics would be impossible, and the time it would take is more than I have. Not to mention, how would I get to the leaders of some of the hostile countries who mistrust any outsider, but most of all, Americans? I don't see how..."

"Daniel, we have not finished giving you our entire proposal," Hobbes interrupted. "We have thought of this, as well as many other problems you would run into, and we are willing to give you certain tools that would assist you in your goal. Even with these tools, your task will not be an easy one. You will encounter hardships, and you may feel that the cost to you personally may not be worth the end result. These are the things you must weigh before you agree to be a part of the experiment."

One of his habits that he used to be unaware of was that he twisted his head slightly to the right when he was curious about something, quite similar to what many canines do under the same circumstances. Carmel had brought it to his attention and had poked fun at him. She called it his Sheena move, after their now-deceased family dog of many years who would do the same thing. Danny's head made that gesture now when he said to Hobbs "Tools? What kind of tools?"

Calvin began "Daniel, here is our entire proposal for you. We have the power to enhance your brain to the effect that you will be using about 35 percent of its potential. This will allow you to heal the sick and dying. You will not be able to control the minds of other humans, but you will be able to sway them to a certain way of thinking. You will also be able to restore their innocence. All creatures throughout the universe are born innocent. It is only through the teachings of their elders as they grow and the experiences of life that create those humans that perpetuate inhumane acts on their fellow man. Daniel, we have studied you long enough to know that you are an atheist and don't believe that humans have souls, but there is a phrase in your language, to "cleanse someone's soul." This phrase best describes the process of restoring innocence. Our hypothesis is that if you use these tools correctly, you can plant a seed in every individual of peace and love for every other living entity on this planet."

"There is, what you would call a catch," Hobbes said. "The only way you can use these powers that we'd give you is to be in direct contact with the individual you intend to affect."

Danny was still frustrated as he said, "Don't get me wrong, the tools that you'd give me would be incredible assets, and, in theory, this experiment just might work, but touching each person in the entire world is still a daunting task. Even if I touched a person for one minute, there are over six billion people on Earth. I would need a calculator to figure out if I had enough years left in my life to get to everyone."

"If you touched one person for one minute for ten hours each day, and if you did this every day for 20 years, that would equal less than five million people," Calvin responded.

"See what I mean? Even if I could do this for 60 years, I just don't have enough time, and you did that calculation in your head, didn't you?"

Hobbes tried to calm Danny down. "Yes Daniel, time is a factor, as well as logistics, and any number of difficulties that will present themselves as you embark on your journey. But we did not choose you because we believe you would not be able to find a way to save your people or would give up once you start. We told you that you were not our only candidate, but both of us believe you are the best person for this task."

He didn't know if it was the steady and even tone of Hobbes' voice, or what he heard in his head and thought of as his voice, or if these guys were fucking with his head. But in either case, he felt his anxiety ebb.

"How long were you two watching me?"

"Years."

"That's a little creepy. Just my luck I have to hook up with a couple of intergalactic stalkers."

"Daniel, our pre-experiment observations were necc…"

"Hobbes, chill out, I was kidding with you." Danny asked with a more serious tone in his voice, "But why did you choose me over the other candidates?"

Hobbes said, "We both felt that, of all the candidates, you possessed the right blend of honesty, common sense, and compassion. Coupled with the fact that we know you are an atheist and, therefore are unencumbered by the complications that religion can bring, and you have an uncanny ability to know what is important in life. You are wise beyond your years, and you are your people's best chance for survival." Hobbes' "voice" actually conveyed emotion on the last sentence.

"That is incredibly flattering. Are you sure you have the right guy?"

"And your sense of humor serves you well," said Calvin.

Danny nodded his head slightly as he said, "Ok, let's do this then. I've lost track of time, and if my wife wakes up in the morning and I'm not there, she is going to freak. If she goes out to the deck, she'll find a half-smoked cigar. And I thought I saw my wine glass fall before your transport sucked me into the twilight zone. Carmel sees that, and she will call a half dozen of my cop buddies and then I will have to explain things before I'm ready to. How long have I been up here?"

The blue aura appeared and Danny heard, "It is 3 am, according to the clock in your living room, Daniel."

"And how long will it take to have this brain surgery that you have planned for me?" asked Danny.

Calvin said, "No surgery, as you know it, will be performed on your brain. We will use a procedure that involves a piece of equipment that you might find similar to what doctors on Earth call an MRI machine. After one hour in this device, we will monitor you for a short time and then answer any further questions you might have. My estimate is that you will be back in your home by 6 am."

"That should work. Carmel usually gets up at about 6:30 or 7 am to get the kids ready and take them to school. Cutting it close, but we do have some leeway."

Hobbes turned toward the wall where the door had been and said, "Then let us precede, Daniel, if you would, follow me please."

He got up from the most comfortable chair in the universe and instantly felt a slight pang of sadness. Danny couldn't get a grip on this feeling, it was as if he missed the chair already and the chair missed him. *Strange chair,* he thought.

The door appeared in the wall once more and slid into the ceiling. All three entered the hall again, and Danny followed Hobbes as he took a left. It was then that Danny remembered a question he'd wanted to ask before they left the briefing room.

He started "I forgot to ask, but how would this second chance work? Once this thing gets going, it doesn't seem like a do-over is feasible."

From behind him, Calvin responded, "Daniel, neither one of us said anything about a second chance. You are correct that it would not be possible. How did you come to believe there would be a second chance?"

"Hobbes said that we wouldn't get a third chance, so I guess I assumed that I would have two tries at this. Sorry for assuming, you guys must have someone else in mind in the event that I fail."

Hobbes said, "Daniel, I apologize if I gave you the wrong impression, but you are your planet's second chance. We were not going to bring this up, but it appears there is no avoiding an explanation at this point. When we told you that Calvin and I were away from our planet when our people came under attack, we said we were conducting another experiment. That experiment was here on Earth. Your people's first chance was over 2,000 years ago."

"Jesus Christ!" Danny blurted.

With some surprise, Calvin said, "Yes Daniel, that was his name."

"What?" The confusion in Danny's voice was apparent. "Whose name? What are you talking about?"

"Jesus Christ. That was the name of the subject of our first experiment on Earth." Calvin explained.

The trio stopped their progress down the corridor as the only human there stood in shock for a few moments. Then his mind raced, and he tried to remember all he knew about the story of Christ. Even though he was an atheist now, that wasn't always the case. He'd been raised a Catholic. As he thought of what he knew about Jesus Christ and coupled it with the new information from the aliens, the experiment story made more sense than if the man was the son of God. As Christ had used the powers he was given, people thought they witnessed miracles. Before this moment, Danny believed there may have been a person named Jesus Christ. But Danny also believed that his actions and "miracles" were embellished as the accounts were relayed orally from village to village and over time. But he never did believe that the man was the son of God. Danny figured he got that one half right. He also began to realize some of the hardships Christ must have had to overcome, and it gave him some insight about what he would also have to endure.

Hobbes moved forward again, and Danny followed. "Daniel, we gave Jesus the same information about the experiment as we did you. What he did with the powers we gave him and the tactics he used were his choice, as they will be yours. Christ did not start out by presenting himself as a religious being but the people he surrounded himself with and the public's interpretation of his actions evolved and seemed to take on a life of its own. Christ did nothing to dispel these assumptions and eventually decided that this was the right tactic to accomplish his task."

Danny said, "Ok, two things. First, I know that scientific experiments have rules and procedures about interfering, but couldn't you at least have saved him from being crucified? And second, so what, you guys are over 2,000 years old?"

Calvin's "voice" sounded grief-stricken inside Danny's head. "Hobbes and I have spoken about this many times. Daniel, we were not here when Christ was executed. We had already been ordered by the council to return to our planet because of the war. That being said, to this day we do not know what we would have done. Interfering would have made the experiment null and void. But Christ's death would end the experiment anyway. We also argued among ourselves about why we wouldn't interfere, and why we might have observed the reaction of the world to the death of the son of God, as they believed him to be. Maybe what he had done to that point would have been enough to change the course of mankind. In the end, Hobbes and I agree that we don't know what we would have done, as we never got the chance to be put in that situation."

"I understand," Danny said.

"And yes, Daniel, we are both over 2,000 of your years in age. Early in our history, our people had a life span of between three and four hundred years. That number rose quickly after we began to develop our minds, and our scientists believe it is the single greatest factor for the increase of our life span."

All three walked in silence for another 20 yards before they came to another nondescript section of the wall at which Hobbes turned to the right, and the usual happened, a section of the wall swooshed into the ceiling, and Danny was shown a third room in the ship.

He had never had the occasion to have an MRI, but he had seen pictures of them and had seen some in TV shows and movies that he had watched and the machine in the middle of the room closely resembled what he had seen. The alien machine was prone, and Danny believed he would have to lie down in it. It was fully enclosed, and he did not see any glass or way to see out of it. He had heard that it was quite common for people to feel claustrophobic in an MRI machine, which he did not believe were enclosed. He was not claustrophobic by nature but the thought of being cooped up in that thing for an hour began to make him a little nervous.

"There is no need to be apprehensive, Daniel," Hobbes said. "You will not be conscious during the procedure."

He watched as the near end of the capsule opened up like a coffin. Another shelf, like the one that had brought him his water, but wider, slid out of the machine about six feet. Calvin gestured for Danny to move toward the machine and said, "Climb up onto the shelf with your head toward the opening."

Danny did as he was told and as soon as he had finished, the shelf retracted into the capsule portion of the machine. Seconds later, Danny saw the capsule door at his feet close and thought, *this has been one big hoax but instead of putting a probe up my ass, they put me inside a suppository.* His last thought was, *but I don't want to know who or what the suppository is for.* He felt all the air being sucked out of the capsule, and his world went black.

CHAPTER 4

Danny regained consciousness back in the most comfortable chair in the universe. He felt like he was waking from the longest and most restful sleep he'd ever had. Danny felt slightly groggy, but only for a few seconds, and then he was fully alert. The first thing he noticed, something he believed was a result of the brain enhancement, was that his senses were definitely heightened. He noticed tiny flaws on the walls of the room, he heard a low hum which he knew were the engines of the big ship that he had not heard before. And the chair felt even more incredible than when he first sat in it, if that was possible. In fact, he thought he'd better get out of the chair before he got a chubby. He saw Calvin and Hobbes standing about ten feet from the chair, staring at him.

"What are you two goons looking at?"

"Daniel, how are you feeling? Are you all right?" No blue or green aura appeared. He knew it was Calvin who had spoken to him.

"Well, I feel great. I never did have the best eyesight, but I was able to get by without glasses. Now I can see things with incredible clarity."

Hobbes said, "Remember, Daniel, that you now have the power to heal. Your subconscious mind has been mending everything about your body that wasn't functioning at its peak performance. Some you will notice, such as your eyesight and some you will not as in the case of your elevated cholesterol."

"Whatever is happening, this is incredible. Is this how everyone will feel after I touch them?" Daniel asked.

"No," Calvin responded. "You are feeling the effects of your advanced brain function, and you will not be able to pass that on to the people you touch. That is not to say that they will not feel anything. Those that you touch will feel both physical and psychological changes. They will experience a sense of peace and happiness."

"I'm going to like this job," said Danny.

"Daniel," Calvin said a little sternly, "do not forget that we have cautioned you that this will not be without difficult times. Think about what Christ must have gone through. And the best laid plans often do not proceed as they should. Remember, Christ did not set out to have religion be the central focus of his experiment, but that part grew rapidly and quite possibly out of his control. Any method that you use to accomplish your task will be entirely your decision, but we advise that you maintain control of your actions and those you surround yourself with. With today's mass media, internet, and TV broadcasts that reach all corners of the globe, you should have an easier time than Christ did in presenting yourself. But those same tools could also cause you trouble. Any mistake that you make will be magnified, as you will be scrutinized by the news, talk show hosts, and any number of websites that will give a voice to any and every one."

Danny was silent for a moment. Then he said, "I do understand that this will be difficult, but I will not be in this alone. I have many friends and relatives and have already begun to think of who I want to help me and be my advisors. Also, there is my wife. Carmel complements me perfectly. If she agrees, I will have her at my side as my chief advisor. I am trying to grasp the enormity of what I have to do and although I don't have a plan in mind, I suspect whatever tack that I take, I will attempt to keep things slow at first. Kinda get my feet wet before I dive into the deep end. I do have a few questions before I go home. How will you contact me? Will I have to come back to the ship? Can I contact you?"

"Daniel, we have given you all that we can. Our Ministry of Science oversees all the experiments that are conducted, and if Calvin or I gave you any further powers or information, that would be overstepping our boundaries. You will not be coming back to the ship, and we cannot leave the ship, due to our physical conditions. Through your enhanced brain function, you will be able to hear us as you do now, but we would only make contact with you in the event of a dire emergency. The success or failure of this venture rests solely on your shoulders."

"That's too bad. I believe that in the short time we've had together, we started to form some kind of bond. But I do understand you can't do everything for me. Is this it, then? Are you sending me back now?"

"Yes Daniel, in a moment we will bring you back to the transport pod and set you back down on your deck. As of right now, everyone in your home is still sleeping. The return trip will not take long, and your landing should not disturb your wife and children."

Danny nodded, and the three proceeded to the wall, which revealed a doorway that did its usual disappearing act into the ceiling. Back into the hall, which Danny didn't know if it was the same hall or not, but they traveled a longer distance than they had before. When Hobbes stopped and another doorway opened, Danny saw what could only be an elevator compartment. The three entered, and Danny discovered that he was not mistaken, as he felt the compartment descend. No buttons or floor indicators were on the wall, so he did not know how far they fell. But he got the feeling they were going quite fast and went down many levels.

When the compartment came to a stop and the door opened, it led directly into a huge area that he believed to be a docking station. The transport that had brought him to the ship hovered nearby as both Calvin and Hobbes angled toward it, and Danny followed.

As they reached the transport, Hobbes turned to him and said, "The first phase of the experiment is complete. The next phases are in your hands, Daniel. As is your people's custom, we wish you luck. Are you ready for the return trip by way of our transport?"

Danny said, "I've been on this ride before, and at least I know what to expect. Thank you for your hospitality. I wish I could shake your hands, as is also our custom, but I know your medical condition doesn't allow for that. And if there is a chance we will be able to converse once more, instead of saying goodbye I'll leave it with, until we meet again."

"I think I can speak for Hobbes when I say we would both enjoy your company, if the future will allow. But for now, the transport awaits."

The transport rose to a height of about 7 feet off the floor, and its passenger took a position under it. Within seconds he was again enveloped in the bubble, and as he looked down he saw lines develop on the floor below him. The floor split into two large doors and one section slid rapidly to his right into the floor as the other section did the same to his left, he was looking at the surface of the moon. He glanced up and only caught a glimpse of the two tall robed figures before the transport accelerated out of the bay door and began its half circle path around the moon.

"Do you still believe it was wise to withhold information from Daniel?" Calvin asked of Hobbes.

"Yes. When we told Jesus that his altered brain functions would cause his life span to increase by several hundred years, he though himself to be invincible. This caused him to disregard the threats on his life, not to take them seriously. Imagine where Earth would be today if he'd been more cautious and was not crucified. We changed the conditions of the experiment to evoke a different outcome. Let us hope it will be enough."

The two robed figures turned and headed for the elevators as the bay door turned back into part of the floor.

# # #

Danny was determined to remain conscious this time and did well as the transport rocketed around the moon, but he felt himself slipping as he picked up speed when the transport straightened out. He wasn't sure if he went out for a couple of seconds, but he did feel the transport begin to slow down, and he was fully awake when his alien taxi entered Earth's atmosphere. A few short minutes later, the craft was hovering above the familiar back deck. The bubble disappeared, and Danny fell the last two feet onto the deck. Being fit and athletic, he should have easily landed on both feet and remained erect. But his left foot came down on the overturned wine glass, and he had no choice but to finish this trip on his ass.

What snapped Danny's head toward the house was the light in the dining room coming on and spilling through the sliding doors that led to the deck. Then he saw the sweet face of Carmel as she stood on the other side of the glass, giving him a stern look. He had to laugh as he mumbled to himself. "Here we go."

CHAPTER 5

Danny had just a few moments to look at his wife with his new vision. At 5'8" and a half, she was only slightly shorter than her husband, which led to the running mock argument that she was just as tall as him. Raven black hair that went a few inches past her shoulders and a slim build with proportionate curves that put her at about 125 pounds. She had the face of an angel, but that was his opinion, and he thought he might be a little biased. At that moment, her green eyes seemed as if they were glowing. He didn't know if that was due to his modified eyesight or the fact that she was bent outta shape. Carmel slid open the glass door too quickly, and it banged against the jamb. Danny knew she was angry, and his moment of reflection on her beauty was broken.

Before she took one step out onto the deck, she was already asking questions but not shouting as the kids were still sleeping. Eleven years of experience as a mom served her well. She knew that if she woke the children too early, she was in for a grouchy clan at breakfast. Still, even though she was talking barely above a whisper, Danny could hear the edge in her voice.

"What the hell do you think you're doing? Have you been out on this deck all night? Just how many glasses of wine did you have? And why do you have that silly smirk on your face when you know I'm upset?

Danny picked himself up off of the floor of the deck and sat in one of the bistro chairs before answering. "Right now I'm sitting on my deck talking to my beautiful wife. I have not been out here all night, as a matter of fact, I just got back. I only had one glass of wine, but the deck had one too. And I'm smirking because in an hour, you'll forget that you were ever angry with me."

"Highly doubtful, Mr. Warburton."

Ouch, he thought. She only called him that when she was really pissed. "Mel please, don't be upset with me. This is going to take some time to explain, but believe me when I tell you that last night and today will be the start of a whole new life for us and our children. Hell, for the entire world, if I have my way about things."

"Have you lost your mind? You sound drunk or crazy! And besides, I don't have time, I have to get the kids up and get them ready for school in a few minutes. And have you forgotten that we made plans to drop the Caravan off at the mechanic this morning?"

Shit, Danny had forgotten about the van. Carmel's six-year-old Dodge had developed a rattle in the engine over the past week, so they had made an appointment to bring it in and have it looked at. He took his wife by the shoulders, and brought her to the other bistro chair, and said, "Listen, have a seat. Give me three minutes inside and when I come back out, things will start to make sense ...sort of."

Danny went into the house, took two steps, and froze. He had touched his wife and felt nothing. No sense of healing or a "cleansing of the soul." He realized that he did not know how his new powers were supposed to work. His head was spinning as he thought, *I'll figure it out,* and then went to the cabinet to get a new glass and pour himself another wine. As he headed back to the sliding door, he grabbed another cigar out of the pack on the kitchen counter. He stepped back out onto the deck and closed the door behind him. As he set the new glass of wine on the small glass-topped table, which was part of the bistro set, he stole a glance at Carmel, who rolled her eyes and let out a sigh. He grinned at her, which made her seethe even further. He took a few minutes as he unwrapped the cigar and searched for his lighter. Danny found it on the deck under the table, picked it up, and slowly lit the Hav-A-Tampa, and took a deep drag.

Now it was Carmel's turn to chuckle before she said, "Go ahead, buster, keep digging yourself into a bigger hole, but don't be surprised when it takes you a week to climb out of it."

"Ok. I'm sorry, I guess I was having a little fun testing your patience. It's just that my mind is going a hundred miles an hour. I have so much to tell you, and I'm trying to organize my thoughts and find a starting point."

"Danny seriously, I have to get the kids ready for school."

"Let the kids sleep in. We can call the schools and tell them the kids will not be in today due to a family emergency, which is not an untruth."

"Should we tell them that the family emergency is that their father has lost his marbles?" Carmel still had an edge to her voice.

"Mel, you know I am one of the most level-headed people you have ever met."

Carmel's voice softened as she responded. "Listen Danny, you are acting a little strange, and certainly this is unlike you but you are scaring me a bit. If you want to talk, that's fine with me, we can sit out here and talk all day if you wish. But maybe we should do that alone. Let me get the kids to school so we can have our privacy."

Carmel stood and took a step toward the door, but Danny gently grabbed her by the wrist. Their eyes locked for a moment, and then he closed his. In his mind, he envisioned a light switch in the middle of a wall plate. He saw his hand move toward the switch and then push the switch up to the ON position. Once that happened, he felt that he could see inside Carmel's body. He started to scan all the major systems, looking for irregularities. Her eyesight was never 20/20, but it would be now. He found a small lump in the left breast and knew without hesitation that it was benign. He was able to dissolve the lump, just to be on the safe side. He discovered slight inflammation to the tendon at her right elbow and the start of carpal tunnel at her right wrist. Both were probably the result of too many hours on the laptop computer. Danny scanned for further problems as he mended Carmel's right arm in both places and realized he was getting faster at this already. He did not encounter anything else inside her body that required fixing and as he was exiting, almost as an afterthought, he cleared up a patch of irritated skin on her left shin. The patch had first been visible about ten days ago and had gone from the size of a penny to the size of a quarter. Carmel believed it was psoriasis but hadn't called her doctor to have it looked at yet. That wouldn't be necessary now.

Danny opened his eyes. Carmel was staring at him, but he could tell by the glaze in her eyes she was not seeing him. Her mouth was slightly open, and her posture was rigid. It looked to him like she was in some kind of trance. He became scared that he'd done something wrong and hurt his wife, so he quickly let go of her wrist. Her gaze and facial expression did not change but only a few seconds had elapsed before he realized that he had forgotten something: he hadn't given Carmel back her innocence. He grabbed her wrist again and closed his eyes. Like the healing process, he did not know how to start this portion of his new powers.

Danny decided that he would try to create an image, as he had done with the light switch. He let his mind travel to the center of Carmel's chest, just to the right of her heart and saw a glowing orb about the size of a golf ball. He didn't know if this was his creation or if it actually existed on some level inside Carmel. Danny saw about six or seven small black dots no bigger than the head of a pin and one slightly larger dot were on the face of the orb. Although he didn't have anything to compare it to, he thought the orb was lacking some of its luster. He visualized his hand coming into view again, but this time his hand held an eraser. The eraser was of the kind you found in every schoolroom resting on the ledge of the large green slate chalk board when Danny was in elementary school. But unlike those old-style erasers, Danny's eraser was not black and was not caked with a years' worth of chalk dust. No, Danny's eraser image was white and dust-free. His mind moved the eraser to the orb, and his hand gently brushed the eraser against the orb, back and forth twice. Not only did the eraser remove the black marks easily, but it also polished the orb so that it was shining brightly.

His hand withdrew, and Danny opened his eyes. He felt confident that he had used his powers correctly and thoroughly on Carmel. Letting go of Carmel's wrist, and looking at her face, he still saw the blank stare and the trance-like symptoms. He continued to look at her face and held his breath for 4…5…6 seconds, and then she blinked. Danny's face lit up with a huge smile, and this time, when she looked into her husband's eyes, he knew she was seeing him.

"Wha…? Wha…?" Carmel stammered but couldn't form any words.

"Sit back down, honey," Danny said. As she did, he thought at least she understood what he was saying, even if she was still in what he hoped was a mild form of shock.

"Just sit for a moment and take deep breaths. I realize you must be confused, but you know I would never do anything to hurt you."

Carmel blinked several times quickly and then did take a couple of deep breaths before she said, "What the hell was that?"

"Before I explain, how do you feel?"

Carmel took a few moments to take inventory. "I feel great. I swear I can see more clearly. I feel like I'm 25 again and could run a marathon."

"Take a look at your shin."

Carmel moved the bottom of her bathrobe to reveal both of her legs up to the knees. Danny grinned and thought, not for the first time, that his wife had a great set of gams. He knew that Carmel was naked under the robe. He also knew that she slept in the nude and probably only had time to throw on the robe when she heard the commotion on the deck. Danny felt the familiar stirrings down below but suppressed them and thought to himself, *Not now, Mr. Johnson, we don't have the time.*

Carmel looked up quickly and said, "It's gone! I know it was there when I went to sleep because I put some anti-itch cream on it." She ran her hand over her left shin and felt smooth skin. "You did this! You fixed everything that was even slightly wrong with my body. I don't know how I know this, but I do. And the feeling of tranquility, peace, inside of me... it's...it's beautiful." Carmel's voice cracked slightly and a few tears fell down her cheeks.

Danny reached out and wiped the tears from his wife's face. "It's ok, baby, I think that's how you are supposed to feel."

"Oh, I know it is." Carmel smiled and a short chuckle escaped her lips.

Danny leaned back into his chair and took a drag on his cigar, followed by two sips of the wine, the slightly smug grin on his face returned. "Ok, I guess it's time for an explanation. This is some wild shit you're going to hear, but you have already felt and seen what I can do so maybe that will help you to believe the story I'm about to tell you. Also, I'm pretty revved up right now. I have been up all night and I should be dog tired, but I think I'm running on pure adrenaline so if I lose you or you don't understand because I'm talking too fast, just let me know. And you can't laugh and call me crazy."

Carmel was looking at Danny and expected him to continue until she realized that he wanted a reply. So she said, "I'm not sure I can promise you that, but I will try."

"Good." Danny paused to take another hit off the wine glass and cigar. "Last night I was about a half hour late getting out of work because of some reports I had to go over. I decided to forget the gym and come right home. When I got here it was my usual routine, out on the deck with wine and smoke. I had finished the first glass of wine and got up to get a refill when I saw a bright light in the sky. I figured it was just a star and went inside. When I came back out, I was shocked to find the light was extremely close to the house. Before I knew it, the light was right over the deck, and I was looking at a UFO. It enveloped me in a bubble of oxygen and took off, with me in tow, and headed for the far side of the moon. I was able to catch a glimpse of a much larger ship that this thing was taking me to before I passed out from the g-force."

Danny paused and took another drag and sip, but that was a ploy. What he was really doing was studying Carmel to see what kind of reaction she was having to his story. What Danny found was his loving wife waiting on what he was going to say next. Not a hint of doubt, he could see it all on her face, and his heart swelled.

Over the next hour or so, Danny told Carmel every detail of his encounter with the aliens. From waking up on the bench and the initial contact, to naming them after cartoon characters and the explanation of the experiment. He told her about the first experiment and the attack on the alien's planet. Danny didn't leave out anything, even the thought that he might get a chubby from sitting in the most comfortable chair in the universe too long. Danny was correct when he thought Carmel would have to slow him down and ask for clarification on a few points, but that only happened twice. After he was done, several moments of silence fell between them. He could tell Carmel was taking in all she had heard and didn't want to blurt out a response.

Finally she said, "That was an incredible story, and I believe every word of it. But really, Calvin and Hobbes? You don't think that beings as intelligent as you make them sound wouldn't know you were poking fun at them?"

"I wasn't poking fun. I like Calvin and Hobbes, and I liked the aliens. I don't think they were offended."

"Ok. They're your friends, you know them better than I do."

Danny grinned. "That's right, they are MY friends. And if you don't stop breaking my balls, I won't ask if you can have a tour of the ship." Danny took Carmel by the hand and said, "Come on, let's get started."

Carmel's tone became serious. "What are you going to do?"

"Well, I figured we would get the kids up, make a big breakfast, and see if we can explain this to them without freaking them out. That way we can take our time. And maybe the act of eating will be enough of a distraction. I...I don't know how to make this easier on them. I'm grasping at straws here," Danny said with frustration.

"No, honey. I meant, what are you going to do with these powers?"

Danny put on his best Ving Rhames voice from *Pulp Fiction* and said, "Oh, that what now." He loved to insert movie lines into his conversations, but sometimes it annoyed Carmel, knowing this did little to stop him.

Danny continued, "Seriously, I don't know. Well, that's not entirely true. I have a general idea of what I want to do, but I haven't had time to work out any of the details. I was hoping you would agree to be my right hand woman and help me take my basic idea and form it into a specific plan. You are intelligent, compassionate, and one of the nicest people I know. I've never told you this, but

I've always felt that because of the type of person you are, you have made me a better human being. Will you help me?"

Carmel smiled. "I wouldn't miss this for anything. As with all that has come before us since we met, I will be by your side."

Danny turned and led Carmel into the house and said "Let's go change the world."

CHAPTER 6

The sixty-one-year-old man sat on the park bench with a hand full of seeds he had produced from the small brown bag on his lap. He'd visited the park on most mornings for the past five or six years and had fed the birds that would gather. At 6′1″ and broad-shouldered, he'd been an imposing figure in his youth. But even then it didn't take people long to learn that he had a gentle soul and a soothing voice. When he spoke in front of large crowds, he held the audience in his hands with his charismatic nature.

But time and circumstances had taken their toll. His hair, although still plentiful, was entirely steel grey. He had put on weight over the years, which showed in pronounced jowls and a pot belly. And the stress of the last 24 months caused the once-broad shoulders to slump and gave him a tendency to walk with his head down. These days, when he gazed in the mirror, he sometimes saw a man who looked at least 70 staring back.

He threw the seeds onto the park path, where the 20 or so birds that had come to feed jostled each other for position. The man reached up and pulled at the white collar around his neck for about the millionth time since he'd started wearing one 42 years ago when he'd entered the seminary at the naïve age of 19. He thought to himself that after so many years, a person could get used to anything, but not so, as the collar irritated him three or four times a day.

Father Padraig O'Malley stood and emptied the remaining contents of the brown bag onto the path, and the birds chirped in delight but continued to jostle, even though there was enough for all. Father O'Malley had lost the simple pleasure of feeding the birds for today. He brushed the particles of seeds from his shirt, crumpled the bag, and threw it into the trash can that was chained to the bench. The bench itself was bolted to a concrete slab. O'Malley noticed that his shirt was rumpled, his pants were wrinkled, and his shoes had a dull finish. This was not always the case, but he knew it was another symptom of the stress he had put on himself.

It had been a rough two years, a time when he'd thought more than once that he might be suffering from depression. He also knew that he should get some counseling before it became too much for him to handle, but he did not want to talk to another priest in his parish, or another priest anywhere else, for that matter.

Father O'Malley began the short walk back to St. Veronica, where he had been the pastor for the last two years. It was not a promotion he'd been prepared to fill. The previous pastor, Father John Spellman, had been accused of sexually molesting 12 boys over the span of 20 years. Actually only two were still boys, the remaining ranged from late teenage to early 30s, and those were the only ones who had come forward so far.

The lead detective on the case for the Philadelphia Police Department, Jayson Padula, had told Padraig that more victims were probably out there, but some would never speak of their ordeal. Padula had mentioned this to Padraig after the investigation had been ongoing for months. This was also after Padraig had been eliminated as a suspect himself and had been cleared from having any knowledge of Father Spellman's criminal activities. But the fact that Padraig did not know of the crimes did nothing for his guilt. Padraig had known all of the victims, some quite well, as eight of them had been altar boys. No, Padraig did not know, but in his heart and in his mind he believed he should have. How could he work so closely with a person and not know the evil in his heart, especially since he was in the good and evil business?

Padraig believed that if he had paid more attention, he would have seen some kind of behavior by either Spellman or the boys that would have alerted him that something was wrong. Even though this had been a problem for years in the Catholic Church in several countries, Padraig believed he had put his head in the sand and thought that something like that would never happen in his parish. And what did those boys think of him at the time of the molestations? Did they think he would do nothing if they came to him? Did they think he, too, was a monster like Spellman and also molested boys? He had failed them as their teacher, as their counselor, and as their priest.

As Father O'Malley thought about these things, he had to stop walking, as his heart ached. He actually felt a pain in his chest, a pain that doubled him over and blurred his vision. His breaths were labored, and a film of sweat had popped up on his forehead. Padraig reached out and found a metal pole that he grabbed to steady himself. Between five and ten minutes later, the pain ebbed, and he was able to stand upright, that is to say, as upright as he had been while walking through the park. Padraig wiped the sweat with the sleeve of his shirt, and his vision cleared. He was able to focus on his surroundings and found that the pole he grabbed held up the walk signal at the intersection of Park Street and Maple Street. Both streets bordered the park, which was at O'Malley's back.

He looked across the street at the steps, the front doors, and then his gaze traveled up the front of the building until he was looking at the gold cross at the top of the spire of his church, St. Veronica. The church was a majestic structure with much scroll work and gargoyles along its edges. It was the biggest and oldest church in Philadelphia, and as Padraig stared at the cross, he felt he might have a moment of epiphany that would lead him back from the brink of faithlessness. But in the end he hung his head with the shame and guilt that he had heaped upon himself and shuffled across Maple Street.

Father O'Malley took the fieldstone path on the left side of the church that led to the parking lot and the rectory beyond. He entered the rectory from the side door, as was his habit for 25 years when he first came to St. Veronica. After seminary, Padraig was assigned to a church in a small town north of Philly in the Pocono Mountain region. The town had the one Catholic church, and he'd been one of two priests. O'Malley had spent 15 years at that small church and developed into the priest, and more importantly, the human being he would eventually become. Padraig thought many times that he would have been happy to have spent his entire career there. But when the transfer orders came for St. Veronica, he surprised himself with his feelings of enthusiasm and eagerness for his new assignment. But what surprised him even more was his lack of feeling any sadness for leaving the place he had grown to love. Sure, he was going to miss the parishioners and the people he had become close to, but he knew that when he saw that little church in his rear view mirror for the last time, he would not look back. Padraig chalked that up to the excitement of a new place, a bigger church, and what he hoped was a larger and more diverse group of people for his interactions.

The side door of the rectory led to a mud room where he took off his shoes and put on a pair of slippers he always kept there. Padraig thought for a second that he should take his shoes to his bedroom and polish them, but he continued on and left them where they were. From the mud room, he entered the kitchen and saw Mrs. Janeski, his housekeeper for the last ten years. Katia, as she'd insisted he call her from the first day she came to work there, was leaving the kitchen on her way to the adjacent living room. She said over her shoulder, "There's a letter on the table for you, it's from the archdiocese."

Padraig sighed, went to the table, picked up the letter, and inspected the return address. Correspondence from the archdiocese had been coming more frequently over the past two years. Most of the letters were instructions for Padraig on how to handle certain situations as they pertained to the Spellman situation. That was all right with him, he did not want to be involved with any of the decision making where that matter was concerned. Padraig tore open the envelope and read the one sheet of paper enclosed. When he was done, he muttered, "Well, how about that?"

Katia Janeski responded from the nearby living room, "Now, that doesn't sound like you got the usual spin doctoring letter from your bosses."

It was apparent to Padraig that at 40 years of age, Katia's hearing had not yet diminished in any way. "They're sending me another priest."

"Who's leaving?"

"As far as I know, no one. There aren't any transfer papers that came with this. With so few entering the priesthood these past several years, I didn't think we had a chance of adding to our staff."

Padraig was still scanning the letter when a thought occurred to him that made him look up sharply. What if they were preparing to force him into retirement? Again, his voice was a little too loud when he said, "They can't do that. I did nothing wrong."

"Do what?" Katia asked.

"Nothing, nothing, I was just thinking out loud," Padraig said too sharply. But he caught himself and moved to the doorway so he could see Katia and said more calmly, "I'm sorry, this caught me by surprise, and I have not been handling the stress very well lately. I think I need to be alone and reflect. Why don't you knock off a little early today, go home and spend a few extra hours with your family."

"Are you sure? I could stay and talk, if you wanted me to."

"Thank you, but not today. Maybe I could get a rain check on that offer though?"

Katia smiled, walked over to him, put her hand on his shoulder and said, "It's a standing offer."

Padraig offered her a half-hearted smile of his own and made his way to his room. On his way down the hall he thought that maybe that was what this place needed, an infusion of new blood, new ideas, and someone not tainted by the scandal. As he entered his room, the half-hearted smile he had for Katia turned into a real grin, small, but real. Padraig also thought he felt at least a twinge of the faith he'd once owned.

Katia put away her cleaning supplies, gathered her things, and left by the front door, which she locked behind her.

CHAPTER 7

Breakfast went as well as could be expected, with three children whose main thoughts were that they didn't have to go to school that day. Danny and Carmel tried to explain to the kids what had happened to their father the night before. Although they did settle down and appeared to be listening, their father didn't believe they understood the severity and enormity of what they'd heard.

It was only after the table had been cleared and the dishes were done, and they took the children into the living room that Kate had begun to think that this was not a joke, that this was not a day off from school to go to Fenway to see a Red Sox game, or to Lake Compounce Amusement Park, or to a local park to ride bikes and have a picnic lunch. Sometimes her parents would do that to have some family time together. They told Kate and her siblings that they liked to do that now, when they had time, because as they got older and were involved with after-school activities, it would become more and more difficult to get the whole family together. No, this was certainly not one of those days. Both mom and dad were acting serious, but there was a look in their eyes that Kate couldn't describe, like they were five years old and had seen their first Disney movie. Kate knew the tone of their voices and that look did not go together. So when her father said he needed to give her a hug, she felt a bit uneasy. Something like a sliver of fear coursed through her. Kate shook her head as if to clear the cobwebs. What was she thinking? This was her dad, a man she knew would walk into a burning building to save any one of his family, a man who would give his own life to protect her. Kate felt ashamed as she flung her arms wide and stepped into her father's embrace. As her father held her tight for a couple of minutes, Kate felt a surge flow through her body. He ended the hug by kissing her on the cheek and whispering that he loved her. She then felt her mother's hands on her shoulder and she was guided to the couch where her mom helped her sit.

Her father said a few words to her mom, who nodded and then both of them had Sandra and Jack sit on the couch next to her. Up to that point, Kate was experiencing tunnel vision, but she was unfamiliar with the term and therefore didn't know what was happening. She thought she was going into shock, which she had heard of, but then her peripheral vision returned. She blinked away the last of the trance as her father was getting ready to hug Sandra.

Kate became worried again, she knew something had happened to her when her father hugged her, but she wasn't sure what. She felt good, at peace inside, and the pain in her left ankle she had twisted while playing soccer in gym class last Monday was gone. Kate put her right index finger on the pimple that had popped up on her chin two days ago. She had developed that habit when she was nervous since the blemish had first arrived. Mainly she covered it up when she was around Trevor Sullivan, who she liked and who also liked her, according to her friend Rachel. But for the first time in three days, she felt nothing on her chin.

As with most eleven-year-old young girls, she was so lost in her own world that Kate was oblivious as to what was going on around her. After searching her chin for a few seconds for the errant zit, she looked up and saw Sandra and Jack in that same half-trance she had experienced. Her father was still on his knees in front of Jack, and her parents were smiling. She knew at that moment that her dad was responsible for removing the pain in her ankle and taking away the golf ball on her chin, as well as giving her the feeling of peace inside.

Kate then thought back to the story her parents had told them at breakfast about aliens and dad being given powers. She'd thought that it was a big joke and believed that her parents would spring the punch line on them later that day. But now she knew that it was all real, and she began to understand what he meant when he said that there were going to be big changes, not only for them, but for all humans. She knew her father, and she knew he would try his hardest to make the world a better place. More than once she'd heard him say how he hated it when someone would say "Life isn't fair." He always told Sandra, Jack, and herself that the only reason life wasn't fair is because people make it that way. He'd go on to say that if people treated each other better, the scales would tip to the fair side more often than not.

A tear fell down Kate's cheek as she jumped from the couch and hugged her father so tight she almost knocked him over as she said "I love you too, daddy."

Kate was even more confused when her mother and father told her, Sandra, and Jack to get dressed and get their bikes out of the shed, as they were going to go to the park and ride around and have a picnic lunch. She thought, *Well, how about that? It is one of those days.*

# # #

Since it was a weekday and still morning, not many people were in the park. Therefore, the kids were allowed to ride in the parking lot in the far west corner. Even during busy times, that was the last lot used by visitors because of its distance from the ball fields and playscape. Still, Mama and Papa bear kept a close eye out for oncoming vehicles as their children raced by and they chatted.

"So, are you going to fill me in on your plan to get started with this?" Carmel began as Danny sat behind her on the small slope of grass next to the parking lot.

He was absent mindedly massaging Carmel's shoulders when he replied, "Family and friends first. Which might take a while, maybe a month or two. You have a big family, and we both have a lot of friends, not to mention there will have to be some traveling, my parents in California, your sister in Boston. But after that anything I do will have to be local at first. One of the problems I see right off is that Calvin and Hobbes may have given me these powers, but they did not give me an endless supply of money. We'll need money to live on and to provide for you and the kids while I do whatever I must. So, for at least the immediate future, I will have to keep working. For now, I do what I can with the people in this general area. And what I'm hoping is, word will get out, and people will come to me. If that starts to happen, then I think some positive publicity would be right around the corner. And staying with the best-case scenario way of thinking, that publicity would put me in touch with the right kind of people, powerful people, people who could get me audiences with governors, congressmen, and the leaders of this country. In turn, they would get me audiences with the leaders of the other powerful countries of the world."

"Ok, that is a quite rudimentary plan. Do you have a guess as to how long this would take?"

Danny hesitated, not because he was calculating the length of time. No, he'd had a number in his head since after breakfast. He hesitated because he worried about the reaction from his wife. Finally he said, "Two or three years. But that is a rough estimate. Sure, things will go slow at the start, but it might speed up faster than I anticipate in the later stages."

"Or the whole plan could go to shit when they throw you in jail for practicing medicine without a license."

"Honey, me? They're going to throw me in jail?"

Carmel sighed. "Yes, they will throw you in jail. You aren't as suave and persuasive as you think you are."

"Well, that is true, I am more suave and persuasive than I think I am. Besides, I know a lot of the cops in the surrounding towns, and once I touch them and do the things that I can now do, they will not want to shut me down. And that goes for the health department or any other agency they send after me."

Carmel nodded. "You have a point there. If you make them feel the way I did this morning, I can't see anyone giving you a hard time. So if we call family and friends Phase 1, when does that start?"

"See, I knew I could count on you! You're already starting to organize this operation, Phase 1, Phase 2, whatever we decide to call it. This will be fun." His voice took on a serious tone. "We will make it fun and do this together. You and the kids go where I go, I will not sacrifice our time together, not even for the rest of the world. But to answer your question, Phase 1 starts tomorrow. We've got one small detour this afternoon, something to sort of get the ball rolling." But Danny was an idealist, and in those early days he hadn't even scratched the surface of the word sacrifice.

Carmel went to the car to get the lunch basket and small cooler while Danny gathered the kids to the grassy area where he had been sitting. They laughed and talked as they all ate ham and cheese sandwiches, except for Jack, who rolled his eyes and stuck out his tongue when offered the ham and cheese. It was a game his mother played with him, as she knew he didn't like ham but she couldn't resist the face he made, and everyone always laughed. Then she would produce a turkey and cheese, and Jack would wipe the imaginary sweat from his brow, another cataclysmic event averted.

After lunch, Danny told the kids they could go over to the playscape until 1:30, which gave them about 45 minutes on the slides and swings. Then they'd take a short ride into Hartford, and he didn't want to get there too late. There was no back talk from his children about the shortened play time, just smiles and giggles.

At 2:30 Danny, Carmel, and their three children walked up to the nurse's desk in the cancer ward at the Children's Medical Center at Hartford Hospital. Danny explained to the nurse on duty that he and his family wanted to visit with the patients on that ward. The nurse told them that due to the nature of the illness that was treated on that floor, only family members or those accompanied by family members were allowed visitation. Danny smiled at her and placed his right hand gently on top of her hands, which were folded together on the desk. Thirty seconds later, the nurse came out of the slight daze she was had been in.

Danny said, "We only came to help."

The nurse responded "I know," as she reached for the button that released the electronic lock on the door that led to the ward.

They thanked her, and then he led his family onto the cancer ward. Immediately they heard the voices of the ill children, but they heard laughing and upbeat conversations. Kate leaned close to her father and said, "Daddy, I thought you said the kids here were really sick and some might even be dying."

"Yes honey, that is true but as you can hear, this is not a gloomy place. I think it is because children are very resilient, and I'll bet the staff tries to keep the mood light so the kids don't dwell on their illness."

While Kate and Danny talked, they had continued to walk down the hall and now were about half way into the ward and came to a u-shaped nurse's station. He had deliberately avoided entering any of the rooms that preceded the station. He guessed that the staff on this ward would be very protective of their charges, and he wanted to deal with the nurses before they caused a ruckus and someone called security. That would take too much time, and his focus here was the kids, then he hoped for a quick retreat. A woman who appeared to be in her forties looked up from the papers she held, and the look on her face told Danny that the door nurse had not announced the arrival of Clan Warburton.

Samantha Rayburn had been the head nurse of the cancer ward for the last twelve years. At 5'5" and 115 pounds, with glasses and mostly grey hair, she didn't strike people as an imposing figure at first glance. But when she had to get tough, it took about two minutes of conversation with Sam, and that would be a one-way conversation, before she would remove all doubt that she was in charge and could handle herself quite capably. As a police officer, Danny had many occasions to interact with hospital staff. He recognized Sam's type and admired that trait.

Sam came around to the front of the station and said, "Good day. My name is Sam Rayburn, and I am in charge here. I have been here long enough to know the families of all the patients on this floor, and I don't know you. Perhaps there was an error that allowed you access to this ward. If you would follow me back to the nurse's desk, I'm sure we can find where you are supposed to be."

A smile was on Samantha Rayburn's face, but Danny knew it was a façade as he saw the steel in her eyes and heard it in her voice. Under normal circumstances, he thought the nurse who had buzzed them in would soon be missing a piece of her ass. But these were anything but normal circumstances. He started to respond that yes maybe they were lost as he touched Sam on the shoulder.

Thirty seconds later he began "Sam, you now know that we don't mean any of the children here harm but we could use your help. I would like to visit all the children on this ward, and I was hoping you could escort us to each room so that the kids wouldn't be suspicious or afraid of us."

Sam said, "That would be my pleasure. Shall we start with Room 1 and work our way around the ward?"

"This is your place, you lead the way."

Samantha Rayburn turned to head in the direction of Room 301. Her right hand went instinctively to the small of her back, where over the years she had developed a constant ache from lifting the children to and from beds and wheelchairs who had become too weak from their illness or treatment to lift themselves. But like Kate and her chin zit, Sam's pain was no more.

She let out a short chuckle as she led Danny, Carmel, Kate, Sandra, and Jack into Room 301 and introduced them to seven-year-old Stevie Johnson. Stevie wasn't the worst case on the ward. He wasn't the best either, but that didn't matter to Danny, who hugged him and at the same time cured him of the disease that would have eventually taken his life. The Warburton family didn't leave the room right away. They all gave Stevie a hug and chatted for about 15 minutes before heading to Room 302. And that was how the afternoon and early evening went. The group went methodically around the floor and met with all of the children, who would soon be leaving the hospital and going home.

After taking care of the children, Danny made contact with the rest of the staff on the ward and then gathered them all, including the patients, in the area near the nurse's station. "You don't have to understand what happened here today or even know who I am. That will all come out sooner than later. But I will ask all of you to keep my visit here to yourselves for now. I assure you that you will not have to keep our secret for very long. You were some of the first, and there will be many more, but I just need a little time so things don't become chaotic. Can you all do that for me?"

Everyone in the group gave their assent by either nodding or by voice. But even with the best of intentions, some people were not born to keep a secret.

Danny said, "Good. Thank you."

One of the older patients, Danny remembered her as 15-year-old Aydan Brewer, said, "No, thank you!"

With that the entire group crowded around Danny and his family and hugged and touched each one. A short time later, the Warburtons left the ward. Jack didn't quite understand why his parents and sisters were all crying, but he wasn't worried. He knew they were what his mom called happy tears.

# # #

Thousands of miles away in space, Calvin was in the engine room of the ship conducting routine calibration tests while Hobbes was in the communication center transmitting a report on the progress of the experiment to their home planet. At about the time that Danny and his family were getting a group hug from everyone on the cancer ward, both Calvin and Hobbes made a facial expression they would describe as a smile. Any human who happened to glance at those unfinished faces, with some exposed bone, sinuous muscle, and still-growing synthetic skin, would either wet their pants in fright or lose their lunch in horror and disgust.

Reprinted article from *The Hartford Courant*
Miracle At Hartford Hospital

The *Courant* has learned that 10 days ago there was a shocking turn of events in the cancer ward of the Children's Medical Center at Hartford Hospital that some are calling a modern miracle. Based on an eyewitness account, a mysterious person entered the ward during the early afternoon hours on that day and visited with all of the patients. He spent about 10 or 15 minutes in each room and spoke to the children and also spoke to the staff on duty that day and then he left. Our witness would only speak to us on the stipulation of strict anonymity but she told us that after this person touched her she felt renewed. She said she no longer needs the glasses she has worn since she was 7 years old, and she has experienced a sense of inner peace since that day. We were told by this source that the mystery man, who she called The Healer, asked that those that he had touched keep his visit a secret, and although she tried, she believed this story too remarkable to not be told.

We spoke to Dr. Lance Hanchin who is the attending physician of the cancer ward at the hospital and he told us that they will be conducting further tests and will still have contact with all of the patients who were on the ward that day but it appears that every child has been cured. Dr. Hanchin said the cancer is not just in remission, it is totally gone in each and every case. The doctor went on to say that 15 of the 19 children have already left the hospital and returned home to their families. The doctor would not speculate as to how this phenomenon had occurred but did say that he is a man of science and does not give much credence to the rumors spreading through the hospital that the mysterious visitor was an angel and this was the work of God.

We did speak to several hospital employees who were not present on the day of the event but did confirm that there have been many theories ranging from angels to aliens circulating around the hospital. But our eyewitness said that although being a religious person, she did not get the impression that the visitor and his actions were anything divine. She described him as a "regular guy" and it appeared that the people with him were his family, wife and children. Hospital administrators have told us that there is extensive video coverage inside and the surrounding grounds of the facility but their contention is that there is no coverage of the visitor and alluded to the fact that the video equipment may have been tampered with shortly after the incident.

This journalist did obtain a list containing the names and addresses of the patients on the ward that day but the decision was made to not make contact or attempt an interview with any of them. It was my opinion that those children had been through enough during their short lives and shouldn't be put in the position to violate a promise they made to the man who gave them a second chance. That list is no longer in the possession of this reporter or *The Hartford Courant.*

If anyone at the hospital knows what actually happened here, they are not saying, but there is a feeling throughout the facility that what the visitor said to the children and staff on the cancer ward is true, that they were only the first, that events such as this one will occur again, and that we will soon know who and what this mystery man is. I, for one, look forward to more of these events because even though it has been shrouded in the unknown, this has been a good thing. If you don't think so, go ask 19 kids and their families.

CHAPTER 8

The next day Danny was awoken by Carmel at 9:30am. She had let him sleep in, but only a little. He had gotten over 12 hours of sleep, as he'd crashed not long after dinner. She knew he deserved even more sleep, as he had been up for over 30 hours the day before but she also knew he wanted to get a few things done before work today.

Carmel whispered in his ear, "Rise and shine, sexy, the kids are all off to school, and there's hot coffee in the kitchen."

Danny was alert immediately. He grabbed his wife around the waist, pulled her onto their bed, and kissed her. He said, "Is the coffee as hot as my wife?"

"Nothing is as hot as your wife." Carmel said as she rubbed one hand through his chest hair and put the other behind his head to pull him down and kiss him back. Then she pushed her husband back onto his pillow, jumped off the bed, and headed for the door.

"Put some clothes on and come into the kitchen, I've got the paper ready for you also." Nine days later Danny would read the first of many articles about himself from that very same newspaper. Five minutes after she left the room he was sitting in the kitchen at the L-shaped section of the counter where they had their morning coffee.

Carmel asked, "What's on the agenda for today?"

"Well, today I thought I would go see my brother and both of my sisters. I'll have to keep an eye on the clock so I have enough time to get back here and get ready for work. I was also thinking that I should start touching random people that I come into contact with throughout the day, like store clerks, people I pass in parking lots, pretty much anyone within arm's length. I might as well, since the plan is to touch as many people as I can. Tomorrow I will visit your brother and my friend Paul from high school. I would like for you to come with me, but I understand that might not be feasible every day. When I go see your mother on Thursday, I really think you should be there."

"Of course I will go with you to my mother's house. I know that since my dad died, she has been a little standoffish with you, and I do not know why. But she does like you, she always has."

Danny sighed. "I know, honey, but lately it seems I never know what to say to her. Our relationship is definitely strained."

"Maybe that will get better. I'm hoping you can bring her some inner peace."

"Me too. Anyway, on Friday after the kids get out of school, I want all of us to get on a plane for California. We haven't seen my parents in over two years. It will have to be a short visit, probably fly back on Sunday afternoon. You up for that?"

"Really, just hop on a plane at a moment's notice? We never were the spontaneous traveler types. Hell, you plan vacations six months in advance. Also, can we afford that?"

"Yes, I think we can get a good last-minute rate, and I also think that making impromptu travel plans might be a bigger part of our future," Danny said as he finished off the last of his coffee. He had leafed through the paper as he spoke to Carmel, but only half-heartedly. He'd scanned the headlines but wasn't at all interested in what was going on in the world or locally.

Over a second cup of coffee, he booted up the computer in the den and made the airline reservations for the trip to California. Carmel had turned quiet, and he knew she was thinking about how this whole thing was going to affect not only their bank account, but more importantly how it was going to affect their children's education. She probably wondered if it was going to take their father away from them.

He finished with the tickets and went back into the kitchen where he found Carmel with her back to him as she washed the few breakfast dishes. He came up behind her, then put his arms around her waist and his lips close to her right ear.

Danny whispered, "Don't worry about us. I said we would do this as a family, and I meant it. I believe we will spend more time together than ever before as this thing gains momentum."

She whirled around with a surprised look on her face and said, "Are you able to read people's thoughts?"

He wrinkled his brow as he gave that some thought, "No, I don't think so, what brought that on?"

"Because that was exactly what I was worrying about."

"I don't think I read your mind, I just sensed that something was bothering you and figured it was about us as a family and all the traveling that will have to be done. And you can chalk that up to us knowing each other so well."

"Maybe, but that did seem a bit too coincidental. Perhaps I will conduct my own little experiment to determine what the all-powerful Oz is capable of."

"Smoke and mirrors, my dear, it's all done with smoke and mirrors." Danny said, just before he leaned in and gave his wife a long kiss as he reached around and cupped one ass cheek. Then he turned and headed for the bathroom to get the day started with a hot shower.

Once he got going, the day flew by. Danny went to his brother George's house first. George was the older of the two brothers and worked second shift as a fireman in nearby Farmington. Having a cop and a fireman in one family always led to breaking each other's balls at almost every family get together, and they'd only had to be separated one or two times over the years. Danny didn't have much time to sit and socialize with George, but he did have time to take care of his left knee. His brother had done serious damage to his knee while playing high school football. Even after three operations, it had almost kept him from becoming a fireman. He now walked with a slight limp and never told anyone about the constant ache. George's wife Kaye was home also. After Danny hugged her, he tried to explain the gift he'd received from his new friends but he got the impression that he left them with more questions than answers.

His next stop was at his sister's house. Kelly was the oldest of the four siblings. She had two daughters who were 15 and 17 years old, and she had been pretty much raising them by herself since her divorce seven years ago. Danny and Carmel tried to help out by taking her girls for an overnight every now and then so she could get out and maybe meet someone, but so far no one has made it past the third date. At least the Warburton children had a blast on those nights. They loved spending time with their older cousins.

Kelly commuted to Hartford every day and worked for one of the big insurance companies. Danny had called her from George's house to make sure she was home, as he remembered that she had taken this week off from work. Kelly had wanted to catch up on some home projects and also to get away from work for a short time.

After a few moments of pleasantries, Kelly became curious and asked him if there was a reason for his visit. That was when he put his hand on her shoulder and found out that his sister was in remarkable shape. He sharpened her eyesight and took care of a little cholesterol build-up in her veins, but that was it as far as the physical improvements. He studied the glowing orb he'd seen in all of the people he'd had touched so far and found Kelly's to be mostly covered in black. This was the worst one he had seen so far. He theorized that this was the result of going through the divorce, working full-time, and trying to raise two teenage girls by herself. Regardless of the cause, the Healer went to work. In a few seconds, the orb had been restored to its original cleanliness and glow.

Danny underestimated the effect of having that weight lifted off Kelly's shoulders and almost didn't catch her as she fell to the floor. He carried her to the living room, laid her on the couch, and held her hand while she shook the haze off. She knew instantly what her brother had done for her and started to cry as she hugged him. Once again Danny tried to explain the hows and whys, as he'd done with George, and Kelly seemed to grasp the explanation much better. As he left, he looked into his sister's eyes and saw a renewed enthusiasm for life that made him wonder how he hadn't seen the sadness in those same eyes for the past several years.

Danny called his younger sister, Candace, Candy to just about everyone she knew, from the driveway of Kelly's house. She rented an apartment in New Haven, where she attended Yale school of law. She would be starting her last year in August, but he knew she always took classes in the summer and might finish early. At 25 years old, she was truly the baby of the family. Danny always suspected that Candy, like his own son Jack, had not been planned. His mother was 40 and his dad was 43 when she was born, and her arrival was a bit more than a shocking surprise. Candy was smart as a whip and the most outgoing of the Warburton children. The center of attention from her earliest days, her lust for life rubbed off on anyone she spoke to for more than ten minutes which was one of the reasons he always loved talking to his younger sister, he felt younger himself for hours afterward.

He learned that Candy was at her apartment, but only for another hour, as she had class and then would go right to work at the bar where she waitressed. He knew he only needed a few minutes of her time and therefore asked her to stay where she was until he arrived.

Thirty-five minutes later, the Santa Fe pulled into the parking lot of her apartment building. As she always did, she met him outside as he exited the car. Because of their unforgiving schedules, a visit by Danny to New Haven was rare and had piqued her curiosity since his phone call. She hugged and kissed him on his cheek before he took two steps away from his car and then inquired as to the out of the blue visit.

"To what do I owe the pleasure of a visit from the greatest detective since Sherlock Holmes?"

Danny laughed before he responded "Thanks for the compliment, but can't I come down to see my baby sister?"

"Great detective, lousy liar."

"Of course there is a reason, but let's go inside. I know you're pressed for time, so I will try to explain as quickly as possible."

As soon as they were seated on Candy's couch, Danny took both of her hands in his and took care of business. He detected a slight irregular heartbeat that he doubted even she knew about and wondered if it could have caused her problems later in life. No matter now, it was an easy fix. Next, he studied the orb, only to discover that he did not need to bring out the eraser at all. Such a contrast to Kelly's made him wonder for a second how each person's attitude on life itself had an effect on their health.

After, he again explained what had happened to him three nights ago. Without hesitation, his younger sister believed him and told him he should use this gift to help as many others as he could. Then she grabbed her book bag and change of clothes bag and told him to lock up when he left, as she was going to be late for class. Danny sat on his sister's couch in shock, then laughed out loud for five minutes before he secured the apartment and headed home.

That night at work, Danny made physical contact with each of his detectives, several people who came to the bureau to be interviewed, two victims, one witness, and one suspected burglar. He also touched three patrolmen who came to the office to ask questions on a particular case and everyone who was at the main desk when he went down on the pretext of checking on a report. Halfway through the shift, he went out for a coffee and took care of the young girl who served him, as well as the other four patrons of the shop.

After the shift, he went to the weight room for 45 minutes, and then took a shower. When he returned to the darkened detective bureau, he ran into the police department night janitor. Danny clapped him on the back and wished him a good night.

The next day went pretty much as planned, Carmel came with Danny as they met her brother at a coffee shop near his office about mid-morning. Danny shook Ted's hand, held on for a few seconds, and then the three of them spent a pleasant half hour getting caught up. What he was beginning to realize that some people understood what was happening immediately, while others, although they felt better, visibly brightened, and experienced all that everyone else that he touched did, couldn't comprehend the fact that it was Danny who had caused the changes in them.

This time, anyone who had witnessed Ted's demeanor when he entered the coffee shop would have been shocked at the transformation. Prior to shaking the Healer's hand, Ted greeted his sister with a smile that looked like one he used for strangers and gave her a half-hearted kiss on the cheek. Then his hand made contact with his brother-in-law. For a few seconds his eyes glazed over, and he stared at the floor but when he came around, he was the Ted that Carmel remembered from their teens. He was once again outgoing and gregarious, his voice was animated, and he flirted with the waitress. When they departed, Ted gave his sister a huge hug and gave his brother-in-law a look that said deep down he knew Danny was responsible for something but Ted didn't know what yet. During their time there Danny excused himself from the table and made it a point to visit everyone in the shop.

Their next stop was to visit his best friend from school, Paul. He was a successful doctor in a busy practice, but when Danny called him he assured Paul that they would only take a few minutes of his time and so he agreed to see them in between patients. As promised, it only took him 15 seconds to heal the doctor. Paul was one of those who understood exactly what had happened, if not the how. He trusted his friend implicitly and did not question right then, mostly because Danny said they would get together soon and he would explain everything.

That night, Detective Sgt. Warburton went to work and made contact with more than 20 officers as he walked around the police station at the beginning of the shift. He put four more victims at ease and two suspects, both of whom were arrested that night. One had a warrant charging him with sexual assault in the first degree. Already there were aspects of this experiment that bothered him, and none were more evident than this case of a rapist. The cop in Danny wanted this asshole punished for his actions. But The Healer also knew that once he was touched, this person would never again commit another crime, so putting him in prison would be counterproductive. He decided that for the time being he would let the justice system go about its daily business.

At midnight he went to the gym, not only because he wanted to stay in somewhat good shape, but also to maintain some sort of stability in what was sure to become a hectic lifestyle.

On Thursday Carmel and Danny went to the home of Jessica McNiff, Carmel's mother and widow of Liam McNiff. When Liam died, Jessica became an angry woman, and for some unknown reason she'd turned that anger on her son-in-law. Since then she had probably spoken all of 25 words to him, none of them pleasant. Jessica did stay in touch with her grandchildren through her daughter, but even Carmel's relationship with her mother was not what it used to be.

When they first arrived, he was reluctant to make physical contact with Jessica because he had become a little nervous around her over the last two years. They had been there about one hour when The Healer, returning from the kitchen, came up behind Jessica and gently gave her a kiss on the cheek. The rest of the day was spent by all three using up the better part of a newly opened box of Kleenex. They ended up spending most of the day with Jessica, getting to her house at 9:30 am and not leaving until 3 pm. The only reason that they left then was because Danny had to be at work at four.

Danny drove to work that evening and went directly into Captain Franti's office. He had not seen his friend all week, as the captain had been at an anti-terrorist seminar in Atlantic City until last night. Danny found him sitting behind his desk, walked over to it, stuck his hand across the desk top, and said, "Welcome back, boss."

Franti hesitated for a second because he knew his friend was slightly germaphobic, and shaking hands was not his habit. But Franti was like most humans, and when presented with another's paw, they took it and shook it.

While Franti was in the trance that was becoming so familiar to Danny, he said, "Sit back down, boss." The big man slowly did.

When Franti cleared the cobwebs, he whispered, "What the fuck was that?"

"Just a little tune-up for that aging body of yours, which I know better than anyone how you abuse the shit out of."

Danny gave his friend the abridged version of how this all came to be, then asked for Friday evening off. Of course, the captain granted the day off and thought he would go golfing this weekend, since he didn't have the lower back pain anymore.

After Franti left for the day, Danny decided to visit one of the city's low-income housing projects. It was a gorgeous summer day, and he parked the unmarked detective car on the outskirts of the neighborhood and began walking. There were still about two and a half hours of daylight left, so he encountered a lot of the kids who lived in the row housing playing, riding their bikes, and shooting hoops on the basketball court. Even the children knew he was 5-0, some because Patrolman Warburton had been to their house back in those days, but even those who had never met him knew he was 5-0 because of the fact that he looked and dressed like a cop.

Danny made conversation with as many of the kids that he could and, of course, he shook their hands. He was going to have to get over his petty phobia. He rested a hand on their shoulders and generally made contact with all those he talked to. After shooting a few baskets, he sat on top of a nearby picnic table and it wasn't long before he had a good-sized crowd of children and teens around him. The kids didn't know what was happening to them, they only knew that they wanted to be near him. This attracted the attention of some of the parents of these kids. Those who were enjoying the weather had already been eying Danny since he'd showed up, as they knew who he was. The adults began to be part of the circle of followers The Healer attracted. At first they came to collect their sons and daughters but Danny stuck out his hand to each one and, like Franti, they couldn't help themselves. One by one the adults who came over became part of the crowd, then even more came who didn't have children but came over out of curiosity.

At 7:30 he addressed the group as one and told them that it was best that they return to their homes because they knew better than anyone that the housing project was no place to hang out after the sun went down. He told them that the days of being afraid in their own neighborhoods were coming to an end and that soon their children would have the same opportunities as the well-off kids from the west side of town, but that would take time, and for now parts of the world were still dangerous. He looked over the group and did not see a doubtful face among them.

The group dispersed. Danny pulled out a cigar, unwrapped it, and lit up. A short time later, the automatic lights in the area began to come on, but not all were working. He began to see small clusters of teens and young men checking him out from a distance. He knew that it wasn't going to be easy with the second group from this neighborhood.

Danny had a second badge on a lanyard around his neck and tucked under his shirt. Now he took it out so it could be seen, not by the gang bangers who were part of the groups now occupying the area, they already knew who and what he was. This was for the others who came into the projects to purchase drugs. After a while the dealers became fidgety. They thought this was some kind of ploy by the police and kept looking for other officers sneaking up on them. After about an hour of watching their backs, they discarded the ambush theory. But they were still unhappy with Danny, as he was disrupting a good portion of their business. It was decided by the highest ranking gang member there, that a contingency of four would confront the cop, the gang's top enforcer would be one of that group. The four approached the detective and slowly surrounded him, all were armed. The enforcer was also the spokesman. He said, "You seem to be all by yourself out here, detective."

Danny lifted up his shirt to expose his belt line, then pulled up each pant leg to show his ankles. "And I came unarmed."

"Well, that doesn't seem to be a very smart move on your part."

"Listen. You know, and I know, you're not going to shoot a cop for fucking up business for a couple of hours, you wouldn't bring that kind of heat on yourselves. I was getting ready to go anyway, but before I do, I want a meeting. Do you have the authority to negotiate?"

The enforcer did not like being made to look bad, but he also knew he could not speak for the gang. "I'll be right back, my three associates will keep you company till then."

Fifteen minutes later, the enforcer came back with the gang president, Hector Garcia. Danny recognized him from the department intelligence memos.

Hector started "My man here says you want to talk. I don't think we have anything to talk about."

Danny went into a long bullshit story about how the violence in the area was hurting the innocent children and how the police department wanted to get the heads of all the city gangs together to form a truce. At the end of the story, he told Hector that they came to him first because he was the president of the most powerful gang in New Britain, he figured it couldn't hurt to butter him up a bit. Hector's demeanor changed a bit. Danny noticed and took the opportunity to capitalize. The Healer stuck out his hand, and even though Hector was a street-wizened thug, he was still human and shook his hand. Thirty minutes later, Danny had turned the entire membership of the South Side Kings into law-abiding citizens. He learned that the enforcer's name was Carlos Cintron, and Danny went with Carlos to his apartment and cured his mother of Parkinson's. From that day forward, the South Side Kings would lay down their lives for Daniel Warburton. And when it came time, Carlos became an integral part of Danny's personal security detachment. Hector vowed that he and his men would atone for their past transgressions by protecting the neighbor and using the money they had earned from selling illegal drugs to help those families who had financial difficulties.

He went home after his shift with a sense that, for the first time, he had used his powers to start to change a little part of the world for the better. He was still smiling when he crawled into bed and fell into a deep sleep.

Friday morning was spent getting ready for the flight to California. The elder Warburtons had left Connecticut and retired to Monterey five years earlier. John Warburton had done quite well as an engineer for Sikorsky in their helicopter division and at the early age of 58 decided he had enough of the northeast weather so he and his wife, Teresa, headed west. Fifty-eight was too early for a man like Jack Warburton to retire, so he'd began his own consulting firm. But he still considered golfing his California job and the firm his hobby.

The flight was uneventful except for the fact that Danny was the life of coach class. He talked to everyone and, of course, made some excuse to make physical contact with each passenger. Halfway across the country, he had everyone talking to each other, telling jokes, and showing family photos like they were long-lost friends. The flight attendants joined in, and it wasn't long before he was invited to visit the cockpit and meet the flight crew. On the way, he took care of first class.

They landed in San Jose, picked up the rental car that had been reserved, and headed south on Route 101. They had taken off from Bradley at 7 pm. Even though they gained time, it was still 11 pm when they pulled into Monterey. Danny had not told his parents they were coming out, as he'd wanted to surprise them. The kids were tired, it had been a long day, and he didn't want to disturb his parents this late, so he decided to get a hotel for the night and drive to John and Teresa's house early the next morning.

Morning came and, as anticipated, Danny's parents were surprised, excited, and overjoyed to see them all. He hugged his father and mother as he entered their home, but he didn't use the gift on them at that time. He wanted his parents to enjoy the company of their grandchildren without thinking about anything else. After things settled a bit, his mom insisted on making breakfast, so eggs and pancakes were devoured heartily. Danny poured himself a second cup of coffee when the feast was over, then laid it all out for his parents. They both looked at him with skepticism, but he didn't let them dwell on it too long before he held his mother's hand and then his father's.

The Healer let the haze clear from his father's eyes before he asked him, "How long have you known?"

John Warburton's face reddened with shame as he said, "Three months, the doctors said it was terminal. I was getting up the courage to tell you, your brother and sisters, but over the phone did not seem the right way. We were going to Connecticut in two weeks." John Warburton had pancreatic cancer and he knew the operative word there was had, as in the past tense. John stood and hugged his son.

Danny thought that this was only the second time he had seen his father cry, the first time was when Candy was born.

The seven of them spent the rest of the day enjoying each other's company. John and Teresa took their son and his family to one of their favorite places for lunch in nearby Carmel by the Sea, a place called Merlot Bistro. Then they walked along the Ocean Avenue area and did some shopping in the Carmel Plaza.

Danny didn't know much about the town except that Clint Eastwood and Sonny Bono were former mayors, but he quickly discovered why his parents had decided to retire to this area. Picturesque seaside towns, beautiful weather, and a relaxed attitude that seemed to permeate the air made him envy his parents a little.

The Healer wondered if he would ever be able to retire, not from his job, but from this experiment. Would he ever be able to relax and enjoy some of the things his parents now enjoyed? These thoughts made him anxious and, being a mother, Teresa Warburton noticed.

"Son, is everything ok?"

"I was thinking how you and dad have a great life out here, but my family's future is so uncertain now. I guess I was feeling the weight of this whole experiment on my shoulders and wondering what I got myself into."

"They chose you for a reason," said Teresa, "and I'll bet one of those reasons was because they believed you could handle it. You're a good man, and your father and I have always been proud of you. If I was one of your little green friends, I would have picked you, too."

"Well, they aren't little and as far as I know, they aren't green, either. But thanks, mom. You always could cheer me up." As Danny finished he kissed his mother on the cheek.

On Sunday there was another big breakfast, but there wasn't much time for anything else. Clan Warburton had a noon flight back home, and they still had to drive back to San Jose. Everyone said their goodbyes, and John and Teresa said they would come back East for Christmas.

Again, those on the plane were all touched by Danny, as well as anyone who came close to him at both airports, the airline counter employees, and a half-dozen TSA workers.

He had planned for his next family visit to be to his Cousin Amanda's house. Mandee and her husband, Ralph, lived about 30 minutes away and had one son, Anthony, who was born with Down syndrome. Tony was not as affected as most who were born with that affliction, and his parents threw themselves into his education as soon as they had trained themselves. They read every book on DS and researched even the most obscure methods on teaching DS kids. Everyone who met Tony complimented Mandee and Ralph on their tireless dedication to giving their son the best possible life they could.

Scheduling issues prevented Danny from getting together with the three of them quickly. But finally, over a week after he returned from California, he went to their house on a Sunday morning.

Ten minutes after he arrived, he took care of Mandee and Ralph and then explained to them how these events came to pass. Then he got down to the delicate issue of Tony. He told his cousins that he had cured many people since his visit to space, but all of the medical problems he'd encountered had been contracted after they were born. He wasn't sure if the gift would work on Tony, and Danny wanted the parents to make the decision about whether he should try. He explained that they didn't have to give him an answer that day, he would come back anytime they liked.

It took them about ten minutes to make up their minds. Tony had been playing in his bedroom, so they brought him to Danny, who was in the living room. Even though he was apprehensive, he didn't hesitate. He hugged Tony. Not since Carmel had The Healer concentrated so hard on getting it right, but although he could take care of a few minor problems with Tony's body, sadly he could do nothing for the boy's damaged brain. After he let go of Tony, he felt exhausted.

Tears were in the eyes of Ralph and Mandee as they led their son back to his room. The boy was as happy as he always was and felt no ill effects of the failed attempt.

It took 15 minutes before Danny could gather enough strength to sit up. More than two hours later, he was able to drive himself back home. Physically, he was at 85 percent but emotionally, he was spent. If there was one person he really hoped he could help it was Tony, a truly innocent child who'd never had an ill thought toward another person.

# # #

Ten days went by. Danny felt blue, first about his thoughts in California about never being able to retire and then his failure to heal Anthony. He went to work, and he still touched those he came into contact, but not with much enthusiasm. By that time, he had taken care of almost the entire New Britain Police Department. There were still a few he hadn't run into which was due to scheduling, and a couple who had been out of work due to injury. As Detective Sgt. Warburton, he did what he had to do on the job and stuck to his routine, but he felt that he had put himself in a rut.

Carmel had noticed her husband's funk and decided to try and help. One day while he was in the kitchen, sitting at the breakfast counter, she came up behind him and slapped him on the back of his head. At the same time, she put on her best Cher voice from *Moonstruck* and said, "Snap out of it!"

Danny gave her a long look then replied "You can't interject random movie lines into a conversation. That's my thing. You can't do my thing. Find your own thing. And that was a horrible imitation of Cher."

Carmel chuckled. "More nasal? Anyway, I am serious. I understand you being a little down, he was the first person you couldn't help. Have you considered that there might be more?"

"Not until after Anthony. I didn't think I would have limitations."

"Well, I have an idea that might help. Let's go to Boston and see my sister. Beth has been calling me asking when we were coming up." Carmel hesitated before continuing. "Truth be told, my mother talked to Beth and told her what you did for her. Don't blame my mother, we did tell her we were going to visit Beth and Joe, and she thought we already did because a few weeks had gone by. Now Beth calls me every other day and wants to know what happened and asks why mom's gone off the deep end. Besides, you need to get away and while we are up that way maybe you would like to stop at that cancer place. I think it's in that area."

"What place are you talking about?"

"You know, the one the Red Sox support. They even have a billboard at Fenway with the name of the place."

"Oh, you mean the Dana Farber Cancer Institute? Yes, I believe it is in the Boston area. Ok, we could spend a day with your sister and spend the night in a hotel. Do some sightseeing the next day and then stop at Dana Farber on our way home."

Carmel thought, *"Mission accomplished."* She heard the excitement in her husband's voice and also saw it in his eyes. "I'll set it up for this coming weekend," she whispered in his ear, and then kissed his cheek.

On Saturday morning, Clan Warburton made the two-hour drive to Boston and, as planned, spent the day at the house of Carmel's sister, Beth. The Healer helped Beth with her daily pack-and-a-half cigarette habit, but otherwise Beth and Joe were quite healthy. They didn't have any children, and that was by choice, but they invited their neighbors and best friends over for dinner, and Danny was happy to help them with their minor ailments, also. After dinner, the men sat on the back porch and kept the conversation light, discussing work, sports, and vacation plans. Danny had a cigar, and after his second glass of wine, he informed Carmel she was driving them back to the hotel.

The next day, they all got up early and crammed two or three days of activities into one long day of Boston attractions. Late in the day, they located the Dana Farber Cancer Institute and discovered that the in-patient treatment was done at Boston Children's Hospital, which wasn't far from the institute. They drove to the area of the hospital and found a restaurant where they had dinner. The restaurant was close enough to the hospital that Clan Warburton decided to walk off their meal in the mild Boston evening.

The hospital cancer ward was not that dissimilar from the one in Hartford, only bigger and with about three times the number of patients. Danny had to work a little faster because of the number of children and the fact that the family had a two-hour drive back home. Again, Carmel and the kids went with him to each room and tried to visit with each child for a short time. In addition to the patients and staff, the hospital had accommodations for one parent to stay overnight with their ill child, so that added many more people to the visit.

It was late when they finished, and it had been a long day, so Danny didn't ask this group to keep everything a secret. He figured with a group this size, someone was going to talk anyway, so why bother with the speech? They thanked him, and his family profusely and were extremely appreciative for what he had done for them. Even though he was tired, The Healer had a smile for each and every child on that ward, and he felt good as they walked back to the van.

Carmel saw in his face that the trip had been a success and said to him, "Welcome back." She drove home and heard slight snoring from the passenger seat before they hit the Massachusetts Turnpike.

The story broke in the *Boston Globe* on Tuesday morning and was on the national nightly news broadcasts on Wednesday evening. As in Hartford, Danny had convinced hospital security to lose the camera footage of his visit. But he didn't count on two ATM cameras and one traffic camera capturing the Warburtons walking to and from the hospital. By Friday evening, his face, albeit grainy, was splashed across the country on TVs and on the internet.

Comparisons were made to the Hartford incident, and that story resurfaced. The similarities were too many, and no one believed this was the work of two separate people. Danny and Carmel watched the news and read the papers intently and waited for the knock on the door or the phone to ring.

A week went by, and that knock on the door did not come. Those who knew that the images on the ATM and traffic cameras were Danny, Carmel, and the kids, were friends and family, and they kept quiet. But he knew it was inevitable that someone would put a name to the face, and he was surprised it had not happened already. He was starting to think that instead of being shanghaied one night at work or having a mob of reporters ascend on his house, maybe it would be better for him to control the how and when the world came to know about him.

He told Carmel and the kids that there was to be a family meeting the following Saturday after breakfast. By that time, Kate and Sandy had a pretty good grasp as to what was going on and what their father was capable of. Jack knew that dad could "fix" people and that he made them happy when he touched them, but beyond that he didn't give it much thought.

Saturday came and after the post-breakfast clean-up was finished, Danny asked everyone to sit in the living room. He started out by saying "We have been doing a lot of good with the gifts I have been given, and there hasn't been any effect on our daily lives up to this point but it is only a matter of time before that changes."

Sandra said, "Dad, your face is all over the internet, and all of ours, too."

Kate added "But the quality is not very good, and I don't think anyone has recognized us. But the things people are saying about you are upsetting to me. They don't even know you, what a good person you are."

Danny cut Kate off, as he could tell she was going to get herself worked up. "Kate, don't get excited over it. I have been online and have read all the rumors about what people think is going on. I'm an angel sent by God, Jesus Christ returning, the antichrist, an alien, I read one that speculated that I was a super hero who had been bit by a radioactive doctor, I think that one might have been a joke. Whatever is being said on TV or written online, we know the truth, so that other stuff is just talk. The problem is that it is gathering steam and is about to turn into a runaway train. I think we need to stop that, and the way we do that is to come out with the truth. My idea is to grant an interview with one of the local TV stations."

Jack said, "You're going to be on TV, dad?"

"Yes Jack, but that doesn't mean that our lives will be just like they are now. You kids may be bothered or teased at school, and the media may still camp out on our front lawn. Our lifestyle is about to change, and I don't think there is much we can do about it except pick the how and when."

Carmel said, "We may experience some inconvenience, but it will be worth it in the long run."

Danny winked at her. "I think you're right, honey. So this is my plan, since I seem to watch Channel 8 news more than any of the others, I propose we all walk into their broadcast center on Monday. I think they might put us on the air right away." He was thinking out loud. "Yeah, us. It will not be just me on TV, Jack. It will be all of us."

CHAPTER 9

"Jesus Christ, Brain! You got your nose stuck in another newspaper," Leo Campisi said only half-jokingly. "Don't you got a job to do? You ain't earning sitting around here reading about what the rest of the world is doing."

Jimmy "The Brain" Santini moved the paper down a few inches and gave Leo a short smirk before raising the newspaper again. Then from behind the paper Jimmy responded "I've already made my collections for the day and had a sit-down with my distributors. Now I'm on my third newspaper with one more to go, and then five news sites on the internet. Maybe if you got your fat ass out of bed before noon you would be able to earn as much as me."

"Fuck you, Jimmy. I've been earning since you were still pissing your bed. And don't think your connections in this family will save you from an ass beatin' if I think you deserve one. A little respect is in order for guys who been made long before you."

"Respect goes both ways. Besides, I thought we were just breaking balls here."

"Just be careful you don't go too far with that."

But Leo was actually the one who worried about going too far. Jimmy's uncle, Sonny Santini, was a captain in the Gambino crime family of which Jimmy and Leo were members of that family, so that connection kept others from messing with him.

The Brain didn't have to rely on his uncle, though. In the ten years he had been with the family, he'd worked hard and done anything that was asked of him. At 28 years old, he had his own crew but still did a lot of the work himself. He had his fingers in loan sharking, and prostitution, but he made most of his money from supplying narcotics to street dealers. He was smart, hence the nickname "The Brain," but he was also tough and had a reputation of not taking any shit from anyone but the top bosses in the family. He had even done two hits at the behest of his uncle and was well-liked by most. Everyone could see that he was a rising star in the Gambino crime family.

At 5'9", Jimmy was of average height, average weight, and had average looks. He didn't dress flashy, and he drove a four-year-old Nissan Altima. The only thing he had spent a lot of money on was his safe haven, the house he bought out in The Hamptons, and the furnishings and other accoutrements he filled it with. He had a couple of girls he saw on a steady basis and took them to places and functions where he knew having a lady companion was expected of him. But he was not the typical Mafioso, his main concern was making money and getting ahead in the organization.

When he was a child, his mother chastised him and told him that he could have been a doctor or scientist, but early on he knew that the family life was in his blood. So he figured, why fight it? Besides, Jimmy knew he was smarter than anyone in the organization and with his connections, he should be running the show before long.

The Brain put the papers aside and powered up his laptop. He would often tell his crew that knowledge was power, and if you knew what was going on around you, in most instances, you could see trouble coming and take steps to avoid any fallout. One of the items that intrigued him today, and which he soon discovered was the lead story on every internet site that he usually visited, was of a person who had gone into a hospital in Boston and cured all the kids of cancer. The article said this man just touched the kids, and now they were cancer-free. It went on to report that there was another incident that was identical to the Boston story that had happened in a hospital in Hartford Connecticut a month or so earlier. The accounts of both incidents were nearly identical, and the reporter who wrote the story was convinced that the same man was responsible for curing all the children in both places.

Jimmy's first thought was that if this guy continued, there would be a lot of people out of work in the cancer business, but he didn't know why this bothered him. He didn't know anyone in the cancer business and even if he did, it shouldn't make any difference to him if they lost their job. But something about these articles cast a foreboding shadow over his thoughts. He couldn't quite put his finger on why, so after a little while he brushed it off and finished perusing the rest of the news sites.

CHAPTER 10

Father Padraig O'Malley waited anxiously in the arrival area near Gate A19 at Philadelphia International Airport for the U.S. Air flight that would bring his new priest to the city. O'Malley knew that the flight was not paid for by the Church, as they sent their new priests to their first assignments by rental car or Greyhound. But Father Paul Sikora had gone back to Saint Cloud, Minnesota, after graduating seminary school for a short visit with his family.

O'Malley had gotten a short bio on his new young priest that was included in a packet from the archdiocese. Sikora's parents were well-off and very active in their local church. They had even donated the cost of repairing the rectory roof, which had been damaged during a severe winter storm several years back.

The report on Paul from the seminary was glowing. His academics were top of his class, and he was described by his instructors as enthusiastic and eager to learn. The only negative mark on that report was that when he was put into a group situation, Paul would most often shrink back and let someone else take control. One instructor wrote that even in a one-on-one, he came off as being timid. When O'Malley read that he thought he would have to help Paul overcome that, there was no room for timid behavior in a big city parish like St. Veronica.

The flight had landed, and the Pastor scanned the passengers as they exited the tunnel. A photo of Sikora was also included in the packet, but Padraig was looking more for the traditional white collar rather than the face of his new apprentice. The packet did not include Paul's height and weight, so Padraig was a bit surprised when he came out of the tunnel at 5'6" and about 145 lbs. The elder priest thought that given his small stature and the report of his timidity, a lot of work needed to be done. As Father Padraig O'Malley extended his hand to his young charge, he chuckled inwardly and thought, *"The pigeons in the park had better find a new lunch spot".*

The ride back to St. Veronica was filled with the same conversation that any two men would have, regardless of their profession. Two people, who until 30 minutes ago had been strangers, were now thrown into a situation where each realized they would be spending much of their time together over the next few years. They spoke of their family, where they grew up and went to school, and their past in general. Although Padraig had much more past to talk about than Father Paul, he was able to get him to do most of the talking by asking the right questions to make the younger man feel at ease.

Padraig was quite surprised by the amount of information he had learned about Father Sikora in the 35 minutes it took to reach the rectory. Once parked, O'Malley carried one of two small suitcases that belonged to the young man inside the rectory and showed him to his room.

After they had deposited the two suitcases on top of Paul's modest bed, Padraig said, "Why don't you unpack later this afternoon? Right now I would like to take you on a tour of the church and the rectory."

Paul responded "That would be nice."

The two headed back through the rectory and into the kitchen, where they intended to exit through the rear door but had discovered Katia Janeski moving about the kitchen.

Slightly startled, Padraig said, "Oh, Katia, I'm glad we ran into you. I would like you to meet our newest priest at St. Veronica, Father Paul Sikora."

Father Paul extended his hand, and Katia shook it. He told her it was a pleasure to meet her and called her Mrs. Janeski. She insisted that he refer to her by her first name, but it would take six months before Paul would break himself of the habit of addressing her by her surname. By then, his emotions would be pulled in so many different directions and the actions he was contemplating were so grave that he hardly noticed when Katia was in the room.

Padraig and Paul headed for the door once again but were halted by the housekeeper. "Where are you two headed? I was about to fix you something for lunch."

O'Malley looked at his watch and saw that it was just after the noon hour "I didn't realize what time it was. Are you hungry, Paul? We could have a bite before we start the tour."

"Actually, I am. I only had toast with my coffee this morning before the flight."

The two men sat at the table while Katia warmed up some tomato soup and made each one of them a sandwich. While they ate, she moved on to other chores, so they cleaned up after themselves when they had finished, and Padraig washed the few dishes they had used. The two left by the rear door of the rectory and headed for the back entrance to the big church.

Describing St. Veronica as big was not an exaggeration. The tour took the better part of two hours and included every corner of every room. Of course, Father O'Malley took his time, showing Father Sikora where things were kept and relating anecdotes about each room that had occurred over the years. When the tour was completed, the two priests went to O'Malley's office, which was accessed by a long hall located directly behind the altar. Padraig kept a coffee maker there, which he now used to make himself and Paul two cups. After they had settled into chairs with their coffee, it was the younger of the two men who started the conversation.

"On our walk through the church, I noticed more than a few areas that have fallen into disrepair."

"Unfortunately, our budget gets smaller and smaller each year. Attendance is down, and that affects the collection plate numbers and donations are diminishing, also. If you noticed the building at the rear of the property, that used to house our school, but declining enrollment made it impossible to operate. The last few years we lost money. But when I first arrived here, the school generated enough funds each year that allowed us to use some of that money in the church. On top of all that, the subsidy that we receive from the archdiocese is cut at each budget meeting."

"You are not alone there. The numbers are down throughout the country. People are leaving the Catholic Church like never before. In seminary, we were shown the diminishing statistics not only for attendance and revenue, but also for those willing to devote their lives to the faith by becoming nuns and priests."

"Yes, I know, but the Catholic Church has been through some tough times in its history and has always rebounded. I believe the church can and will recover from the scandals that have plagued us over the last decade. Even this grand church was not untouched by the problems that have surfaced of late."

Father Paul looked down at his shoes and said, "I am aware of the accusations against Father Spellman. I hope you don't consider this prying, but when I learned that this would be my first assignment, I googled St. Veronica and read everything about her that had been printed for the last ten years."

Padraig hesitated before he responded "I'm not sure if I find that prying or not. I was not brought up in an age where so much information is available just by typing in a few words on a computer. And by contrast, you haven't known a time when there wasn't an internet. I guess it was only prudent of you to find out as much as you could about the place I hope you want to call home for years to come."

Father Paul smiled and said, "I hope so, too."

Padraig wanted to bring the conversation back to a more positive note. "You know, Paul, I think you are just what this church needs; a young and fresh perspective and an enthusiasm that will bring the young people back into the fold."

"That is exactly what I want to do. I have some ideas, such as hosting a dance for the 18 to 25 age group. I was thinking maybe there would be some space in the school building for that event." Paul said, his voice rising as he spoke.

The Pastor said, "That does sound like a good idea, and we can look into using the school."

Paul continued "I also thought that we could use the classrooms in the school to give free instruction to teens and older youth on life issues, such as job hunting, filling out an application for a job or a loan, managing finances, planning a future, and sexual responsibility. I'm guessing that half the battle is getting the people to come here, so if we provide a wide range of activities and get a least a few to participate, then hopefully word of mouth will help us expand. Once they are here and talking to us, we can show them that we are much more than mass on Sunday."

Padraig stared at Paul with his mouth slightly open. He wondered where the timid person who attended the seminary had gone. He finally blinked a couple of times and said, "Those are some really grand ideas, Paul. We might have to squeeze the archdiocese for a few more dollars to implement some of them or maybe find funding in other places. Either way, I believe I have your first assignment. All of your ideas will have to be reduced to a written proposal, in which anything that might cost even one dime must be included."

"Actually, I did have some thoughts about keeping costs down. Would it be possible to hand out a questionnaire on Sunday asking our parishioners if they would be willing to donate their time and expertise on some of these projects? For instance, maybe we could get someone who works in an HR office to give a class on resumes, applications, and interviews. I was hoping with volunteers we'd keep the costs down to a minimum. Oh, and for the record, these are not all my ideas. Some are mine, and some I gleaned from brainstorming sessions we had at the seminary. You see, Father O'Malley, these are the types of things they are teaching at the seminary these days, ways we can bring people back to the church."

Father Padraig O'Malley was smiling when he responded "I think myself and this church were quite blessed when the decision was made to send you to us."

Paul blushed and looked at his feet again. They finished their coffee, and he asked to be excused, as he wanted to unpack and rest before starting on the proposals. They walked back to the rectory and parted ways at the kitchen door.

Padraig had wanted to take a walk through the park, but he didn't bring any food for the pigeons, because he associated that with being depressed and he was feeling far from depressed today. He felt it in his bones: today was a new beginning for him, both as a priest and as a man. So Father O'Malley strode around the paved path that meandered through the park with his head and his spirits held high. He greeted joggers with a "hello" or a "good afternoon" and stopped to chat with the mothers with strollers and anyone else he encountered on the path, for that matter. Later that night, as he retired for the evening, he tried to remember the last time he felt good about himself and eager to get up the next morning. He had to go too far back for that and drifted off to sleep before he found the answer to his own question.

CHAPTER 11

Clan Warburton sat in a lounge-type room in the New Haven studios of the ABC affiliate in Connecticut, WTNH. They had walked into the offices 25 minutes ago at 4:15 pm and announced to the receptionist that they were the family that had visited the two cancer hospitals. The receptionist, Jennifer Chase, politely explained to the Warburtons that the station had been swamped with calls from people claiming responsibility for the hospital incidents and at least a dozen more who had come into the offices. Jennifer explained that if they left their name and address someone would get back to them.

Danny smiled and took hold of her hand. "Could any of the others do this?" Seconds later, he informed her that she and her husband could stop looking for a surrogate to carry their child, as Jennifer was now able to carry her own pregnancy to term.

That got her attention, and minutes later they were shown to the lounge. The hour of their arrival was not random, Danny wanted to give them just enough time to set up an on-air interview for the five o'clock news but didn't want to be subjected to hours of questioning prior to the live broadcast. He knew that with only 45 minutes to put something together he made them scramble a little, but he guessed this was not the first time they'd come upon a good story they needed to plug into the news on last-minute notice. He had bought a new suit for the occasion, dark blue pin-stripe with a light blue shirt and a grey tie with thin red horizontal stripes. Carmel looked stunning as usual, and the girls wore their best dresses. But it was Jack who was the most dapper of the group, with a black suit and black shirt with a white tie. Two days before, they'd held a dress rehearsal, and

Jack had noticed that Kate and Sandy both were wearing summer hats that went with their dresses. The youngest Warburton decided that he also needed a hat so he would fit in with his sisters. So Carmel hit the stores and somehow found the perfect accessory, a white fedora with a black band that fit Jack's six-year-old head perfectly. Already word had spread, and three of the female office employees of the television station had stopped by the lounge and doted over Jack, who, of course, loved the attention.

At 4:45, the station manager, Clifford Lavin, entered the lounge and told Danny that they had been going over the camera coverage from the Boston incident and it certainly looked like the Warburtons. But he hadn't been certain until he'd talked with Jennifer Chase, and then he was convinced.

Lavin began "So this is the plan. We are going to run our top two stories that we had scheduled before you came in. Then we announce the interview with you, which will be done on a side set next to the news desk. The whole thing will last about five or ten minutes, and at the end we want you to introduce your family and bring them onstage. How does that sound?"

"First off, my family will be with me from the start of the interview. And secondly, don't even ask how I came to have this gift and do what I am able to do. I will address that at a later date. Also, I don't know anything about a live news broadcast. I've been a cop for most of my adult life, but I'm thinking that you might want to block out about 30 minutes for this interview. You cut this short and with the amount of calls you'll get, you might cause the cell towers to shut down due to the volume and also cause a meltdown at the phone company."

Lavin responded, "Ok. We will get more chairs for the set so that your family can be with you. As far as how long the interview will go, let's play that by ear. Now, what will you talk about?"

"I don't think we have time to go over everything that is open for discussion. But during the interview, if there is a question that I am not comfortable answering at this time, I will certainly let you know about it."

"Well, I will not be the one on the set with you, you may be familiar with our nightly news anchor, Karen Ayala? She will be your interviewer."

Five minutes later Danny, Carmel, and the kids were seated on the set to the right of the news set. The lights over them were dim, but they were able to see the two news anchors seated at the adjacent set. They heard the director count down from five to one and watched him point to Ayala as the red light on the camera came to life.

Karen led off the broadcast with a story about the state budget deficit and when she ended, the camera panned to her co-anchor. She quickly got up, walked around the cameras, and approached the Warburtons. She nodded to Danny, then shook hands with the rest of the family. She told him that she had a few hasty notes and was aware of the one issue that was off limits. He did not have a chance to respond, as the director told Ayala that 10 seconds remained before the interview would start. This time, the director did not count down from five, but instead held up one hand with all five fingers up and brought each one down until there was one left. At that point, the lights above the set came on and as the director pointed once again to Ayala, the red light signaled that they were all on live TV.

Karen began "By now, with numerous news stories and over one million internet hits on the video coverage, you would be hard-pressed to find someone who has not heard of the incredible events at the children's cancer centers in Boston and Hartford. We here at Channel 8 are proud to have an exclusive interview with the man responsible for the miracles at both of those hospitals. Welcome Mr. Daniel Warburton, who is accompanied today by his lovely family."

The camera panned back to show the entire set and all who were seated there.

"Good evening, Miss Ayala," Danny said. "Let me first introduce my family. This is my wife, Carmel, my two daughters, Katherine and Sandra, and my son, Jack. Thank you and the entire staff here for having us and treating us so well."

"You're welcome, Mr. Warburton. Now, we all know that the events in Boston and Hartford were real. Those children were cured of cancer, that is a documented fact, and there has been much speculation as to how anyone could do that. Also there have been thousands of people who have claimed they did these miracles. Why is it that we should believe you above all those others?"

"First off, call me Danny. And please stop referring to them as miracles. This had nothing to do with God or any religion. I'm just a man who has been given a gift, the source of which will be revealed at a later time, and nothing that I have experienced over the last two months has led me to believe that this is religious in nature. And if you need a reference, go talk to your receptionist who I cured of her infertility when I arrived."

"I did speak with her, and so did our station manager, and it was the description of her encounter with you that ultimately tipped the scales to give you this interview. So our audience is aware, you came to us, Danny, and asked for this interview to be live. Is there some message you wanted to specifically give to our viewers and, eventually, to the world?"

"Yes there is, Karen. Up until a short time ago, I was just a regular guy but I was given a gift and also, in a way, a task. The donors of the gift told me that we humans are in trouble. What with crime, greed, and apathy, we are headed down the wrong path, possibly to our own destruction. In some countries, over half of the population lives in poverty, but the governments there do nothing to help. As a group, we don't care about each other. My fear is that if we continue this way, what will we be like in the future?"

Danny paused to gather his thoughts. "And when I say our destruction, I'm not here to predict the end of the world, that would make me sound like a lunatic. No, I believe that people will be on Earth for a long time, but if we don't turn ourselves around, will we still be able to look in the mirror and call ourselves human?"

Karen interjected "You must admit, though, that there are hundreds of organizations and hundreds of thousands of people who give of their time and money to help others who are less fortunate."

"Yes, Karen there are good people in this world, and I'm sure many lives have been impacted by those you have mentioned. But even the large organizations do not have the power to help everyone. And as long as there are governments that allow their own people to die from disease and hunger, the hard work that those charities do is like shoveling sand back into the ocean. We've all heard about provisions being sent to third world countries and those items never making it to the people who it was intended for."

"But what can you do about the way people treat each other? You can heal and cure, but how can you change attitudes?"

"Curing disease and generally mending people is not the only gift I was given. I can also return the innocence we all had at birth. I know that might be difficult to understand and those who gave me the gifts described it as a cleansing of the soul. Now, I am an atheist and don't believe in a soul, but what I can tell you is that those I have already touched go through a transformation. They describe it to me as a sense of peacefulness. Let me give you an example. A housing project in New Britain was run by a local gang and was not a safe place after dark. I was able to reach into the heart of that gang and make contact with every member. Those young men now protect their neighborhood and have used the money they made from drug sales to help families struggling to make their bills. And therein lies my task. To change the world, just as I did to that neighborhood."

"You said that these changes in people came after you touched them. Do you need to have physical contact for your gifts to work?"

Danny sighed. "That is correct, Karen. And that is where my task will become quite difficult for me. Over seven billion people are on the planet. People who are a lot smarter than me can do the math and figure out how many years it would take for me to touch everyone. But just because that might not be possible doesn't mean I won't try"

Now it was Karen's turn to sigh. "It sounds like you will not be getting a whole lot of sleep in the future. Have you thought about how you will get started?"

"I've already started, don't you read the papers?" Danny said facetiously. "But to answer your question, I do have somewhat of a plan. My guess is that it would be easier and quicker if people came to me. So for now, here's what they need to do. There is an abandoned department store on Farmington Avenue in New Britain, and I have already made an agreement to use that building. What I intend is to gut it and make it one big room with a lot of chairs. I will be there 16 hours a day and touch as many people as I can each day. It is my hope that word will spread and more people will come to see me. To all those that I have helped so far, forget the part where I asked you to keep it a secret, tell everyone."

Karen said, "Yeah. I'm going to reiterate that sleep comment I made a few minutes ago."

"Which brings me to another point, I've told you I was just a regular guy before this. I have been a police officer with the New Britain Police Department for 15 years. If I am to help as many people as I can, I will have to quit my job. This presents a problem, and here is where I am going to sound like a scam artist, I still will have bills to pay and a family to feed, so I am asking those that I help to please give a donation so that I can continue and help others. Give what you can, if you can't afford to give anything that is fine too. No one will be turned away."

"Are you set up and open at that department store now?" Karen asked.

"Not yet. We have a shipment of chairs coming tomorrow, and we plan to clear a small wooded area that is to the left of the building for additional parking. But that can be done while we are open, so let's say this Wednesday morning at 8 am."

"I do hope you the best, Danny." Karen turned to Carmel and asked "Mrs. Warburton, what do you think of all this? And how will your husband's endeavor impact you family?"

Carmel was a little surprised to be addressed. The way the interview was going, she did not believe Miss Ayala was going to talk to anyone but her husband. But after a few moments, she collected her thoughts and said, "This is not what I would have chosen for our family. I suspect there will be some degree of notoriety, and although we have already done some traveling because of my husband's gift, I think those short trips were just the tip of the iceberg. I am worried how those two factors will affect the children's education and our home life in general. I guess I would have been perfectly happy being a police officer's wife and mother to my children and living anonymously. But I am Danny's wife and will follow him to the ends of the Earth because I believe in him and his mission. And, like him, I feel that we should do this as a family and stay together whenever possible. I was the first person my husband used his gifts on, so I know what he is capable of. With me and the kids at his side, there is nothing he can't accomplish. And, like my husband, I also prefer to be called by my first name. It's Carmel."

Now it was Karen's turn to hesitate. She felt the love this woman had for her husband and also a sense of protectiveness. Finally, she turned to the Warburton children and said, "Kids, I'm sorry we didn't have a chance to speak with you today, especially because you girls look so lovely and young Jack is so handsome. I heard that you have already captured the hearts of several of the girls who work in the office, Jack. Unfortunately we are running out of time, unless there is something else you would like to say Danny?"

"No, I think I accomplished all that I had set out to do today, except maybe a demonstration."

Danny's and Karen's chairs were close to each other and before she could react, The Healer reached across and took hold of her hand. The cameras caught it all as the news anchor slumped slightly in her chair and her eyes closed. Her head lolled forward for a few seconds, then their hands were no longer in contact. Karen blinked a few times, a reaction Danny had become quite used to seeing, and then she came fully aware. She jumped up and gave him a huge hug.

Karen addressed the audience. "This is incredible, this feeling of serenity. I feel like I'm 21 again. Every little medical issue I had is gone, every ache or pain vanished. I am here to report to all who can hear my voice that this man is not perpetuating a hoax, this is no scam." Tears started to fall down her cheeks as she sat back down. She continued "I'm feeling a little overwhelmed, could we send it back to Doug at the news desk?" The red light on top of the camera went off, Karen Ayala stood back up and gave The Healer's hand a squeeze before she headed off to the dressing rooms.

Clan Warburton headed for the parking lot. On the way, they discussed where they would stop for dinner, as Carmel had already informed Danny that it was much too late to expect her to start cooking when they got home.

CHAPTER 12

Monday night Danny called Captain Franti and informed him that he would not be coming back to work. The captain told his friend that he'd known that this day was coming, and he wished him well. They spoke for a few more minutes, and before Franti hung up, he asked Danny if he had seen all of the coverage his interview generated. Danny said he had not, because when they arrived home from New Haven, he'd kept the TV and computers off and had even taken the phone off the hook until he'd made the call to him. Franti advised him to get ready for the media blitz that was coming his way. Little did the captain know that he, too, would be waist deep in the hectic world that The Healer's life would become before too long.

Tuesday was mostly uneventful. Carmel stayed home with the kids now that school was out, but Danny cautioned them to stay inside for at least the morning, in case the media descended on the house. He went to the building that would become his second home during what he called Phase 2 of his plan. There wasn't much to do to the inside of the old department store, all of the clothes racks had been taken out, and the main floor was empty. While he waited for the chairs to arrive, he swept the floor and cleaned up the restrooms, then stocked those rooms with toilet paper and paper towels. At 9 am the crew arrived to clear the trees for more parking space. Danny came out to greet them and to let them know what he wanted done, and to touch each one of them.

Not long after they got started, a tractor trailer pulled into the lot and went around back to the loading dock. After the truck had backed in, the first thing that was unloaded was an electric fork lift that Danny had purchased from the chair company. Danny and Rick, the driver, unloaded the chairs. As Danny worked the fork lift, he banged into a few corners until he got the hang of the new toy. Rick had a similar fork lift of his own but didn't hit anything. Two hours later, the truck was empty, and Rick was back in the cab of the truck. He had thrown the heated seat cushion he always had onto the passenger seat, the back pain the cushion was there to ease was gone.

The truck pulled out and as Danny watched it leave, he noticed several people standing on the sidewalk on the far end of the lot. One news van and crew was setting up near the guys clearing the trees. He didn't worry about anyone wandering in, as all of the doors were locked. Next he started the task of putting all the chairs into rows. Danny did not want to have to put all the chairs back into rows at the end of each day, so he zip tied each chair to the next one in line.

At 5 pm, the tree crew left. The TV crew and the few spectators had moved on earlier in the day. At 6 pm, his cell phone rang, it was Carmel. She was out in the parking lot and told him that she and the kids had brought him supper. He hadn't eaten since breakfast and suddenly realized he was ravenous. Carmel had brought him a chicken parmesan grinder from Gino's Pizza, their favorite pizza joint, and it took all of 15 minutes for him to devour the grinder and a side of fries. She had also brought him two beers, one of which he drank with his meal, and the other while she told him about their day. She said there had been about three or four news crews parked on the street in front of their house from 10:30 in the morning until about 3 pm, but they did not attempt to contact anyone inside the house. Danny told his wife that he wanted her and the kids to be with him when he opened up Wednesday morning, at least for a few hours, and she agreed. He apologized for being rude, but he wanted to finish setting up before it got too late. He walked his family to the van and gave everyone a kiss goodbye.

Danny was alone to finish the monotonous chair task. By 10:30 pm, he had zip tied the last row. He still had about 50 chairs left but had absolutely no room for them on the floor. He figured on nice days he could put them outside along the front of the building, if the crowd got that big.

At 11:15, The Healer dragged himself into his house and went directly to bed; no cigar, no wine. He fell asleep seconds after his head hit the pillow, and the already-sleeping Carmel curled her naked body around his.

Wednesday morning the family woke up early and went to IHOP for breakfast. There was electricity in the air that even the children felt even if they did not fully understand. Danny thought, *"This is it, the real beginning, the point of no return had been crossed on Monday."*

While they waited for the food to arrive he looked around the table and was a little nervous. He may have taken on the task of fixing the entire world, but his first priority was to the people surrounding him at that moment. He hoped his decision would not interfere with the responsibility he had to them. Then the food came, and the mood lifted. They talked and laughed while they ate, and for that short time they were just Clan Warburton enjoying a meal.

Thirty minutes after they pulled out of the lot at IHOP, they drove into the lot of the old department store. Besides the crew who were still clearing the trees, there were seven cars already in the lot. Danny was slightly discouraged but thought seven was better than none.

Kate broke the silence. "Dad, what did you do here yesterday? The place still looks abandoned."

"I put up all those chairs that you saw. That took all day and most of the evening."

"I know that but I thought you were going to put up a sign or something"

"I can't afford a sign. Besides, what would the sign say?"

Carmel said, "You know dear, Kate has a point. We need to make the place more inviting, even if the sign was just a sheet with spray paint letters. Hey kids, that could be our project for the day."

Danny responded "That sounds like a great idea, but the question remains: what will we call our place?"

"That is part of the project. We will throw some ideas around this morning, hopefully make the sign this afternoon, and if those tree guys are still here maybe we can get them to use their bucket truck to put the sign up."

Sandra piped in excitedly, "How about The New Ark?"

Danny responded as he parked the van in the rear of the building, "That has a religious connotation, and I really want to stay away from anything like that."

The conversation continued as he unlocked the back door and they entered the building. He closed and locked the door, then reached for the bank of switches that turned on every light in the place. They walked past the office area and onto the main floor.

He sighed "I didn't notice before, but this place is drab, which is compounded by its size."

Carmel said, "Project number two. Ladies, you will have to get your creative juices flowing and come up with ways to decorate and brighten this place up. Jack, we will need some of your famous refrigerator paintings to hang on the walls. Honey, you just might be stuck with us until the new school year starts. There is a lot of work to be done."

Sandra, undaunted by the rejection of her name for the building, with even more excitement said "Music! We need speakers and a sound system. People need something to listen to in case they have to wait a long time to see you, daddy."

Danny smiled at his middle child. "That is a wonderful suggestion, Sandy, but I am not paying for a DJ."

"No, daddy. You have to get a CD player that can hold a lot of discs and plays them one after the other."

"Ok, I think we can do that. But no loud or obnoxious stuff. Soft music, to put people at ease."

It was now Kate's turn to sigh. "Not your smooth jazz stuff, dad."

"You're not old enough yet to appreciate good music, young lady. Anyway, we can work out the details later. Let's go see if anyone is at our door."

He took his keys out again and unlocked the front door. The sensor over the automatic door registered the movement, a red LED light flashed on, and the doors slid open. Danny reached up and pushed the switch to kill the power and hold the door open. The Healer looked out into the parking lot and saw 11 cars, but no one was exiting them.

Carmel must have been thinking the same thing as her husband, because she said, "The first sign we need is one that says Open."

Danny said, "Let's go back inside, see if we can find some cardboard and a Sharpie. Maybe the people in the lot are a little scared. Let's give them some time."

They all walked back inside, past the floor and the rows of chairs, to the first set of offices. Danny had found a desk in one of the back offices on Tuesday and had moved it to the front office. He had planned to use this space to see the people who showed up. He checked the drawers of the desk but didn't find what he was looking for. He then walked back out to the floor and intended to help Carmel and the kids search the rest of the offices for sign making material and found three strangers standing together by the first row of chairs.

The elderly black man who stood in front of the other two appeared to be the leader of this small group. He stood about 6′4″ but looked to weigh only 125 lbs. He wore a suit that was a bit outdated in style, and it hung on him as if he had been much broader in the shoulders and chest when he had first purchased it. Behind and to his right was an elderly black woman, and The Healer knew that these two were husband and wife. The third person in the group was a white male who looked to be in his mid-30s. He wore jeans and a faded concert t-shirt, so faded no one could ever make out the name of the band. His hair was too long for his age, and Danny thought it made him look like he was trying too hard to be 21 again.

After a few awkward seconds of a staring contest, the leader said, "Looks like you were expecting quite a few folks today."

"That was my hope."

The leader continued "My name is Cook, Terrance Cook and this is my wife, Adele. And I don't know this other gentleman's name, we met coming in the front door. Are we the first ones here?"

"Yes, you are," Danny said as he took two steps toward his first visitors and stuck out his hand to Cook. "My name is Danny War..." He stopped in his tracks as the three people in front of him moved backwards two steps. They moved in such unison that it appeared choreographed.

"I guess if I were in your shoes, I might find this whole thing a bit frightening also. My wife and children are in the back rooms looking for something to make an "open" sign. I'm going back there to help them search. Why don't the three of you have a seat, talk things over, try and relax. When I come back, if you're still here, we can talk. You have already come this far." He then turned and started to look for the rest of his family.

He found Carmel in one of the offices. She had located an old Magic Marker. But when she tried it out, the ink was dried up, and it wrote faintly. Kate arrived from another back office and had some materials, as well as her sister and brother.

"I found some cardboard but nothing to write on it with. But I also found some white paper. So if we have to, we can cut out letters in the cardboard and use the paper as a backing to highlight the cutouts."

Danny said, "Smart kid. I have some scissors in the desk in my office. Honey, could you cut the letters?"

As Clan Warburton turned and headed for what would now be called Danny's office, Carmel replied "I think I can handle that task."

"Oh, and so you are not startled, while you were back here three people came in. They seemed a bit skittish when I first approached them, so I gave them some time to think while I came looking for you guys. Let's go see if they are still here."

As they came onto the floor Danny was pleasantly surprised to see four more people sitting with the original three. He told Carmel where she could find the scissors and asked her to take the kids with her.

The Healer addressed the small group. "Good morning. My name is Danny, but you may already know that. Did you all come here today because you saw the interview on Channel 8 Monday evening?"

The group nodded in unison, and he heard a few softly spoken assents.

"Please, try not to be afraid, only good will be done in this place." He paused for a few seconds and continued. "So my plan was to meet with anyone who came here in the office behind me. That would allow for some degree of privacy. But if you want to have someone with you, that would be fine, too. Mr. Cook, I believe you were first in line. Would you and Adele like to come into my office?"

Terrance replied "We talked it over and decided that we would trust you."

All three went into the office, and Danny saw that Carmel and the kids had already been and gone. A few minutes later they came out of the office, and both Terrance and Adele told the people waiting that there was nothing to fear, and they were going to tell everyone they knew to come to this place.

Danny thanked them and then took concert t-shirt into the office. When they came out, another new arrival was waiting.

And that was the way things went for most of the rest of the day. People trickled in, and The Healer took care of business. He had put a large jar on the desk in his office for donations, and the amount of small bills in the jar grew steadily as the people came and went.

Just after noon, Carmel took the kids to get the stereo and a couple dozen CDs. When they returned, they also had lunch. Danny took 20 minutes to eat the sandwich his wife had made for him from cold cuts and other supplies. Two visitors waited for him, so they were invited to have something to eat with Clan Warburton. A short lull in traffic after lunch gave Danny and the kids a chance to get the stereo hooked up. So the next person to enter the old department store was greeted by the saxophone of Boney James.

Later in the afternoon, Danny looked toward the door and saw Terrance and Adele Cook coming in, followed by a group of about 20 or 25 other people. He went to meet them, shook Terrance's hand, and got a big hug from Adele.

Terrance said, "I hope you don't mind, but we brought a few family and friends by to see you."

"Mind? This is exactly what I was hoping for. I didn't think it would happen on the first day. Please, everyone come in. Welcome."

He finished with the few who were already waiting, then went to work on Terrance's group. By the time he was done and said goodbye to the Cooks, five more waiting. Before he could speak with them, Carmel approached him and said, "Danny, the kids are getting restless and tired, and I've got dinner to get started at home. How long were you planning to stay?"

"I hadn't given it much thought, but I guess I should set some definite hours of operation." He looked at his watch and saw that it was 5:45 pm. "I didn't realize it was getting this late. Why don't you take the kids home, feed them, and get them their baths. I'll be home in a few hours."

"How are you going to get home?"

"I'll call one of my guys in the Bureau."

"They are not your guys anymore. Remember? You quit."

"They would still give me a ride home. Mel, are you getting upset? Because we talked about this."

"I'm just tired. Go ahead and finish up here, and I'll see you at home."

Danny walked Carmel and the kids to the van and saw them off. As soon as they were gone, he felt lonely. Even with the trickle of people in and out for the rest of the evening, he still couldn't shake that feeling. At ten minutes after eight, no one was in the waiting area as he came out of the office with his last visitor so he walked her to the door and took the opportunity to close up shop. He took down the "open" sign, which had been attached by a string to an old flag pole bracket on the side of the doors and locked up. He called the New Britain Police Department Detective Bureau and got a hold of one of his favorite detectives, Tim Grey. Tim was all too happy to come and get his old boss and give him a lift home. Danny walked through his front door at 8:55, and Carmel warmed up the spaghetti sauce and made him some fresh pasta. The children were asleep already, they'd had a long day, too. And that was all he wanted to do after he ate, but he also wanted to spend some time with the lovely Mrs. Warburton. So he poured two glasses of wine, and they sat on the back deck and talked as he savored a cigar and the company of his wife.

Day two of the store started with The Healer getting up early and having toast and coffee for breakfast. The night before he had convinced Carmel to sleep in, along with the kids. They would take two cars from now on, and that would allow her to take care of a little business. Today she was going to the bank to deposit yesterday's donations, which totaled nearly $800. Danny didn't keep an accurate count, but he guessed he was visited by about 150 people on day 1. Carmel had also planned on picking up some spray paint to make the big sign for the front of the building. They still did not have a name for the place. Danny thought that the tree crew would be finished soon and, without their lift, putting up the sign would be a problem. He cleaned up his few breakfast dishes and left a quiet house.

He arrived at the old department store at 7:45 am, and there were about 30 or 40 cars in the lot. He said out loud, "Now that is more like it." He stopped at the tree cutting crew and spoke to the boss. The crew was finishing up their coffee and about to get started for the day. He asked the boss if they could help with putting up the sign, and he was all too happy to be of assistance. Danny had brought his laptop, and set it up in the office before he opened for the day. He wanted to check the news every so often to prepare for any trouble coming his way.

At 8 am he unlocked the front door and hung out the open sign. There wasn't much hesitation, as most of the people came right in and sat in the first few rows. The stereo had already been started, and this morning's guests were greeted by the beautiful voice of Sade. The morning went smoothly and much more steadily than the day before.

At 11, Carmel and the kids arrived with lunch, the sheet, and spray paint. Danny was on his way into the office when he first saw them coming down the back hallway. He stopped in his tracks, and his heart skipped a beat when he got a better look at his wife. She was wearing a pair of shorts and a form-fitting t-shirt with sandals, and she looked fantastic. The kids looked well-rested and were excited to see their dad. After hugs and kisses all around, he could see that Sandra was more excited than the rest and about to burst.

Danny laughed and said, "What has gotten into you, Sandy?"

Sandra giggled and spoke so fast her father could hardly understand her. "I have another suggestion for the name of your place, daddy. And I know you're going to like this one. It came to me during breakfast this morning, and I haven't told anyone yet. I wanted you to be the first one to hear it."

He had to cut off his middle child for fear she would forget to breathe "Ok honey, slow down, I'm listening." At the same time he looked at Carmel for a clue, but she raised her eyes like she didn't know what Sandra was talking about.

Sandra took a deep breath and let it out slowly, after which she said just one word. "Hope."

Danny knew this was huge for Sandra, so he bent down, kissed her cheek, and whispered, "I love it, Sandy. It's perfect."

He told Carmel and the kids that he had to get to his guests and he would let them find a place to spread out the sheet and paint the sign. Thirty minutes later, Carmel reported to him that the sign was done, but the paint was still wet. He suggested that he take a break and have lunch with them and maybe the paint would be dry by the time they were done eating.

The line to see The Healer had slowly gotten longer during the morning, and just before lunch there were about 80 or 90 people waiting on the floor. Carmel noticed this and whispered to her husband that she did not bring enough to feed everyone as she had done the day before. Danny told her not to worry and that if today was any indication, they couldn't afford to feed everyone everyday anyway. He hoped that people would bring their own snacks.

After lunch, Carmel checked the sign and found the paint was dry. She shouted to Danny from down the hall that she was going to talk to the tree crew about helping her put the sign up. He began to yell back at her that he had already arranged for their assistance, but she had turned to head out the back door. Danny thought that the crew would only have to get a look at her long legs in those shorts and they would be falling over each other to honor her request. He chuckled and brought the next person into his office.

The afternoon of day two went on that way for some time, The Healer saw one guest after another in his office with a few things in between to break the momentum. First, Danny heard the sounds of the lift in front of the store as the sign was raised. It took a few minutes to change the CDs in the stereo, and finally Danny took the time see Carmel and the children off when they left for home at about 5:30.

At 7:30 pm, Danny addressed the crowd on the floor. He told them that he was closing up but that he was going to give them each some kind of receipt so that they could be first in line tomorrow. He went back into his office to look for something he could give those left in line. He came back out a minute later with a pad of Post-It notes. He approached the first person in line, wrote the number 1 on the first page of the pad, put his initials under the number, gave it to the young blonde woman in the first chair, and went to the second person in line. The last number he wrote that day was 153. He saw number 153 out the door, collected the open sign, took the donations jar out the back door, and pointed his car toward home.

Day three started with The Healer opening up the doors to a crowd of over 200. The number of people was growing faster than he had anticipated. While the people filed in, Danny turned on the stereo. The sound of a saxophone once again filled the air, but this time it came from the talented Mindi Abair.

He took those with a Post-It note and his initials first and in order, and 152 were there first thing in the morning. The last Post-It noter came in a few hours later. Carmel and the kids showed up earlier than expected, loaded down with paints, chalk, and poster board. After the hugs and kisses session with the family, Carmel informed Danny that today was decorate the walls day. She also told him that she made the deposit of yesterday's donations on the way over. He hadn't counted the money the night before, he and Carmel had gone straight out to the deck with their wine and his cigar. She told him that the deposit was just over $3,000, which caused his eyebrows to rise. Maybe lunch for everyone would be affordable.

He had several visitors that day who were not necessarily looking for his healing touch. The first ones were the city fire marshal and the health inspector. They came together, but they had stopped at the police station to inquire about an escort. They were told by the lieutenant on duty that there would be no escort. If there was a problem, they should back off and then the police would respond. Both men told the lieutenant that they were going to see the mayor about this. The lieutenant responded that he thought the mayor wouldn't escort them either, but seeing that it was a free country they could ask him anyway. The two men had stormed off, and the lieutenant had turned to the desk officer and said, "I'll be damned if I will order one of my men to accompany those two jerks on a ball breaking expedition when the target is Danny Warburton." Seconds later, the ex-Detective Sergeant got the heads up on his cell phone. He didn't have time to play games, so he took care of business as he greeted the pair of city officials with a hand shake.

The other visitor was Channel 8 news anchor Karen Ayala, accompanied by a cameraman. She arrived mid-afternoon, and the chairs were nearly filled. The look of astonishment was apparent on her face. She asked Danny for a taped interview and also asked him if he was ready to reveal how he had come by his gifts. He acquiesced to the interview but only as he saw or in between guests. He also told her the timing was not right to tell his whole story. They stayed for about 30 minutes, as they wanted to get back to the studio so they could air the segment on the 6 o'clock news.

Before Carmel and the kids had left for the day, Danny had sent her out to get some white plastic poker chips. She came back with three packs, one hundred chips in each pack. He had told her why he wanted them, and she and the girls wrote the numbers 1 through 300 in black marker on those chips while Jack continued to create masterpieces with paint and poster board.

At 7 pm, Danny closed and locked the front door and tried to see everyone who was still inside. At 7:50 he stopped for the day and handed out the poker chips to the remaining people. When he was done, he still had numbers 78 through 300 on his desk. All that was left of day 3 was to bring the donations jar home and enjoy what was turning out to be a nightly session with Carmel on the deck.

After his first glass, curiosity got the best of him and he and Carmel counted the donations jar: $11,345, largely due to a check for $5,000. He guessed they would be able to make the mortgage payment next month.

Day 4, Saturday, the place was crowded all day long. The Healer was starting to learn that he had to take time out from seeing people to handle business. First CD of the day was from Corinne Bailey Rae, her debut album. He inserted the disc into the stereo and had taken two steps away when "Like a Star" floated into his ears. Danny started with the leftovers from the day before and then called home. He wanted to talk to his wife before she left the house for the day. She answered on the third ring, and he asked her to pick up some stencils, both letters and numbers, and paint on her way in today. A non-stop flow of guests came in and out of his office until 12:15, when Carmel showed up with lunch.

She greeted him with a big kiss and explained why she was alone. "The kids seemed like they would be a little bored here today, so I dropped them off at your sister's house so they could visit with their cousins. Then I stayed and chit-chatted with Kelly. She is doing so much better and even has a date next weekend."

"Well, that is good news. I'm glad for her."

Danny and Carmel went into his office and closed the door for a private lunch. He hadn't been eating well over the last four days, and his hunger became overpowering at the aroma of the food. He had wolfed down half of his grinder before he realized it and looked up at an astonished Carmel.

"I'm guessing you approve of my choice of lunch for today."

"To tell you the truth, I don't think I even tasted it.

She couldn't hide the concern in her voice when she responded. "This gift must have ramped up your metabolism. Did you know you have lost weight recently?"

"Yeah, I know. But it may be due to the fact that I have been eating less lately."

"Could be, but it is certainly something we will be watching. Anyway, why did you want the stencils?"

"I want to put the store hours on the door. What do you think of 8 am to 8 pm Monday through Friday, 8 am to 1 pm on Saturday, and closed on Sundays?"

"That sounds good. I was beginning to think you were going to be here seven days a week."

"You know better than anyone that I'm a bit of a workaholic, but these last four days have kicked my ass. And even though you and the kids have been here much of the time, I have been busy and haven't been very good company. I miss you guys."

Carmel smiled and kissed her husband on the cheek. That signaled the end of lunch. After they cleaned up, she offered to paint the hours on the front door. Danny took her up on that, and he went back to seeing his guests.

Carmel busied herself the rest of the afternoon by changing the CDs in the stereo and talking to the people waiting to see Danny. At 4 pm she told him that she was going to pick up the kids and head home. He told her that he was going to stay until 7 tonight, and the hours on the door would start tomorrow.

He arrived home at 7:30 and had a quick bite to eat. He visited with the kids until their bedtime, and then it was out to the deck with Carmel. Before midnight they retired to their bedroom and, although they were both tired, they found the energy to make love. After, each satisfied, they spoke for a few minutes and agreed that they needed that, and it had been a long week. Then they both drifted off to sleep and didn't wake up until just before noon.

CHAPTER 13

Jimmy Santini watched the coverage of Danny's interview on Tuesday, after it had been picked up by the network newscasts. When it was over, he immediately began to pace around the spacious living room of the mini-mansion he owned in The Hamptons. The Brain was more agitated than he could ever remember in his adult life, and it bothered him that he couldn't understand why. The interview seemed sincere, but the demonstration of the guy's abilities looked like a bad piece of theater with the Ayala woman in on it. It was plain, and lacked pizzazz. If Warburton was trying to convince people that he had the power to heal, he did a piss poor job of it. He thought that they should have had the lights go down when he grabbed the news lady's arm and then had a humming noise in the background and maybe even made the video feed wink on and off. Then when he let go of her, all those things would go back to normal.

Still, Jimmy continued to be bothered and thought that Warburton would somehow cause him trouble. He even considered a road trip to Connecticut to see the guy at his abandoned department store, but that would have to wait a few weeks, as he was too busy with a problem that had arisen. One of his distributors was skimming from his profits. Other wiseguys would send one of their crew to handle such an indiscretion, but Jimmy was the hands-on type and believed in the concept of leading by example. He wanted his crew to see that he would be willing to do anything he would ask them to do.

Finally, he knew what he had to do to calm himself from the irritation caused by the interview. In the barn behind the house he kept a few pieces of workout equipment, which included a heavy bag and pair of boxing gloves. He changed into sweats, went out to the barn, and hit the bag for over an hour. When he returned to the house, he was drenched in sweat but no longer agitated. He showered, had an early dinner, then retired and hoped a good night's sleep would clear his head of this Warburton thing.

As Jimmy Santini tried to figure out why Danny Warburton had gotten under his skin, just under 100 miles south and slightly west, Father Padraig O'Malley was anything but agitated. He was extremely pleased with the way Father Sikora had plunged into the Lord's work in his new community. He had already organized one youth dance at the school gym and had another planned for the weekend before the kids went back to college. Father Sikora had only a few volunteers to help him with his life classes for the local teens, but he was getting a schedule together and working with what he had so far. Father Paul had proved to be a most enthusiastic young priest and was far from the timid person that Padraig had expected.

The older priest was becoming more content as each day passed, and the park pigeons were forced to find food elsewhere. But that didn't mean he was a stranger in the park, not by a long shot. Father O'Malley spent at least an hour each day walking in the park and speaking to all that he encountered. Some days Father Paul accompanied him, but most days he started his walk alone. Padraig's mind and psyche were not the only things that were healing and getting stronger. The daily park excursions caused him to feel better physically, as well. He was also getting back to old habits that he had once enjoyed. Reading was one of his passions that he had let slip over the last few years. Not only did he read scriptures, but also for pure enjoyment he read mysteries, science fiction, and even the macabre from authors such as Stephen King and Dean Koontz.

Padraig didn't watch much television, occasionally he caught the first half of a Phillies game but would start to fall asleep in his chair around the fourth or fifth inning. Not this evening though. He planned to work on his next sermon and after dinner read a few chapters in the novel he was currently involved with until he retired for the night. He certainly did not expect to be watching a YouTube video on Father Sikora's laptop that would disrupt his reading and push back his usual bedtime.

Father O'Malley did work on his sermon that evening. After helping Katia clean up after dinner and seeing her to the door, he sat down with his book, but had only read two pages before Father Paul came knocking on his door. It was Thursday, and neither one of them had watched any television since Monday. Paul hadn't even checked the news on his computer, as he did about four or five times a week, because he was so busy with his various projects. But tonight he had time and found several articles about a man who claimed to be able to heal the sick. Paul was leery, but the articles were from reputable reporters. Although the reporters were not totally convinced themselves, the general feeling he got from the writers was that they lent some credence to this man's ability. The articles gave his name as Daniel Warburton and explained that he had given an interview to a local TV station on Monday. Paul was no stranger to the internet and found it easy to locate the full interview on YouTube. An hour and a half later, he was at the pastor's door.

Paul showed Padraig the YouTube video of the interview between Danny and Karen Ayala that had aired on Monday night. He then gave his mentor a few minutes for it to sink in. Finally, Paul asked excitedly, "Do you think this guy is for real?"

"Well, I haven't had enough time to form an opinion, but from what I know of the internet there are many manufactured videos, hoaxes, and those who will do anything to get their 15 minutes of fame."

"I agree, but before I brought this to you, I spent about an hour researching Daniel Warburton and found information from both before and after this interview. Certainly much more after, but he seemed like an ordinary man just a few months ago. And now he has been identified as the person who went into a hospital in Hartford, Connecticut, and Boston and cured every cancer patient there. There are hundreds of posts online that attest to the validity of his claims."

"Remember, Paul, that the information age, as wonderful as it can be, can also be used to dupe a greater number of people than ever before. Hoaxes have always been revealed for what they are in the end, but I am a bit concerned that you seem to be very excited by this story, maybe overly so."

"I know I'm showing more emotion than I should, and I came in here and dumped this on you without warning. But I can feel this electricity inside me, and I don't understand why. I have this unexplainable feeling that this event will be a turning point in the Catholic Church."

"Father Paul, by your own admission you have only known about this for a few hours. It is getting late, and I think you need to calm yourself so we can discuss this rationally. So I suggest you go back to your room, maybe have a glass of wine and read some of your favorite passages in the Bible, and sleep on it for now. We will find some time tomorrow to gather information on this story and talk it over."

"Yes, Father. Please excuse my impetuousness. I will take your suggestion and see you in the morning." Father Paul left the room and softly shut the door behind him.

Padraig sat stunned for a brief moment. He had not seen this type of behavior in Paul before. He reminded himself that he had only known Father Sikora for a few months, and he was still a young man, prone to outbursts of emotion. He assured himself that he and Paul could reason this story out in the morning when they could look at it with fresh minds.

Padraig decided that he would find the comfort of his bed now, without any further reading. After washing up and changing into his pajamas, Father Padraig O'Malley lay down on his plain but reposeful bed and closed his eyes. But the hook was already set, and sleep would not come. Since he'd started to ready himself for bed, he'd thought only of Danny Warburton with increasing curiosity. He continued to play certain parts of the interview he had watched over and over in his head until he knew that his pillow was not his friend right now.

There was an outdated desk top computer in his office in the church. Although not as fast as Father Paul's laptop, it was connected to the internet, and Padraig wasn't clueless when it came to navigating cyberspace. So he put on his slippers and a cardigan, not because the late July night was chilly, but to avoid looking completely silly while walking around in just his pajamas. He took the path from the rectory to the massive church.

At 3:15 am, with a slight headache from staring at the computer monitor for so long, Padraig found his pillow again. He had read about Danny Warburton for over five hours, watched the interview two more times, and viewed the opinions of those in the media that he thought were trustworthy, before finally shutting off the computer at 3 am. This time he fell into a deep sleep only seconds after crawling into his bed but he had time for one last thought. He now felt that he understood a little of what Father Paul was so agitated about. But as his new priest saw this as something positive, Padraig believed that Warburton could be troublesome for the Church.

CHAPTER 14

Danny felt a little guilty for sleeping in on Sunday, but the kids said they understood. And Clan Warburton proceeded to have a great day together. They didn't do anything spectacular, spent a few hours at the park, had a game of miniature golf, and went to a go-cart track, where Jack had to ride in his father's lap. But doing these things as a family was all that they needed. They topped off the day by getting three pre-made pizza doughs, cheese, and pepperoni and made a mess of the dining room table and floor as they joked and laughed while putting together their dinner, especially when Jack put more of the shredded mozzarella in his mouth than he did on the dough. After diner they watched a little TV until it was bedtime for the kids. Even Danny and Carmel retired early, but it was not because they were tired.

Monday morning, back to the building called Hope, and the constant flow of people. Norah Jones was the first artist of the day on the CD player. Carmel had called around and set up a meeting with a caterer for 11:30 that morning. She showed up at ten, with the kids and a Tupperware tub filled with activities for them. But by the afternoon, the kids were done with the games and cards and coloring books and told their mom that they wanted to be out with the people who had come to see their dad. So that afternoon, the three of them went out front and "worked" the crowd. As the oldest, Katherine decided she would be the host and greet the guests at the door. Sandra was under orders to keep her brother close to her, so the two of them walked through the rows of chairs and engaged those seated in conversation. Sandra had a talent for spotting the nervous ones and spoke to them a little bit longer, telling them that she had known her father her whole life, and he would never harm them, he was here to help. And, of course, everyone loved Jack, who didn't have to say a word, just flash that Warburton smile. Mama bear stood off to one side with a few tears running down her cheeks and a lump in her throat as she watched her children grow up before her eyes.

Monday went smoothly. Danny told the caterer he wanted a daily order of coffee, juice, and Danish until 10 am and then a spread of fixings for sandwiches and a few hot items like little meatballs and pasta until six in the evening. They negotiated a price for the five-and-a-half days that Hope was open, and the caterer couldn't wipe the smile off his face as he walked out the front door. He knew he wouldn't need another gig as long as this one lasted.

Carmel and the kids stayed for the entire day, but when it was time to lock up, everyone was tired and hungry. Danny stopped on the way home and picked up Chinese food. After they all had their fill, most got a second wind except for little Jack, who was crashed on the living room couch by 9 pm. After the kids settled down and hit their beds for the night, Danny told Carmel that he thought he wasn't getting to some of the people who needed his immediate help. He told her that he was going to start opening late on Fridays so that he could visit the methadone and rehab clinics to try working on the drug problem, at least in this area, to start.

Hope looked like a circus on Tuesday morning. With the serving of coffee and Danish, the guests no longer sat in their chairs and waited their turn. They were up, walking around, and talking with each other. With all of the conversations going on, Danny wasn't sure if anyone could hear the sensual trumpet of Chris Botti coming from the stereo speakers when he first turned it on. Carmel showed up at noon with lunch for Danny, her, and the kids. He decided that they wouldn't have their lunch in the office, but instead he had set up a table in front of all the chairs so he could feel closer to his guests. Many of the people waiting to see him also visited the caterer's tables at that time and had lunch with Clan Warburton. After they ate, Carmel told him they would not be staying. She explained that several stores had sales, so today was back-to-school clothes shopping day.

As it turned out, the fire marshal and the health inspector wouldn't be the ones who complained to the mayor. The health inspector's second-in-command knew of the initial visit to Hope and felt his boss dropped the ball. So he spoke to the mayor, who in turn spoke to the chief of police, James Fordwell. The chief told the mayor that he would speak to the lieutenant. But what he didn't tell His Honor was that their talk wasn't going to be about the lieutenant's rudeness to the two other city employees. So technically, Jimmy didn't lie to the mayor. But everyone has a boss, and that meant the chief was tagged to accompany the mayor to Hope.

After lunch on Tuesday, Chief Fordwell drove to city hall to pick up the mayor. He was informed that the mayor was going in his city-owned Town Car, which was always driven by one of his aides. As Fordwell headed to Hope, the empty passenger seat in his cruiser was another reminder why most people who knew him thought the mayor was a dick.

Mayor Greg Dubois was waiting in front of the old department store when Chief Fordwell arrived. He only had to look into the mayor's eyes to know that he hadn't waited to go in out of courtesy for the chief. No, the mayor was scared of the man they came to see.

Dubois said, "Chief, this man worked for you, so you know him. I think it would be best if you went in first and explained to him the reason for our visit."

"That would be fine by me, if I knew the reason for your visit."

The mayor stammered. "The deputy health inspector informed me that your ex-officer is in violation of several health codes and several more fire codes. We are here to shut him down!"

"You have no idea what the man is capable of, but you're the boss, I'll go in first. Give me five minutes, and then you come in and we'll have a sit-down." Fordwell didn't wait for a response. He turned and entered Hope.

Danny and the chief greeted and shook hands, but nothing happened. The Healer had visited the chief weeks ago for that part.

Fordwell frowned and said, "Danny, I apologize, but I've got the mayor outside. He wants you to close the shop because of health and fire code violations, and he's being a dick about it."

Danny's response surprised Fordwell. "Oh, good. I have been waiting for this."

"You knew the mayor was coming?"

"Not the exact time and date, but knowing His Honor, I knew he couldn't resist a chance to exert his control. Jimmy, the mayor is just a conduit to those who are much more powerful than him. This whole thing was set up not only to help people, but also to lure the mayor or some other politician to me."

"Well, it didn't take long. It's been just over a week since your interview on TV."

"Yes, things have progressed more rapidly than I had anticipated. So let's keep the ball rolling and bring the boob in."

Fordwell turned in the direction of the door as Mayor Dubois entered. Ever the vote-seeker, Dubois saw all the seats were filled and started to introduce himself and shook hands with those on the ends of the aisles. As the mayor reached the front of the row of chairs, where Chief Fordwell was standing, The Healer stepped from behind the big cop with the stars on his shoulders and offered his hand to Dubois. The mayor was so far into politician mode that he didn't immediately recognize Danny and, without hesitation, he accepted the outstretched hand. Jimmy Fordwell held the mayor up as he began to slump, but it was only for a few seconds, as Danny was done, and Dubois regained his composure.

"What was that?" the mayor asked a little breathlessly.

The Healer clapped the mayor on his back and said, "Just a little internal housekeeping, there was a bit more black in there than most. Sorry I sprang that on you without any warning, but look on the bright side, you're no longer a dick." Which of course made the chief laugh out loud.

Danny said, "Anyway Greg, do you think you can do something for me in return?"

Dubois realized what had happened to him. "Just name it, Mr. Warburton."

"Call me Danny. I would like an audience with the governor. Could you set up an introduction?"

"I haven't really gotten along with him in the past, but I think he would be interested in your work here. Give me a few days."

"That would be fine, and tell him to bring along anyone else in state and federal government that might also be interested. Hell, we'll make it a party. I close the shop on Saturday afternoons, so try to schedule it on one of the next few Saturdays."

Dubois shook Danny's hand again and said, "I will."

Danny turned to Fordwell. "Always a pleasure Jimmy, but if you two gentlemen would excuse me, a lot of people are here who need a few moments of my time. Greg, I'll be waiting to hear from you." He turned to the next person in the line of chairs and began to talk to her. The chief and the mayor found their own way out.

That night, while outside on the deck, he told Carmel about the mayor's visit. "You should have seen his face, Mel. He was looking around, and it was like he was actually seeing people for the first time."

"Did you really tell him that he wasn't a dick anymore?"

"Yeah, I did. It was worth it to see Fordwell with tears of laughter on his cheeks. And Dubois wasn't even offended. But his visit just kicked things into high gear. Phase 3 will be here sooner than I thought, which means more travel and a more hectic life for our family." He knew this was a sore spot for her, and he waited for her response.

Carmel took a sip of her wine and gazed out into the blackness of the back yard. She took a deep breath, let it out, and then turned to the man she chose to spend her life with. "I reserve the right to be cranky a few times during our family's upheaval, but I can't say that I didn't know it was coming."

"I suspect you won't be the only one to be cranky at times, so before all that starts, let's take the kids to Six Flags on Sunday. I haven't seen much of them these past two weeks, and I miss them. And who knows, maybe you'll like traveling the globe. We certainly will see places that we never would have prior to the gift. It would be nice if some big corporation donated a private jet to us. Then we could fly in style and comfort, enjoy a big screen TV, a bar, and maybe even have a bedroom in the back. Then I could make you a member of the mile high club."

"You say that like you already are a member."

They had come into the kitchen from the deck as they talked, and Danny was at the sink rinsing out their wine glasses. He said, "Me?! Now, you know that's not the case, Mel. But we could play pilot and stewardess in bed tonight. I could show you around the cockpit, and then we'd pretend we're in the club."

Carmel was right behind him and slapped his ass so hard her hand stung. "You sexist pig, who says you'll be the pilot?"

Danny laughed and rubbed his smarting ass cheek as they headed for their bedroom.

CHAPTER 15

Father Sikora was a little concerned that Padraig was still sleeping at 10am, the morning after he showed him the Warburton interview. He had noticed that since his arrival, Father O'Malley had seemed to improve both physically and mentally. But he also had learned of the stress that the older man was under over the last two years, and he still worried about his new friend. Paul was sitting at the rectory's small kitchen table nursing his second cup of coffee when he decided that if he didn't hear from the pastor by 10:30, he was going to knock on his door. And if there was no answer, he was going to enter.

Five minutes before his plan of action was to commence, Padraig shuffled into the kitchen. He was still in his pajamas. Padraig saw the look on Father Sikora's face and said, "About what time did you start to think I was on my way to heaven?"

"Father, no. I didn't think you were dead. I......I didn't know what to think."

"I do appreciate your concern. Frankly, Paul, lately I have been feeling a renewed purpose in my life and my faith, and you are a big reason for that. So I believe I'll stick around for a little bit longer."

"That is a high compliment indeed. But are you feeling ill at all? It is not like you to rise so late in the morning."

"I'm feeling fine. The reason I'm up late is because I didn't get to sleep until 3:30 in the morning. I'll tell you all about it, but first, how old is that coffee?" Padraig inquired as he pointed to the coffee maker.

"It's a couple of hours old. Let me make you a fresh pot."

Padraig sat down at the kitchen table while Paul busied himself at the coffee machine. When the coffee was done, Paul poured Padraig a cup, then poured himself yet another one and hoped it wouldn't make him jittery. He brought the two cups to the table, then sat opposite Padraig, and waited for the explanation as to the pastor's late night.

After a few moments and a few sips of his coffee, Padraig started "I must have caught a bit of the Warburton bug from you last night. After you left my room, I tried to go to sleep, but that interview you showed me was nagging at my brain. So I went to my office in the church and used the old desktop to do some research of my own on this healer. Paul, I stayed there half the night and still didn't see a portion of what is on the internet about that fellow. But what I did see leads me to ask you, why do you think this man will be such a positive influence on the Church?"

"Honestly, I don't know. Some of the excitement has ebbed, probably from a good night's sleep and my concern for you this morning. But I guess it was a gut feeling I had from watching the interview and from a few other items on the web."

"Oh, there is no doubt he is a charismatic individual. He appears very down-to-earth, he knows how to talk to people, and his smile is infectious. I imagine he comes across as a very likable person. But it has been my experience that sometimes appearances can be deceiving."

Paul asked cautiously, "Even after looking at hours of information on him, you still think he is a fraud?"

"I'm not sure yet if he is for real or not, but I can say that I do not get the same positive vibe that you get from him."

"Like I said, those feelings have subsided a bit. But I still think his ability to heal is genuine."

"Well, we may disagree on that subject, but either way, he is way up in Connecticut, and we have to take care of our business here at St. Veronica. And if he does impact the church one way or the other, that would be for those in a higher office than us to worry about."

"I understand that, but if it's all the same to you, I would like to continue following the story. And if you would like, I could keep you updated, unless you would rather I keep it to myself."

"That would be fine, Paul. But for now, I will let you get back to your work here. After I shower, I'll be in my office in the church, if you need me."

The two men parted, each knowing that they had lied to the other one. Paul would not just follow the Warburton story, he would delve in with every spare moment that he found. And Padraig would be on his old desktop with his office door closed almost every other day looking for the latest downloads on anything pertaining to Warburton. He would even contemplate taking a trip to Hope to see what was going on with his own eyes.

Both priests did quite well keeping their research from each other for months, but eventually they each confessed to the other of their secrecy. On that day, the first threads were woven together of a plan whose origins came from hell.

# # #

Jimmy The Brain Santini made most of his money off of the drug trade. He tried to keep his operations close to home and had most of his distributors in the boroughs of New York. But a few were out on Long Island, and he had a few more who came down from Connecticut that he would supply. All of these mid-level dealers gave Jimmy his cut every week, and he watched the numbers carefully. His main concern was that those same dealers skimmed some of his profits, but he also wanted to track the current trends of the drug trade. Things like which drugs sold better than others and in what areas. So when he saw a steady decline in sales of all types of drugs in Connecticut, he didn't think it was a result of skimming. He knew that his dealers were not smart. When one decided to steal from him, it was usually larger chunks of money that were immediately noticeable. They had no patience. No, Jimmy knew this for what it was, less drugs sold and less drugs being used. He set up a meeting with his crew to find out why, but in the back of his mind the name Warburton kept popping up.

The meeting was short, mainly because no one had a clue why the numbers were down. Santini decided to send Sal Giordano to Connecticut to get some answers from his dealers there. The next morning, Sal drove to New Haven. He took along one of the soldiers of the Gambino family, not because he was going to lean on anyone and needed the muscle, but because Sal had never liked drug dealers. He looked on them as a sleazy bunch who would get a kid hooked on that junk just to make a buck, and they shot each other up more than any wiseguys Sal ever knew.

As with any legitimate retail business, the drug trade was no different. It started at the top with manufacturing a product and then trickled down in an ever-widening pyramid-type structure until the product reached the consumer. The mid-level dealers who received their supply from Santini's men then brought it back to Connecticut and sold it to several other dealers, who in turn had their own platoon of street distributors who dispensed the product to the consumer. The amount of levels depended on the amount of product being moved and the size of the organization.

Today, Sal was meeting with the people who came to New York and bought the drugs from Jimmy. All they could tell Sal was that the street dealers were not re-upping their supply as often as they used to, and the major decline was coming from the middle of the state.

One of the mid-levels told him that there was a story about a guy up that way who could cure people's addiction. This same guy was going to rehab clinics and even curing people on the streets. He said this guy rehabbed people just by touching them. He also told Sal that he thought the story was bullshit. But not because he didn't believe it, he did. But because he didn't want to look stupid in front of the New York guys.

Giordano told the dealers that they'd better start looking into the real reason they were not moving the product like they used to, because Jimmy Santini didn't like losing money. And he sure as fuck didn't want to hear some story about a guy curing addicts by some miracle and any other voodoo shit. The two mobsters left with the threat that if this current trend continued, they would be back.

Sal was grateful that the traffic on I-95 wasn't as bad on the return trip back into the city. He drove directly to the building that housed the base of operations for the crew, a pool hall that Jimmy Santini himself owned. The business was located in the heart of the Gambino family territory, at a busy intersection in the Bronx, about five blocks from Yankee Stadium. Most days, Jimmy was in the spacious back room of the pool hall.

When Sal arrived, he found a couple of the guys out front playing pool, but the boss wasn't at his desk. Sal called Jimmy's cell. When Jimmy answered, Sal was about to tell him what had happened in Connecticut, but the boss said he wanted to hear it face to face and told Sal to stay put.

Jimmy had been driving his car when the call came in from the pool hall. Five minutes later, he noticed that the speedometer had inched up to 50 mph. Prior to talking with Sal, he had been going 35 in a 25 mph zone. He backed off the accelerator and then registered the anxious feeling that was coursing through his body. His hands were clenching the steering wheel, and it felt like every muscle in his body was tense. As he drove, he struggled to find the source of his anxiety, but the reason eluded him. He calmed himself somewhat by the use of some steady breathing and relaxation exercises, and by the time he reached the pool hall, he was in control, at least on the outside.

Jimmy took Sal to his office in the back and said, a little too sharply, "What did you find out? What's the problem up there? Tell me everything they said."

Sal was taken aback by Jimmy's demeanor and didn't answer right away. He didn't understand why this was such a big deal to Jimmy, but he quickly realized that it was. So he took a serious tone when he said, "Boss, those mooks didn't have any information for me."

Through clenched teeth, Jimmy asked, "You mean to tell me that they didn't say anything to you, and you left, satisfied with their answers?"

"No, Jimmy, that's not what I'm saying. They told me that sales are down in the center of the state, but they didn't know why. They're losing money too, but they don't know what to do about it."

Santini was standing behind his desk with his hand splayed out on the polished top. He knew he was overreacting and tried to force himself to be calm. "Sal, it appears that I am a little out of sorts today. I should know better than to expect my distributors to know anything about the bigger picture."

Sal was relieved. "No problem, Jimmy, we all have bad days. Hey, this might make you laugh. One of those guys said he thought the diminished sales were due to some guy he'd heard about who was going around curing addicts just by touching them. He said he didn't believe the stories, but looking at his face, I think he does."

Santini was as white as a ghost as he mumbled, "I knew he was going to be trouble."

Sal's worry was evident in his voice. "Boss, what did you say? You feeling okay? You look like you've lost all your color."

"I'm fine. You can leave now."

Sal didn't say anything more, and he turned and headed for the door. He did turn to look at Jimmy as he opened the door to the hall and saw him pacing behind his desk and heard him mumbling to himself again.

CHAPTER 16

Even though Danny was putting in long hours, up early most mornings, and not hitting the sack until around midnight after quality time with Carmel on the deck, the weeks seemed to fly by. The positive thing was that on his trips to the methadone clinic, fewer people were there. And even fewer addicts than usual were on the streets. On the flip side, there wasn't an empty seat at Hope from the time the doors opened until he dragged himself out to the Santa Fe each night. Traffic was backing up on Farmington Avenue, and the caterer was having a problem keeping the coffee urns filled in the mornings and the food trays during the day. More than a few times Danny had to go outside and help an elderly person who had passed out due to the heat of the day.

Conditions became so bad that he enlisted the aid of Carlos Cintron and several other ex-gang members for crowd and traffic control. Carlos had been stopping by to visit with Danny over the last few weeks, and Danny thought it his good luck that the ex-South Side King enforcer was there when he decided he needed some people to help with the logistics. He hired Carlos as his security advisor and told him to round up about 10 more, both men and women, who could work both inside the building and in the parking lot to assist in making things run smoother. Within three days Carlos had the security staff wearing bright yellow golf shirts with "security" across the back and their names stitched over the breast pocket. They had rain gear for foul weather days, flashlights for the evening hours, and radios to communicate with each other. Money was not a problem, as donations were still pouring in.

The young men and women that he brought in were enthusiastic and had a fierce loyalty to both Carlos and Danny. They had all grown up in the same housing project that Sgt. Warburton had first visited, and they were witness to what he could do and how he could make things better.

The Healer was getting a little anxious waiting for Mayor Dubois to get back to him with a date for the meeting with the governor. He hadn't heard word one from the mayor and suspected that he was intimidated by the governor and was having trouble working up his courage to go see him or even call. The governor had a very powerful personality and usually got his way in the legislature. Some might even call him a bully, but although Danny wasn't a fan, he had to admit the guy got things done.

He thought he might bypass the mayor and go see the governor himself. It would be easy for him to get by the capitol police and any other security that was in place, but Danny couldn't be sure when the governor was in his office, and finding time was difficult. He decided to give the mayor until the end of this week, and then he would reach out to Dubois.

Monday of the following week, the kids would be going back to school. Danny and Carmel had planned to spend as much time as they could with them over the weekend doing the little things they like to do, going to the park, out for ice cream after dinner, and staying up late watching scary movies with all the lights off.

Danny figured that they probably wouldn't finish the school year at their current schools, as Clan Warburton would most likely be on the road by then, but he had already planned on that. Deidre Lorre had come to Hope with a health concern, a heart issue she'd had from birth. She had been a teacher in Baltimore, Maryland, for ten years before her heart condition worsened and had forced her to leave that job. Prior to her learning about The Healer and the things he was doing at Hope, she was on a list for a new heart, but her rare blood type was making it difficult to find a donor.

Deidre was single, and Danny thought she would be perfect to fill the role as private tutor for his children when Phase 3 started. After their brief visit in his office and the question was asked, she said she would be delighted to teach the kids when the family began to travel. He advised her to go back to Baltimore and take care of any business she needed to and pack a couple of suitcases, as he believed that point would be reached sooner than later.

On Thursday of that week, an incident occurred during the afternoon hours that unnerved Danny. The morning went as most mornings would in those days. Throngs of people were waiting as soon as the doors opened, and some of whom had traveled for a day or two to reach Hope. The coffee was fresh, but it was always fresh, as the caterer continued to struggle to keep up. Danny grabbed the privilege of the first cup each day prior to setting up the CD changer. Today it was Dave

Koz leading off, and then to open the doors. His security crew at their posts, both inside and out, and Carlos stationed by Danny's office.

It happened around 1:30 that afternoon. The Healer had taken a lunch break between noon and 12:30 pm, and now he was waist-deep in visitors. He had just introduced himself for the 2 or 3 hundredth time to the next person in line, when he felt a shiver run up his spine. He didn't know where this feeling was coming from, but after about 30 seconds he was able to pinpoint the cause. At the very back of Hope, which in its previous life would have been referred to as the front of the store, about ten yards to the left of the doors, a man stood as close to the wall as he could without leaning against it. But Danny knew that this person would never lean against any wall.

He was nondescript, Danny's height but a little thinner, dressed in khakis and a short-sleeved, button-down shirt, average looks and the hairstyle of thousands of other guys. Danny guessed that he was in his late 20s, but had the confidence of someone older. The Healer got all this from exactly 3 seconds of eye contact with this person, which made him think about Carmel's remark about reading minds.

He felt some kind of connection with the person until the crowd intervened and eye contact was lost. The perception of this man that he felt was not a good one, and Danny had learned to trust his instincts even more since he met Calvin and Hobbes. He turned to locate his security chief, and when he did, he waved him over. Then turned back to find his mystery guest but could not see past the crowd. He excused himself to the person sitting in the first chair and asked him to get up. Danny then stood on the chair just in time to see the back of the man's head as he went out the door. He gave Carlos a description of the man and explained to him that his people were only to watch this man, in no way were they to approach him. He then headed for the door as fast as he could but was slowed down considerably as the aisles were filled with his guests. When he did finally make it to the door and outside, Carlos was only two steps behind him.

Cintron saw the concern on his boss's face and was not going to let him out of his sight. Danny stood outside the front doors and scanned the lot. After a few seconds, he asked Carlos if he saw the man. The head of security had not and was in the process of checking with his people; all reports were negative.

Danny said, "How could he have disappeared? If he had a car waiting, he'd still be trying to get out of the lot and if he was on foot, we would have seen him walking away."

Carlos was a bit confused. "I don't know, boss. What was with this guy, anyway?"

"I can't put my finger on it, but I got this strong vibe from him, even before I saw him. And it wasn't good."

"Maybe it is time to install a camera on the front door. Then we would have a picture of everyone coming in. In case something like this happens again, or if this same guy comes back."

"Not a bad idea, Carlos. I'll think about it."

After a few more minutes of staring out into the parking lot, they both went back inside to murmurs throughout the floor. Danny saw that he had to calm the crowd, so he put on his best negotiator's voice and had them at ease in a short time.

Carlos went back to his post, but his eyes drifted to the front door more often that day. The Healer went back to seeing his visitors, but also snuck glances at the spot he first saw, who he would refer to as the intruder, all that afternoon and into Friday.

Jimmy Santini knew that he had been made by Warburton and used the crowd to try and become invisible. He knew where every one of the security officers were when he exited the old department store, found three people who were just leaving, and blended into their small group. As he neared his car, he peeled off and slid behind the wheel. He crouched down and saw security talking on their radios and looking around the lot. He didn't believe any of them were armed, but he didn't see the security chief close up. Even so, he probably wouldn't have seen the smallest of bulges in the front of Carlos' baggy shirt. Jimmy then saw Warburton and some spic come out of the front door and start to look for him. Santini decided that he would stay put for now, as he knew he wouldn't get far in the traffic of the lot. If they found him out, he would have to put a bullet into Warburton's head right now and try to escape during the chaos. That wouldn't be the optimal plan for killing him, so he was relieved when the two went back into the building. Jimmy waited for another 45 minutes before starting his car and easing out of the lot.

The next day, with his mind still half occupied by the intruder, Danny almost forgot that this was the day of the unofficial deadline he had given the mayor to call him back. He wasn't thinking about the mayor or the governor as he poured his first cup of coffee and rifled through the pile of CDs. He was going to have to find time to buy more, as he was starting to double and triple up on some of them. Then he found one of Sade's earlier works that he hadn't played for a few weeks. Somehow it had become lost at the bottom of the box where he kept the collection. It was her first album, Danny thought it came out in 1986. He kept with the debut theme and loaded in Ricki Lee Jones' self-titled first from 1979 in the second slot.

It was 2:30 pm the first time he remembered that he wanted to call the mayor that day. Danny decided to take one more guest into the office and then make that call. One turned into six more, not because he forgot about Dubois, but because saying goodbye to one visitor and introducing himself to the next flowed as it had been for weeks. Sometimes he couldn't bring himself to keep people waiting. Even though he was using his gifts on those who came to see him, there was a part of his mind that was thinking about and focused on Greg Dubois.

# # #

Some distance away, in a dimly lit ship surrounded by the blackness of space, Calvin felt a twinge in his advanced brain. Hobbes was in the same room, and Calvin turned to his partner, but Calvin knew that it was not Hobbes' energy wave he had picked up on. Calvin waited a moment but did not feel anything further, so he continued with his current task.

# # #

Danny was finally able to get a few minutes to dial the mayor's cell phone when he had to attend to the CD player. After he reloaded the machine, he pulled his cell from his pants pocket and headed for the hall that led to the back offices. He had taken three steps in that direction when his phone rang. He kept walking as he answered and heard the voice of the former dick, Greg Dubois.

"Mr. Warburton, this is Mayor Dubois. I'm sorry it took so long to get back to you, but the governor had been avoiding my calls. Apparently he was still holding a grudge from that comment I made about him over a year ago. So I ended up going to Hartford and spoke to one of his aides. I told him the matter was of the utmost importance, but even that didn't impress him. I had to resort to dropping your name, and within minutes I had an audience with the governor. I hope you don't mind, but I believe that he wouldn't have seen me otherwise."

"You did fine, Greg, and you can call me Danny. So tell me what became of your meeting."

"One week from tomorrow, Governor Martin Acevedo is coming to Hope. He will be there at approximately 2 pm, and he is bringing about 50 family, friends, and other state politicians."

"Outstanding, Greg. I couldn't be happier, but the caterer won't be. I hope you and your family will attend. I want to make this slightly formal, not suit and tie, but I do want you to introduce me to the governor. Then we will see how `Martin the Bully' reacts after shaking my hand."

Dubois chuckled, and the two men said their goodbyes. Danny went back to seeing his guests and had Carlos get word to the caterer that he wanted to see him. All in all, he thought the day was very productive. He sensed that it would not be long before Hope returned to its former life as an abandoned building. The Healer felt bad that he wouldn't be helping individuals as much, but he had to stick to the plan. If he could reach all of the leaders of the world's governments and get them to care about their own people, then change could happen on a global scale, and he would have affected lives even without touching them. Maybe then he could come back to Hope and reopen her. Of course, Danny thought that several years would go by before that was even a possibility.

CHAPTER 17

The week seemed long to Danny, he was anxious about his meeting with Governor Acevedo. He saw it as a major stepping stone in his plans and wanted the day to go off without a hitch. Carmel knew every mood that her husband possessed and could usually figure out what was going on with the most subtle of clues, but she would have had to be brain dead not to pick up on his nervousness about Saturday afternoon. He would talk about it while they ate lunch together at Hope and every night on the back deck.

By Thursday, she'd had enough. So when he once again started saying something about the food selection for Saturday, she picked up a plastic knife from the bag of take-out that was spread over the top of his desk and held the knife to her wrist and said, "Go ahead. Mention Acevedo one more time."

Danny laughed. "That bad, huh? You should have given me the Gibbs slap to the back of the head days ago."

"I didn't want to be that rude, and I know how important this meeting is for you, but you should have more confidence in yourself. Even before the gift, you could talk most people into doing what you wanted them to do." Carmel put down the knife and took her husband's hands into hers. "Clear your mind of Saturday, concentrate on the task at hand, helping those people out there. They deserve your undivided attention."

"Lately this has become so second nature that I can take care of the visitors and also be thinking about other things. Quite a change from when I first was learning to use the gift. But that doesn't matter. You're right, I have no reason to fret about the governor." At that second the CD player stopped, and he continued "That is my cue, lunch must be over." Danny and Carmel picked up the trash from their meal, and he went out to reload the music.

On Friday he tried not to think about the next day's meeting. He did this the same way he always calmed himself, with music. He loaded up the CD player with the voices that soothed him the most, Norah Jones, Sara McLachlan, Corrine Bailey Rae, and, of course, lots of Sade. Then he dove into his guests. He talked to them more than he usually did, he took time out to mingle with the crowd, and he and Carmel took their lunch out in the main room so he could be even closer to the people who came for his help. The combination of keeping himself busy and his sultry ladies of song were enough to keep Saturday afternoon in the back of Danny's mind.

But Saturday morning was a different story, and he knew that it would be. He couldn't keep his nerves quiet with the meeting just a few hours away. As he knew he would, Danny made it through the morning and just before he closed the doors to Hope for the day, Carmel and the kids arrived. They weren't in their best clothes, because he'd held fast to the plan that he didn't want this to be a formal affair. But Mama Bear had them looking good, and Danny's smile, when he saw them come out of the back hall, conveyed all the pride he felt for his family.

Saturday afternoon came and went, and most of it was a blur to him. He was so busy with meeting everyone. The governor didn't bring 50 people, he brought 150, which was fine with The Healer. He was surprised to see that Acevedo had invited one of the U.S. senators from Connecticut, who was right there with Acevedo when Dubois introduced the governor to Danny. Thirty seconds later, he was his old confident self, as he now had the most powerful man in the state and a conduit to the United States congress telling him they were at his disposal and would help in any way that they could in his crusade.

As afternoon turned into evening and some of the party goers, because that was what it had turned into, a party, were starting to depart, Danny went looking for one particular guest. He found Karen Ayala conversing with one of the governor's aides and Greg Dubois. Karen had kept in touch over the weeks. He was sure that the calls from her started because she meant to hold him to his word of giving her an exclusive interview. But he was also sure that the most recent calls were because they were becoming friends. No one objected when he stole Karen from her small group and brought her to an area of the room where they had a little privacy.

"Karen, I don't mean to torture you with my next request, but I want to give you time to prepare and to hype this. I am ready to tell my story, how all this came to be. Can you have a crew here next Saturday, right after I close Hope for the day?"

"A week?! You can't possibly expect me to wait seven days..."

Danny cut her off. "I know, I know. It will seem like an eternity to you but, if you haven't noticed, I have become quite busy. Besides, I think you will be grateful for the time to get yourself ready for this, and I promise, no question will be left unanswered."

"A week? I'll be ready in two days. After that, all I'll be doing is pacing the floor at work and at my apartment."

"Then my best advice to you is to wear comfortable shoes. I will see you next Saturday." Danny turned and walked away before Karen could protest any further and looked for his wife and children.

# # #

Jimmy Santini was pissed for days after his encounter with Danny Warburton at Hope. He was pissed at himself for turning and running from the situation. Even though he knew it was the right course of action at the time, self-doubt still crept in until he was calling himself a coward each time he saw his own face in a mirror. More than once he asked his image if he was afraid of Warburton. From the internet articles he had read, he knew that the man was an ex-policeman and detective, and therefore might be armed, but Jimmy had faced down armed men before and hadn't flinched. No, there was something different about Warburton. And that something he couldn't quite put his finger on, but it had him spooked as well as pissed. Back at the department store, when their eyes locked, Jimmy had felt something from Warburton. And Jimmy knew, in his well-above-average brain, that the man was on to him, that he knew the mobster's intentions. He couldn't understand how, and it defied the logic and intelligence that Santini prided himself on, but still, he believed it to be true. Whatever it was that Warburton possessed, Jimmy now had no misconceptions that he could do all the things he claimed he could do. From now on, The Brain had to keep his distance from this man. In no way could he let himself be close enough where Warburton would have the chance to touch him. He would have to find a way to kill him from a distance.

Jimmy didn't leave his house for four days after his visit to Hope. During that time he mostly walked around the cavernous mansion, usually still in his pajamas and robe. But there were more than a few times, he found himself sitting on the patio that faced the rear yard and the woods beyond and not knowing how long he had been out there. He would sit on the patio and stare into the wooded area and let his hatred for Warburton seep into his bones. He would think of ways to kill his nemesis without getting close to him. Certainly a knife was out of the question, and maybe even a handgun was too near the man. He wasn't good enough with a sniper rifle to attempt it with a kill of this importance, but then Jimmy thought that a remote-detonated, well-placed bomb might be the answer he had been looking for.

Santini knew he probably had only one shot at killing Warburton. He had seen his security staff, a bunch of kids from the ghetto. But if he failed to kill Warburton the first time, his security would be drastically enhanced, and therefore much more difficult for a second attempt.

Every time he sat on the patio, his thought process went through the same weapons menu. But once, there was a different idea, one might say, "a moment of clarity." Jimmy "The Brain" Santini actually stopped weighing the pros and cons of which method to use to kill Danny Warburton, and questioned why he hated this man so much. The mobster was still making boatloads of money off of his illegal ventures, so the dent Warburton put into his drug activity was minor compared to the big picture. But he got around this by telling himself that he wasn't going to kill Warburton because of what he had done. No, he was the only one with a little vision when it came to this situation. He knew Warburton could cure people of their addictions, so it only stood to reason that he could stop people from gambling and visiting his whores, also. He knew if that asshole were to operate unchecked, it wouldn't be long before the organization's whole empire crumbled. That was why he must put an end to him, to stop his future actions.

On day five, Jimmy cleaned himself up and put himself together enough to go into the city and meet with his crew. It wasn't as if he had no contact with anyone during his Hamptons lock-down. He had called his second-in-command, Vincent Golino, several times over the last few days but there hadn't been occasion for Jimmy's personal attention. He knew the day-to-day stuff would take care of itself, and if there was an issue, Vincent knew how to get a hold of him.

The Brain had found the perfect guy to be his right-hand man in Vincent Golino. He had no aspirations of having his own crew, and he was completely loyal to Jimmy. Vincent was six feet tall, 240 pounds of all muscle, and had a sledge hammer of a right hand. Jimmy liked having his own monster. He had seen Vincent's handiwork plenty of times, but none more impressive than the first.

Golino did not like to be called "Vinny", he thought it made him sound too gangster, and he desperately wanted to be looked on as more intelligent than that image. Not long after Vincent had joined Jimmy's crew, there was an incident with another young tough who'd wanted to make a name for himself in the family and thought he would show everyone how big his balls were. This idiot, Jimmy couldn't even recall his name now, decided to pick on the big, dumb Vincent Golino. After the third time the big man told him that his name was not Vinny and asked him not to call him that, the sledge hammer came from right field and connected with the idiot's left cheek. It was the only punch thrown in the fight, but it sent the idiot for a five-week hospital stay. No one ever saw him again, but there were rumors that he went from the hospital to the airport and moved in with his parents in Deltona, Florida.

# # #

When Jimmy walked into the pool hall that morning, everyone took notice, and loud greetings came from all over. No one wanted to question where the boss had been for four days, but the elder statesman of the crew didn't fear the boss as the others did.

Sal Giordano asked "Where you been all week, boss? We wuz startin' to get worried."

Jimmy was about to tell Sal that it was none of his fucking business, but then recognized the sincerity in his underling's voice and said, "Just feeling a little under the weather. Besides, Vincent and I were in contact, and I trust you guys to take care of shit when I'm not here."

"You can count on us, Jimmy," Sal said.

There were assenting murmurs from the rest of the crew, who believed Jimmy, and they went back to what they were doing before he had arrived. But Vincent knew better. The boss wasn't sick. Vincent didn't know what was bothering him, but Ida Golino's youngest son did know when to keep his mouth shut. Another quality Santini liked about him.

The Brain continued toward the back of the hall and as he passed Vincent, he told the big man that he didn't want to be disturbed. Vincent only nodded, but it was more fuel for his suspicion. Jimmy hadn't come into the city in nearly a week, and he didn't want to get any updates from his guys? Vincent watched his boss as he went through the door that led to the back offices.

Jimmy sat at his desk and powered up his laptop, his intention was to use a search engine to gather information, but he had second thoughts before the machine had finished the start-up functions. He knew the government monitored the internet, and certain words or combination of words would send a red flag to those prying eyes. Bomb, explosives, how to, would most assuredly warrant a visit by the feds. He would have to learn about bomb making from another source. The trouble was, Jimmy had never had occasion to work with someone in that field. After a few moments, he decided that he didn't even want his crew knowing what he was doing. Not yet, at least. So the only other person he could trust right now was his uncle, Sonny. He dialed Sonny's cell phone, and the Gambino captain answered on the third ring.

"Santini Construction, how can I help you?" Sonny was always cautious that the local, state, or FBI listened in.

"Uncle Sonny, its Jimmy."

"Hey kid, I was going to call you this morning, I got word you weren't around all week, and I wanted to know if there was a problem."

Before Jimmy answered, he thought, *"Fucking guys can't keep their mouths shut"* but showed no signs of being ticked when he spoke to his uncle. "No problem, Sonny. I think I caught a bug or something, feeling more myself today."

"That's good. So, is this a social call?"

"I'm always interested in catching up with my favorite uncle, but I also have some business to discuss."

"Then you better not be contagious, because you know I only conduct business face to face."

"I know that, Sonny. The usual place, say, in about an hour?"

"See you in one hour." And then Sonny ended the call abruptly.

Jimmy wasn't offended, he knew that was his uncle's way. He went back out front and told Vincent to bring the car out to the street in 30 minutes. Golino acknowledged the order and felt a sense of relief. This was more like the boss, when he had a business meeting, Vincent would often drive him in a Lincoln Town Car they used for such events. He mistakenly thought that things were going back to normal.

Forty minutes later, they were on their way to a small coffee shop 13 blocks away from the pool hall. Sonny liked to talk at the shop because it was popular and, therefore, packed with people and noisy. He wouldn't sit in the same booth twice in a row and believed this venue too hard for the police to bug. The capo was already seated when his nephew arrived, as was his habit with any meeting, to be in place and have his guys watching both inside and out prior to the other parties arrival. As Jimmy approached the booth, Sonny stood and hugged his nephew. In a world where one had to watch his back because the feds had the ability to turn anyone into a snitch, Sonny knew without a doubt that he was safe with this boy.

"The boy genius! You continue to impress our friends in high places. What can I help you with today?"

"I am in need of knowledge. Do you have someone you can trust that can teach me about a rather large fireworks display?"

Sonny didn't hesitate to give his nephew the information he requested. He had an uncanny memory when it came to names and phone numbers, he took a napkin from the tabletop dispenser and wrote just a first name on it, accompanied by a cell number. He folded the napkin and pushed it across the table. He wasn't worried that Jimmy was doing something stupid. And even if his actions were questionable, Sonny would find out from the man whose name was on the napkin.

The younger Santini knew when he accepted the note that anything that transpired between the fireworks expert and himself would get back to his uncle. Jimmy thanked Sonny, and the two had coffee and talked, but not of any more business.

CHAPTER 18

Karen Ayala was off by a few days on her prediction as too how long it would take her to get ready for her second interview with Danny. She was in her office on Sunday, which was not the norm for her, checking the availability of the cameramen on the following Saturday. She knew who she wanted behind the lens as well as in the booth and was pleased to see they were both free on the day of the interview. She put a Post-It note on her computer screen to remind herself to line up her crew first thing Monday morning. She then spent the next few hours jotting down notes about everything from the background color on the set, whether to use chairs or a couch, what she would wear, and when to get her hair styled.

Karen knew this interview was going to be historic. Danny had been so entrenched in that building of his, he hadn't really taken stock of how much his story had spread. People were coming from all over the country to see him, and she knew of at least a dozen others who'd traveled from Europe, Asia, and South America. The Healer knew of the extent that people were going to come see him, Karen knew this because when she did call her friend she would always ask how far the longest distance was someone had traveled to see him that day, and he always knew. She guessed that the significance of that information didn't register with him because after that person had left his office and the next had entered, he was focused on the task at hand.

But the enormity of the story was not lost on Karen. She had been following its progress on all forms of media, but mostly on the internet. Newspapers were dying out, and even local and national TV news programs were losing viewers. But the information highway was growing, and that was where a majority of those between the ages of 18 and 30 went to learn the events of the day. So much had been written about Danny on the internet that she could not possibly read it all. Articles were on news sites, blogs, postings, and interviews with some of the people who had visited him at Hope, and comments were posted from nearly every country in the world.

But even with all this attention, Karen was astonished by the fact that the media had not descended on Hope. Being a reporter herself, she knew her kind were naturally curious, and some would stop at nothing to get a story. So why weren't at least ten remote feed vans parked outside of the building each day? It was a mystery to her. She could speculate all day as to the reasons, but in the end she counted herself as the luckiest of them all that this fell into her lap, so she didn't want to screw this interview up. Karen knew she was good at her job, but also knew she wasn't the best, so she thought that a meeting with Cliff Lavin and the rest of the news crew for a brainstorming session could only help her. After making a few more notes about the things she needed to get done over the next few days, she finally called it a day and headed home.

Danny also stayed busy that Sunday, but it was not anything to do with work. Clan Warburton started out the day going to a little diner for breakfast, then had a two-hour drive into New York for an afternoon at the Bronx Zoo. The weather was gorgeous, sunny with a slight breeze which was perfect for walking around the expansive zoological garden. They bought lunch at the zoo and ate at one of the outdoor tables. Father and son took a ride on an elephant, but the girls didn't want to get near the smelly thing.

When they all climbed into the min-van for the trip home, it was nearly 6 pm. Even though they were all tired, the first hour of the ride was filled with their voices as they all took turns relating to the others, about their favorite part of the day. With all the chatter and laughter, the kids didn't realize they were halfway home until Papa Bear pulled onto an off ramp to find a place for dinner. The second half of the ride was more subdued, and Jack took the opportunity to catch a nap. By the time they reached home, the sun had almost completed its trip across the sky and was well on the way to starting the day on the other side of the planet.

Danny was pleased with himself for not once thinking about the week to come and the interview with Karen on Saturday. He also didn't use his gifts on anyone. He had made a promise to himself weeks ago that he would give his family his undivided attention on the only full day he had with them. He sensed that some of the other zoo patrons recognized him, and he'd also caught a dozen or so staring and pointing in his direction, but none approached. He was surprised at this, but also thankful that he was given his privacy. What The Healer didn't realize was that he was the cause of this. His mind was putting out a message to all who thought to approach he or his family, nothing menacing, just a subtle hint that this was not the time nor the place. Danny's mind was not powerful enough to send the message very far, maybe 100 or 200 yards in all directions, so it began to fade as soon as it left his mind. For that reason, his unusual brain activity did not reach the radar of Calvin and Hobbes and therefore did not cause them any concern, at least, not yet.

Monday morning found the kids back in school, Carmel running a few errands, and Danny back at Hope, which was as crowded as ever. As Kim Waters played his saxophone from the CD player, The Healer saw to his visitors. But as was his habit lately, another part of his mind thought about what was yet to come.

He knew that the interview on Saturday was important, and he had to present his story in such a way as to not offend too many people. He knew, however, the tale would be told and there were going to be those who would be upset and vehemently describe the events that led to his gifts as bunk. This group might include the truly faithful, the Catholic Church, hell, maybe all religions, for that matter.

But even so, he couldn't help himself by often thinking three or four moves ahead. He kept hearing his old high school football coach giving the team advice about a weaker opponent: "If you're not thinking about the next game because you've already counted it as a win, that weaker team will rise up and bite you in the ass because you will be ill-prepared. Keep your head in the present." Danny tried to relate that long-ago speech to the events surrounding his life today and concentrate on his visitors and only ahead to Saturday. But in his mind, the third or fourth move in his future would be a sit-down with the President of the United States. And just as he had a mayor, a governor, and a U.S. senator working to help him on his journey, he felt that if he had the president on his side, it wouldn't be long before he had the entire U.S. government at his disposal. Danny was sure that with those kinds of resources, he couldn't fail.

Each night that week, with a cigar in one hand and a glass of wine in the other, he excitedly told Carmel that they were so close to the time when his plans really took off. Although she never knew the Pulaski High School football coach, she would come eerily close to repeating the same words her husband heard when he was but a scrawny slot receiver with good hands. Carmel would do her best to keep him grounded, but she knew that when her husband was this excited about something, she had very little influence over his actions.

By Wednesday, Karen believed that she had taken care of everything that she possibly could have in preparation for Saturday's interview. But she was also aware of the unknown. She had no idea what Danny was going to say and therefore must be able to think on her feet and form questions as the interview progressed. She had done only one "blind" interview before, but she was confident in her skills as a reporter. And as her friend, she knew that he wouldn't intentionally try to trip her up.

Mr. Lavin was quick to give her anything she needed and let her have more input than he usually gave reporters about even the most minor aspects of this assignment. More than one meeting was held with Lavin and the news staff. As a matter of fact, they had seven meetings over three days. After the third meeting, the attendance grew to the point that the last few involved every employee at the television station, from the station manager to the secretarial staff and even the cleaning crew. No ideas or comments were stifled, which made for some lengthy sessions. Those long meetings were one of the reasons Karen put in 12-hour days on Monday and Tuesday and 14 hours on Wednesday.

When she arrived home that night, she kicked off her shoes and lay down on the couch in the living room. Her intention was to rest for a few minutes before she poured herself a glass of wine and got ready for bed, but she didn't wake up until 9:30 am Thursday morning, still in her clothes from the day before, and still on the couch. She called Lavin and told him she needed the day to herself and then she stripped down, set her alarm clock for noon, crawled into her bed, and fell right back to sleep. When she awoke, she showered and then had a light lunch at a café several blocks from her apartment. The remainder of the afternoon was spent at the mall doing the activity that took her mind off of everything else, shopping; a new skirt, several blouses, a CD, and a book from Barnes and Noble that she didn't think she'd have time to read. Karen searched for the outfit she would wear on Saturday. After several stops in different stores, she found the perfect set, a dark blue suit jacket and just-above-the-knee skirt with a light purple blouse that she thought was business attire but also had enough of a feminine look to please her.

As she was on her way out of the mall, she passed a shoe store and remembered Danny's advice. She had to try on eight pairs of shoes but finally found what she thought were the most comfortable she could find. They were a pair of soft leather moccasins which were a little overpriced, but she bought them anyway, even though she didn't think she would do any pacing at this late date.

On the opposite side of the spectrum was Danny, who did absolutely nothing to prepare for the interview. Carmel tried to tell him to put the story down on paper or at the least write some notes on index cards. But the few times she did this, "arrogant Danny" responded.

"Come on, honey. I know the story. Remember? I was there. Besides, I could tell the world that I got the gifts from eating chocolate cake, and they would still love me. Look at me, who wouldn't?"

This invoked a sigh and a roll of the eyes from Carmel, which was the reaction he wanted "Chocolate cake might be more believable than aliens, and by the way, you're not going to tell people that you named those guys Calvin and Hobbes, are you?"

"Well, maybe you're right about that. I might keep that to myself. But that is all I will hold back. I am not positive that this is the right time to tell the whole story, but I do know that it has to be told. If people discover that I am holding anything back, it will only make them suspicious of me and my motives, and quite possibly, the motives of the aliens. I am prepared for some backlash, but in the long run, it should only be a minor speed bump in my plans."

Carmel stood from her chair on the deck, walked the few steps to Danny's chair, and bent down so her mouth was right next to his ear. "Whatever decisions you make, I'll be there right beside you." She stood, drained her glass of wine, and said, "Let's go inside now." Which they did, but their Friday night would not end for another two hours.

CHAPTER 19

Saturday morning was no different than any other over the last few months for The Healer. He opened Hope to the usual crowd and saw as many people as he could until closing time. He had agreed to do the interview in the Channel 8 studios, which meant a 45-minute drive from New Britain. Carmel and the kids had met him at Hope at noon. The Santa Fe was left parked behind the ex-department store, and they all got into the van. He had anticipated stopping for lunch and therefore told Karen that they wouldn't arrive until at least 3 pm.

Karen made it to the studio by 9 am, which was way too early but she couldn't spend any more time in her apartment that morning. She tried to kill time by going over her notes and finding the best way to sit in the overstuffed chair on the set, as they had decided against the couch. She spent time having her hair and make-up touched up. But eventually she found herself back in her office reaching for the bag under her desk, that she had brought from home that morning, pulling out a shoebox, and slipping into the expensive moccasins. Karen Ayala muttered, "Damn you Warburton," out loud.

She walked, or paced, depending on who you asked, around the studio and pretty much pestered everyone until 2:45 pm, when she went back to her desk and put her three-inch heels back on. She briefly thought about burning the moccasins just so that Warburton never knew about them, but decided that they were way too expensive and way too comfortable to wear once.

She was the first to greet Clan Warburton as they entered the front door of Channel 8, but then everyone wanted to shake Danny's hand and hug his wife and children. It took 20 minutes for them to make it to the set. He saw that his family was settled into chairs just off-camera with a good view of the stage, and he took his seat next to Karen. She informed him that some developments had occurred over the last few days that she had learned only that morning.

He cocked his head, gave her a half-smile, and told her to hit him with the surprise, which turned out to be that the interview would be live, and all the major networks and a half dozen cable stations had agreed to simulcast the event. It was Karen who was surprised by Danny's calm reaction and the fact that his demeanor was infectious, the nervousness melted from her shoulders as the cameraman announced that they had five minutes until air time.

The red light at the top of the camera came on, and Karen introduced herself and the man sitting to her left. She told the TV audience that they were broadcasting live from their studios in New Haven, Connecticut, and then listed the other networks that were also broadcasting the live feed. She turned to Danny and said, "Good afternoon, Daniel. It's nice to see you again."

Thirty feet away, Carmel thought she saw something in Ayala's eyes, and a twinge of jealousy ran down her spine. Just as quickly, she let it go. She knew her husband was an attractive man, and Karen wasn't the first woman to give him a second look. But the bottom line was that she trusted her husband, and that was all that mattered.

"Hello, Karen. I hope your week went well. Did you find it necessary to take my advice?"

Karen gave Danny a smirk and said, "Yes, I did, and my wallet is $75 lighter for it. But I didn't need to use them until this morning."

"I'm glad you stayed busy. Shall we get to the reason we are interrupting everyone's afternoon?"

"Direct as usual, Daniel. So we shall. When we set the date for this interview, you told me that no question would be unanswered, and I plan on holding you to that. But let's start at the beginning. I'm sure what is on the mind of most people is, how did you attain the gift of healing, and your other gifts as well? And my boss has said that we have all the time we need, so give us as much detail as possible."

"I will, Karen, but understand that some viewers might be upset at what I'm about to reveal, but you will know, as well as everyone else I've had contact with, that what I say here today is the truth. Some of the things I tell you I have experienced and, therefore, know as fact. And others, I have been told by those who gave me the gift, so I have no personal knowledge. Nonetheless, I do believe what was related to me. That being said, here is my story.

"It was early June, just after 1 am. I had finished my shift as a Detective Sergeant with the New Britain Police Department. I had gotten out a little late, and when I arrived home my family were all asleep. As was my habit, I took a cigar and glass of wine out to the back deck. I was winding down, enjoying the wine, and before I knew it the glass was empty. So I went inside and poured a second glass, and when I went back to the deck, I noticed a bright light in the sky. At first, it didn't seem very strange but my attention was diverted to movement in the back yard, a deer or some other animal, and when I looked up again, the light was a lot closer. It came in fast, and I didn't have time to react. Then it was right over me, and I saw some kind of device or machine."

Karen interrupted "A UFO?"

"Yes. The…UFO emitted something from under it that enveloped me in a sort of capsule that allowed me to breathe as it took off back into space with me in tow. I don't know how fast we were going, but we come up on the moon pretty quickly. I saw a much larger ship as we went around the moon, but that was when I passed out from the g-force. It wasn't a stretch to figure out that the big ship was our destination. I awoke while lying on a bench in a round room that was completely white. When I got up from the bench, it disappeared into the wall. I went looking for a door, but I couldn't even see a seam in the wall. Before I got too far, a portion of the wall slid into the ceiling and two aliens entered the room. They were quite tall, but I can't tell you anything else about how they looked as the robes they wore revealed nothing of their person."

"Daniel? If I could interrupt once more…did you have your off-duty weapon on you? And if so, did you think to use it?"

"I actually reached for it, as it usually sits on my right hip but it wasn't there. The deck chairs I have are thin, and my gun gets shoved into my right side when I sit down. So I always take it off before I go out to the deck. That turned out to be a good thing, because I was scared at that point and don't know what I would have done if I'd had it.

"The aliens communicated with me by telepathy. Their race is hundreds of thousands of years old, and they have developed their minds to the point where they don't much need their appendages. I, of course, still had to use my mouth to talk to them, and they understood me. And I heard every word they said in English. At first, the conversation among us didn't go as they had planned, mostly due to the fact that I was scared and on the defensive. But it was only a short time before they had put me at ease, and the more they explained to me why they had brought me to their ship, the more I became intrigued. I was only up there for several hours, and for another hour or so after that, I was unconscious again. But the three of us gained a mutual respect, and I count those two as among my friends.

"Sorry, I'm straying from the story. Let me get back on point. They told me that they were here to conduct an experiment on the human race. Now, I know that may sound arrogant to some, like they look at us as lab rats, but that is so far from the truth. They are here to help us. They explained to me that there are hundreds of inhabited planets in our universe, and they are members in an alliance with most of these other worlds. Together, they promote peace and knowledge, and they help each other out when needed. They have been watching us for some time and told me that we are in trouble. Many of the other planets believe we are too violent a race to bring anything productive to the alliance, and there are many who do not want anything to do with Earth. The two aliens that I met convinced their science ministry to give us one more chance, and they were given permission to conduct this experiment. Their goal is to determine if one man, given a few advantages, could make a difference on an entire world. Most of you watching have at least heard what I am capable of doing, and their goal is now my goal."

Karen didn't hesitate. She wasn't in awe of Danny's fantastic story, because she knew that he spoke the truth. She had no facts to base this on, but deep in her heart she knew her friend was not lying. So she was quite calm when she asked her next question. "How did they give you these powers, Daniel?"

"They brought me to another room and put me in this machine. The best I can describe it is that it looked like an MRI machine. They told me that long ago, their species was similar to us, in the way that they walked and talked like us, and they developed physically and technologically at about the same rate as humans. But there came a point where they turned their efforts inside and looked for ways to develop and enhance their brain function. Over many years, they were able to train themselves to use a greater portion of their brains, which then led their technology to expand tenfold.

"As humans, we have been told that we use only about 10 percent of our brains. The aliens told me that it is more like 7 percent. The machine enhanced my brain function so that I use more of it. They told me that I use about 35 percent now, so the aliens gave me a taste of what they have. Now I use my mind to heal people and cleanse them of their biases and hatred they feel for their own kind. As I told you in our first interview, I have to be in physical contact to accomplish this. Do you have any idea how long it would take to touch every human being on the planet? Rhetorical question, Karen. I don't know, but I do know it would be longer than a lifetime. All I plan to do is the best that I can."

"Did they tell you why they chose you?"

"Now you're going to make me talk about myself, aren't you? Believe me, Karen, I'm just a regular guy. I was a cop for 15 years before all this. I went to work and tried to provide the best life that I could for my wife and three children. I was nobody special. But the aliens said they had studied a group of people who were down-to-earth and had a lot of common sense, people who had traits such as integrity and honesty. Now, these are their words, remember. They told me that I displayed these characteristics and that I was their number one choice, go figure. They also said that the fact that I am an atheist was a factor in their choice, because they believed that I wouldn't be encumbered by any religious aspect of this. You know, the whole healing and cleansing part of it."

"I didn't know you were an atheist."

"I usually keep it out of day-to-day conversations, tends to cause arguments. Nothing polarizes people more than talking about religion. I am of the opinion that everyone should be able to believe in whatever they choose and not be hassled about it."

"You make it sound as if these aliens are atheists also. Are they?"

"The few hours that I spent with them were rather overwhelming. Number one, I really didn't think to ask. And number two, I would refer you to my last answer, i. e. day-to-day conversations. But I did get the impression that if they did believe in a supreme being, it wasn't like humans do. That is just a hunch, though."

Karen felt that she was onto something, but she wasn't quite sure yet "Really, just a hunch? Did the aliens say anything about the way humans worship or about any specific religion?"

Daniel hesitated for so long that Karen was about to say something else but before she could he finally replied, "Yes, they did."

Karen waited for Daniel to elaborate. When he didn't, she smiled and said, "Daniel, when I bought those comfortable shoes, I also picked up a crowbar. Do I have to go get that now?"

Daniel laughed. "No. No, you don't. I said no question would be unanswered, and I keep my word. You remember when I told you that some people were going to be upset with some of the things I say tonight? Well, here it comes. I hope you have operators standing by. I am not their first experiment on Earth. They told me they had been here before. As a matter of fact, it was the same two aliens, and had given the same gifts to another man. They told me that they were called back to their planet on an emergency and were not present for the end of that experiment."

"Hold on, Daniel. Nowhere in any history books is there a chronicle of anything like this happening before. Don't you think that something of this magnitude would have been written down by someone?"

"Oh, but there are volumes written about the man. He chose not to reveal how he came by his powers. Even the aliens don't know why he took that path. They told me they were not sure if his actions were deliberate or if events took on a life of their own, and he did nothing to dispel the popular notions of what and who he was."

"Volumes, huh? Did your new friends tell you what this guy's name was?"

"Jesus Christ." Daniel didn't say anything more. He wanted Karen and all those watching to digest that before he went on.

"Damn it, Daniel! I don't want to believe you. What you are saying is so far outside the box and like a dagger to the heart to all Christians, including myself. But even if you hadn't touched me after our first interview, which means that I am positive you are telling the truth, everything I learned in my journalism classes at UCONN about reading a subject during an interview, you're telling the truth. Your words, body language, and eye contact, they all point to the fact that you are being truthful. You are right, in that this will cause a stir. Being that you are still in the early stages of your plan, do you think this was the right time to make this revelation?"

"I don't know what the fallout from this interview will be. But I do know that if I were to keep that information a secret and it were to be revealed at a later date, and all secrets eventually are found out, wouldn't you think that would do more damage? People would look upon me as dishonest, like I was trying to hide something. And remember, I am just telling you what I was told, but like you believe me, I believe them. On the other hand they did not say anything about God or a supreme being, just that Christ was our first chance, and I am our second chance, and there will not be a third."

"Well, I'm pretty sure that puts a period on our talk. Anything else that I ask would seem anticlimactic. Before we sign off, however, I would like to give you a chance to say whatever you would like in a closing statement."

"Thank you, Karen. I would like to say that I hope the information about Jesus Christ won't cause some to look on me unfavorably. That was in the past, and we must look to our future. An invitation to join this alliance of planets could catapult our race years into the future. They would help us out with technical and medical advancements and afford us protection against any other alien race that is not so benevolent. This could mean our very existence. But first, what I have been tasked to do must be completed. And for that to happen, I need the cooperation of those who are in power to help me streamline my plans and make me more efficient. And by those in power, I mean the leaders of the countries of this world. My guess is that I will have to wait for them to come to me. In this day and age of heightened security everywhere, I don't suppose an ex-cop from a small city in the middle of Connecticut can easily get an audience with the President of Russia, or the Prime Minister of Great Britain, or even the President of the United States. So I hope they are watching and reach out to me. That is about all I have, except that I want to thank everyone who decided to watch. And Karen, again, thank you and everyone here at Channel 8 for helping me attain my goal."

Karen leaned over and put her left hand over his right hand. She said, "We will always be here for you, Daniel."

Karen turned to the camera and thanked the television audience again for watching. The set went dim, and 20 seconds later the light on the camera winked out. Both of them stood, and Karen leaned into him and gave him a hug as she said, "Great interview Daniel. Just the right amount of shock and awe. You came across as the regular guy you wanted everyone to see." The two separated.

"You think so? The whole Christ thing wasn't too much, too soon?"

"Like you, I don't know. But I have a feeling that we won't have to wait long to find out."

"Very funny. Anyway, thanks again. You've been great. My days might get a little busy in the near future, but let's try to stay in touch."

Karen smiled and said, "You can count on that."

Danny left the stage and went to his family. He hugged his kids and his wife.

Carmel said, "If I didn't know better, I'd say you two were almost flirting at times up there."

"Mel, Karen and I are just friends."

"I know. I'm just teasing, and maybe a little jealous."

"You know you don't need to be, but it's flattering anyway. Besides, that's what you lead with after an interview of such importance? What did you think?"

"Well, let's see. You've alienated every Christian, and told the rest of us we are all a bunch of Neanderthals who can't control our rages because we are only 7 percenters."

"I knew I could count on you to see the bright side. Let's hope I didn't create too much of a shit storm."

The family's moral compass then chimed in as Kate said, "Daddy! Your language in front of the young ones." She motioned to her two younger siblings.

Clan Warburton had started to make their way toward the front door, and they all got a good laugh at Kate's comment.

Karen Ayala went back to the dressing rooms, sat at one of the make-up stations, and looked into the large mirror. She was proud of herself. No doubt that was the best interview she had done in her career. She started to go over it in her mind, the questions she asked, some of her comments, and her interaction with Daniel. She was still thinking of the latter when she decided to wear her new moccasins home. As she reached down to unstrap her heels, she thought of her on air-greeting of Daniel, the way she touched his hand, and the hug she gave him at the end. She sat bolt upright, again looked at her reflection in the mirror, and said out loud, "Oh shit, Karen! Damn it all, you have a crush on Danny Warburton."

CHAPTER 20

Jimmy Santini had just pushed the off button on the remote control he still had in his right hand. The screen of the 60-inch LCD TV that was mounted on the wall over the fireplace was blank, which matched the stare of its owner. He put the remote on the oak coffee table in front of the leather couch where he'd been sitting as he watched the Warburton interview. Jimmy began to laugh out loud at the ridiculous tale he'd just heard from the surround sound system that was hooked to his television. The Brain stood and paced around the living room as he talked to himself.

"Maybe I won't have to kill this guy. If he is going to step on his dick every time he gets in front of a television camera, it won't be long before he fades away. He'll have his 15 minutes of fame, and then people will tire of him. Aliens! Does he really think people are going to believe him? And that whole thing about Jesus Christ? Wow! He pissed off about half the world with that one, and the Vatican is going to roast him. At least now I can forget about this asshole and get back to business."

Jimmy poured himself a glass of 12-year-old scotch and decided he would call one of the few women he sometimes dated and have dinner out tonight. He felt like celebrating.

# # #

Jimmy Santini wasn't the only one with a blank stare on his face as the stage went dark in the New Haven studio. If anyone had decided to do a survey on the subject, they would have found a little under 90 percent of those who watched the interview live, and that totaled in the millions, had the same stunned look. Two of those were currently in the Jesus Christ business, trying to save the souls who lived in the Philadelphia neighborhood where St. Veronica stood.

The two priests did not watch the interview together. Both still kept their interest in Warburton a secret from one another. Father Padraig O'Malley watched on the small television in his office in the church, and Father Paul Sikora was in his room at the rectory, watching on his laptop. Like Santini, the younger man paced the floor of his bedroom. But unlike the mobster, no laughter was heard from either of those who wore the collar.

Padraig shut off his television when the network news took over after the interview and began to talk about every word that Warburton said. He knew they'd hash and rehash and analyze the entire interview for the next several hours, he was not in the mood. He wasn't even sure what he thought about Warburton's story. He was initially shocked, of course, as he guessed most people were, even those who were not Christian.

His faith was just returning, he was happy again, due to a large part by the arrival of Paul. He stayed in his office for the next hour and thought about the implications this would have on the Church. He tried to stay positive, but he lost count how many times he stopped his thought process and said to the walls, "What if he speaks the truth?"

Not only had the two men become mentor/teacher, protégé/student, but also became close friends. Usually they took dinner together at the end of the day, and lively chatter was shared across the table.

Katia joined in most nights and was so happy for Father O'Malley. Paul had led him from the brink, and she could once again see the zest for life and faith in the older man's eyes. She worried that if something were to happen to Paul, or if their relationship was damaged, Padraig would fall back so far as to be unreachable. These were her thoughts on that Friday evening when the men hardly spoke two sentences over their meal. They both picked at their food, and neither ate more than the pigeons in the park. Katia Janeski never took a psychology course in college, but she thought any fool could see there was something unspoken between those two.

Thirty minutes after dinner, the silence was still unbroken. Katia brewed a pot of coffee and had sliced two pieces of her homemade apple pie, which the two men took into the living room. Halfway through his piece, Padraig decided he felt foolish enough and addressed his new friend.

"Paul, I have a confession to make."

"Shall we go to the confessional?"

"No, it is not so much an infraction against God, as it is against you."

The surprise in Paul's voice was evident. "Me? You have been nothing short of completely gracious since my arrival. I am blessed to call you my friend."

"Yes, and therein lies the rub, the fact that we have become friends. These last few months, I have kept a secret from you."

"Father, you certainly do not have to tell me everything."

"True. But this is a subject that we had discussed before, and I have deliberately avoided discussing it with you again. Remember that fellow from Connecticut, Daniel Warburton, whose interview you brought to my attention? Well, I have been following his story on TV and through the internet this whole time. I don't know why I didn't say anything about him to you, but perhaps it was because you were quite excited when you first told me about him. Being fresh out of seminary, I know that sometimes the real world is not always what is taught in a young priest's training. I knew that you would have your hands full adjusting to your new life here at St. Veronica as both a priest and a person, and I didn't want something like Warburton to interfere with your transition. I hope you can understand that, Paul."

Because of his embarrassment, Padraig could not look Paul in the eyes as he was speaking. But now that he had finished his confession, he turned his face to the younger man.

On the other hand, Paul could not take his eyes off his Pastor until Padraig finally looked upon him. Sikora then looked down at his hands that still held the small plate with his unfinished piece of apple pie. He didn't respond for some time. That seemed like an eternity to Padraig, who mistook his silence for anger, which couldn't be farther from the truth.

Paul had never had a stuttering problem, but he did now over his first few words, as he couldn't get his thoughts together. He took a deep breath and started again. "Father O'Malley, if you feel that you have committed some sort of sin against our friendship, then I am equally guilty." Paul raised his head, and looked his mentor in the eye, and continued. "I have also been investigating Daniel Warburton using any and every form of media available to me. I kept this to myself because I didn't want to appear weak in your eyes, and your opinion of me means more than I can express in words."

Katia couldn't believe her ears as it had been years since she'd heard Padraig laugh so loud and long, that she almost couldn't place the sound from where she stood at the kitchen sink washing the evening dishes. A tear ran down her cheek as she said to the soap bubbles, "It certainly took long enough for those two stubborn men to get over whatever was in their way."

Paul chuckled only because Padraig was laughing so loud, but he really didn't see what was so funny. A few minutes passed before Padraig was able to get a hold of himself. He wiped the tears from his eyes and looked at Paul.

"Oh! Oh Paul, you mean to tell me that all this isn't amusing to you?"

"No Father, I do not see the humor in this. We could have damaged our friendship simply by not communicating with each other."

Padraig was laughed out, and his voice became serious. "But we didn't. And I'll tell you why it was funny. We were both doing the same thing, not telling each other about it, and both of us had the same reasons for keeping it from the other. Coincidental? I don't think so, but ironically funny. And the fact that our reasons for remaining silent were also identical speaks volumes about the strength of our friendship. But really, what you and I find funny or not is inconsequential compared to what we heard tonight, don't you agree?"

And just like that, Paul was back from his guilt trip, the excitement returning to his voice. "For most of the interview, I was mesmerized. You were right to call him charismatic, but I was also shocked at times and couldn't believe some of the things he was saying."

"Yes, the sheer enormity of the entire situation. We as humans think that we are so advanced both technologically and in our benevolence to others. To be told that we are on the brink of being shunned by alien beings because they think us barbaric, well it certainly would knock our arrogance down a few pegs."

"Father, I'm not sure that I believe anything that Warburton said. If we believe the part that aliens granted him these gifts, then we must believe everything he told us. And I surely don't believe our Savior was a lab rat."

Padraig could hear the anger in his protégé's voice. Father Sikora had been subjected to a gambit of intense emotions during the last 15 minutes, more than Padraig had seen from him since his arrival, and O'Malley thought he should try to focus the younger priest so they could continue their conversation with more of a logical basis.

"Father Paul, give me a moment. I think we will be up later than usual discussing the events of this afternoon, and I want Katia to put on another pot of coffee before she leaves."

He went into the kitchen and spoke with his housekeeper for a few minutes. Paul discovered that he still held the plate with half a slice of apple pie on it and finally put it down on the end table next to his chair. When Padraig returned, he could tell from the look on the young man's face that he was still torn inside by what Warburton had said.

"Paul, if we are to continue our discussion, we must control our emotions. I understand that you feel that Warburton has attacked our faith, but there is little we can do about that tonight. What we must prepare for is the turmoil this will cause our parishioners. They will be looking to us to allay their fears and answer any questions they may have about all this. Don't forget that we have a job to do, and we have been entrusted with the souls of all who enter our church."

What Padraig had learned about Paul in the short time he had known him was that he took his responsibilities very seriously. He hoped that his last comment would snap Father Sikora out of his anxiety.

Paul took a deep breath and let it out slowly. "Forgive me, Father, I wasn't thinking of our charges, only of the impact to the Catholic Church as a whole. Like you always tell me, stick to the basics."

Padraig smiled. "That's right, one can only build on a solid foundation."

"But I do still want to talk about Warburton. Looking at what has been written about him and his past, he doesn't seem like the type of person who would deliberately attack the church for no reason."

"Ok, we can discuss Warburton. And I agree with you, he appeared to be a hard-working family man. By his own admission, he is an atheist, but we have no evidence he was an active one, but there were a few things about the interview that disturbed me. First off, when he said the aliens told him Jesus Christ was an experiment, he seemed genuinely embarrassed or sorry that he had to be the one to tell people. And the reaction of the reporter, Ayala, she wasn't shocked at all, and she didn't attack his story with probative questions. You would think that if someone said something so outrageous to a reporter that she would have at least acted stunned. I can only conclude that she immediately believed him, and that troubles me more than his statements."

"He touched her during the first interview. Is it possible he is brainwashing people somehow, like a cult leader?"

"I don't know Paul, but that doesn't sound right. The people he has touched and cured are not following him around, living in a compound, and thinking he is some kind of messiah, like a traditional cult. They go back to their lives, and his actions are not motivated by money. There are accounts of those he has cured who have given nothing, because they had nothing to give. I am at a loss as to a theory of his motivation. So let's look at his actions so far and maybe, since we have done so much research on this guy, the two of us can put our heads together, compare what we have learned about him, and try to figure out his goal."

Paul picked up the plate from the end table and decided that he did want to finish his pie. "That sounds like a great idea. And we should also try to figure out why he would want to make such disparaging remarks against Jesus Christ and the Christian faith."

"Let's first look at what we know. There wasn't much in newspapers or the internet before he began to cure people. Wedding announcements, one-line birth announcements when his children were born, and several articles about investigations of major crimes he was involved in when he was with the police. A regular guy, by all accounts."

Paul said, "But since he first cured those kids in Hartford, his notoriety has exploded. I probably had the time to read only about 25 percent of what has been written about him. And there are over a dozen websites devoted to his actions, as well as 20 or 30 blog pages, each with at least 50 new entries daily. The first interview went viral, and tonight's was broadcast on major networks and on the internet, and not just in English. He has been gaining momentum at an incredible rate. But do you think his, literally, out-of-this-world story will hurt his cause, whatever it may be?"

"It appears that those he has touched and cured will stick by him, no matter what he claims, evidenced by the reporter's reactions. But he will pick up skeptics due to his story. And you're right, Paul, about his momentum, but that, too, will slow. I believe he agreed to do the interview to speed up his plans and to get the word out to those he really wants to meet, the heads of state around the world. Now, put yourself in the shoes of those powerful people. Would you want this man to touch you? I'm willing to bet that many will be very cautious, and more than a few might prescribe to your brainwashing theory, or something close to it."

"I do hope you are right. Maybe if he is slowed down some, we can have more time to decide what to do about him."

"Paul, what do you mean by we? What is it that you think we can do about Mr. Warburton?"

"Not we as in you and me, I meant the Church, the Vatican. Surely they must respond to his allegations about Jesus Christ."

"They might not respond, at least not right away. It is possible those in Rome will want to see how this will play out first. Right now, I wouldn't be surprised to hear from one of the Pope's advisors that they are setting up a committee to study the situation and also invite Warburton to Rome to clarify some of his statements. I don't believe that the Church would want to be adversarial with a man who is only doing good. Right now, the public sees Warburton as a man who can cure people of their ills, even cancer and AIDs. If the Church attacks him for what he said, the public might think the church has ulterior motives, and we would grow even further from our flocks."

"What ulterior motives could the church possibly have? I think the people would see us as defending our faith against false accusations."

And then Father Padraig O'Malley shocked his young friend with two words: "Are they?"

"I don't understand what you mean, are they what?"

"The accusations, are they false?"

"Are you saying that you think there is a chance that Warburton is speaking the truth?" Paul said as the excitement returned to his voice.

Padraig tried to speak calmly in the hopes that his demeanor would rub off on Paul. "As far as Warburton is concerned, he does think he is telling the truth, and so do all those he has touched. And if he reaches his goal and touches everyone on Earth, and then everyone on Earth believes his statements about Jesus Christ, then doesn't that make them true?"

"If a thing is wrong, then it should not matter how many believe, it is still a lie." That was when Paul stopped short and seemed to be staring at a spot just above and to the left of Padraig's head. He mumbled something, mostly to himself, but O'Malley picked up on a couple of words, "great deceiver." Father Sikora rose from his chair and began to pace the floor of the small living room.

Padraig thought that all rational discussion was over for this night, but he tried anyway. "Something has obviously caused you agitation, Paul."

"Let me ask you a theological question, Father, do you think it possible for Satan to possess the body of a human?"

The pastor sighed. "I can see where you are going with this, and I have to tell you that I don't know. Certainly, there have been accounts of possession throughout history, and there was a time when the priests performed exorcisms. But there isn't enough evidence to prove or disprove demonic possession. And even if you could, how would you know that the possessor was Satan, not just a minor demon? There have also been theories that Jesus Christ was not the son of God, but God himself who possessed a human body because he wanted to know what it was to be human and also to walk among his people. Those who have subscribed to this theory have surmised that

God told the people that he was the son of God and of the flesh so that they would more likely accept him and not be in awe, and therefore he could live among his followers."

"So it might be possible for Satan to do the same?"

"But Satan is not a God. He is an angel who was cast out of Heaven, and, therefore, not an equal to God."

"You must admit, though, that the Church paints him to be nearly an equal to God."

He decided to stop dancing around the young man's theory. "Correct me if I am wrong, Paul, but you are about to tell me that you think it is possible that Satan has possessed Warburton?"

Father Sikora had stopped pacing and was now standing in front of the still-seated Father O'Malley. To his credit, he appeared calm and in control of his emotions. "I don't know what I believe at this point. But given our profession, I believe it makes more sense that Satan is trying to destroy God by the use of a normal family man and former police officer than aliens conducting an experiment. With all that has been written about Catholicism and Jesus Christ, and even the physical evidence that has been brought forth over the centuries, how can we believe that it was all manufactured? Padraig, you and I know Jesus Christ was the son of God, to think otherwise is crazy. I have very little experience as a priest, and maybe thinking that Satan is making some kind of move here and now is also crazy. But I have this feeling of dread, and if you are right and the Church doesn't immediately denounce Warburton, then maybe it is up to those like us to act. Sometimes timing is everything, and it is possible Satan knows that, too. Our teachings tell us that in the past Satan has tried to sway humans to the side of evil, his side, but if I were in his shoes, I might think it was time to try a different strategy. Hide among the humans and don't try to convince them that the Church and God have abandoned them, give them an alternative. I think that people would have a hard time turning their backs on God unless they were given an out, the Catholic religion was just a big misunderstanding. And as I said timing, given the recent troubles of the Church and the fact that people are leaving in large numbers, accompanied by the majority of people who now believe that there are other intelligent beings in the universe, it would seem that now would be the opportunity for Satan to destroy all religion. In the last 20 years, the public has been introduced to more benevolent aliens through television, movies, and novels, than ever before. During the last census, when asked their religious affiliation, thousands wrote in "Order of the Jedi," and if you aren't familiar with that, it is from the *Star Wars* movies. So if I have hit upon something here, and Satan is behind this, then he is using a form of brainwashing. But not to turn people to evil. He is using acts of good and crediting other worldly beings to get people to question the existence of God. Soon people will start to ask themselves, why hasn't God sent us someone like Warburton? And they will logically conclude that God did not because he doesn't exist. Satan's attack on Jesus Christ and his role as the Son of God is only his first step to eradicate all religion. Ingenious really, because in the end if Warburton/Satan is not stopped, no one will even know that it was Satan who destroyed, not only religion, but I think his end game is to destroy the world."

Padraig sat stunned and at first and didn't know what to think of Paul's theory. He was about to open his mouth and try to shoot holes in it, but then he thought of Warburton's account of the aliens. He'd said that the aliens told him that humans would eventually kill each other off without their help. He interpreted this to mean that humans were inherently evil, bent on destruction of their enemies on Earth even if it meant their own destruction. Sure, there were evil men, well-documented throughout history, but Padraig believed that man was not evil at his core, that most people were good, and there was plenty of documentation about those who gave of themselves every day to help others also, even some who even gave their own lives. Ether the aliens were wrong, or there was something to Paul's possession theory. But in the end, Padraig did not want to jump at this theory just yet.

"Ok Paul, some of what you have just said has caught my interest but, it is still only a theory. We do not have any evidence of a possession and have no authority to act on any of this. I say this because at the end of your speech, it did sound as if you have already made up your mind that Warburton is in the hands of Satan."

"I may have gotten ahead of myself, a little."

"Then we must slow down. What I propose we do is continue to monitor Warburton via the media and internet. Determine if his plans hit a snag because of his story, or does he continue to gain momentum. Maybe even go to New Britain and observe him directly. But, and I cannot stress this enough, any trip will be taken together. And we will work as one on this, full disclosure to each other. We should take time out, let's say after dinner each night, and meet to discuss anything of significance regarding Warburton."

Father Paul seemed to have curbed his anger and excitement as he responded "I agree that further investigation is necessary, and I will acquiesce to your experience in these matters."

Padraig chuckled. "I have no experience in these matters. This isn't something anyone has seen or heard before. And I have to tell you, Paul, if this is Satan that we are up against, I'm not sure I am physically and spiritually up to the challenge."

"Well, I could argue against that statement for the rest of the night, if you want. And I have to tell you that if this is the work of Satan, then I think that we are as strong a team as you will find to take him on. With my youth and fresh-out-of-the-seminary knowledge, and your vast experience and years of studying scripture, at the end of the day, he will know he was in a fight."

Padraig sighed. "Let us hope that it is not Satan, because I don't think mere men can kill him. The best we could hope for is to somehow drive him out of Warburton and back to Hell."

Father Sikora nodded with a sober look on his face. The two men headed toward their own bedrooms, renewing their vow to meet after dinner the next night to discuss the reaction to Warburton's claims. They both told themselves that they would continue to look for evidence of Paul's theory, but in their hearts they had already started to lean in the direction that Satan had taken up residence in New Britain, Connecticut.

CHAPTER 21

On the Monday after the interview with Karen Ayala, Danny arrived at Hope at his usual time to find the biggest crowd there to date, and the media seemed to be everywhere. He glanced at some of the television trucks and vans as he steered the Santa Fe toward the back of the building and found that the media had not only came out in force today, but had decided that it was time to stop hanging back. The cameramen and reporters, which he saw had come from around the globe, were lined along the front of the building. Some had even tried to follow the Hyundai to the rear doors.

Carlos Cintron and his small security crew did their best to hold back the reporters and keep the rest of the crowd in some sort of orderly line that started at the front door. With The Healer safely through the back door, Carlos left the front in the hands of his captains, and he used his key to enter a side door. He found his boss at the stereo.

Carlos said, "You really kicked the hornet's nest on Saturday, boss."

"I found a CD of a new singer, Lianne La Havas. Have you ever heard of her before?"

"I don't think so, boss. My crew is having a hard time with the crowd and all the media out there. We might have to bring in some more people if this is how it is going to be from now on."

Danny didn't seem to be concerned with the crowd or the security problems as he responded to Carlos. "That would be fine. Whatever you think, Carlos. You know, I have a couple of CDs from Diana Krall, but I don't remember playing any of them yet. That's strange. I'll lead with Lianne and play two from Diana this morning."

Carlos was a little unnerved with Danny's apparent disconnection with the circumstances. He was always on top of things here at Hope, but today his mind seemed far off. "Boss, you ok? Did something happen over the weekend?"

"Thank you for your concern, Carlos, but I am fine. I just feel that this is coming to an end very soon, and I'm not sure I want it to. I knew I would have to move on from this place if my plan is to be successful, and as chaotic as this place is at times, I still will miss it. You bring in as many bodies as you need to keep things running as smooth as they can. When it is time to move on, we will have to let them go. But I would like you to stay on. Are you up for a little traveling?"

"Anywhere and anytime, I am at your disposal."

"Thanks again, Carlos. As far as today and our newfound media frenzy, I am not doing a press conference right now. But I guess we should give them something so they will go away. Get a few of your people, and when we open the doors, herd the reporters and their crews to the right side against the wall. I will address them as a group, maybe take a few questions, but then let it be known to them that we have work to do here. They can stay and watch, but if they get in the way, they will be asked to leave. I suspect that most will get some file footage and then get bored enough that they will leave on their own."

"You got it, boss. Give me a few minutes to get my crew in position before you open the doors."

"The show must go on, Carlos. You have five minutes." Danny raised his voice to be heard as the security chief already hustled toward the side door he had entered, on his way to coordinate with his troops.

He spent 15 minutes with the media and after a short statement, he answered three questions, then cut them off. During that time he made a few jokes and was his usual gregarious and confident self. When he told the group of reporters that he had to get back to attending to his guests, none of them complained or tried to ask more questions. Most of them stayed and became part of the line to have their few minutes with The Healer in his office.

After Danny left the reporters, he went to the front of the rows of chairs and greeted the first person in line, as he had done countless times before. The rest of the day was uneventful, if you call curing cancer, diabetes, and blindness, as well as numerous everyday ailments that his guests came in with that day, as not worthy of mentioning.

During his time at Hope that day he took a few minutes to call Carmel. He asked her to hold dinner until he got home so that he could sit down with the whole family. While they ate, Danny talked and laughed with his wife and children, but Carmel noticed moments when he was staring off into space. After the kids were long asleep and their time on the back deck was over, husband and wife made love. It was good, as it usually was between them, but again she felt a sadness in her husband. She was going to let it go and chalk it up to his tiredness, but then decided to ask him before he drifted off.

They were both lying on their backs when she propped herself up on one elbow and put a hand on his chest. "Did something happen today? Both at dinner, and now in bed, you seemed to be far off at times."

"Oh shit, honey. I'm sorry. I should have been giving you every ounce of my attention."

"I agree, but it does say something when you can push me over the edge without even trying. But we will talk about that later. Right now, I am more worried about your state of mind."

"There must be a problem, because Carlos also said I was disconnected today. I don't know, I have this feeling that something is just over the horizon that I can't quite see and it's giving me a sense of dread. I can't put my finger on it, and nothing has happened that points to impending trouble, but I can't shake the feeling, either. Maybe I'm feeling a little down that I didn't get a phone call yesterday or today."

"Who did you think was going to call you?"

"The governor, the senator, someone from Washington. I'm pretty sure they all were watching on Saturday."

"Honey, did you forget who you're talking about? Politicians! They don't make any decision quickly, and they have to form a committee and discuss it before they do anything. I know you are anxious, but it has only been a couple of days. You and I both know your plan is solid, but it is not going to happen overnight. Please be patient before you drive me and the kids crazy."

Danny knew that his wife was right, so he tried to shake off his current mood. He smiled and said, "Did you know that while you were talking, the sheet slipped off of your shoulder, and now your nipple is winking at me?"

"And I was worried about the kids and me going crazy."

# # #

As it turned out, he didn't have to wait another whole day for the call he was expecting. At 10:30 am on Tuesday, Governor Acevedo dialed Danny's cell. He was leading a guest out of his office and told the next person in line to excuse him, as he had to take the call. He went back in the office, shut the door, and sat behind his desk before answering his phone. He didn't have Acevedo on his contact list, so only the phone number showed on his cell's display, but he knew who it was.

"Good morning, Martin. Good of you to call."

"Hello, Mr. Warburton. That was a hell of a story you told everyone on Saturday."

"One hundred percent the truth, and call me Danny."

"Yes, I know it is the truth. I don't know how I know, but I do. The problem is that those you wish to meet are skeptical and if you ask me, I think they're a little afraid, also. I have been in contact with the White House both before and after your speech on Saturday. You may have pushed the president back a few steps with that story. His people, mostly his military advisors, are worried that the aliens' true goal is to take over Earth, and you are just a way of getting to him."

"For chrissake, Martin. If Calvin and Hobbes wanted to take over the Earth, they could come down here and be done with it in about an hour. They certainly would not need me."

"Calvin and Hobbes?"

"It's just.....I had to give them names, call them something."

"Ok. Strange names, but that is your business. Listen, Danny, you probably didn't watch the political talk shows on Sunday morning, but the president's advisors were on every one. All the moderators wanted to know was when was he going to sit down with you. Likewise, the network morning shows yesterday and today were also putting pressure on a meet between you two. I think he knows a meeting with you is inevitable, but he is being told by his people to use caution. I have been told that he will hold a press conference in a few days and announce that he is working out the details of bringing you and your family to the White House, but that trip might still not happen for a week or so. He is listening to his advisors, and he will heed their words to take things with you slowly. I have some experience in politics, so if you would allow me to be your advisor, I would tell you not to push him on this. Let the president take the slow track here, and it will work out in your favor."

"Thank you, Martin. One, for being such an advocate for me, I didn't know you had been in contact with the president on my behalf. And two, for giving me your advice in this matter. I will let the president dictate the pace of our relationship. This is too important to screw up, I need him as an ally. If you could please continue to be my liaison with Washington and keep me abreast of your progress, your efforts would be greatly appreciated."

The two men said their goodbyes and disconnected the call. Danny sat at his desk for a few moments and thought, *"A week, two at the most, and his plans will be nearly unstoppable."* He chuckled to himself and said to the empty office, "What goes around, comes around. I guess I should call Karen and ask to borrow her pacing shoes."

The Healer got up, opened the door to his office, and went back to the business of the day.

Two days after Danny's conversation with Martin Acevedo, the President of the United States, Adam Douglas, held a press conference in the Rose Garden of the White House. Just as Acevedo had told him, among other things, Douglas told the crush of reporters that it was his intention to reach out to Danny and invite him and his family to the White House. He went on to say that it was his hope that he and Mr. Warburton could come to an agreement as to how best to use the talents he had been given, keeping in mind the interests and well-being of the United States and its people.

The president's speech was broadcast in prime time, so Danny was home, sitting on his couch in the living room watching the television with Carmel and the children. Katie and Sandra were excited that the president was talking about their family and that they would get the chance to go to the White House. Jack was excited because his sisters were.

Carmel saw the brief frown on her husband's face before he joined in with the kids, talking about what they would wear, their travel plans, and what else they should do while in Washington DC. She marveled at the way this grown man sometimes acted and talked like his children, just to be part of their world for a short time. The girls knew it was only dad being goofy, but they enjoyed it as much as he did. Carmel wasn't going to forget about the frown, though. She would bring it up later, on the deck.

When the laughter died down and the giddy, excited talk of their impending trip also came to an end, Danny noticed Jack rubbing his eyes and the girls trying to hide yawns. Mama and Papa Bear brought them to their bedrooms and tucked them in, then they retired to the bistro chairs on a night where the temperature had cooled with a hint of the soon-to-be autumn season. Carmel waited until Danny had put away half of his glass of wine before she broached the subject of the president's speech.

"I noticed that while you were listening to Douglas, your shoes were still on."

He took a long pull on his cigar and starred at his wife before answering. "What are you talking about, woman?"

"This is what you have wanted for some time, but I sensed disappointment. Duh, you weren't jumping out of your shoes."

"Fucking politicians! Douglas thinks I'm going to his house and enter in some kind of negotiations about how to use my gifts for the good of this country. I served my country and wouldn't want to live anywhere else, but this isn't about who is the best, who has the most land, who has the most powerful military, or who has the biggest dick. I don't care about countries, this is about the individual and about society as a whole. I am not going to let him screw with my plan."

"Baby, I didn't mean to rile you up," Carmel said, as she leaned toward her husband, put her hand on the side of his face, and smiled. "And you know that whatever you decide, I will be at your side. But remember, politicians often say things in front of a camera because they believe it is what the public wants to hear. Douglas might be willing to go along with your plan as it is. But I implore you not to be closed minded and on the defensive during your meeting with him. It wasn't so long ago that you were telling me about your supervisor training at the police academy, and you said that the best leaders surround themselves with intelligent, common sense advisors and then heed their advice."

"I have already done that. You are my chief advisor. You are smart, compassionate, one of the kindest people I have known, and you have a lot of experience telling me what to do."

"You are an ass."

Danny turned to an invisible third person on the deck and said, "Give a girl a compliment, and she calls you names."

"I can see you're out of your mood. But all kidding aside, the people in Washington are used to dealing with the international community. At least listen to what they have to say about the best way to move your plan beyond our borders."

"I will, Mel, and you keep pulling me back down to earth when I start to think I can do all this by myself."

Their glasses were drained, so he took one more drag on the cigar before snuffing it out. Danny and Carmel held hands while on the way to their bedroom, quietly undressed, and fell asleep in each other's arms.

CHAPTER 22

Danny wasn't the only person upset by the words of President Douglas that night. In his mansion on Long Island, Jimmy Santini had thought that the Warburton problem was behind him until the president's speech. None of the general public, except maybe Clan Warburton, knew what Douglas' speech was going to be about, but Santini made it a point to watch every speech this and every past president made on national television since he was 13 years old. And even though he was upset, the remote control did not find itself smashed against the face of the big screen TV. To his credit, he didn't break, punch, or kick anything when he heard the president's plan to see Warburton, hell, he didn't even swear. Part of his restraint stemmed from the realization that he would have to go back to his original plan to kill the meddling son-of-a-bitch. But his self-control might also be attributed to the fact that he had company.

One of his female acquaintances was in the game room playing pool by herself while Jimmy watched the president. She had no interest about what politicians had to say, so she'd excused herself to the game room when Douglas appeared on the screen. Usually he didn't have people in his home, but he was trying lately to be more like a regular gangster and thought he needed to get laid more often. So he called his lady friend and invited her to dinner at his house. She understood what it meant when he told her to pack an overnight bag. Jimmy told himself he didn't care what the bimbo thought of him, but then again, he didn't want her to witness him having a temper tantrum.

He went into the kitchen to make himself another drink, then joined his guest in the game room. He made a mental note to dig out that name and number his uncle gave him a few weeks ago.

The following morning, as soon as the cab left on its mission to take Jimmy's date back to her apartment in the city, The Brain took the folded napkin that his uncle had given him out of his wallet where it had sat since his meeting with Sonny. Since he hadn't looked at the napkin in the coffee shop, this was the first time he saw the name printed there. "Eamon," Jimmy said to the napkin. "What the fuck kind of name is that? It certainly doesn't sound Italian, sounds Irish. Well, Eamon, you must know how to keep your mouth shut if my uncle trusts you like a family member."

Jimmy didn't know the half of it. Eamon Flannigan was born in Belfast, Northern Ireland, when that corner of his country was still part of the United Kingdom. Eamon's father worked long hours for little pay, and this resulted in Eamon learning most of life's lessons on the streets. He was a vandal at a young age and recruited by the Irish Republican Army not long after his 15th birthday. Inside the ranks of the IRA, he fell under the tutelage of one of the most knowledgeable bomb makers of that time. And eight years later, when his mentor was killed when a bomb he was making blew up in his own garage, Eamon became the primary bomb expert for his organization.

As time went on and tensions softened between England and Ireland, the need for Eamon's talents abated. When the English government began the process of reuniting Northern Ireland with the rest of the country, Flannigan saw the writing on the wall. He "retired" to the United States and planned to live out his life in anonymity. He had enough money to do so. But his reputation followed not long after he arrived in New York, and it wasn't long before those in the killing business looked him up. Growing up poor, money was always a motivator for him, so when his phone rang, he usually collected a consulting fee. When the price was right, he occasionally would make the device, but he never planted it or witnessed the destruction it caused, not anymore.

So on that late summer morning when his phone rang and he heard the caller give his name, Eamon Flannigan made an appointment to see Sonny Santini's nephew. He had been given a heads-up by Sonny about a week or so ago that Jimmy would be calling, and he'd asked Eamon to give him all the courtesy that he would afford the elder Santini.

The conversation was short, as no business was discussed over the phone, just the details of the meet. Jimmy didn't want to go to the Irishman's house in Queens, and he told Jimmy that he was too old to drive all the way on the other side of Long Island. They came to an agreement to meet in Central Park in two days at 10 am. Eamon told the younger Santini that he would be at the Bethesda Fountain, sitting on the wall/bench that was closest to the pond and eating peanuts out of a brown paper bag. After the call ended, Jimmy thought, *"Fuckin' crazy old Mick got me running around Central Park."* But he had to admit to himself that he liked the idea of an outdoor venue, it made electronic surveillance that much more difficult.

# # #

"I can't believe we haven't heard anything from Rome yet. It has been days since Warburton made a mockery of our religion. They didn't even send a communique to the archdiocese around the world to give us some direction as to how they want us to respond. Our parishioners are going to be asking questions, and we may even get a visit from the local media. If they want us on the same page, they should at least contact us at the church level." Father Paul ranted over the morning toast and coffee.

Padraig let the younger priest have his say. He had watched Father Paul become more and more agitated since Warburton's interview and the president's speech. In Paul's eyes, the speech had given credence to Warburton's blaspheme. He tried to placate him when he got this way, but Father O'Malley was wrestling with his own confusion. Why was it taking so long for the Vatican to make a statement about the subject? And even though he at first thought that Paul's possession by Satan theory had some merit, Padraig was now questioning the sanity of that way of thinking. But he'd had more experience with the Church and its ways, and he also had to be the voice of reason lately. So he collected his thoughts and spoke in a calm manner to his friend.

"Rome has not said anything to us, and that says that we are not to say anything to the media. It has long been the practice that on major issues, those at our level wait for the Vatican's opinion before we give ours, no matter how long that might be. I suspect that they are waiting for Warburton to make some kind of fatal mistake so they can disparage him and his story. But I agree with you that they have waited too long on this one. I suspect we will hear from them any day now. But don't get your hopes up. My prediction that the Church will be non-confrontational with Warburton still stands. They have always been a conservative bunch, and they probably won't go out on a limb this time, either. And since the president has invited Warburton to the White House, an invitation to the Vatican is just around the corner."

"Like giving the fox a key to the henhouse." After a few moments of silence, Father Sikora continued. "Have you given any further thought to what we have discussed in the past?"

"The possession theory? I have been thinking about what you said recently and, I just...I just don't know if we are on the right track there. Some of what you have said makes sense. But the whole situation is so…Old Testament that it is hard to imagine that something of that magnitude could happen in this day and age."

"That is exactly why Satan would choose now to make a move, we have become too complacent. My guess is that he has been waiting a long time for these exact set of circumstances, the steady decline over the past ten years in church attendance, the molestation scandal that has involved so many priests in a number of countries, and the fact that people are looking elsewhere for answers. Remember, it was you who pointed out that these aliens of Warburton's have told him that humans are so violent that we will eventually kill each other off. You and I both know that there is more good in this world than evil. Also, if a race of aliens wanted to help us barbaric earthlings, wouldn't they go to the governments of the world with their proposal of assistance? No, this alien story just doesn't wash. It is a lie, as is the part where Jesus Christ wasn't the son of God. So if that is a lie, where does that leave us? Maybe my theory that Satan has possessed Warburton is wrong, but I don't think so. Every day, I feel more and more that I am right and if no one else is going to do anything to stop him, then it falls to us."

"I'm not sure the two of us can do anything to stop whatever is going on, we are too removed from the situation. And I think that we would have to get close to Warburton and witness his actions first hand and talk to him to make a final determination about whether your theory is correct or not."

"I don't think getting close to him would be wise, but we can discuss strategies at a later time. For now, I will defer to your experience and wait for Rome's guidance and recommendations."

"Thank you, Paul. I know we hoped that Warburton's momentum would slow, but that doesn't seem the case now. So I appreciate your temperance in this matter. We must be positive before we commit ourselves to a course of action where we can't afford to be wrong."

# # #

On the day that Jimmy Santini was to meet Eamon Flannigan in Central Park, he arrived 30 minutes early and took a position where he could observe the wall by the pond and the most likely avenue of approach. The mobster had never been to the fountain before, but recognized the exact spot he was to meet Flannigan by the man's description of the area. He wanted to observe the bomb maker and size him up before they met, and also see if he brought any muscle with him.

At five minutes before ten, Jimmy noticed a man carrying a brown lunch bag enter the fountain area from the paved path to the right of the pond. The guy was big, about 6'2", with a broad chest and a bald head. He wore jeans and a black turtleneck shirt under a grey blazer. The man made a beeline for the bench and began to shell and eat peanuts from the paper bag.

The Brain left his vantage point in the shadows under the stairs that faced the fountain and came out on the opposite side. He then went to the top of the stairs and came down like he had just arrived. Once in view, Jimmy also went straight to the bench and sat a few feet from Flannigan. Not offering his hand to shake or even looking the Irishman's way, Jimmy began the conversation. "Mr. Flannigan I'm…"

Flannigan cut him off. "Jimmy Santini. I've done some work for your uncle, and I can see the family resemblance. Sonny and I have a mutual trust of one another. He tells me that you are what he calls a stand-up guy, and he would put his life in your hands. I don't know you son, but a recommendation like that from Sonny Santini goes a long way in my book. What is it that I can help you with today, boy-o?"

Jimmy's first thought was that he needed a translator, Flannigan's brogue was so thick he was sure he had missed a few words that came out of the Irishman's mouth, but he understood enough, and he didn't believe that their conversation would be lengthy.

"My uncle tells me that you are the best at what you do. What I need is some knowledge and an object big enough to take out a car and the occupant."

"You want me to teach you how to make this object?"

"No, I don't have time for that. I would like you to make the device and teach me how to set it and activate it."

"I can make it real easy for you to set it, boy-o, but that would mean someone would have to be within 100 yards to detonate it with a remote. Or I could show you how to wire it to the starter or a pressure plate under the driver's seat. But that would take some time to first instruct you how to do that and second, time to set it. What'll it be?"

Jimmy didn't need any time to think about it. "Make it as easy as possible to set, and I will take care of the remote, I have to make sure the right person is in the car, anyway."

"So be it. Call me again in three days." Without waiting for a response, the big man stood and walked toward the path that had brought him there, brushing the peanut shells from his pants as he went.

CHAPTER 23

After the president's speech, Danny knew that he would have to play the waiting game. So in the meantime, he did what had become very routine for him. He went back to Hope every day, listened to smooth jazz or women with sultry voices oozing from the CD player, and touched as many people as possible.

On Wednesday of the next week, he arrived at Hope and, like every other day, he let the caterer in and put in the first of many CDs. He was in his office when he heard his security chief use his key to enter through the side door. Carlos and his security team had gone back to the usual coverage since the media frenzy that had occurred when Danny got a shout out on TV from President Douglas had subsided. Without looking at his watch, Danny knew that the time was 7:50, because he heard the ex-gang enforcer briefing his crew, which he did at precisely the same time each day, next to the caterer's tables so his people could grab a quick coffee and a bite to eat before they went to their posts.

Five minutes later, Danny pushed his chair back from the desk and headed to the front doors to unlock them for the day. His cell phone rang, and he answered it as he always did. "Danny Warburton."

"Mr. Warburton, my name is Franklin Nickerson, and I am Adam Douglas' press secretary. I have been instructed by the president to contact you and set up a date when you and your family can be the Douglas' guests at the White House for a few days. Unfortunately, the president left this morning for London, as he's had meetings scheduled with the British Prime Minister on his calendar since last month. President Douglas will be back at the White House one week from today, and he asked if you could be in Washington on that Friday."

Even though this was the call he had been anticipating for some time now, it still took him by surprise, so he stalled for time to gather himself. "Um…sorry. You said your name was Mr. Nickerson?"

"Yes, Franklin Nickerson."

"Ok. Well ….I guess you don't tell the President of the United States that you have to check your date book, so next Friday it is. Will you be calling back with the details, or do I walk up to the front door and knock?"

"We do have a gate and a few security checks, so no one just walks up to our front door. But from what I have read, with your talents, you might make it that far."

Danny chuckled. "You know what they say, don't believe anything you hear and only half of what you read."

"Mr. Warburton, you must already be aware that we have spoken to your family, friends, and ex-colleagues at the New Britain Police Department during our extensive background check on you. We do that for everyone who will stay the night at the White House."

"That's funny, no one called to tell me the government was poking around in my life. And you can call me Danny."

"What's funnier is that we received the same response from everyone we spoke to when we asked that they not contact you about our background investigation. Almost to a word they said that you could take care of yourself and didn't need a heads up from them."

The Healer didn't want someone this close to the president to be suspicious or think him a danger, so he decided to close the conversation out before he said something stupid. "Mr. Nickerson, please excuse me, but I was about to open up shop for the day when you called. And now I find myself five minutes late. Please call me back around the middle of next week to confirm our stay and to tell me what to do once we arrive in Washington DC."

"I will be in contact soon, and you can call me Frank."

Danny heard the sound of the call disconnect and put his phone away. He stood in the center of the chairs and looked around the large room. A bittersweet smile formed on his face, and he made a mental note to tell Carlos and the caterer that next Wednesday was the last day Hope would be open for a while, maybe for good.

He stayed busy all morning and tried to keep his mind on his guests, but he had developed the ability to sort of "separate" his thoughts. One part of his brain was thinking what he had to do, such as in this case he was making a list in his head about the notifications he'd make about closing Hope, during his lunch break. The other part of his brain was healing the person he was in physical contact with at the moment. Danny found that the only problem was a few seconds of what he called "static," which occurred after a diagnosis of his guest was made and before he actually started healing and cleansing. During that time, his other thoughts weren't making it through, but he didn't think this was a big problem, as his secondary thought process resumed right after he disconnected with the current subject.

When lunch time came, he grabbed some sweet and sour meatballs from the caterer's table and went into his office. He put the plate down at his desk, then looked at his belly. He hadn't worked out or ran for four or five months, but he hadn't gained any weight. He guessed that the enhanced brain activity must be burning those extra calories. Danny popped a meatball into his mouth and called Carmel's cell phone. He only spoke to his wife briefly and told her of the phone call from the White House and his plans to close Hope the following Wednesday. They ended the call after they agreed that they would work out the details of the trip to DC during their nightly back deck session. His next call was to his friend and ex-boss, Captain Michael Franti.

Danny dialed Franti's office phone, as he knew it was Michael's habit to have his lunch at his desk, also. The captain answered on the first ring "Detectives, Captain Franti."

"Sorry to interrupt your lunch, but I don't get much free time these days."

"Danny! Good to hear from you. I understand you have been making friends and influencing people with the Catholics."

"Oh, you saw that interview, huh?"

"Of course I did. I knew it would be memorable. Maybe it would have been best to keep all that alien and JC shit under your hat for a little while longer. You getting any death threats yet?"

"I have been getting more than the usual hang-ups lately, and there have been two or three callers who said I should die, but those could have been from people who really know me. How are things going at the PD?"

"This place is a fucking ghost town, thanks to you. You're curing the junkies, and you all but solved the gang problem. We haven't had many new cases in the bureau, so I have been looking into some cold cases. But even those haven't been a challenge. For instance, last week I call up this guy we liked for a homicide four years ago and before I can ask him to come in for an interview, he confesses over the phone. It turns out he had already visited you at Caldors and got the blue light special. He came in and put his confession on paper, and now he is locked up on $250,000 bond. The thing is that I know he has been…let's say, rehabilitated. So what do I do with him now? Put him in prison on the taxpayer's dime when I know he won't do it ever again? Frankly, I don't know what to do with him, so I'm going to dump it in the prosecutor's lap."

"I'm glad that I at least have caused you a moral dilemma. And it isn't Caldors anymore, it's called Hope, you fucking ballbreaker. Anyway, I didn't call you to hear that all you have to do is play solitaire on your computer. I called to offer you a job."

"I already have a job. But for how much longer, I don't know, thanks to you."

"See, perfect timing. You won't have a job anymore, and I am offering you a new one."

"Doing what?"

"To tell you the truth, I've had more than a few death threats, and a couple of protesters, as well as, someone spray painted a nasty message for me on the back of the store two days ago. I was thinking you could head up my security team when I hit the road, which is in less than two weeks, by the way."

"Don't you have Carlos for that?"

"Carlos has been great, but I need someone who can conduct background investigations on the people who have been sending the threats, to determine which are legitimate and cause for concern. I will give you a signing bonus, enough to pay off your mortgage, and a hefty yearly salary. The only drawback would be the traveling, but you don't have to give me an answer now. Go home, talk it over with Gina. Just let me know before Sunday. And who knows, a few months down the road, maybe Gina and the kids would want to travel with us. I'm bringing along a tutor for my children, your kids could join the class."

"This is a lot to think about, but I will call you on or before Saturday."

"Great! I'm going to let you go, I've got to make several more calls and finish my lunch. I'll talk to you soon." Danny didn't wait for a reply from his friend. He already felt an urgency and could almost see time creeping up behind him.

Sometime that afternoon, he stopped by the caterer's table to grab a snack and a bottle of water. But it was actually an excuse to tell the man who had fed him and his guests so many meals that his services were no longer needed starting the following Thursday. The caterer took it well and thanked him for his generosity.

The rest of the day seemed to go by quickly, and before he knew it, he was locking the front door. As he walked back toward his office, he called to Carlos and asked him if he could see him in his office. As he entered, Danny sat behind his desk and asked Carlos to close the door.

"Carlos, I wanted to tell you that I appreciate all that you and your crew have done for me over these last months."

Carlos interrupted his boss. "You got the call you were waiting for."

"I got the call."

"I suppose we all have to start looking for new jobs, as of when?"

"We close up shop next Wednesday, but hear me out. I have a proposal. You and your people have learned a lot about the security business in a short time. But if you're going to start your own business, all of you need some formal training. So this is what I was thinking. I put up the seed money for you to open your own security company, but before you take on any clients, your entire crew attends classes. I have already looked into it and found a training academy not far from here. Hire a few more people if you have to, and you can use this building for your offices. What do you think?"

Carlos was floored, and the tough ex-gang enforcer almost came to tears. "You have been so good to me, boss. This is more than I can ask of you."

"You didn't ask, I offered. But there is one problem."

"What's that?"

"You are going to have to find someone you trust to run the company while you're away. I am going to Washington DC next Friday, and that might be just the start of extensive traveling. I would like you to come with me as part of my security team, and I could use two of your best to come along, also. From what I have observed, Luis and Cassandra would fit that bill. So you would still have the problem of finding the person who could run your business for you. But it's not like you would be away for years at a time, I anticipate that there would be some down time, and you wouldn't have to be at my side 24/7. You would be able to come back to check up on the business from time to time. So that is my proposal. You don't have to answer now, but time is short. Let me know by Monday morning."

With that, Danny stood and came around the desk to where Carlos still sat. The young man was still processing all that his boss had said to him, but Danny didn't have time to sit around while Carlos pondered his future. He shook Cintron's hand and pulled him to his feet at the same time. He then ushered him to the side door, bade him good night, and left him in the driveway that led to the back of the building. Danny headed back to his office to close up for the night and hoped that he wouldn't be passing his current security chief, still standing where he left him in the alley, as he drove toward the front of the building on his way home.

Dinner that night was quiet, and Carmel kept glancing at her husband and wondering when he was going to tell the kids about the trip to Washington DC. Every so often she would catch his eyes and give him a look that said, "What gives? Say something already." But Danny would smile at her and resume clearing his plate. When he didn't acknowledge her by the third glance was really a glare, she gave up and thought to herself, *"I swear he does these things just to drive me crazy".*

After the table was cleared and the dishes done, Papa Bear announced that they were all going out for ice cream. There were picnic tables in the rear of the local Dairy Queen, and that was where Clan Warburton settled to enjoy their dessert. Even though fall was in the air, ice cream melts, which meant Jack had more on his face and hands than made it into his mouth. When they had finished their treats, Danny dropped the bombshell and told the kids they would be sleeping in the White House for two nights, or so he thought at the time. Katie and Sandy were ecstatic and let out short, high-pitched squeals, and Jack celebrated by wiping his hands on his shirt and shorts. Carmel looked at Jack and shook her head, she then turned to her husband and suggested that they head home because a bath was in his son's future, and she really wanted to make it to the deck for a glass of wine before it got too late.

When they got home, Danny saw to the girls as they washed up, put on their pajamas, and brushed their teeth. He tucked them into bed and promised that their mother would stop in to say good night. Meanwhile, in the bathroom, Carmel stripped Jack of his chocolate-covered clothes and plopped him into a quickly drawn bath. He protested the fact that he couldn't have play time in the bath with his toy boats, but deep down he was happy that the bath only took 15 minutes, as he was tired and wanted sleep more than bath toys.

Husband and wife waited 15 minutes to make sure the kids were asleep before they headed for the back deck, each with a glass of wine, and, of course, Danny with a Hav-A-Tampa. For a short time, neither spoke. When there was a silence between them, they were usually comfortable with it.

He was looking up to the clear night sky and the thousands of visible stars, and Carmel looked at her husband. It was a cool night, but not unpleasant, and she thought that in a few weeks, she would have to bring a sweater with the wine. She broke the silence. "Thinking about your new friends up there?"

"As a matter of fact, I was. With all the space between us, they can feel me down here, and sometimes I swear I can feel them, too. Although I don't think I'm supposed to."

"What do you mean by that?"

"I don't completely know, but I get these strange images in my head every so often of both Calvin and Hobbes as they move around their ship. And they don't seem to realize that I have that capability."

"From what you have told me, how could they not know?"

"Like I said, I don't know." Danny had been still looking into space the whole time he was talking to Carmel. After a short pause, he snapped his head down and faced his wife as if he had to forcibly stop staring toward the stars. "Anyway, we have some plans to make for next week. How do you want to travel to DC?"

"I think driving would be a little tedious, and everyone will be too anxious to get there. Eight to ten hours in a car would take the fun out of the trip. I guess flying would be best. What do you want to do?"

"The airport is always such a pain in the ass, but once we're on the plane, it would be the easiest way. We'll fly then. Could you make the reservations and buy the tickets online tomorrow? Oh, and call Deidra, the tutor, and let her know we need her services soon. Not for DC, but not long after that."

"Sure, I can take care of those two things. And you can pick up something for dinner on your way home, because after the kids get out of school I am taking them clothes shopping. We have to look good for the president."

"Like you need a reason to shop."

Carmel smiled and drained her glass, rose from her chair, and headed for the door. "Finish your cigar, and I'll meet you in our room."

He poured another glass of wine and smoked the cigar down to the nub. As he entered their bedroom, the lights were dim, but he could see that the object of his desires was in bed with just the sheet covering her. He could tell she had nothing on under the sheet, as her nipples swelled and protruded noticeably against the fabric. Danny was hard in an instant and joined his wife moments later. Sleep wouldn't come until several more hours had passed.

CHAPTER 24

Several days after the President of the United States gave a speech inviting Clan Warburton to the White House, the Pope conducted a press conference at Vatican City. The event was short, as the Pope was getting on in years and did not have the strength to stand for long periods of time. He read a prepared statement and did not take any questions from the small corps of reporters. For the most part, Rome's message was that they would also like Warburton to visit with the Pope and his advisors face to face. The Catholic church was concerned with the statements made by Warburton in regards to the Son of God. The Church believed that he may have misconstrued the message conveyed to him by those who bestowed his gifts, and it was the Pope's wish that Warburton could tell his story and give a word-for-word account about what the aliens said to him about Jesus Christ to a group of theologians. The Pope's statement included the comment that after the alien's story was investigated by those who have dedicated their lives to understanding the scriptures, a reasonable explanation could be found for Warburton's confusion on that part of their account.

Father O'Malley and Father Sikora, of course, watched the broadcast together. After the camera left the Pope and went to the so-called network experts to pick apart every word of the speech, Paul used the remote control to turn the television off. He waited for the elder priest to make the first comment.

Padraig snorted, and a wry smile crossed his lips. "I hate to say I told you so son, but this is what I predicted would be Rome's response weeks ago."

"Yes, their stance is exactly what you said it would be. How did you know their response to the letter?"

"I've been around a long time. I've seen three Popes come and go, but it really doesn't matter who wears the big hat. The Vatican is the Vatican, and it takes decades for Rome to change its ways even one inch."

Father Paul leaned forward in his chair and folded his hands together. His voice took on a deeper tone and was much calmer than it ever had been over the last few months as he responded to his mentor. "Where does that leave us?"

"Well, the way I see it, that leaves us to check on things ourselves. My back won't let me sit in a car for long, so we will have to make frequent stops. For that matter, if it wasn't my back, it would be my bladder causing us to hit every rest stop from here to Connecticut. And you will have to do all of the driving. Not tomorrow, but the day after should be fine. Are you up for the trip?"

Inside, Paul was like a ten-year-old being told he was going to Disney World for the first time. But once again, his voice displayed calmness. "I am ready for that trip. We should take tomorrow to come up with a plan of action once we are there."

"No action. This trip will be for observing, I think the military call it reconnaissance. You have to promise me there will be no confrontation."

Father Sikora swallowed hard and said, "You have my word."

The two men parted and didn't speak of Warburton the rest of the day or during their supper. When Paul Sikora retired for the night, his mind was still racing. He thought he would never get to sleep, but if he were to ask the man he believed to be possessed, he would have been told that using ones brain that much expends a great amount of energy. So eventually, he did succumb to sleep due to exhaustion. Of course, if Father Sikora ever did address Daniel Warburton, the conversation wouldn't be so mundane, because the young priest would be convinced he was not speaking to another human being.

The next day went by quickly as Paul kept himself busy with his youth programs. An hour before dinner, O'Malley sought him out and when he found him in the first pew of St. Veronica, he didn't ask what he was praying for. He gave him the keys to the church-owned Ford Taurus and told him to top off the tank, as they would be leaving at 7 am the next day.

Padraig skipped the evening meal, which brought a knock on his door by Katia. It took a few minutes to convince her that he was feeling fine and his absence was only because he wasn't hungry. Katia stared at his face for a few moments trying to read him, but found she didn't have anything else to say. So she left the man, who she considered her second father, as he wished.

They left at 7 o'clock as planned, and very little conversation was shared between the two. Paul was lost in his own thoughts and wasn't even aware of the silence in the car. Padraig had brought his Bible, which he read as they travelled north through New Jersey. After about an hour of reading various passages, the older man's eyes began to close periodically, and before they reached the George Washington Bridge, he was completely asleep, with the Bible still open on his lap.

Paul estimated they were about 15 minutes outside of New Britain when he decided he had to wake Padraig, because he needed help with the directions to Warburton's shop.

"Father O'Malley? ....Father O'Malley?"

Padraig stirred, sat up, and then used his right hand to hold the Bible to his thighs as the book tried to escape his lap. The older man blinked several times and looked around in an attempt to figure out where he was. "Where...? Paul...? Oh right, how far out are we?"

"Between 10 and 15 miles is my guess. I didn't want to wake you, but I need help with the directions. I wrote them down on the paper which is in the cup holder in the center console, but I didn't want to be driving and reading at the same time."

"Of course, it's the least I can do after you have done all of the driving, and probably had to put up with my snoring. Besides, I have to shake the cobwebs off before we get to our destination."

O'Malley put his Bible in the barren glove box and read the directions to Paul. A short time later, they pulled into the parking lot of the former department store and saw the sign "Hope" above the front door.

The place was busy as usual, with a constant flow of people going in and coming out. The two priests stood together next to their car and took it all in. Some of those they saw entering the big building were in wheelchairs or were helped along by other people. In contrast, those exiting were talking and laughing animatedly. None needed assistance by human hand or device. Padraig thought they all literally beamed.

The two men glanced at each other and then started for the door. After a few steps, Paul stopped dead and grabbed at his collar. Padraig turned to see why there wasn't an idealistic, young priest walking beside him any longer.

"I didn't even think about it this morning. I put the collar on as I do every day. Do you think it is wise to go in there with them on?"

"This is who we are, son. If you are right and the creature who is running this place recently relocated from a warmer climate, then he has an agenda, and harming us in front of all these witnesses is not part of it. We will be all right." Padraig continued toward the front entrance of Hope.

The two entered the front door and came to a halt, in a state of semi-shock. First, it was jammed with people at 10 am, and all of them seemed to be talking. Second, music was coming from a cheap pair of speakers on a table in the far corner. And third, the entire left wall was lined with tables that held several coffee urns, trays of Danish, muffins, and toast, as well as three kinds of juices in pitchers that were in tubs of ice. Padraig was surprised at the party atmosphere but snapped out of it enough to realize that those trying to enter behind them were being blocked. He moved to his left, behind the last row of chairs and noticed Father Sikora still being a hindrance, standing with his mouth agape in the middle of the aisle. O'Malley reached out, gently took him by the arm, and guided him to the back wall.

Regaining his composure, Paul asked, "Do you think it is like this all day, every day?"

"I believe it is."

Danny Warburton came out of his office at that moment, shaking hands with three others who had also just exited the office. He started to speak with the elderly woman who was seated in the first chair, but the music stopped. It appeared that he excused himself from the woman and headed for the stereo. Warburton put a CD in the player, and Padraig heard a blast of saxophone emanate from the speakers. He pegged it as a form of jazz and thought that at least Satan had good taste in music.

The Healer returned to the first chair and the woman, who then stood up but they didn't turn and head for the office. Instead, he was looking over the woman's head and seemed to be scanning the back of the crowd. Seconds later his eyes locked onto O'Malley's. Everyone else who happened to be looking at Danny at that moment saw his usual smiling face, and at first, that was what O'Malley saw. But as the seconds clicked by and time seemed to stop for the old man in the collar, he felt as if someone or something was looking into his mind. Later he described the feeling to Paul as if another presence was inside him. O'Malley became frightened but couldn't pull away from the powerful stare of the other man. Panic almost set in as Padraig came to believe that Warburton was reading his mind and knew what the two priests thought of him and the reason for their visit, to find some way to stop him. If you'd asked him, Father O'Malley would swear that he was locked in that gaze for five minutes or more, but actually it was more like six or seven seconds. It was Danny who broke the connection as his cell began to ring, and he answered it.

He saw the name of the caller on the display screen, and a smile lit up his face despite the uneasy feeling the priest at the back wall had given him. "Karen, it's good to hear from you. I thought you lost my number."

"Even if I had lost your number, what makes you think I couldn't find it in a matter of minutes? I'm a pretty good reporter and have my ways of obtaining information. Seriously though, I knew you would be busy getting ready to go see the president. Has he contacted you yet?"

"His press secretary called, we are going down to DC on Friday. So yeah, I have been busy, my excuse for not calling you. How are things with you?"

"I also have had a lot on my plate, I'm not in Connecticut anymore."

"What! You quit Channel 8? Where are you?"

"Not long after our last interview, CNN called and offered me a job as a field reporter. I know it's cable but it's still CNN. Right now I'm down in Atlanta getting my apartment set up and learning the ropes here. They probably won't send me out on assignment until next week. Maybe I'll see you at the White House. My new bosses know we are friends and most likely will ask me to take advantage of that."

As Karen talked, Danny stole a glance to the back wall to see if the priests were still there. They were, but they seemed to be arguing quietly.

"You will not be taking advantage and congratulations on the new job. Listen, Karen. I hate to cut this short, but I have a situation here that requires my personal attention. Come up to Washington on the weekend and have lunch with me and Adam."

"Don't get cocky, Warburton. I'll try to make it there by Sunday. Bye bye for now." Karen Ayala hung up and immediately cursed herself. She said to her new, mostly empty desktop "Jesus Christ, Karen. Bye bye for now? You sound like some high school girl talking to the quarterback while twirling her hair around a finger." She then turned to her left and saw another reporter at his desk five feet away staring at her.

Karen pointed a perfectly manicured finger with a fiery red color covering the nail at him and said, "Not one fucking word."

The other reporter put up his hands and went back to his work. CNN's newest reporter opened the bottom drawer of her desk, pulled out the comfortable pair of moccasins, replaced her pumps, and tried to relax and organize the few things she had brought from home for her new work station.

Father Padraig O'Malley was rattled by his encounter with Warburton, and he wanted to leave. Paul argued that they had just arrived and learned nothing of what was going on here. Father Sikora wanted to stay but could also see that Padraig was distressed, as his hands were shaking and beads of sweat had formed on his forehead. After several minutes of trying to convince O'Malley that they needed to stay and gather information, he saw that the Pastor was in a near panic and relented to the elder priest. Paul was actually surprised when his mentor grabbed his shoulder and needed assistance to walk to the car.

He was able to get Padraig to the passenger side of the car, pull out his keys, and unlock the door, when both conspirators heard a voice very close behind them.

"Leaving so soon, fathers? We didn't even have a chance to talk."

Paul whirled around and let go of Padraig, who almost fell to the ground but was able to use the side of the car to stabilize himself. Neither one of them were able to respond to Daniel, both too startled and stunned by the fact that their adversary had sought them out.

Danny tried again. "I'm sorry, I just assumed you were emissaries from the Vatican and didn't understand why you left without saying a word to me. But I can see now that the elderly gentleman is having medical difficulties" The Healer took a step toward the two, raised his hand, and continued. "If you would allow me, I can help."

A groan escaped Padraig's lips, and Paul said too loudly and too harshly, "Don't you touch us! We don't need help from the likes of you."

"I'm sure I don't know what you mean by that."

"We know who and what you are. You cannot deceive everyone. So you can just keep your distance." As Paul was talking, he also opened the passenger door and helped Padraig inside. He made his way to the driver's door, never taking his eyes from the person he saw as a creature from hell. Once Father Sikora had opened the door and was about to get behind the wheel, he addressed Warburton again. "We are no one special, just two parish priests who were able to see through your façade, so I believe there will also be others who can see the evil that you are. We will stop you."

"Evil? Have you paid attention to anything I've done so far? How, by any stretch of your imagination, can you describe me as evil?"

Father Sikora said nothing. He quickly got into the car, started the engine, and sped out of the parking lot, leaving Danny standing there shaking his head. He did happen to notice the plate on the Ford was from Pennsylvania but couldn't read the tag numbers or letters.

As he walked back to the front door of Hope, he passed off the two priests as religious fanatics. For a second he wondered if they were even real priests, but then he recalled their faces and the way they acted and knew those two were actual clergy. What surprised him was, without even knowing it, he had tried to read the older one's mind and did, in fact, catch glimpses of thoughts. They were nothing he could make sense out of, the image of a creature surrounded by fire Danny assumed was the priest's idea of Satan, the front of a large church, and a group of pigeons on a park path. Those images were replaced by the feeling of pain in the old man's chest just before he broke off contact. He wasn't sure if the uneasiness he felt from his two visitors was due to his ex-cop instincts or from the brain tinkering he went through in space, but even though he had a bad feeling about them, he mistakenly decided that they were probably harmless and would never see them again.

CHAPTER 25

Jimmy Santini was anxious on the inside but didn't show it on the outside for the three days since his meet with Flannigan. On the third day, he called the Irishman using the same phone number his uncle had given him.

Flannigan answered on the third ring. "Who's calling?"

"It's the man from the park. You got that item I ordered?"

"It's done, but this time you have to come to me to pick it up. I will not leave my house with it. Come this morning at 11 am, get the address from your uncle. And boy-o, bring 25 large."

The call was disconnected before The Brain had a chance to respond. He called his uncle, Sonny who gave him the address of Eamon Flannigan and elicited a promise from his nephew that what he had planned would in no way hurt Sonny or the family. Jimmy assured him that his actions could only help the organization.

The Brain ended the call to his uncle and leaned back into his chair behind the desk in the back of the pool hall. He used the desk phone intercom and buzzed the phone in the front room. The clerk behind the counter picked up the phone and spoke to Jimmy briefly. When he hung up, he yelled over to Sal, who was playing at one of the tables. "Giordano, the boss wants to see you."

When Sal came through the door, Jimmy sat up in his chair but waited until the door was closed before he began to talk. "Sal, there is a job in Connecticut that calls for my personal attention, and I will need your assistance. Go home and pack a bag for three or four days. I've secured hotel rooms for us."

"Do I need to bring anything special?"

"No, I have taken care of that. Just a handgun will do."

"Can I know what the job is?"

"Sal, you are one of my best men, and I know I can trust you. That is why I am taking you on this job. It's a hit on a guy who lives in a city called New Britain. This guy has the potential to ruin our business because he cures addicts and does something to people so they don't want to take part in our other endeavors as well. If he is left to continue, eventually our family and our ability to earn will cease."

Sal responded with some distress in his voice. "I think I know who you're talking about, boss. Is his name Warburton?"

"Yeah, that's the shitbag."

"Jimmy, I know about this guy because I was going to bring my father to see him. As you know, my father has diabetes, and his health is going downhill fast. Two weeks ago he lost his sight, and the doctors say they can't do anything more for him. Warburton may be his last chance. You can't kill him, boss."

Jimmy went from zero to 60 in three seconds. "Can't? Who the fuck are you to tell me I can't do anything I want to do? I'm the smartest wiseguy in this family and the only one who has the foresight to realize that this asshole will fuck us up! You disappoint me Sal. I guess you are not as trustworthy as I thought. Looks like I have to do this job by myself."

As Jimmy spoke, Sal was becoming increasingly nervous and looked into The Brain's eyes. So he didn't see the hand ease the 9mm semi-automatic from the top drawer of the desk. When Jimmy was done talking, Sal's gaze dropped to his soon-to-be ex-bosses right hand and saw the weapon. He didn't have time to raise his head and look at his murderer, but he did hear the loud reports of the shots as two bullets slammed into his chest. The big man fell backward onto the floor. Santini came around his desk and put another round into the head of the already dying Mafia thug just as three others from his crew came through the office door with their own guns pulled.

Vincent Golino looked down at Sal, whose last act on earth was to make a mess of the throw rug in front of the desk, and gasped, "What the hell happened here, boss?"

Without a trace of emotion in his voice, Jimmy said, "Sal thought I didn't know what was best for this crew and the family as a whole. I didn't see any other way to convince him otherwise. Now I have business elsewhere and will be out of town for a few days. You three clean this shit off of my floor....and get me another rug. Any questions?"

The three gangsters exchanged glances as they put away their weapons and all murmured that there would be no question and answer period from them. Jimmy Santini left the pool hall and headed for his car. He needed to go home and hit the heavy bag, then shower and be in Queens by 11 o'clock.

At 10:55 am, The Brain pulled into the driveway of the modest two-bedroom Cape Cod-style house that Eamon Flannigan had called home since a few months after he arrived in the United States. The big Irishman opened the front door as Santini reached the top step and said, "Come in."

Flannigan had already turned and gestured for Jimmy to follow him. He went to a door just off the kitchen that led to a set of stairs to the basement. At the bottom of the stairs, he turned right, and Jimmy saw that the basement was cut in half by a wall that held a steel door at the far end. The door was fashioned with a hasp and padlock, as well as a deadbolt. Eamon pulled a set of keys from his pants pocket and disengaged both locks. Before he opened the door, the Irishman hit a light switch on the outside of the room and both men entered.

A workbench was along the left wall, and a set of four floor-to-ceiling cabinets were on the opposite wall. One stool on wheels was under the bench, and a beat-up stereo cassette player was in the far corner. Jimmy saw a lone box in the middle of the workbench under a bright florescent light fixture, otherwise the room was spotless. Flannigan pulled out the stool from under the bench and sat down in front of the box, which looked like an ordinary corrugated container. One big paw reached into the box and pulled out a device that was about as big as a brick, and the other paw pushed the box aside. Flannigan put the bomb down in front of him and motioned Jimmy to get closer.

Eamon said, "This is as simple as I could make it. The bulk of it is C4, or plastic explosive. On the one side, you can see the blasting caps and the receiver that will set off the explosion." Flannigan turned the bomb over and continued. "The other side is a powerful magnet with two prongs that are set into the C4 itself."

Jimmy interrupted the big man. "How will I…?"

"Shut the fuck up, and I will tell you all you need to know."

Jimmy's anger flared for a moment, but he brought it under control, because he needed this mick, and he didn't think Sonny would look too kindly on him if he killed his uncle's favorite bomb maker. "I apologize. I'm a little on edge and anxious to get this job over with."

Flannigan glared at Santini, but then his look softened. He said, "Now, where the fuck was I? Oh yeah, the receiver is powered by a battery and has an on/off switch." Eamon moved the switch up and down a few times. "As you saw, a small red light comes on when the device is armed. So this is what you do, boy-o, when you get the chance. You put this thing under the chassis of your target's car. The magnet will hold it to the metal of the car's frame. Put it wherever you want, but if the target is going to be driving, I suggest you put it in the area of the driver's seat. Just make sure you turn it on." Flannigan pulled the box close to him again and pulled out what looked like a small cigar tube with a short antennae coming out of the bottom and a button on the top. "This is your remote detonator. It also has a battery inside and an on/off switch. When the switch is turned on, another red light will shine under the button on top. You must be within 100 yards for the signal to reach the bomb. Once the target is in position, all you do is push the button. I made this one slightly big because the blast has to penetrate the vehicle's frame, but you could be as close as 50 yards and there would be no danger to you. The magnet is strong, but I wouldn't take any chances that the car wouldn't hit a pothole and dislodge the bomb. Best to set it off before the target gets going. Put it under the driver's seat to kill the driver, but make no mistake. No one inside that car will survive. Any questions?"

"No, you explained all I need to know about it. Sorry I interrupted earlier."

"Never mind that. You have my money?"

"I have it out in the car."

"You go get it, and I'll box this back up. I'll meet you back in my kitchen."

A short time later, Jimmy Santini was back behind the wheel of his car, the box with the bomb was safe in the trunk. He steered the car in the direction of I-95 and thought he was finally on his way to pulling the thorn that had been in his side for months. The smile didn't leave his face until he was ten miles from the old department store in New Britain.

# # #

Monday night, with Hope being operational for only two more days, Danny and Carmel sat on the back deck. But very little talking was going on. Husband and wife were content to look out on the back yard and contemplate their own thoughts.

Carmel broke the silence as they both worked on a second glass of wine. "Let's blow off the airport. How's this for an idea? We leave a day early, on Thursday, and we take the train to DC. The kids have never been on a train, and I think they would get a big kick out of it. If we leave early enough, maybe we can get some sightseeing in late Thursday and Friday morning."

Danny smiled around the wood tip of his Hav-A-Tampa and replied, "That is a great idea, honey. Hell, I'll get as big a kick out of it as the kids will."

Carmel reached out and touched her man on the shoulder. "Then it's settled, we will take the first train out of New Haven Thursday morning. Tomorrow I will get us a hotel room in Washington for that night."

On Tuesday, when he got a few moments to himself, Danny called Carlos into the office. Cintron had already told his boss that he would take him up on his offer to seed the security business and the continued job.

"Carlos, the wife and I have decided to travel to DC by train, and we are leaving a day early. I still would like you to fly out of Bradley on Friday and meet us when we go to the White House."

"Shit boss, I was going to talk to you today about that. My car crapped out on me over the weekend. I've been getting a ride to work these last two days with Cassandra. I wanted to know if I could ride to the airport with you and your family, so you see I don't have a way to Bradley."

Danny thought for a moment and said, "Actually this works out. Mel can drive the mini-van here tomorrow, and I'll come in my Santa Fe. Then you can take her home in my car and keep it. That way you can take that to the airport on Friday and leave it there in long-term parking. We will take the van to the train station and have a vehicle waiting for us whichever way we decide to travel home. But wreck my car, and it will come out of your paycheck."

"I'll treat it with kid gloves. But boss, I didn't make any flight arrangements, and it seems kind of late for that now."

"You don't worry about that. I will call my boss and have her work on it. You may have to fly at an odd hour, but I'm sure she can find something."

After Carlos left the office, The Healer called his wife right away and got her working on a ticket to DC. A few hours later, she called back and reported that luck was on their side. She explained that at first she couldn't find a flight on Friday using the airlines websites, so she decided to call the airport. After a few misses, she spoke to a ticket agent for Southwest who happened to visit Hope several weeks back. With the agent's help, Carmel was able to get Carlos on a flight leaving Bradley at 3:17 pm.

Before he left for the day, Danny made one more call to Captain Franti, who had yet to let his old friend know if he was going with him on the road. The captain answered his cell phone on the third ring with his usual opening "Detectives, Captain Franti."

Danny's reply was only semi-joking. "I should come to your office right now and kick your ass. I have been waiting for three days for your call."

"I know, I know! It's not like I was avoiding you. I have been trying to persuade Gina that this is the right move for us for the last four days, but she's not buying it. It's a big change, and she is scared that the money will dry up, that we will be separated for long periods of time, and if she and the kids do join us, that the kid's education will suffer. So for now, I'm going to have to decline your offer. But I'd like the opportunity to accept it at a later date, if I can change Gina's mind. Is that ok?"

"Buddy, the job is yours any time you want it. Carmel, the kids, and I are taking the train from New Haven to DC on Thursday morning, and we should be back on Monday. How about I give you a call on Monday afternoon? And if you're free, we could meet for a drink."

"That sounds good. Tell those assholes in Washington to quit screwing around and get to fixing this country, and I'll see you on Monday."

Wednesday morning found Clan Warburton at their favorite local diner having an early breakfast before all of them headed to Hope in two cars. When they arrived, Danny began his pre-opening ritual for the last time, greeting everyone he came in contact with, getting a cup of coffee from the caterer's table, starting up the stereo and selecting the first CD, Esperanza Spaulding was the opening act on this last day, and then unlocking the front door. Although Carmel wanted to head home for some last-minute laundry and packing, the kids were having a ball hanging out and interacting with the people who had come to see their father that day, and he was in no hurry to have his family leave. He was painfully aware that a chapter in his life was coming to an end, as well as a portion of his plan that he enjoyed immensely, so he selfishly wanted his family nearby.

Not long after they ate lunch together, Carmel put her foot down and told her husband and her children that it was time they headed home. The kids protested. Papa Bear didn't say anything when he received a look from his wife that said, "Back me up on this one." He smiled, which drew a roll of the eyes from an exasperated Carmel.

Always the quick-witted one, Sandy stepped forward and became the spokesperson for her siblings. "Mom, I think it would be a great idea if we stayed with daddy. You could run the errands and also take care of those last-minute things at home without having to worry about us. You could get so much more done. And we could help daddy around here, greet his guests, change the CDs, and pick up the paper plates and cups."

"Who will watch you and take care of Jack? Your father is busy, and all of the security people have their job to do. Right, dear?"

At the risk of getting another look from Carmel, Danny said, "They wouldn't be any trouble, Mel. Besides, they haven't spent a lot of time here lately, and it is the last day. Kate and Sandy can look after their brother, and I have two from security posted by the door at all times now." He turned to his two oldest and said, "One of you will have Jack by her side every minute from now until we leave."

The two girls nodded profusely and turned their hopeful eyes on their mother. All Carmel could do was chuckle and shake her pretty head. She knew when she was being ganged up on. She went behind the desk and kissed her husband, then whispered in his ear. "If our days on the road start with a trip to the ER to stitch up the head of one of my children on the night before we leave, no one will be going anywhere." She put her finger on his lips as an indication that he shouldn't reply if he knew what was good for him.

The mother lioness kissed and hugged her three cubs and went off in search of Carlos. When she found him and was told that he was driving her home now, he didn't hesitate or ask questions. He did, however, understand why Danny sometimes referred to this woman as his boss.

If she had waited another 30 minutes, maybe things would have turned out differently. But then again, maybe not. Within the next 30 minutes they missed passing another vehicle entering the parking lot of Hope. The Nissan Altima was nondescript, and even with Carlos' senses turned up to full volume on the last day of operation, he probably wouldn't have noticed the man behind the wheel and recognized him as the same one who caused a security ruckus at Hope a few months back. But he never got the chance to test his powers of observation because of those 30 lousy minutes.

# # #

Jimmy The Brain Santini drove into the parking lot of the old department store, chose a spot near the rear, and backed in so he had a view of the front door. He looked at his watch and saw that it was about 2 pm. He figured closing time was either six or seven, and he would have to kill four or five hours. He thought that maybe someone might notice his car parked in the same spot all afternoon and briefly planned on leaving for an hour and parking in a different spot when he came back. But on the off chance that Warburton left early, he didn't want to miss him. So he decided to take the chance and stay right where he was until closing. Jimmy didn't need to follow Warburton home to get an address. That information was all over the internet. But in the event that there were two or more cars in his driveway tonight, he had to identify which one the guy drove to this place.

As he waited, Santini watched the cars come and go. All of the cars in the main lot belonged to the people that came to be healed. A side lot to the right of the building looked out of place, and the pavement was newer than everywhere else. Jimmy noticed that some of those cars did come and go, but several in the back were there all day. *One of those could be Warburton's,* he thought, and surely most of them were his security. Maybe he had a private spot elsewhere, like in the back. No, he had to wait it out and watch Warburton drive out of the lot. He might only have one shot at this.

Time dragged on, and around 5:30 pm two of the security people came to the back of the lot and headed for the entrance. Jimmy became slightly concerned that they would see him, but once they got to the street they were too occupied in stopping traffic coming into the lot to notice him. He saw this as a good sign, as he believed this was a precursor to closing. The lot began to thin out as no new cars entered, but enough remained in the lot to mask the Altima's lack of movement.

Unbeknownst to Jimmy, Danny had decided to close up one hour early on his last day. Carmel waited at home for the rest of Clan Warburton, and the kids needed a good night's sleep. They had a long day tomorrow. After Carlos returned from the safe transport of Mrs. Warburton, Danny asked him to close the lot at 5:30 pm. That should give The Healer enough time to see everyone left in the building.

He was off on his estimate by 16 minutes. After he locked the door at 7:16 pm, it still took him another 20 minutes to get out to the van. The extra time was spent with hugs and tearful goodbyes to the staff.

Drying his eyes as he loaded his children into the van, Danny climbed into the driver's seat and pointed the vehicle to the front of the building and the street beyond. Everyone else had made it to their cars and were ahead of the van leaving the lot. He looked in his rearview mirror at Hope one last time and did not notice the last car in the lot still parked in the back. At this time of the year and at this hour, it was almost full dark, and no one else saw the car, either. Carlos never forgave himself for that lapse.

Jimmy Santini saw the mini-van emerge from behind the building and knew in his heart that Warburton was inside. He decided to be sure, so as the van drove toward the exit of the lot, the Altima swung out of the space it had occupied for hours and the headlights came on. Santini hoped the headlights would illuminate the inside of the van, as his car pointed at the side of Warburton's vehicle.

As the Nissan got closer to the van, Jimmy saw Warburton behind the wheel and saw a young girl in the passenger seat. As he looked further into the passenger compartment, he saw another child, or maybe two. A rare moment of morality crawled up his spine, and The Brain worried that Warburton's kids went with him to the store every day. He tried to think back on his first visit, but he didn't remember seeing the girl from the front seat that day. He could have missed her back then. Or this day could have been a fluke, and the kids didn't usually come with him. Santini decided that it didn't matter. If the kids were with him in the morning, there would have to be collateral damage. Jimmy would play this out under the assumption that one chance was all he would get.

He pulled in behind the van as it exited, and he watched it turn right. To avoid suspicion, the Altima turned left and headed for a nearby hotel to get a few hours of sleep before putting his plan into action.

# # #

The alarm on the cell phone that was on top of the cheap night stand only sounded for a few seconds before a hand reached out from under the sheets and silenced it. The display on the screen read 2:30 am. Santini was out of bed immediately but still felt groggy. He decided to use the hotel shower, but mostly to wake him up. The gangster thought that if there ever was a time that he needed to be alert, this was it, no mistakes.

Once he was dried off, he dressed in all black; pants, turtleneck, light jacket, and topped off with a black watch cap. Jimmy had brought the device that Flannigan had given him into the room in the same small duffle bag that held his change of clothes. He took it out now and hefted it. The magnet looked and felt snug against the C4, but he pushed the two items together to be sure. He put the bomb back into the bag and gathered the rest of his stuff, making sure he forgot nothing. He had registered under a false name and paid the clerk in cash. He had no intention of going to the desk to check out. He left the keys on the bed and headed for his car. His watch told him it was 3:10 am before he fired up the Nissan and drove out of the hotel lot. Jimmy figured he would be in Warburton's neighborhood by 3:30.

The Nissan passed Clan Warburton's house at 3:32 am while going about 20 mph. Jimmy wasn't looking for the number on the house. He only needed to see the mini-van in the driveway.

When he saw it, he let out a stress-releasing sigh and applied a bit more pressure on the gas pedal. Santini noticed that other houses were close to the Warburton home, across the street and on the right side. But a small copse of trees was on the left that ran for about 75 yards before the next crossing street. He thought the trees were dense enough to conceal him while he waited for his target to enter the van.

He turned right onto the first street past the house and parked his car at the curb about half way from the intersection and the first house. He shut the car off and slunk down in the seat, and he waited 40 minutes just in case he was noticed and the cops were called. When enough time had passed, he gathered the bomb, the remote detonating unit, and his night binoculars. Jimmy Santini entered the wooded area and headed straight for the driveway that held the Dodge van. The leaves had already begun to fall, so the intruder had to be careful to make as little noise as possible. But he could have run through the trees as the crisp night air kept the windows closed in the nearby houses. Even if someone did hear his movements, they were used to hearing small animals traveling through this copse.

The intruder made it to the edge of the Warburton property, then he stepped onto the pavement of the driveway. He used the van as cover and came up on it from the far side. For all his worry about the placement of the bomb, it turned out to be a simple operation. Jimmy flipped the switch to the on position, and the light winked on. He lay on the ground, and even though he was on the passenger side, he was able to reach under the van and put the bomb under the driver's seat with little effort. The magnet was stronger than he realized, and it stuck solid to the undercarriage with a thunk.

He eased back into the trees and went about 45 yards until he found the tree he wanted. Jimmy sat down behind the one with the widest trunk he could find, one that would hide him from sight and also shield him from the blast. He reached into his jacket pocket and felt the detonator inside, in the off position. The watch was checked again, this time reading 4:25. He would stay with his back to the tree until about 6 am, observe the van from behind the trunk, and wait.

# # #

Their plan to take the first train out of New Haven on Thursday morning was short-lived once they found out that the trains started to run before five am. The revised plan was for Danny and Carmel to be up at 4:30 am, both getting quick showers, and then get the kids up at the last minute before they left. The children could stay in their pajamas for the ride to the train station and get dressed in the van when they got there.

The night before, when he went out to the back deck the fall air had such a nip that he went back inside and got a sweatshirt to put on. Weeks later, he remembered that as he sat on the deck and sipped wine, he had hoped Franti would call and say he was coming to DC with them. Knowing he hadn't missed a call, Danny still pulled out his cell phone to visually check it, only to discover he was right in the first place. He put the phone in the pocket of the sweatshirt. A short time later, when he went inside, he hung the sweatshirt over one of the dining room chairs, forgetting the phone. Fortunately, he remembered where it was before they left for the station.

Papa Bear was the first to be ready, so he roused the kids as he grabbed their backpacks from their rooms. He went out to the van and packed the rear compartment with their bags. Mel was not long behind him and finished getting the kids moving. They groggily grumbled but moved their feet, and all grabbed their pillows so they could nap on the drive to New Haven. Three sets of shuffling slippers came out of the front door, down the steps, and across the driveway to the waiting van. The children climbed in as Danny closed the back hatch door.

Carmel was right behind Jack, and Danny said, "I think I have everything. Are you ready to go?"

"All except for my coffee, which we will stop for prior to getting on the highway. Right?"

"Of course! I'm jonesing for one, too."

Carmel got into the front passenger seat, and Danny climbed behind the wheel and started the Dodge.

The intruder was surprised that he heard noises coming from the Warburton driveway so early. He slowly turned, peeked from behind his cover, and saw his target put three backpacks and two suitcases into the van. He had to think quickly, as it looked as if they were going on a trip, not to the store. Jimmy saw the kids and wife come from the house and get into the van, while Warburton was in the driver's seat. Santini turned and put his back to the tree again. He really didn't want to kill the wife and kids, but he knew this was his best chance. If he didn't detonate the bomb now, it might be found later. And then Warburton would up his security to the point where no one would ever be able to get this close again.

# # #

It is strange how the universe works. Maybe Calvin and Hobbes knew more about such things than Danny, but in retrospect, he thought about how some people's fate is decided by mere minutes.

On Wednesday night, as The Healer was finishing his wine and cigar and about to head to his bedroom, Captain Michael Franti broached the subject that had frosted his wife for the last five days. They were in the living room of the large house they owned in Avon, Connecticut. They both worked hard and were able to afford the house with the in-ground pool in an affluent town due to the fact that Michael had been earning captain's pay for the last three years, and Gina had been an RN for 15 years. She was comfortable where she was and saw Danny's job offer as a threat to her way of life.

"I'm not saying I'm taking the job, Gina, but I have a boatload of vacation time coming, and my friend is going to DC without any backup. I will only be away until Monday."

"That is what you say now, but I can see one trip turning to two, and two turning to ten. And I'll get the same argument about your friend not having anyone to watch over him. You and I know what he can do. He doesn't need a babysitter. He can take care of himself."

"I have already told you that I turned down the job, and this one trip is all that it will be. Danny is my friend, but not my family. My place is here with you and our children. But I have to tell you that I've got a bad feeling about his trip. I can't put my finger on it, but all I can say is that I think he needs me on this one."

The emotion and caring in her husband's voice tipped the scales, and Gina Franti relented. "One trip, Michael. Now, go call your friend and tell him your wife said you can go out and play."

Franti smiled and said, "That'll be the day when I let him know I ask my wife for permission to do anything."

He got up from his lounge chair and headed for the kitchen to make the call. He didn't even stop when he felt the couch pillow hit him in the back of the head.

After trying Danny's cell phone three times over the span of 20 minutes and getting his voice mail, Michael decided that he was probably asleep, and he would try again in the morning.

Franti knew his friend would want to get an early start. So he also arose at an obscene hour, showered and dressed, and dialed the cell phone again. This time, Danny was stepping into the shower. His cell was still in the pocket of the sweatshirt and set to vibrate, which no one was around to hear. Michael decided that he would continue to try the cell several more times, but from the front seat of his car as he began the 35-minute drive to Clan Warburton's castle. As he entered the ramp to the highway, the feeling of urgency became almost oppressive, and he took the speedometer up to 85 mph.

As Danny started the van, Jimmy Santini contemplated his next move from his hiding place behind the tree. At the same time, an unmarked police car owned by the city of New Britain and assigned to the head of the investigations bureau made a right turn off the highway exit ramp and was only three minutes from its destination.

Inside the Dodge minivan, the driver made a final check and realized he did not have his phone. He mumbled under his breath, "What did I do with my cell phone?"

From the front passenger seat came a response. "What did you say, honey? I couldn't hear you."

Carmel didn't get a response because her husband was lost in thought, backtracking to when he last used his phone and where he put it. After a couple of seconds, he snapped out of it and faced her. "Shit, I left it in the sweatshirt I wore last night, and that is in the dining room. I'll be right back."

The Healer got out of the van and walked toward the front door at a brisk pace. Inside the van, Carmel jumped into the driver's seat and said to her children, "Your daddy always drives, but today I feel like being behind the wheel."

As she put the gear shift into reverse, none of her kids said anything, as they were almost all back to sleep in their reclined chairs. Carmel turned the wheel and backed up so she could at least have the van facing the street before Danny came out and kicked her back to the passenger seat.

And at the same time, Santini turned and faced the Warburton driveway again. He didn't see the target, who was nearly at the first step of the front stoop, because by then the van was close to being sideways and blocked his view of the front door. He didn't even know that the van was light one passenger. Jimmy The Brain believed that the Warburtons were starting their trip to wherever they were going, so he pulled the remote detonator from his pocket and flicked the power button to the on position with his thumb. Although his eyes were fixed on the Dodge in the driveway, his peripheral vision picked up on the muted light that indicated the detonator was activated. Jimmy pushed the button.

The explosion was deafening and actually lifted the vehicle several feet off the ground. The resulting fireball reached a height of about 20 feet in the air and the same distance in a circular radius across the ground, destroying the three rose bushes Carmel had planted on the back edge of the driveway a few days after each of her children were born. Mercifully, all of the occupants were killed before the van came back down to earth. None of them suffered, but their bodies were unrecognizable, as the van burned at incredible temperatures for the next 35 minutes.

The most significant injury that happened to Danny was caused by a piece of the van's frame. After it broke off, it was propelled by the force of the blast and hit him on the side of his head. That chunk of metal cracked open his skull and not only exposed his enhanced brain but damaged it to the point that any normal human being would have been left in a vegetative state.

But that wasn't the only damage he suffered. At the time of the blast, he had put his left foot on the second step. He was thrown sideways into the metal railing, which broke his hip and tibia in three places. When he landed, his right shoulder took the brunt of the impact and shattered, as well as his right wrist. Because his body was thrown over ten feet, the burns he incurred were minimal and confined to his left side.

Earlier, Danny had wondered how mere minutes could seal a person's fate. But it only took an instant, and Clan Warburton was no more.

CHAPTER 26

Michael Franti guessed he was about a quarter mile from his destination, but the rest of the way was flat. If the van pulled out of the Warburton driveway now, he would see it. Then the silence of the crisp morning air was shattered by an explosion. Franti could see the fire ball contrasted against the still-dark sky and knew where it had come from and also knew that his friend was in trouble. He stomped on the gas pedal. As he approached, he aimed the nose of his car at the mouth of the driveway, but then thought that fire and ambulance crews would soon need access to that area. So he continued another 20 yards and parked against the curb.

The veteran cop was out of his car before it came to a full stop and approached the house from opposite the blazing van. As he ran across the Warburton front lawn, he pulled out his cell phone and dialed 911. Franti gave the dispatcher all he had and ended the call as he reached the front steps. Because of the heat, he could only get a few feet closer to the fire, and he knew he could not help anyone inside the vehicle. He was about to go inside the house in hopes of finding the Warburtons safe and sound when he noticed the metal railing. Michael had to lean closer to it to determine that the thing hanging from the railing was a scrap of denim material and what looked like blood stains.

Quickly making the connection, he turned to his right and saw a figure lying prone in the grass, not moving. Franti went to his friend and saw that he was badly injured, then discovered the gash in his head and thought Danny was dead. A hand in front of the injured man's mouth told the captain that he was still breathing, but when he leaned over to do that, he got a good look at the head wound. What limited medical knowledge he had went back to classes at the police academy, but he decided that the wound needed to be covered, to at least protect the brain—which Franti was able to see clearly.

Michael didn't have anything to use as a bandage and thought about what he had in his car, but there was nothing. He didn't want to leave his friend, but Danny was unconscious, and the medics were on the way. He went to the top of the front steps and planted one big right foot at the location of the dead bolt and shattered the door frame. It only took him four minutes to find some gauze in the spare bathroom on the first floor, but to him it seemed like an hour. When he returned to the chaotic front yard, he heard the sirens in the distance, and he let out a sigh.

It didn't hit him until after he had put a makeshift bandage on Danny's head that the house was locked and empty. In his heart, he knew Carmel and the kids were in the van when it exploded. Michael Franti was on his knees beside his friend and found that he couldn't bring himself to look at the burning van. Even if he did, he would have had a hard time seeing it through the tears that filled his eyes and streamed down his cheeks.

The medics arrived first, and Franti showed them where Danny was lying. Fire crews were not long behind and began to extinguish the fire on the van, which had suffered extensive damage from both the explosion and the ensuing fire. As moments ago the van was consumed by fire, so was Michael Franti consumed by grief. He didn't want to, but his feet seemed to have a mind of their own and shuffled to the heap that once transported a family to their destination. The charred mass was devoid of flames but still radiated heat. It continued to smoke and hiss and, as he got closer, the big cop saw the burned figure of a human being in the driver's seat. He quickly turned his head, as he did not want to see the smaller figures in the back.

It took a couple of minutes for Franti to regain his composure. When he looked up, he saw the ambulance crew loading the gurney holding Danny's body into the emergency vehicle. He hurried over as the wheels of the gurney clicked into place on the floor of the unit.

Michael grabbed the arm of one of the medics, probably a little too hard, and said, "Do you know who this is?

The medic was in his early 20s, and this scene was the most gruesome he had witnessed in his young career. He looked Franti in the face with "deer in the headlights" eyes and couldn't form any words. He just nodded his head, no.

"This is Danny Warburton. Do you know the name and what he can do?"

Again, no words came from the medic, but he gave a nod in the affirmative this time.

"Then you know how important this is. You keep him alive and tell the doctors in the ER who they are working on. I'll be along shortly after I secure this scene. My name is Captain Michael Franti, and this is a murder investigation, so don't fuck anything up."

Another nod came from the medic as he climbed into the back of the ambulance. Michael slammed the door and banged his hand on the side to let the driver know it was clear to go.

Three patrol units had arrived while Franti was talking to the medic, and he called them over. He told the patrolmen that they were to secure the scene and no one was to enter until he was called. He would notify his detectives and even they were to contact him before they started processing anything.

The uniformed men nodded that they understood. They all knew who lived at this address, and they also knew about the relationship between the owner of the house and the big captain in front of them.

At the hospital, the doctors and nurses were informed of the name of the patient before he arrived. Several of those on staff that morning had personal contact with Danny, and a dozen others knew someone who had.

Doctor Russell Levesque was told of the head injury when the medics called in that they were on their way. When he actually saw the wound, however, he was taken aback at the severity. During his five years as an emergency room doctor, he had not seen head trauma this bad, and he wasn't sure he had the expertise to fix this patient. Levesque was stunned for a moment, then barked orders to the rest of the staff. He called for multiple IVs with antibiotics and pain killers and also said to get the patient to the OR stat.

The doctor intended to go to the nurse's station and contact the hospital's chief neurosurgeon. But as he turned, a hand shot out from the gurney and latched onto Levesque's wrist. The doctor looked down and saw that his patient had grabbed him. The doctor thought that for a man who should be dead, he had an incredibly strong grip. The patient's eyes were still closed, and his face was turned away from Levesque, but the doctor somehow knew that the patient was trying to communicate with him. He leaned over to put his ear closer to the man's mouth. Levesque heard a whisper emanate from the gurney.

"No operation will be necessary. All I require is a secure room and some time. I will heal myself...please."

Every word was heard by Levesque, as well as another doctor, three nurses and one orderly, who was cleaning behind the station. The orderly stopped what he was doing when he heard the whisper and looked at the man on the gurney. He was the only person there who noticed that the voice came from the patient. But the patient's lips were not moving.

Levesque wasn't entirely sure of what action to take. Doing nothing went against his training and ethics, but he also knew who his patient was and had read quite a lot about him. He motioned for a veteran nurse to come to the gurney and spoke softly, so only she could hear him.

"Admit this patient under the name David Drake. Take him to the seventh floor and put him in Room 712. Draw the curtains and lock the door when you leave. Put a note in the computer and on his chart that I am to be called before anyone else sees him—and no IVs. I am counting on your discretion."

The nurse said nothing, but a nod was all that Levesque needed to assure him that his orders would be carried out to the letter. Room 712 was used by the police department when they needed to secure a prisoner who required medical attention. It had been retrofitted with a door lock and was the only patient room with that type of lock.

Next, Levesque went to the office that was used by the ER doctor on duty and made a call to the hospital chief of staff. He wanted to keep this as quiet as possible, and that meant telling very few people, but it would blow up in his face if he didn't have the support of his boss.

Fifteen minutes later, a big man with soot on his face, dirt and grass stains on his pants, and traces of blood on the cuff of his left sleeve, burst into the ER like a hurricane, waving an open wallet with a police badge pinned inside to everyone who was in ten feet of him. He demanded to know where the head wound patient was located. Levesque had just come back from the seventh floor, having spoken to the staff there about the unusual circumstances in Room 712. The doctor intercepted the badge waver, but for one second he also thought the big cop was going to knock him over and keep walking. He scanned the badge quickly and found what he needed.

"Captain!" said Levesque firmly. The big man's eyes locked onto his. "It appears that you have come from the same place as the man you are looking for. Are you injured as well?"

"No, do I look injured?" he snapped back.

"Quite frankly, you do. Please come into my office, and I will fill you in on the patient's status and location. I understand the need to keep this under wraps."

The captain hadn't expected this response from the hospital staff, so he decided to see where this went and followed the doctor to the office. Levesque sat behind the desk and motioned for Franti to also have a seat.

The doctor said, "As you know, I must consider the privacy of my patients. Therefore, I must ask if you are a relative of the man you are inquiring about."

It took quite an effort for the big cop to keep his ass in contact with the chair. "Listen to me, doctor. That man is an ex-cop who worked for me, on top of being my friend. His wife and children were killed this morning by the same explosion that injured him. That makes it a criminal investigation, of which I am in charge. I am filled with anger over this and have nowhere to direct it, and you've decided to get in my way. See where this is going? I suggest you tell me everything you know about his injuries while we are on our way to where he is."

The good doctor was not the first person to feel his stomach drop in the presence of the veteran officer. But Levesque was able to keep his nervousness out of his voice as he rose from behind the desk and said, "I'm sure you know the way, but I will take you there and cooperate with your investigation."

On the way to the seventh floor, Dr. Levesque told Captain Franti all he knew about the patient's injuries. He relayed everything that had happened in the ER. Although no x-rays had been done, he knew about the damage to the patient's bones and the minor internal injury. He said he knew who Daniel Warburton was and the story of his powers, and that was why he did not conduct any medical procedures and why he was isolated.

By the time the doctor finished talking, Franti knew where they were headed. He was familiar with the only patient room equipped with a lock on the door.

Michael looked down at the doctor with a face that reflected a new sense of respect for the man and said, "You did good. When he grabbed your wrist, did you feel anything? Maybe black out for a second?"

"I don't think so, but I did know immediately that what he told me to do was the right course of action."

The elevator door opened onto the seventh floor, and Franti thought the damage to Danny's brain could have affected his powers. At that time, only the ER orderly could have eased the captain's worries. Levesque unlocked the door to Room 712 and opted not to turn on the lights as they entered. The room was mostly dark, but some muted lights were on over the bed. He could see Warburton.

The first thing that Levesque noticed was that when the patient had been put in the bed, he was placed on his back. But now the patient was on his side with the head wound facing up. He was also in a slightly fetal position. Levesque shared that with Franti but received no response, as the cop stared at the figure on the bed. Eventually both men grew tired of standing in the room and feeling helpless, so they returned to taking care of other duties that they had control over.

# # #

After the explosion, Jimmy Santini's initial plan had been to enter the driveway from the wooded area and make a quick search for Warburton's body to ensure the man was dead. If there were any signs of life, he was going to empty a clip into his head. But the big guy in the unmarked cop car caused Jimmy to hesitate. Knowing Warburton's past, this guy probably was a cop and, therefore, armed. He figured the unmarked cop had been on his way here already. It had been much too early to be responding to the blast, and he wasn't patrolling the area, not in that car. Santini decided that a confrontation with one of Warburton's pissed off cop buddies was not in his best interest. Besides, he thought, no one could have survived that explosion. So he headed back in the direction he came and exited the woods a short distance from his car.

No one noticed him coming from the tree line or as he got into the Altima. And no one noticed the car as it turned out of the side street and headed for the highway in the opposite direction from the destruction and carnage the operator had left behind him. The speedometer climbed steadily until it reached 67 mph, the speed where Santini decided to set the cruise control. He realized that his shirt was soaked with sweat, and he felt like he was overheating. He turned on the air conditioner and leaned back into the chair for the ride home. Despite the uncomfortable wetness of the shirt, he felt that he was safe from capture, that he had gotten away with murder.

CHAPTER 27

Ever since coming out of the machine on the big ship that was the temporary home to his only nonhuman friends, Danny had known that his memory was getting better by the day. His memory was photographic since the ship, and he recalled things that had happened in his life as far back as when he was six months old. But after the explosion, when he came to, not consciously, but there was a part of his brain that "woke up", he had some memory gaps. He thought he was in a hospital, but he couldn't be sure. He didn't know how he got there, but knew he was hurt badly, and in some far off place he did feel pain.

The last thing he remembered was closing Hope for the last time in preparation of the family visit to the White House. He didn't know how he sustained the damage to his brain and body. Was it a car accident on the way home that last night? But after what he thought was two days trying to figure out how, he decided that he needed to stop using his brain for that and let it concentrate its full power on healing himself. Then he could really wake up, and he would be able to ask others what happened. Danny felt himself go deeper into the center of his brain, to the core, where he symbolically closed his eyes and rested while his brain did its magic on his own body.

# # #

"He has gone into survival mode while he heals himself."

"Is he aware of the deaths of his spouse and offspring as of yet?"

"No, his memory is sporadic at best, but it will not be long before he is fully healed. I suspect he will regain all of his memory."

"This could present a problem. The human psyche is very fragile, news of his family's deaths could affect him detrimentally. The gifts that we gave him could be used in a negative way. We may have to step in and end the experiment if something like that occurs."

"I agree, Calvin, but that may not be our only issue with Daniel. When I touched him in his hospital room, I scanned what had occurred over the previous 24 hours. The doctor who first saw him in the emergency room had every intention of calling in a neurosurgeon to conduct some kind of operation. But Daniel communicated telepathically to the doctor that would not be necessary."

"How could that be, Hobbes?" The space travelers had begun to call each other Calvin and Hobbes not long after Danny left the ship. "His brain doesn't have that capacity."

"You and I both know that, but he doesn't. Without further analysis, my best guess is that it could be the result of some kind of mutation due to the injury to his brain and his will to survive. And if it is a mutation, there is no telling when it would stop."

"His brain could become as powerful as ours?"

"Or surpass ours."

"We will have to take a more active role in monitoring his actions from this day forward. The potential and the temptation to abuse powers of that magnitude would be like a crushing weight to a human. Hobbes, please draw up an intervention plan in the event we must terminate this experiment."

"I will. But to employ one of their words, I hope we never have to use it."

# # #

The lock on the door proved unnecessary. No one had entered Room 712 for days, not even Dr. Levesque. As he had done in the past, Danny was sending out a vibe that told others that he needed his privacy during this critical healing process. This vibe was picked up mostly by the hospital staff, because there were very few people who knew who was in that room.

Three days after the bomb went off, news leaked that Carmel, Katherine, Sandra, and little Jack were killed. There was much speculation that Danny was also among the fatalities, but there were just as many rumors, mostly on the internet, that he was still alive. Dead or alive, no one knew where The Healer was. The few humans who did possess that knowledge had kept their word and remained silent. That small group met twice, once in the hospital and once at the New Britain Police Department. Maybe those in attendance felt keeping that secret was the right thing to do, or maybe they were all a bit intimidated by big Mike Franti who ended both meetings by reiterating the importance of keeping Danny's location quiet. Nobody wanted to poke that bear with a stick.

The patient stayed in the same position for eight days, and even at the subconscious level he wasn't aware of anything around him. He wasn't aware that he was keeping everyone at a distance with his mind, nor was he aware that most of his brain was involved in repairing the part of itself that was damaged by the bomb, along with closing the gap in his skull. He was in the deepest form of a coma, but his brain activity was off the charts.

On day nine, the patient opened his inner eye, if not the outer ones, and reached out to the closest human he could find.

"Dr. Levesque, I have a message for you.

Levesque looked up from the chart he was going over at the large opening to one of the ER examination rooms. The woman in front of him was obviously a nurse, and he had seen her around the hospital, but he couldn't recall her first name. "Okay." He held out his hand for the written note. Hospital policy stated that all third party correspondence was reduced to writing to avoid confusion and mistakes. When none was forthcoming, he said, "Where is the message, nurse?"

"Sorry, doctor. I didn't write it down. It didn't come to me from any usual channels."

Russell was tired and a little terse with the young woman whose name he just remembered. "I'm not interested in excuses, Nurse Muralo. Give me the message and who it came from."

"It came from the man in Room 712. And this might sound crazy, but I heard his voice in my head. What's crazier is that I know it came from inside that room and believed immediately that the patient was talking to me like he was standing in front of me. He said he needs to see you."

"Did you go into the room?"

"No, I was at the seventh floor nurse's station."

"How long ago did you hear the voice?"

"Five minutes. I came to you without delay."

The doctor was much more calm when he replied, "Thank you, Amelia. I am sorry for my tone with you earlier. Can I count on you to keep this to yourself?"

"Of course. I need to go back to my assignment now."

"I'll be coming with you."

The doctor entered Room 712 and eased the door closed. He was trying to make as little noise as possible, as not to disturb the patient, but he had no idea what to expect. He passed the restroom and saw that the patient was still in the semi-fetal position. Exactly as he was the last time Levesque saw him, over a week ago. And then he heard the voice.

"My recuperation has been moving at an accelerated pace, but I now require sustenance to continue the healing process. My condition prohibits intake of solid food at this time. Could you provide an IV with double the usual nutrients?"

"Of course I can. How many?"

"Keep those cocktails coming as long as my body can accept them."

And so, over the next four days, the good doctor administered IVs at a rate of one bag every two hours. When he was not at the hospital, one of the trusted nurses continued the treatment. Since she was usually assigned to the seventh floor, Nurse Muralo became one of the Room 712 inner circle.

Thirteen days after the bomb went off and devastated his world, the patient opened his eyes and looked around the room he was in. His brain was completely healed, as was the crack in his skull. All the bones that were broken or crushed were still in that condition, but taking care of that was like putting a bandage on a minor cut to others. As part of his mind reached out to Levesque and Franti, another part started to work on mending the rest of his body.

When Captain Franti heard the voice in his head, he looked up from his desk, half expecting to see Detective Sgt. Daniel Warburton standing in the doorway, like he did countless times when the man worked for him. Then he realized where the voice came from, and a wry smile came to his lips. He knew his friend was going to be all right, at least physically.

The doctor was at his house, 25 miles from the hospital, when he received the message from Danny that he was out of the coma.

The problem was that the patient wasn't used to sending out messages with his mind, and he didn't have the experience to pinpoint his transmissions. So when the captain and the doctor learned that he was out of the coma, several hundred others did also, and the word quickly spread. The hospital was next to a park, with wide open spaces, ball fields, and parking lots, which were transformed into RV and tent cities within 48 hours of the patient regaining consciousness. All followers of the man with the healing touch.

Danny was up and about by then, eating solid food, and showing no physical signs of his injuries. He was still weak and had decided to spend a few more days in the hospital. But he could see part of the park from his window and saw the masses of people there. Franti told him that there were a few traffic problems and sanitary issues, but everyone in the park was behaving themselves. Still, he knew he would have to address those people before long.

Since he had opened his inner eye, Danny was regaining his memory in chunks. By the time his broken bones were healed, he was aware that his beloved Carmel and his three children were dead. His heart was heavy, but even though he knew he would never see his family again, he also knew he could not give up on his responsibility to finish what he had started.

Franti had cited security reasons for not telling John and Teresa Warburton, as well as George, Kelly, and Candy and Carmel's extended family, any information about Danny. The elder Warburtons had flown in from California, and John was somewhat appeased because he surmised that his son was still alive or security wouldn't be so tight.

So when he called Kelly from the hospital to inquire what had been done with his family's remains, she was somewhat in shock to hear his voice.

"Danny, what the hell? We didn't even know if you were dead or alive. Dad said you had to be alive because of the secrecy, but we really weren't sure."

"Kelly, I can appreciate how confusing all this is but I really need to know what was done with Carmel and the kids."

"Oh. Well…their bodies were so," Kelly sobbed and said, "No one knew where you were, and Carmel's brother wanted to have a service for her and the kids. Danny, they were cremated. Their ashes are in your house, in an urn Ted picked out. Mom and Dad are here, they are staying at your house, also. We were all worried…"

"I know, Kelly. I'll be leaving the hospital in three or four days, and I will let everybody know what I intend to do. I will call you again on that day, and I will be going to my house if everyone wants to gather there. Tell them all not to worry." He hung up.

The day before he went home, the patient addressed the throng of people in the park. Their numbers had swelled to over 5,000, and all other activity in the park had come to a standstill. Danny had Michael contact the Parks Department and set up a makeshift stage in the corner of the park closest to the hospital. The platform was equipped with a microphone and ten huge speakers that spread out from the stage, five on each side.

Twenty undercover police officers were positioned throughout the park, and they helped spread the word that the one they were all here to support was going to make a speech in one hour.

People flocked to the area of the speakers until the crowd was so big that those in the back couldn't see the stage or the man who seemed to appear before the mike, flanked by Franti and Cintron.

A brief cheer filled the air, and then a hush fell over the crowd. "Your support touches me deeply, thank you. As I look out on your faces, I have to ask you... no, beg of you, not to make this a religious thing. It is not. I'm just a man, and now I am a man who has lost his wife and children." Several tears ran down his face, and he needed a couple of seconds before he could continue. "Please understand that I..." Danny choked up and wiped the tears away before continuing. "I will need some time to grieve, but I promise you all, and the rest of the world, that I will not quit. I took on a responsibility and plan to see it through to the end. I am going home now, so I suggest that you all do the same." He turned and headed for the stairs at the back of the platform. As he hit the bottom step, he heard a woman's voice coming from the barricades that had been hastily set up in front of the stage.

"Please, sir. My boy won't last much longer, he has leukemia."

Danny turned and located the owner of the voice, then saw the waif-thin child standing next to her.

Franti put one meaty paw on his shoulder and said, "Not now, Danny. Security will be compromised, and I don't have the manpower..." He felt his friend pull away from his hand. "Oh shit."

The Healer went directly to the sickly child, put his hand on the boy's head, and completely cured him. He was astonished at how quickly he was able to use his gifts. It only took him one or two seconds, and he was done. He then took the mother's hand, and one second later The Healer was done with her. He began to walk along the barricade, touching everyone within his reach for a second or two.

After about 25 or 30 people, he felt Michael's hands on him again. But this time, both hands were on his shoulders. His old boss whispered in his ear, "Danny, please. We just got you back."

Danny turned, looked at the big man, and said, "So you don't end up swallowing your tongue, we can leave now."

He let himself be led away by Franti back to the hospital. But on the way, he thought of his encounters with the boy and the others in the crowd. Yes, it was much faster than before his injuries, but he still had that period of total blackout when he was using his gifts. He knew that he had gained additional powers, and those that he had already possessed had been amplified, but he was discouraged to learn that he still had those moments of total unawareness when he was healing.

His last night in the hospital was spent in anticipation of a visit from the giants from space. He had waited up until midnight, but by then it didn't appear they were coming. Danny was surprised at the no-show. They must know of his new and improved talents, so he expected at least a word of caution about their responsible use. Just before sleep took him, he thought that maybe Calvin and Hobbes were waiting to see if his grief over the deaths of Carmel and the children would derail the experiment.

John Warburton spent the better part of two weeks making sure that there was no evidence of the event that had cost his son so much. Not that Danny would have noticed, he was concentrating on keeping it together from the passenger seat of the Santa Fe. Carlos drove that car as Luis and Cassandra followed behind, and bringing up the rear was Franti. He was starting to feel like a kid who couldn't take care of himself, having bodyguards was already becoming annoying. He did snap out of it some when he saw how many people were at his house to welcome him home. It seemed his entire extended family was there, as well as Carmel's, and there were even some of Katherine and Sandra's friends from school.

His father was closest to the door, and he gave his son a big hug and said, "I hope you don't mind everyone here, so many wanted to be here to show their support that I couldn't say no."

"It's okay, dad. Better than being alone."

The elder Warburton didn't want to cry in front of his son, so he gave him another hug and drifted into the crowd. Danny tried to say hello to everyone and actually found a few that he had not seen since he became a reluctant space traveler. He, of course, used his gifts on them, not even realizing he did as it was second nature and effortless to him now. After about 30 minutes, he was struck by the notion that this is what it would have been like if he had been awake for the gathering for his wife and children.

Ted McNiff approached and was full of apologies about Danny not being able to attend the services and then showed him the urn he had picked out. As was his way, The Healer told Ted not to worry and that he would have chosen the same receptacle for the ashes of his family.

A few moments later, he spotted Mandee and Ralph, who he hadn't seen since his failed attempt to help their son. She breeched the wall between them.

"Danny, I am so sorry for your loss, and for being such a shit the last time we saw each other."

"No, no, it should be me saying sorry to you. I came to you and gave you false hope that I could help Anthony. At the time, I didn't know that I couldn't."

Mandee threw her arms around his neck and said, "Maybe both of us needed to ask forgiveness, or maybe neither of us did and it was just part of life."

"Is Anthony here today?"

"Yes, he is in the basement playing with some of the other kids."

"I'd like to try again"

"But it seemed to hurt you last time, and aren't you weak from your injury still?"

"I'm fully recovered, and things are different since then."

"I don't know Danny..."

Before she could say anything further, he said, "Bring him to my bedroom in five minutes. If you are not there in 15 minutes, I'll understand."

He watched as Mandee and Ralph headed for the basement stairs, already deep into a discussion. He headed for his bedroom, and the first thing he saw as he entered the room was the framed wedding photo of him and Carmel hanging over their bed. He stared at it for a few moments before he spoke to his wife. "I hope you understand, Mel, I have to get right back into this thing. If I don't have something to do, I feel the grief will send me into a deep depression. Baby, I will be thinking about you and the kids every day for the rest of my life."

He wiped a tear from his eye as the knock on the door announced Mandee's and Ralph's decision. Danny told them through the door to come in. When they did, Anthony broke away from his father's hand and ran to his uncle with a welcoming hug.

With the muted voice typical of his affliction Anthony said, "I missed you, Uncle Danny. I know what you tried to do for me, and I wanted to thank you."

The surprise on his parent's faces told The Healer that the boy had not spoken of the earlier attempt to either of them.

"Well, you are very much welcome Anthony, but to tell you the truth I have been lifting weights and have become much stronger since that day and if you would like, I could try again."

As usual with DS children, he smiled his ever-present smile and said, "Okay."

Danny hugged Anthony back, and both found the process amazingly quick. The boy sprang backwards from his uncle's embrace and turned to his parents.

With a voice of perfect clarity, and sounding like any other young man his age, Anthony said, with tears in his eyes, "Mom, dad, everything is working just as it should. Before, it was like an eight cylinder engine with only two working, but now they are all sparking. I tried, I tried so hard before, but my brain couldn't figure a lot of things out. I feel like I have been set free from a dimly lit room." He then turned back and offered his hand to his uncle, who promptly shook it. "Thank you, Uncle Dan. If there is anything I can ever do for you, do not hesitate to ask."

"I will certainly keep that offer in mind, and you're welcome."

After several minutes of tears, thank yous, and hugs, the small family left the bedroom. Anthony then proceeded to wow those in the rest of the house.

The Healer turned to the portrait over the bed again and said, "Nothing could ever make it worth losing you or the kids. But that right there is as close as it's ever going to get."

CHAPTER 28

"I don't like this, I should be going with you," the driver of the car said in a voice that was becoming increasingly agitated.

"Michael, we have been over this numerous times. I need you here to use all of your contacts to find the person or persons responsible. I will have Carlos, Luis, and Cassandra with me at all times, on top of the fact that all of my senses have been amplified, and I can read people's minds. How can anyone get close to me to do me harm?"

"How close was the last guy?" Then Franti realized what he had said. "Shit, I'm sorry Danny, I didn't mean to be so callous. I'm just worried about you."

Warburton reached over from the passenger seat and put a hand on the captain's shoulder. "I know, I also know you would go to the end of the Earth for me. You don't have to say it, I can feel that. You are a good friend Michael, but your talents best serve me here right now. When that part is over, you and your family can join me if that is what you and Gina decide."

"Well, I want to say here and now that I protest your decision."

"Are you fucking kidding me, that's all you've been saying since you picked me up 30 minutes ago."

Franti laughed. "Fuck you, I wish I still out ranked you."

The mood was much lighter in the car for the rest of the ride to Bradley Airport. The two vehicles parked, and Danny's bodyguards exited the rear car. As they all entered the terminal, Franti pointed one thick finger at the trio and told them they better stick to their charge like glue. They listened intently as they truly believed the captain outranked them.

Michael's other bitch was why his friend had to travel so soon after being discharged from the hospital. He tried to explain to the big man that Frank Nickerson had called him three days in a row since he left Room 712, and next week the president's schedule was going to get very hectic. So that was why 48 hours later he was headed for the White House.

The Healer couldn't help himself, he touched everyone in the terminal that he came within 20 feet of, both travelers and employees alike. That was the reason Franti was able to accompany them to the gate, with his sidearm strapped to his hip, and how his security trio could bring their weapons onto the plane.

They were about to board when Franti pulled his friend off to the side for a private chat.

"There is no doubt in my mind that I can get you the name you want, and I will abide by your wishes and make no contact with that person. But do you know what you will do with that information?"

Danny hesitated for a long time. "I mull that question every day, but I haven't made up my mind. And even if I had, maybe it would change by the time there was a confrontation. I don't have an answer for you because I don't have an answer for myself."

"Have a good trip, call me when you get back." The captain turned and walked away.

# # #

Father Padraig O'Malley spent three weeks in a Philadelphia hospital after having triple bypass surgery on the day he and Father Sikora returned from New Britain. His condition may not have been so severe if he'd received treatment when he had the heart attack, in the parking lot of Hope, but Paul was scared and didn't know where else to go but back to Philly. Once there, he drove Padraig directly to the emergency room at Pennsylvania Hospital, and 15 minutes later, the elder man was in an operating room.

Paul visited his mentor every day, but recovery was slow. He didn't wake up for several days and couldn't speak for several more. Sikora was wracked with guilt for not getting medical attention sooner, but eventually came to believe that the fault rested mostly with Warburton, who he thought gave O'Malley the heart attack in the first place.

The elder priest was not conscious for the news reports of the bombing and subsequent death of Warburton's wife and children. Sikora was watching intently and at first was shocked by the news. But that quickly turned to suspicion as there was no word of the fate of Daniel himself.

As Padraig slowly regained some of his abilities, Paul became more and more certain that Warburton had survived the explosion. So when he watched the live broadcast of the speech outside of the hospital, he wore an "I told you so" smirk on his face. He was alone in his room and said to the eight-year-old, 22-inch TV, "What did you expect? You can't kill Satan with a poorly placed bomb. Maybe the body he now occupies was damaged a bit, but that is just flesh and bone, easy for the Dark One to repair." He let out a gust of air as he shook his head and continued "Somehow I knew that I was to be the one who has to take care of this problem."

Although, deep down he felt an urgency to take some kind of action regarding Warburton, Paul knew that he had to be patient. He surmised that security around the demon would be extremely tight, and at this point he didn't even have any idea how he would get close to him. He also didn't know how he would expel the spirit from the human form it occupied. Paul thought that he didn't possess the tools to try an endeavor like that. Satan was powerful, and an exorcism seemed out of the question. No, he believed that destroying the host body was probably his only option.

Sikora genuinely cared for his mentor, but no longer believed he could help in what must be done. He also didn't want news of the bombing and Warburton's escape to upset Padraig and hinder his recovery, so he did not mention the event to him and asked the doctors and nurses not to say anything either. The elder priest would find out soon enough after he left the hospital, but it was Paul's hope that he would be strong enough to handle it by then. So Father Sikora put the whole Warburton thing on the back burner for now. Maybe after some time had gone by, an opportunity would present itself and he would be in a position to take advantage, but that wouldn't be for a while.

# # #

Jimmy The Brain couldn't believe he was watching and hearing a dead man on the television. He was in the back room of the pool hall, that of the clean floor and new throw rug, but had missed the live version. Of course every news agency and TV station had rerun the speech every chance they got. It was during the morning broadcast of the local news that Santini had caught the latest reports of Warburton's survival. He was alone in his office but that didn't stop him from speaking out loud to no one.

"How the fuck did this happen? I saw him get into that van. His face was lit up by the security lights that came on in the driveway. Look at him, not even a scratch." Days ago when the reports of the deaths of the wife and kids came out, Jimmy wasn't concerned that there was no news about Warburton's status. It didn't even cross his mind that he had lived. But now, after seeing the man speak, the idea that he had failed began to sink in. As he'd said before, now his security would be near-impossible to breach. It would be suicide to try a second attempt. He still couldn't believe the son of a bitch made it out of that firestorm unharmed. His failure would eat at his insides as the small empire he had built would crumble on the outside due to his neglect, only the most loyal of his crew sticking by him. But even they eventually saw the light, and Jimmy Santini died with not one living person to mourn him.

CHAPTER 29

He sat alone in a room inside the building that represented the seat of one of the most powerful people on this planet. He had told Carlos and the others that if he wasn't safe here, he wasn't safe anywhere, so they had relented and waited in the hall outside the door. He was in the bedroom they had set up for him while he stayed at the White House, and he was sitting on the edge of the bed and the comforter that he was sure cost over a thousand dollars. He tried not to let his tears hit the expensive covers. These bouts of extreme sadness were down to once every couple of days, but this one was unavoidable. They had been on their way to this place, and it was supposed to be the start of a journey where they would be spending much of their time together. But life, being as cruel as it is sometimes, put him here all alone, even when he was surrounded by those he now called friends.

The tux he wore was a perfect fit. Just before noon that morning, several people came in and measured him for the suit, and here it was a few hours later. He had not met the president yet, but spent half of yesterday and most of today with Nickerson. He immediately took a liking to the press secretary to the point where they shared a drink last evening on one of the balconies. Danny had been given a sweatshirt with the presidential seal on it to ward off the night chill. The official meeting with Douglas was to be at the dinner party tonight, him and about 200 others. He wasn't sure of the president's agenda, but The Healer was going to touch everyone he met this evening. Time to get this show on the road, with that thought he shook off the blues, wiped his eyes, straightened his jacket, and headed for his destiny.

Back in the same bedroom at 1 am, Danny reflected on the entire affair and thought that it couldn't have gone any better for him. When he'd entered the area where they had the cocktail hour before dinner, President Douglas had been on the other side of the room. He thought that was planned but wasn't sure. Dozens of politicians and their wives were present, some he recognized and many others he did not. They all expressed their condolences and shook his hand. Danny thought this was going to be easier than first imagined. He guessed that these Washington types, being egotistical and arrogant, would be afraid of his touch, but he found them to be just the opposite. Most of them were open and took his hand without hesitation. Maybe he had misjudged these people. He had decided that he wasn't going to seek out the President, this was his house and it was up to him to introduce himself. Cocktail hour actually stretched to cocktail hour and forty five minutes before one of the White House kitchen staff entered the lounge and announced dinner. Another staff member approached Danny and told him he would be escorting the guest of honor to his place at the table. He and his small entourage followed the young woman in the white jacket and matching gloves to the table at the head of the dining room. They sat at the round table that accommodated eight which left four empty seats. A few moments later he heard a familiar voice behind him and turned to see Adam Douglas standing behind his chair.

"Good evening Daniel, I'm sure you have figured out that I have been avoiding you for the past two hours. Frankly I am unsure if I want to shake your hand, probably due to a little fear more than anything else. I don't know why, Nickerson can't stop telling me how wonderful he feels and what a stand-up guy you are. What the hell, now is as good a time as any. Will it make the food taste any better?" Douglas finished and offered his hand to his guest.

Danny stood and gripped the man's hand firmly. After a few seconds had passed and the business of the gift was over, he said, "Yes, the food will taste better, and you will be able to play the piano again."

The president knew the joke and smiled his widest politician smile, which was actually genuine. "I feel fantastic, now that that is over. Let's just enjoy the meal and forget about the future of the world for a few hours, what do you say?"

The Healer returned Douglas' smile, it was infectious, and agreed his idea was splendid. After dinner, many of the guests returned to the lounge-type area where once again drinks were served as well as a small band played. Several couples took advantage of a dancing area. By that time he believed that he had touched everyone who had attended, but another person had also been avoiding him.

For most of the rest of the evening he and his trio of security sat at a small table not far from the dance floor. Danny had been nursing his second glass of wine since dinner ended and he was about to say his good nights and go back to his room when he looked up and saw a woman crossing the dance floor in a shimmering green gown. He didn't recognize her until she was about 15 feet from his table and then his eyes grew wide and he stood to greet his friend.

"Oh my God, Karen, I'm used to seeing you in business-type attire, and I almost didn't recognize you in that gown. You look amazing. How long have you been here? I'm sure I haven't seen you, because I would have at least noticed a beautiful woman in a stunning dress."

"Thank you. I've been here most of the night, but I didn't want to bother you earlier. You were busy doing your thing with everyone else and then I was involved with some other people on the far side of the room. I did want to stop by before the end of the night to say hello and again offer my condolences, this time in person." Karen had called him the day he went home from the hospital, and they had spoken briefly.

She closed the few steps that were in between them and gave him a hug. "I'm so sorry, Danny. If there is ever anything you need, please call me."

"I appreciate that, and I will." They separated. With a lighter note in his voice, he said, "I was about to retire, but I suppose I could have one more glass of wine. If you would join me, we could catch up."

"Oh shit, I would love to but I was on my way out. I have a 5 am flight back to Atlanta and a long day tomorrow. Can I get a rain check?"

"Any time, you know that Karen." This time it was his turn to lean in and give her a small kiss on the cheek as they said their goodbyes.

He didn't need his enhanced perception or his mind reading capabilities to know that she had developed deeper feelings for him. It was all over her face, her body language, and the fact that she was nervous around him when she never had been before. He guessed that was her reason for avoiding him all night and lying about that and her early plane ride. She didn't know how to act around a man who she was falling in love with who had just lost his wife. She was going to have to figure that out for herself. He was so busy and didn't need that type of complication right now.

Despite being in a strange bed, he slept like a rock and was well-rested when his cell phone alarm went off at 7 am. Breakfast was at 8, and then President Douglas was going to take him to congress, where Adam had called for a joint session of the senate and the house. That meeting wasn't scheduled to begin until 11 am, but Douglas brought Danny over right after eggs, bacon, hash browns, and toast, washed down with two cups of coffee. The president introduced him to as many congressmen as he could, this mostly done in the offices of those men and women, all of whom happened to be political allies of Douglas, which didn't bother Danny, he probably would have done the same thing.

When both houses of congress did come together at 11 the room was jammed. Secretaries, pages, aides, and anyone else who was in the building wanted to be in the room. All of the doors were propped open, and the crowd spilled out into the hallway. Adam Douglas addressed the throng, and at first started waving the flag, saying the United States was the most caring and giving nation on the earth, which, of course, was met with loud applause. He went on to say that our great country was on the forefront of every major event in human history over the last 200 years. Just as Danny was starting to worry where the President was going with this, Douglas focused on why he had called this joint meeting.

"I want to introduce to you a man who you've probably seen on the news, or read about in the papers or online. A man who has suffered and sacrificed more than anyone should have to, and yet he has vowed to continue on his quest to bring a better way of life to all humanity. I am here to tell every American and the rest of the world leaders that I will support Daniel Warburton any way that I can. I will offer him money, although I don't think he needs it, I will offer him the use of the Secret Service, I am giving him the use of Air Force One for as long as he needs it, and anything else he needs to continue on his journey safely. I believe in his quest, and I believe that with all of our help, his goals are attainable." Douglas turned to Danny and motioned him to the microphone as he began the ovation himself.

He was thinking about the day when he and Carmel were bantering about a private jet and the mile high club after Douglas mentioned Air Force One, and a bittersweet smile splayed across his face. The memory threatened to send a lump to his throat, but he wiped away the one errant tear, swallowed back the lump and went to the President's side.

Adam shook his hand vigorously, and both men had to wait for the crowd noise to abate before saying anything.

"Thank you, Mr. President, for your support and your generous offer of assistance. I will certainly take you up on some of those." He then addressed the throng and said, "By now I'm sure that you all have read about where I'm going with this. I will not live long enough to be able to touch every person on this planet, so my plan is to at least make contact with the leaders of the world as they, and you, are in the position to help make positive changes for those I can't get to. So for today I would like to go through the crowd and meet everyone here tonight."

More applause as Danny left the podium and began to mingle. Even in the middle of hundreds of people, he was able to see things everyone else would miss. He saw as many as two dozen congressmen and women move away from him and leave the room. He probed the minds of several of those who were leaving and found that five were just scared and the other six were upset with the religious part of the alien's story. He wasn't going to seek them out later to change their minds, he was curious about their reasons.

He could have touched everyone in only a few hours, but he took his time and spoke to most of the people there which stretched the session to six that evening. Danny took a quiet dinner, alone in his room, but even after the long day, he wasn't tired. He wanted to take a walk, sans a half dozen others with bulges under their jackets. At about 9 pm he was able to slip out of the White House with minimal use of his new talents and went looking for a lively night spot. When he did find one it didn't take him long to be the center of attention in the establishment. The Healer made contact with all of the bar patrons, had two glasses of wine, and found another new twist to his gifts. He had been standing at a table and speaking with a group of young revelers when he noticed the waitress coming his way with a tray of drinks. A rather large gentleman stood up as the waitress was passing his chair and the tray started to go over. Danny wasn't even aware of what he was doing until he was already done. He used his mind to right the tray and the drinks that would have surely drenched the big guy who had stood. No one else noticed and the waitress was puzzled but passed it off to a close call. He thought that he should call it a night after that. When he returned to his room, he learned that his escape was discovered and Carlos was pissed at him. He knew that it was only Carlos' way of being worried and caring for him. But it wouldn't be the last time he went off on his own, which would eventually cause fits for his security team and his friend Franti.

The Healer spent ten more days bunking in the White House. Sometimes he went with Adam to meetings with other high ranking government types, but when he wasn't doing that he would often walk around the Mall area and talk to as many people as he could. He promised Cintron that he wouldn't ditch his bodyguards, and he was true to his word but insisted they give him some space and not scare those he met along the way.

Captain Franti was in telephone contact with him every other day, and seven days after he mingled with congress, there was another call from the New Britain Police Department.

"Do you want me to send the rest of your things to the White House?" was how Franti said hello.

"How you never got a job as a stand-up comedian is beyond me."

"I guess my true calling was to be a pain in your ass. Seriously, what are you doing down there?"

"I'm trying to relax and put some of the recent past behind me, basically getting my shit together. Besides, I really like these guys. Adam, Frank, and I have a drink every night out on the balcony, who knew politicians weren't all assholes?"

"Danny, had it ever crossed your mind that might be a byproduct of knowing you?"

"On to other issues, what have you found out?"

"I have a couple of leads, as you know many bomb makers use the same type of materials and make-up of their devices which gives them a signature. From what was recovered at the scene we know that this bomb was simplistic in its design because of the way it was attached by magnets. But the rest of the bomb was not, this lends us to believe that it was made by a pro, but for someone else. Bomb signature databases have grown over the last ten years but they are far from complete. My contact at the FBI, has been searching for similar devices with the information I have given him, and so far he has come up with two similar bombs. One was used in Miami on a boat at a marina seven years ago. And get this, the other was in Northern Ireland in the 70s. FBI says the Miami incident was a mob hit, and the other was just what you would think, IRA. Due to the geographic and time factors, these hits might be coincidences, but we will run them down until we are sure."

"Thanks Mike, I have all the confidence in you. There is no one else I would want on this job."

"Well, I'm trying to do my best, but I get distracted by phone calls telling me that you are out bar hopping in DC by yourself."

Silence was on the line. "Sometimes I think you have Carlos believing he works for you. You don't know what it's like having people around you all of the time, protecting you. I got a little claustrophobic and needed to get out."

"Danny, your security people are there not because you pay them, they are there because they care for you and want you to be safe. Don't do that again. I will call again in a few days."

The two friends said their good byes and ended the call.

That night in his room he continued to work on developing his ability to move objects with his mind. He had been doing this since the bar, mostly in his room where he was assured privacy, but there were a few occasions, when no one was around, that he used his extra gift in public. He was going slow, at first moving small, lightweight items, but recently he lifted the dresser in the bedroom, which probably weighed 200 pounds. The thing was made of oak with ornate carvings and an attached mirror six feet wide by three feet tall. He lifted it a foot off the floor and held it there for about five minutes. Danny felt no strain on his mind during or after these exercises, and his confidence in his abilities grew each day. He started to wonder what other kinds of abilities would pop up. He believed that the telekinesis was a result of his brain injury from the bomb shrapnel, it just didn't show up right away. His mind reading was sort of there before, but now it was at the point where he could pull out others thoughts that were in the deepest parts of their minds. Tomorrow he planned on continuing to develop his ability to communicate with another human without talking. He had been working on his precision and getting his message to only one person, just as Calvin and Hobbes did with him on the ship. He looked up to the sky and thought about the boys in robes up there. They had to know what had happened to him and what he could now do, but still no contact. Not even a "Wish you were here" post card from the far side of the moon. Danny decided he couldn't waste any more time wondering about his space buddies. They could send their taxi anytime they wanted.

In the time he was in Washington, The Healer must have touched 5,000 people. But except for congress, they were not the influential people he wanted to meet. Douglas had promised a trip to New York to visit the United Nations, but so far that had not materialized. Adam said it was due to the fact that many of the ambassadors were not in New York, but they were gathering, and a majority should be there in a few days. And then, the day after he had asked Cassandra to please go and get him a glass of raspberry ginger ale, without speaking, Adam told him they were going to the UN in the morning. The trip involved flying in Air Force One into JFK airport and then after the visit to the UN, President Douglas would leave Danny the plane to go wherever his plans took him. A short time after he had relayed his request, Cassandra had brought him a pail of raspberries. He decided he had to work on his brain's annunciation.

The trip to New York started out with a motorcade from the White House to the airport. Danny had packed all of his things, as did Carlos, Luis, and Cassandra. They wouldn't be back any time soon.

Air Force One wasn't actually the name of the plane they flew on. That designation is the call sign of either of the two planes that shuttled the President of the United States to destinations around the world. So Douglas wasn't going to have to thumb a ride from now on, he had a back-up. The Boeing 747 was huge, with 4,000 square feet of living space, conference rooms, kitchens, and several other areas on three levels. Enough suites for its new owner and his traveling companions to have their own. Adam told Danny that his offer of use of the plane also came with a full staff, which included pilots, chefs, and even a medical staff. He thought of telling the president that he didn't see much use for doctors and nurses but then decided not to say anything and let those people come along, it would be like a vacation to them.

At JFK, they were met by another secret service motorcade, which took them all to the One UN New York, a hotel virtually next door to the UN. The rooms were luxurious and impressed the four Connecticut natives. Danny was used to staying in nice hotels when he took his family on vacation but nothing of this caliber. Yet his reaction was nothing compared to Cassandra's. She was the third daughter of African American parents and like her mother and father, she grew up in the housing project and had never been exposed to a bedroom like the one she was in now. They were all in their rooms when the boss came back out into the hall and gathered Carlos and Luis. The trio then went to Cassandra's door and knocked. They wanted to discuss dinner plans but had to wait, as she was not answering. Luis waited a few minutes, then knocked again. Cassandra opened the door this time and had on a huge, plush bathrobe that seemed to swallow the petite woman.

Carlos said, "Cassy, what are you doing? Remember, we were going to have dinner together?"

Cassandra had the face of a five-year-old on Christmas morning. "Do you have a bathroom like the one I have? Have you even seen the tub? I can't leave right now. You boys go to dinner without me. Perhaps I will call for room service after I take an hour long bubble bath." She closed the door so softly the latch barely made a noise when it engaged.

The three men looked at each other and at the same time burst out laughing. They weren't making fun of their colleague and friend, but they were shocked at the 180 degree change from the usual tough exterior that this woman presented.

Cassandra wrapped herself in the same robe when she got out of the bath and did order room service. She thought it was the best meal she had ever tasted. Later that night she turned out the lights and crawled into bed naked. She wanted to feel the soft, cool sheets over every inch of her body. She drifted off wearing the same face she earlier had answered the hotel room door with.

The next day they accompanied President Douglas to the United Nations. It appeared to Danny that the event was nearly a carbon copy of the meeting with Congress only with a much bigger group. To start off, the main room was larger than the one which was used in Washington, and there were at least a dozen more rooms filled with chairs and a movie-type screen in each that broadcast the goings on in the main room. Adam once again gave a speech and introduced Danny, who didn't know what to say. So he gave the same general statement as he had in DC, but he put an international spin to it. Then, just like before, he went through those in attendance and touched all who wanted him to do so. This time, though, he noticed about four dozen delegates leave. Most of those were from Middle Eastern nations. He didn't want to, but he couldn't help himself. So when he did probe the minds of those leaving, he found a good portion did so due to religious reasons, and the others left because he was American and had the backing of the United States government. Some people just didn't like the USA.

The Healer tried to work quickly but also wanted to make solid contacts from all of the countries represented here, therefore the process of getting to everyone who remained was a long one. He went all the rest of the day and past the dinner hour until Carlos whispered into his ear that it was getting on near 8 pm. He looked at his watch and couldn't believe he had spent seven hours and only had gone through the main hall and half of one of the big screen rooms. Part of the delay was that he had found the hallway leading to the first movie room jammed with people. The UN had their own security force which tried to make a path in the hall for Danny, but without much luck. He thought that he could clear some of the people out if he touched them and then sent them on their way. That plan worked for the most part, but it still took over an hour to get to his destination. He left that evening with the promise to return the next morning and make contact with anyone who wished him to. On the ride back to the hotel, Adam Douglas said he would be going back to DC in the morning. Danny was sorry to hear that and invited the president back to his room for one last drink. He also expressed his disappointment that he had not met the Chinese ambassador in the main room.

Douglas said, "The Chinese and the United States have had a strange relationship for many years now. We do a tremendous amount of trade with them, and yet we still don't trust each other. I wasn't surprised that they didn't stick around, but I was equally surprised that the Russian delegation did."

Danny chuckled. "Anton grew up poor and worked on his father's farm ever since he could remember. He joined the army at a young age, and the only reason he was appointed ambassador was because he was a decorated war hero and the people loved him. It was strictly a political move for the president to gain favor with the voters. He was one of the most down-to-earth people in that room today."

The next morning, they had a big breakfast and headed back to the UN. They set up shop in the main room, Carlos was happy, his job was easier with a stationary Daniel, and had people in and out all day. The decision to call it at 6:30 pm was a mutual one, but as before, The Healer made plans to return. It was Luis who announced the time of 4:45 pm on the fourth day at the United Nations when he had touched the last person.

"I would hope that all this isn't for nothing, I must have touched 5,000 people over the last four days from about 140 of the 193 countries that belong to the UN. That has got to turn into diplomatic dividends down the road."

Cassandra, back to all business, asked, "Where to next, boss?"

"Well, I'm thinking that we deserve the next two or three days off, this was exhausting. You guys cut loose, do whatever you like, and put it on my tab. Cassy, take as many bubble baths as you can. Who knows when you will get the chance to get another one."

Cassandra smiled. "What are you going to do?"

"I think I will sleep for at least the next 14 or 15 hours. Then, I don't know. Maybe some quiet time in my room. But to answer your question, I'm looking at an extended tour of Europe. I can't say how long, but I sure would like all three of you to come with me."

Carlos, Luis, and Cassandra all nodded profusely and spoke at the same time, relaying the fact that as long as he needed them, they would be at his side. He saw the look in their eyes and knew that Franti was right. These three would lay down their lives for him even if he never paid them a dime. The boss got up and coughed to clear the lump in his throat and started to walk toward the door as he said, "Come on, we are going to Ruth's Chris steak house. The finest steak in Manhattan is the least I can do for you guys."

CHAPTER 30

Father O'Malley was out of the hospital for nearly two weeks, and each day got better for him. A visiting nurse came in twice a week to check on his progress, which completely ruffled the feathers of Katia. She felt that she was more than capable of tending to the father and knew him better than any of the nurses the agency sent. Padraig was able to get around the rectory and also to his office in the church and, therefore, to his computer. Paul couldn't keep the news of the attempt on Warburton's life and the death of his wife and children from him any longer. The elder priest was upset at Father Sikora for not telling him the whole story but understood when he was told that he was kept in the dark for health reasons.

As he grew stronger, Padraig spent more and more time in his office, until Katia put an end to it. She thought it best that he didn't wander so far from her sight, so she made arrangements to have his computer brought to his room and to have the necessary hook ups installed so he could access the internet. Katia didn't understand why he needed the internet when he was supposed to be recovering, but she also didn't know that Satan was running around earth, making friends with the world leaders.

After several days in his room catching up on what had happened in the world and what was going on with Daniel Warburton, Padraig didn't know what to think of the situation anymore. He had just finished the last news report of the meeting at the United Nations and how this man had come back for four days to use his gifts to heal as many of those who wanted his help. He was sitting at the small desk that held the computer, and sat back in the chair, thinking. Every time he believed that Paul's possession theory was correct, like in the parking lot of Hope when his heart seized, he learned information that planted the seeds of doubt. For instance, if this was a move by Satan to take over or even destroy the earth and humanity, where was God? His interpretation of the Bible was, if there is to be a final battle for the souls of humankind, that both sides would show up. He supposed that the death of the Warburton family could have been set up by Satan to elicit sympathy, but from what he read, he didn't need any ploy. At the time, he was on his way to the White House and then possibly the Vatican after that. To O'Malley, things just weren't adding up, but right now there was nothing he could do about any of this. Paul hadn't mentioned any sort of plan of action against Warburton, and Padraig thought there was little chance that the two of them could get close enough anyway. He decided that he would have a talk with Father Sikora and convince him that there wasn't enough evidence to prove his theory and even if there was, he could be of no help to him, given his current health.

Father Paul Sikora was, for all intents and purposes, running the parish since O'Malley landed in the hospital. He hadn't imagined all of the mundane day to day activities that Padraig had taken care of before, that involved the smooth operation of the church. He thought that it must be very much like running a business, ordering supplies such as wine and wafers, replacing hymnals that had become torn or unreadable, getting repairmen to come in to fix things that simply don't work anymore or that break. And he was getting no help from Katia, whose one and only focus was to see that Padraig's recovery went as planned. With each passing day he became more tired, mostly due to the fact that he was sleeping only a few hours each night. After taking care of his church responsibilities, he would be on his laptop until three or four in the morning, searching the internet for any and all information he could find on the being who now occupied the body of Daniel Warburton.

The two priests spent little time together anymore. They would have breakfast in the rectory, as they always did, and there was some conversation, but it wasn't anything of substance. They spoke of having the furnace cleaned, renewing the contract of the snow removal company, and starting to accept applications for a new organist. Mrs. Braxton was getting on in years, and the arthritis in her hands was causing more than a few faces to cringe on Sundays. But not once was the subject of Satan, Warburton, or what happened at Hope brought up. Padraig was dealing with his misgivings about their earlier take on the situation, and Paul was of the opinion that his mentor was in no shape to help him in what he believed had to be done so why upset him with the details of a plan that he wasn't even certain of yet.

So that was how the two priests lived for the time being. Days turned into weeks and weeks turned into months with not much change. They both kept tabs on the activities surrounding their favorite human/demon via the internet and the television but they had reverted back to a time when they had done so without speaking to each other about it.

# # #

On the other hand, life for the object of their obsession changed almost hourly, or so it seemed to him. Danny and his security staff had three great days in New York City. They ate well, spent hours seeing the usual sights such as the Empire State building, the Statue of Liberty and several museums. They took in a Broadway play one evening and on two nights wound up in a dance club after dinner. This wasn't the boss' thing, but he enjoyed watching the three younger people having a good time on the dance floor. It appeared to him as he watched, that some chemistry was brewing between Luis and Cassandra, which made him think back to the day he met Carmel for the first time. A few minutes later, his thoughts turned to Karen Ayala, and he wondered how she was doing. That was the last night before they left for Europe and later, when Danny was back at the hotel, Karen had gathered her courage and called him. He couldn't help but wonder if somehow when he was thinking of her, his brain had sent some kind of signal out. He decided that sounded egotistical and answered the cell.

"Hello Karen, believe it or not I was thinking about you just a couple of hours ago. I was wondering how you were doing. We didn't talk much at the White House."

"Hi Danny. Yeah, the Washington dinner thing was my fault. Time for my confession, I was avoiding you that night. I didn't know what to say to you and I didn't trust myself to not say something stupid. You see ....I have developed deeper feelings for you than mere friendship." Danny started to interrupt but she cut him off. "Please, don't say anything yet. Let me finish before I lose my nerve. That all happened before...your loss. Back then, I knew what to do, push those thoughts way down and never let them surface. And then after, I wanted to be there for you, as a friend, but like I said I didn't trust myself, which made me feel shitty. So at the risk of appearing to be a lousy friend, I avoided you. And for that, I am sorry."

There was a pause, so he thought she was done and he almost began to talk, but she continued. "Funny, I didn't call to talk about this. My boss wanted me to get an interview with you, about how your plan was progressing, especially after meetings with the President, Congress, and now the

United Nations, but once I heard your voice, I had to get that out of me. And I apologize again if I have made you uncomfortable."

He knew it was his turn to speak. "There is no need to apologize, Karen. Since the damage done to my head as a result of the bomb, I have been able to read people's minds. But I didn't need to read yours to know how you felt. It was evident by your body language, the tone of your voice, and how you don't make eye contact with me anymore. You can't help how you feel, but you don't have to avoid me, okay?"

"Okay."

"Which brings us to the interview your boss wants. Unfortunately, I am leaving for an extended stay in Europe tomorrow. But if CNN will spring for the air fare, we can meet next week some time, and we can talk about everything."

"I'm sure they would send me anywhere for that interview. So you can read minds, any other talents develop?"

"Maybe a few more, I will tell you all about them but it will be strictly off the record, as is the mind reading, agreed?"

Karen's tone was completely serious "You know I would never go behind your back, you tell me something is not for the public, it stays with me."

"I trust you Karen. Call me when you get the ok and I'll tell you where we will be."

"I will, good bye Danny, see you soon."

He disconnected the call and immediately thought of Carmel and how much he missed her. Maybe being around Karen or even talking to her wasn't such a good idea if it was going to bring out memories of his wife, which inevitably would cause him some degree of depression. He poured the rest of his glass of wine down the bathroom sink and went to bed.

Air Force One landed at Orly the next afternoon, and a car was waiting for Warburton and his security team to take them to the American embassy in Paris. Adam Douglas had sent orders to all embassy personnel to attend to the needs of the visitors with no exceptions. Flying across the Atlantic chewed up most of the day, so no meetings were planned until tomorrow. After a brief sit-down with the American Ambassador to France, and the time it took for The Healer to use his gifts on all who were at the embassy that day, the four were driven to their hotel in the heart of the City of Lights.

The French government consists of a President, the National Assembly, and a senate, Danny thought it was very similar to the United States. He met with the president first and then the Senate but the meeting with those of the National Assembly wasn't scheduled until the following day. With the French government taken care of, he planned to spend the next week walking the streets of Paris and making contact with as many people as he could. Visiting the ruling bodies of most of the countries of Earth was a priority for his plan to work, but he still wanted to be accessible to the everyday citizens also. He thought it unfortunate that he couldn't stay longer and travel to several cities in each country, but time didn't allow for that.

The Healer had been to Paris before, when he was stationed in Germany during his military stint. At that time he found the French people a bit standoffish, but that was more than a few years ago, and this trip was much different. At each restaurant, tavern, museum, or any other establishment he visited, the people were gracious and friendly. He remembered Franti's words about the DC politicians and decided that he didn't care why, he just wanted people to be happier than they had been.

Danny had conferred with Carlos, and the two had come to the conclusion that using the plane to travel Europe didn't make much sense. So they rented a large SUV and made arrangements to leave Air Force One at the airport. They were all set to drive to their next stop, Belgium, when Karen Ayala called. She had finally received authorization to meet Danny in France that day, and she would be flying out the next morning. The group put their Brussels plans on hold until the interview was done.

He drove the rented SUV to the airport and was waiting at the gate when she deplaned and entered the terminal. There was an awkward moment as they were face to face and Karen put her hand out to shake and he leaned in to give her a hug.

"Karen, there is no reason to be nervous around me." He then hugged her.

"I know, but talking on the phone is a little different than seeing you in person."

They collected the one bag of luggage she had besides her carry on and as they headed for the car Danny filled her in on what he had planned. The cameraman she brought along sensed these two wanted their privacy and hung back a few steps

"I'm going to drop you off at your hotel so you can freshen up and then I'll be back at 7 pm. I have reservations for the two of us and we can talk over dinner."

"That works for me. I really only have one day here. My return flight is tomorrow afternoon."

"You came all this way for one day?"

"Not quite, I go from here to Rome. CNN wants me to get a reaction from the Pope about you, since we figured you would be in his neighborhood soon enough."

"I'm going to give you an exclusive, and you're going to stir the pot with the Vatican before I can get down there? Thanks a lot."

"I'm sorry, this wasn't my idea. I still have a job to do and orders to take." Karen looked at her feet as she spoke.

"Hey, I'm kidding. Actually, I would like to know what he thinks of all this, might give me an edge, if and when we meet."

They had reached the car and loaded the bags into the cargo area. As he drove, they got caught up on what they had both been up to since they last talked. At her hotel, he walked her into the lobby, and they separated at the elevator.

A few hours later he was back in the same lobby waiting for her to come down from her room. He happened to be facing away from the elevators when she got off, and he didn't know she was there until she tapped him on the shoulder. He turned around and raised his eyebrows at the sight of her in a spaghetti strapped, mid-thigh, form-fitting, black dress. She blushed as much as her Hispanic complexion would allow.

Dinner conversation went beyond the meal, so they found a couple of seats at the restaurant bar and talked for another two hours. Danny was very clear as to what was on, and off, the record, and she stopped taking notes when he indicated certain information was meant just for her. Near the end of their second drinks, he asked her if she wanted to discuss what she had confessed when they last spoke. Karen smiled and told him that the night had been going too well, and she didn't want to risk ruining it. She said they could bring that subject back up at another time.

Back in the hotel lobby for the third time, Karen called up to her cameraman's room, and he came down to meet them. She had put together a list of questions she would ask Danny, and they would tape the interview in the hotel lobby. Forty-five minutes later, the camera was packed away, and its operator went back to his room. Karen said she would take the hotel shuttle back to the airport the next morning, so goodbyes were exchanged in the lobby. They promised to call each other, because no matter what, they were still friends. And when they hugged, Danny gave her a light kiss on the cheek, turned, and left.

The drive to Brussels took about three hours. On the way, the leader of this small group explained to the others that the plan for Belgium was the same as France, a day with the leaders of the country and then a week walking the streets of the capital city. In fact, that is what he envisioned for every country they visited in Europe. It was possible that they would have to spend another day with the government types of some of the larger countries, so he told them the plan was flexible and they were not on any deadline. Danny spoke to the others from behind the wheel while Carlos occupied the shotgun seat. Luis and Cassandra sat in the back, and as he spoke, he glanced in the rear view mirror and saw them smiling and eyeing each other and it made him smile. He was glad for their budding romance and hoped they could find love and happiness within. It made him reflect on the night before and dinner with Karen. He wondered if it was too soon. He was still mourning the loss of his wife, his family. Was he disrespecting the memory of Carmel by thinking of another woman so quickly? He tried to shake off those thoughts. Besides, he was going to be busy for the next several months, and that bridge wasn't in sight yet.

So that was how they traveled through some of the oldest countries of the world. Occasionally, when the trip became too long, Carlos took over the driving, but it was rare when Danny gave up the wheel. After Belgium, they were on to the Netherlands and Amsterdam. The following week was spent in Berlin, Germany. Even though he had been stationed there for two years while in the army, he'd been on a base that was in the Saar region and never got the chance to visit Berlin. This was one of the places that needed two days with the ruling bodies, and he had wanted to take the other three to the area he did know in Germany, but the week went by too fast and the opportunity was missed.

Their trip took them to Poland next and then south, through some of the former Soviet Republics. Danny had decided that they couldn't visit every country in that area due to time constraints. As it was, they were into full winter by then, and they had to adjust their schedule a few times because of heavy snow. But the cold and the snow were the only setbacks so far. On the way to Romania, Carlos had mentioned that he was surprised they hadn't had any resistance at all.

"Boss, have you realized that we have not encountered any groups protesting us? None of the media over here are reporting anything disparaging, and not one individual has voiced his displeasure since we landed in France."

"You were expecting trouble?"

"Well, not so much trouble. But think about countries like Poland. As a people, they are very religious. But not one renegade priest is giving us shit about your Jesus Christ comments."

"I don't have an explanation for you, but wait until we go to Vatican City, China, or the Middle East. You may have to earn your keep there. And how do you know what the media is saying about us? You don't speak all of the languages we have encountered, do you?"

Carlos laughed. "No, still only English and Spanish, but I have been checking out the internet. Several sites in English that report on our progress daily, and they also report on the local reaction to us. But when we get to Spain, Puerto Rico, and almost all of Central and South America, I will be able to get information right out of the papers."

Danny was silent for a moment "I hadn't thought that far ahead yet. I think we should take a break after Europe. You guys have lives, family you want to see, and we might all be a little tired of traveling by then. We can talk about future trips later."

Carlos let the conversation die. He knew when the boss was going into deep thought about something and this was one of those times.

As they promised each other, Danny and Karen kept in touch by phone. Sometimes she called him, and other times the opposite, but they spoke at least once a week. While he was in Belgium, she called to tell him she would be going back to Atlanta without an interview with the Pope. She was told that he was not feeling well so she waited a few days and then was told that he was preparing for a trip and there was no time, she was invited back in the spring. This wasn't her first rodeo, she knew a brush off when she heard one. So he would have to go to Rome without the information he was hoping for. Maybe the Pope wouldn't give him an audience either. He would find out when he got there.

Romania and Bulgaria were next on the itinerary, and the quartet marveled at the architecture and the detailed, intricate carvings that were found on both the interior and exterior of the older structures, some of which dated back over a thousand years. Then they moved into a region that had seen some of the most recent wars and atrocities toward humans. First Kosovo, then Bosnia and Serbia, where there was still evidence of the conflict that had occurred nearly 20 years before. Danny did what he could for those people and at least he left feeling confident that the governments in that area would begin to put aside their differences.

If they had been enamored by the old world charm of Romania and Bulgaria, they were blown away when they left the Baltic peninsula for Austria. Vienna was amazing and the people there were as welcoming as the rest of Europe had been. It was agreed upon that they would spend a few extra days in Austria and visit some of the famous castles of that country.

By the time they reached Switzerland, the winter was winding down. In that part of the world there was still snow on the ground and still falling on the Alps. They didn't have the time for skiing on those well-known mountains, and those peaks were not the place for first timers such as three ex-gang members from New Britain. Again they were struck by the beauty of the country where, in some areas, it seemed time had stood still for a century. Half way through the week of meandering around the streets of Bern, a phone call from the desk of Captain Michael Franti disrupted the trip and put Danny in a somber mood. He gathered his security team in his hotel room and told them that he had been called back to the states on an emergency mission. He wanted his three friends to stay in Switzerland, enjoy themselves, and take a well-earned rest. He would rejoin them in about a week. He told them he had to take care of some business that needed his personal attention, but didn't say anything about the details. Within hours, he was on a flight from Bern to Paris, where the crew would dust off Air Force One and fly him into Bradley airport in Hartford. As the small jet climbed to cruising altitude and pointed its nose toward Orly, Danny kept playing the conversation over and over in his head, the same words coming from Franti. "We found the source of the bomb."

CHAPTER 31

The captain was waiting for him at the gate. Danny was the only person who got off the big bird with the presidential seal on the tail. The two men shook hands and went directly to the city-owned vehicle parked outside the terminal in the lane for passenger pick-up. It wasn't until they were off the airport property and on the highway that either of them spoke.

"Do you want me to go over the information now, or do you want to get a good night's sleep so we can talk over breakfast?"

"I'm well-rested, you should see the inside of that plane, several large bedrooms with king-sized beds and attached bath. Tell me what you have so far."

"We started with the IRA bomb which really took some digging because the records were old and since hostilities are at a minimum in Ireland these days, the British have long since disbanded their anti-terrorism unit for Northern Ireland. But I was able to speak to an officer who used to be in that unit and although he was in his 80s, he had an uncanny memory. It helped that he specialized in bombs and bomb makers of that era. He didn't remember the particular bombing that we were interested in, but he did tell me that there were only a few good bomb makers who were part of the IRA at that time, and he was able to remember all six of their names. He was a pretty amazing old guy. Anyway, we had these six names and it turns out that two are dead, one is still in Ireland and the other three emigrated to the U.S. but nothing on them since they moved here. Then we concentrated on the Miami incident, which was more recent and still an open case. The Miami cops kept much better records and reports but they never developed a solid suspect. What they did tell us was they believed that the hit was a product of a beef with the Gambino crime family in New

York. When I heard that I knew we were on to something, one of the IRA bombers that came here now lives in Queens, his name is Eamon Flannigan. With the help of the FBI and NYPD, I started to go through phone records, and discovered that Flannigan is friends with Sonny Santini who is high up in the Gambino family. Sonny has a nephew, Jimmy, who is also in the family and he had phone conversations with Flannigan in the week prior to the bombing at your home. Bringing these guys in for questioning would be a waste of time at that point, we didn't have enough, so I started to look at other ways to track Jimmy Santini. I found out that he has an EZ Pass account and was then able to determine that he used the EZ Pass on the only toll from the Bronx, which is the Gambino strong hold, to Connecticut on I-95. From that info it was easy to get a photo of him in his car going through the toll gate on the night before the bombing, the stupid shit used his own car. I don't know his motives, but Jimmy Santini is the man who killed your family Danny."

Franti handed his friend a folded piece of paper, and Danny took it without saying a word.

"NYPD Organized Crime Task Force gave me the information on that paper. It is Jimmy Santini's home address in The Hamptons and the location of the pool hall where he conducts his business, he has an office in the back room."

Again, not a word from the passenger seat, the paper still folded.

Franti went on "Listen buddy, I don't envy your position. Remember the day I gave you shit about creating a moral dilemma for me? Well, I can't imagine the decision you have to face. All I can tell you is that whatever you do, you have my full support."

His silence broken, Danny said, "Thanks Mike. I do have a lot of thinking to do but I have a feeling I won't know what path I'll take until I confront him, but there will be a confrontation." There were a few moments of silence where neither man looked at the other, and then the ex-sergeant turned toward his old boss and continued. "You know we really haven't talked about much else for months, why don't we catch up, tell me about your family and what's happening at the PD, and then I'll tell you about Europe."

For the remainder of the forty five minute drive from the airport the two men talked as friends do who haven't seen each other in a while. Franti spoke of his children and how they were deep into the school year and doing well. He raved about the new car he bought for Gina and his amazement of the fact that her cell phone was synced to the car and she could make a call by speaking into the microphone mounted in the roof next to the sun visor. When he switched to the police department he told Danny that the winter had slowed things down even more than they had already been. But the extra time was being used to implement programs to get the police and the public to interact more.

They were about ten minutes from their destination when Danny began to share some of the highlights of the European trip up to the point where he left the others in Switzerland. He wasn't as long-winded as his friend, but he did touch on some of the charm of the older countries and spoke of the interview with Karen Ayala, and how he was hoping to get some inside information from her when she interviewed the Pope, but that never happened. He didn't feel it was the right time to say anything about the crush she had developed.

Then they had arrived, and Franti pulled the car into the driveway. The Captain grabbed the small bag from the back seat and then noticed his friend starring at his house. The big man sensed the sadness creeping up on Danny and thought that he shouldn't be alone.

"I drove all the way out to pick you up, you could at least invite me in for a beer."

He shook his head "You're right, but I don't even know if I have any. I might have a bottle of wine."

Franti made a face "You can drink the wine. Let's go inside and see what you have."

To their surprise, they found four bottles of Sam Adams in the fridge, and Mike drank half of them while Danny had his wine. For the next hour the two men recalled cases they had worked together and the funny and strange things they encountered as cops. Franti drained the second beer and said he had to be going. They walked to the door and shook hands and then the Captain had the last words.

"You unfold that piece of paper and decide what you are going to do. I won't be calling you. When you're ready to go back, get a hold of me and I'll bring you to your ride."

The only response was a nod.

The next morning he took the still folded paper and put it in his wallet, behind a photo of his wife. John and Teresa Warburton had gone back to California so there was no time to visit with them, but he did want to see as many of his family and friends as he could before confronting Santini. He didn't think there was any way that the mobster or any of his crew could get to him, but then again, he didn't think that was the case before and look what happened. He thought that since he was away for some time, he wanted to get caught up with his people first.

So the next several days were spent visiting, first his sister Kelly who told him all about meeting and getting to know one of the girl's teachers. They have been dating for a few months and things were going great, and the girls adored him. Danny deflected the inevitable question as to why he was back from Europe so soon and told her that this was just a short interlude and he would be continuing the trip in less than a week. He had stayed for longer than he intended at Kelly's house so when he arrived at George's, his brother was 30 minutes away from heading to work, but Danny was happy he was able to see him, if only for that short time. He called his baby sister and found out she was already at the bar. He decided that he would make the drive anyway and have a drink there, maybe he would catch her on a break.

His in-laws took up most of the second day, and the third day was earmarked for the police department. He hung around the main desk and visited all of the separate offices. He poked his head into the chief's office to say a quick hello and planned on doing the same to Franti, but the Captain wasn't in. He went to lunch with Tim Grey and filled out the rest of the afternoon in the detective bureau, he had been in that unit when he left and felt a little closer to those guys.

Each of the three nights he would eat a light dinner and have a glass of wine before bed. On the third night he found a half of a pack of his cigars in the drawer he kept the corkscrew in. He smiled and grabbed one and headed for the back door that led to the deck. The rear door had a window in the top half and Danny could see the two chairs of the bistro set before he opened the door, he stopped in his tracks. He told the door knob, "Not until I take care of some unfinished business." He put the cigar back and drank his wine in the living room.

Morning coffee brought the realization that this was not a pleasure trip, this was a business trip and it was time to get down to it. He went to the bedroom and got his wallet before pouring a second cup of joe. He was sitting at the center island in the kitchen with the folded paper next to his cup. He wasn't afraid of it, he just wanted to make a decision about what he would do once he saw Santini face to face, before he looked at the two addresses. Several more sips from the mug and still his course of action eluded him. Finally he picked up the paper and unfolded it. He had to think for a moment to get the day of the week, Thursday, definitely a work day for the mobster. Figuring the time it would take him to get ready and drive to New York, it would be nearly noon. So it was the office at the pool hall. He told the half full cup of coffee "Good, I didn't want to drive to the fucking Hamptons anyway." Danny's mood was getting darker and a shower did nothing to change that.

He left the city streets and took the ramp to the interstate, only then did he put in a CD. Even his favorite saxophonist, Mindi Abair, couldn't raise him out of his funk. He listened to half of the CD and then pulled it out of the player, the rest of the ride would be in silence. The only other things he brought with him were a bottle of water and the directions to Santini he had printed off of the computer.

Two and a half hours later he turned onto the street that was printed on the last line of the computer paper. He slowed down considerably, looking to his left, waiting for the pool hall to come into view. He saw it when he was still two doors away, a young, what he assumed was an Italian man, exited the business and got into a black Dodge Charger. Danny heard the engine roar to life as he passed it, checking his rear view mirror to see if anyone else was getting in, the muscle car pulled away from the curb carrying one occupant. Not that he knew what Santini looked like, Franti did not have a photo, but he thought he would just know the person who had killed his family when he saw the man. He took the next right and planned to circle the block and come back on the same side of the street as the pool hall and park in the spot vacated by the Charger. Minutes later he got out of his car and locked the door. He was unarmed, he didn't believe he needed a gun and he wouldn't be able to shoot all those inside anyway, he wasn't that fast or good with his sidearm. Danny guessed that while Santini was in his office he probably kept half his crew out by the tables, just for security. So the negotiator put on his widest smile, opened the door, and walked in.

He did a quick inventory, five thugs occupied the main room, one behind the counter, which also served as a bar, two sitting on stools at the bar, one playing at the farthest table from the door, and the last sitting beside a door which he guessed led to the back room, and the man he came to see.

The counter thug said, "What can I do for you?"

"I'm in town on business, had a few hours to kill, and thought I could find someone in here that wanted to play a few games."

"It's $20 an hour, you pay up front."

"Ouch, that's kinda steep"

"Go someplace else then. You gonna play or not?"

Danny pulled two twenties from his wallet and handed them to the guy he would now refer to as dickhead. For his money he received a plastic egg crate type holder filled with the correct amount of balls and was told to pick any table with the same shitty attitude as dickhead had thus far displayed. As he headed for a table he called out loud enough for everyone in the room to hear him and asked if anyone wanted to shoot a game with him. All four of the other mobsters turned and starred at him, but none responded.

He racked the balls and started to clear the table in numerical order. He was talking out loud to himself, phrases such as "Nice shot" when he sunk a ball and "Oh shit" or "God dammit" when he missed. He was trying to be annoying so one of the gangsters would approach him, it only took 15 minutes.

Danny felt a hand on his shoulder and the voice behind him say "We're closing for the day, time for you to go."

He didn't turn around or shrug the man's hand off of him before responding "Vinny, you're starting to hurt my feelings."

Vincent Golino started to grip the man's shoulder and said, "How do you know…"

But the "my name" part never made it past his lips, because Danny was applying his original talents. After which Vinny removed the offending hand and apologized. "I hope I didn't hurt your shoulder"

"No harm, no foul. Why don't you call your friends over so I can meet them, too?"

Less than three minutes later the five former gangsters were standing around, wondering what to do next.

Danny gave them a suggestion. "Why don't you boys go get a couple of pizzas for lunch, I need a few words with your boss."

Golino said, "I don't think he is our boss any longer, you guys feel the same?"

They all nodded, murmured their agreement, and walked to the door. Dickhead stopped at the counter, reached over and took a handful of cash, and announced that lunch was on Jimmy.

Sitting behind his desk in the next room, Jimmy Santini knew nothing of what was going on by the tables. Since the failed attempt on Warburton's life he had fallen into a funk. He was neglecting business, drinking to excess five nights a week, and treating his crew like shit. They, in turn, tried to avoid him and were not giving him his cut of their earnings. Word got around, and soon enough Jimmy's other enterprises were skimming off the top also. It wasn't as if he didn't know about his people holding out, he just didn't care anymore.

When the office door opened and he looked into the eyes of his nemesis, the Brain only had a few sips of his first, and what would be his last, drink of the day and therefore was lucid and sober. He was instantly pissed off that this son of a bitch had the balls to walk into his office.

"What the fuck do you want?"

Danny's response was so soft it was almost inaudible "I want my family back. But I know that is impossible."

"Then why come here? You gonna try to kill me?"

"I don't know what I'm going to do with you. I do know that I had to look you in the face before I made my decision."

Santini spit out his response. "Fuck you! You just try to get near me."

Jimmy The Brain reached into the top drawer of his desk, wrapped his hand around the semi-automatic pistol, and brought it to bear on The Healer. The man on the wrong end of the gun barrel had honed his mutated skills over the last six months and could have used his mind to yank the gun out of Jimmy's hand. Even if the gun went off, he could have stopped the bullet in mid-flight. Instead, he reached inside Santini with his thoughts, past the rib cage, to his heart, and before the chance was there to pull the trigger, that heart exploded. Jimmy Santini's lifeless body fell to the ground, and the gun skidded harmlessly away.

Danny Warburton bent over, put his hands on his knees, and let the anger ebb from his core. He knew he didn't have to kill Santini, but in his mind he wondered how long it would take for Calvin and Hobbes to end the experiment. Well, he thought, if that was the case then let it end where it started. He stepped outside and gazed up into the clear early spring sky, climbed back in to the Santa Fe and headed for the back deck of his house. The ride back went quick, or so it seemed to him. His mind was racing, so many thoughts went through his head that he practically drove home on auto pilot. It was just past 4 pm when he took the off ramp that led to his home town. He knew there wasn't much to eat in his cabinets, and he told himself he wasn't hungry anyway, but he forced himself to stop at a pizza place and get a grinder, mostly because he hadn't had anything all day. Once sitting on the couch in his living room, he turned on the TV and unwrapped the food and found that he was a little hungry. He flipped to the local news, Channel 8 of course, and began to eat. Nothing was on the news about Santini's death, but he watched the broadcast intently while taking bites of the grinder. After the 30-minute local news, the network news show came on and he was surprised when he looked down and saw he had eaten most of the sandwich. He made it through half of the network show and then became antsy. Time for a glass of wine, a cigar, and wait for the inevitable.

When the first cigar was smoked to the nub he waited for his glass to be empty before he went in and replenished both. When his glass emptied first he didn't wait for the cigar, he went in for a refill right away. By the time he had smoked four cigars and had drank six glasses of wine, the watch on his left wrist, although fuzzy, indicated it was 10 pm. He had already moved from the bistro chair to the full-length beach chair Carmel used to use to sun herself. Shortly after draining his glass, he passed out, still waiting for the taxi to the moon.

At 4 am the night chill woke him up. Danny was shivering, had a hangover, and had a taste in his mouth that was roughly the equivalent of a camel's ass. He dragged himself inside, stripped his clothes off as he made his way to his bed, and covered himself up to his chin with the heavy comforter. He was back in a deep sleep before he even warmed up.

CHAPTER 32

Danny didn't wake up until well after 11 am. He quickly took care of the pounding in his head and drank three glasses of water to try and get rid of the dry mouth. He thought back to the previous night and vaguely remembered, somewhere between the fourth and fifth wine, standing on the deck and yelling into the night sky, inquiring why his off-world friends were taking their sweet time ending this thing.

He went out to the deck to get his wine glass, looked up and said, "Oh well, I gave you guys your chance. I'm going back to where I left off and continuing with the plan. I'm too busy to fiddle fuck around, you want to, you know where to find me."

The Healer had no guilt for killing Santini. It was what he had to do, for himself. He washed out his glass, got cleaned up, and called Franti for a ride to Air Force One.

He called his people in Switzerland and told them to meet him at the airport in Rome, he would be there in about ten hours. Carlos hung up the phone and looked up how long it would take to drive to Rome. He discovered that they would get there at about the same time as the boss, he went to find Luis and Cassandra to tell them vacation was over.

As it was, Carlos didn't know how close his guess would be to his group and Air Force One getting to Leonardo Da Vinci International Airport. Danny landed 20 minutes after the SUV parked in the passenger pick up lot. The same deal was made as in France to house their aircraft until they needed it again, and then they all drove to a nearby hotel for a quick dinner and then sleep, they were all exhausted from the traveling. Over dinner he explained to the others that Italy was going to be different than any other country they had visited so far. Not only did they have to visit the Italian government, but they had to deal with the Vatican, the Pope, and the Catholic Church as a whole, who he had already pissed off. They would probably be here for two weeks or more.

They visited the Italian government first, which took two days, and then went into Rome for one week, just like they did with every other country. It was Danny's intention to treat Vatican City like another country, which it kind of was.

By this time, everywhere they went, The Healer was recognized immediately, and it was no different when he entered Vatican City. What the group wasn't aware of, prior to that morning, was that this sovereign state had its own government, the head of which was a president. They had decided to start there and with a little direction, located the building that housed the offices of that person. They met little resistance getting into the building and when they did encounter a guard, Danny took care of that with a mere touch. He did the same when he was introduced to the president and it was his plan to use this man to get an audience with the Pope. That plan only got them into the front door to where His Eminence actually resided. They were met by one of the Pope's advisors who said the pontiff was a very busy man and they should have made an appointment because he was not free to meet with them today. Danny inquired when the Pope was available and he was given a one hour window, three days from then. The president tried to intervene and there were some heated words in Italian but in the end the president raised his arms in defeat and explained to the group that he could not help expedite the meeting. The five of them began to walk back to the entrance and Danny thought they were getting the same treatment as Karen received. They would come for the meeting in three days and be told that the Pope didn't feel well or some other excuse, He knew when he was being lied to.

Danny stopped, turned around, and headed back toward the priest while he talked. "Listen, I'm not here to make anyone do what they don't want to. If the Pope doesn't want me to touch him, I won't. But please don't waste my time with the promise of a meet that will never happen. If the Pope gave you orders to shine us on, give me the courtesy of telling me the truth, we will leave and not return, but if I remember correctly the Pope himself came out and said he wanted to talk to me."

"Mr. Warburton, I will be putting your appointment with his holiness in the book, but occasionally situations arise that require his personal attention and schedules must be altered. That being said, every effort will be made for you and the Pope to meet three days from now."

The Healer chuckled "You know who I am and the fact that I have certain powers, things that I can do, part of which are heightened senses. Let's just say that I know when people are lying to me. You were slightly harder to detect than most, you must be very good at it. Tell the Pope that we won't be coming back, I'm sort of busy myself."

Danny made it to the exit and had his hand on the door handle when he heard another door open to his left, from inside the building, and then saw the Pope, dressed in his usual all white, in a wheel chair, being pushed by one of the Swiss Guards.

In a shallow voice his Holiness said, "Please, Mr. Warburton, come back inside. I do not wish you to leave with such a negative opinion of us."

The man in the chair seemed weak and frail, not what Danny was expecting. "Pardon me sir, but it wasn't that long ago that I saw you on television and you appeared to be quite healthy then. Has there been a change?"

"Back a few months ago I could still stand for short periods of time. I have been diagnosed with Cancer. The doctors tell me that it started in my liver and has spread to several other organs. I found out not long before the press conference I gave concerning you. I had hoped to keep this news to myself and therefore the reason to come up with excuses to cancel meetings and appearances."

"I am sorry." Danny moved closer to the sickly pontiff. "If you believe everything you read, I can help you with that."

"I have thought of that, but also have thought that you might be disrupting the natural order of things."

"I never really thought about it that way, I believed I was helping people live a better quality of life. Look at the way the world is today, man has screwed it up pretty good, maybe I am restoring the natural balance."

The Pope looked as if he was contemplating his response. "But death is the natural order, without it the world will become overpopulated and we will be unable to house and feed everyone."

"Sir, there will still be death, but I must disagree with you on the fact that we would not be able to feed the entire world. If man were to put as much effort and money toward fixing the social problems of its own as he does in waging wars, then I think there would be incredible advances in agriculture and livestock."

"You think you can stop all wars?"

"Not today, but tomorrow, yes I can."

"Then I will accept your assistance. I can see there is no deception in your eyes, you truly believe you can do the things you say."

The Pope then reached out with his hands, taking hold of Danny's right one and pressed it to his forehead. Seconds later the Pope rose from his chair, leaned into The Healer's right ear and with tears falling down his cheeks said, "The pain is all gone! Thank you, even though we Catholics rejoice in the eventual meeting of our father, death is still frightening. I still believe in God and the fact that Jesus Christ was the son of God."

"As you should, I don't change people's religious beliefs or opinions."

"Some here in the Holy City thought otherwise. Would you and your friends stay a few more days as my guest, there are several others that I would like you to meet."

"Sure, we can do that. My research shows that Vatican City has about 1,000 residents, I can meet with all of them if you would like, it wouldn't take long at all."

"I can assure you that some of them will not shake your hand, but we can set it up and they can make their own decision."

"Exactly"

The following morning a hasty press conference was called by the leader of the Catholic Church. Even though it was late notice, over 30 news agencies from around the globe were in attendance. The Pope looked healthier than he had in months as he told the cameras that he had met with Daniel Warburton and although there were still points of disagreement between them, in the interest of peace and harmony in every corner of the world, he was giving his full support to his cause.

# # #

Across the Atlantic, in a rectory that was behind one of the oldest churches in the country, two priests had very different reactions to what they had just heard come from Rome. One of them sighed deeply as another pillar to the younger priest's theory had fallen. This was a good thing, there were no demons or Satan himself involved, the old man started to question if there was a devil at all. He could finally put this thing to rest. The other priest sat in shock, he felt a mixture of despair, disgust, and anger at everyone involved in this mess. He asked himself how he could be the only one who saw the truth of this situation. Maybe this was how God chose to fight this fight, through a lowly priest not long out of the seminary. Then and there, Paul vowed to do whatever he must to resolve this Warburton situation and not let down his Lord.

The next morning Padraig and Paul met for breakfast, as they had done for nearly a year. He saw that the younger priest was agitated, no doubt due to the Pope's press conference, and he tried once more to convince Paul he was on the wrong track.

"Father Sikora, not much of an appetite this morning I see. I know you feel that I am not up to the task, but my health improves daily. Let me help you with your burden, tell me what is troubling you."

"Did you watch the Pope's speech yesterday?"

"Yes I did."

"Then you know what the problem is. Satan has the endorsement of our highest office. He has been running around Europe brainwashing the leaders of practically the entire continent and now Vatican City has fallen. And we sit on our hands and do nothing."

"There is nothing to do. I do not subscribe to your theory that Satan has possessed Warburton any longer. The evidence is just not there. Don't you think someone in Rome would have also thought of this, those who also could see through the façade? Logically I must conclude that we got it wrong, that this is exactly what Warburton claims it is."

"And what of his blaspheme of the Son of God, have you forgotten about that?"

"I truly do not know about that part of it Paul."

"So, on one hand you say you don't know and on the other you are sure, you contradict yourself. If you don't have the stomach for what has to be done, then stay out of my way and I will do it myself."

Sikora's voice rose to what was close to a yell as he spoke his last two sentences. He got up from the table and stormed out of the kitchen. Padraig sighed and shook his head as Katia entered the room.

"What was all that about?"

"Father Sikora is still young, and he gets quite emotional on certain subjects."

"He still needs to show respect to his elders."

"Not to worry Katia, he will get over his issues and will be back to his old self soon."

Katia made a noise and went back to her cleaning and Padraig began to believe what he had told her. Paul would get over this because there was nothing he could do about it and eventually, as time went by, his obsession with Warburton would fade.

Later that day Father Sikora approached his one-time mentor and apologized for his outburst at breakfast. He also suggested that he might need some time to himself and asked for two weeks to go home and visit family, and contemplate his priorities. Padraig smiled and thought this a grand idea, and the two men agreed that Paul would leave for Minnesota on Monday.

Sikora rented a car for the trip home not because he wanted to drive for 20 hours one way, but there was a specific reason he did not want to fly. He cut the trip in half, spending a night outside of Chicago and arriving in St. Cloud late on Tuesday. He had notified his parents that he was coming home for a visit and they were waiting to greet him and of course happy to see him. His mother was devout and could not be more proud that her son became a priest. His father went to church only on the holy days and that was just to appease his wife. Pitor Sikora also told his son that he was proud of him but Paul saw through the white lie. He knew his father wanted him to be a normal guy, with a normal job, and to find a girl to settle down with and give him at least one grandson who he could teach those things Paul was never very interested in, like baseball, football, fishing, and hunting. It wasn't as if Paul didn't try to be pals with Pitor, he went hunting three times and was actually a good shot to his own chagrin. The first two times he had to deliberately miss the deer he fired at, but the third time the deer moved into the vacant area Paul had aimed for and took the shotgun round in the hind quarter. The deer no longer had use of its back legs and fell where it was. Paul was as white as a ghost when they reached the fallen prey and Pitor's smile couldn't have been wider, until he put one into the suffering creature's head and his son turned and puked up breakfast. That was when Paul was 13, and his relationship with his father went downhill from there. It wasn't as if Pitor didn't love his son, he did and would always, they just weren't meant to take pleasure in the same activities.

Pitor and his wife were not at retirement age yet and still needed to work. Therefore, on Wednesday morning both of them left the house early and wouldn't be back until dinner time. This left Paul the opportunity to accomplish the task that was his real motivation for coming home. Being the hunter that he was, his father had close to a dozen rifles and shotguns, but he also kept four or five handguns in the house as well. He was not a collector, but did think it prudent to be proficient with different types of firearms just in case the need for one arose. It was one of those handguns that was Paul's target.

People, as a whole, were creatures of habit, and his father was no different. Growing up, Paul knew where the Sikora arsenal was kept and it was no surprise that it was in the same place. The gun cabinet was made of a sturdy metal and bolted to the wall of the basement, the spare key hidden behind a photo of Pitor holding up the head of an extremely large elk by the antlers, the elk, having recently expired was not smiling as Pitor was. The photo was on a six foot high shelf that held several other pictures of dead animals, on the opposite wall from the cabinet.

He selected a Sig Sauer 9mm semi-automatic which he knew nothing about and had never fired. He had never fired any handgun for that matter, but figured he had time to learn. He also selected two boxes of ammunition that were labeled 9mm, so he was sure the bullets would fit the gun in his hand. He took the hand written note out of his pants pocket that he had wrote the night before and placed the folded paper where the gun used to be. He wasn't sure how often his father opened the gun cabinet, but he didn't want Pitor to report it stolen to the police. Maybe by the time he noticed it missing, his father and mother would have already seen their son's face on the news and in the papers. Father Sikora took the gun and ammo up to his old bedroom, where he would be sleeping for the next few nights, and wrapped them in towels which went right into his suitcase, where they would sit until he was back at St. Veronica.

CHAPTER 33

The globe-trotting quartet did spend an extra week in Rome, taking in the sites, and sampling the local wine. Danny touched everyone he could, inside Vatican City and when he ventured out to the streets of the capital city. As he was with the politicians of Washington DC, he was pleasantly surprised by the residents of the Papal State. The people he met there represented the upper echelon of the Catholic Church, and considering the fact that all a person had to do was read one article about The Healer and they would know that he was an atheist, coupled with his comments on the life and times of Jesus Christ, he thought there would have been at least a few who'd shun him and several more with nasty looks. But of the 950 to 1,000 he had met who lived there, not a one was rude, and the two, a number far lower that even the Pope expected, who declined to partake of Danny's gift did approach him and spoke at length, they smiled, said no, and went on their way.

Eight days after the Pope's press conference, they packed the SUV and headed north, back through Italy and into Spain. The calendar advised all that it was the beginning of summer and the Spanish countryside was visually amazing. Carlos and Luis were much more comfortable here, which anyone would be who knew the language. Even though both of their ancestors came from Puerto Rico and the Spanish spoken there was somewhat different, they had very few problems with the local dialects.

The crew got back to the pattern they had developed when they started this trip of eight days in each country as long as the governments only took up one day. Spain and Portugal were that way and then they needed a day to travel. They went back through France and found a ferry to take them and their vehicle across the channel to the United Kingdom. Two days were spent on the government in London, one for the royal family, and then onto Scotland. They left the SUV in Scotland and took another ferry to Ireland. Warburton was an Irish name and Danny wanted to feel sort of at home, like Carlos and Luis did in Spain, but he didn't speak the language. Not that it was a problem as most of the country spoke, what he could only describe as a form of English. There were times over the next week that no matter how many times the Irishman who he was speaking to repeated himself, Danny still could not understand their words through the accent. He also had never done any research about what part of the island his ancestors came from and didn't know if he still had relatives living there today.

The ferry dropped them off in Northern Ireland and they rented another car for the drive to Dublin. Danny let Carlos take the wheel and as he looked out of the window at the passing towns he thought of the man who was from this land and who had made the bomb that had killed his family and he was reminded of a novel he read years earlier, Trinity, by Leon Uris. In that book Uris described Ireland as "a terrible beauty," thinking of Flannigan and witnessing the countryside, Danny began to understand what Uris was talking about. This place should have been better for The Healer, being Irish, he always wanted to come here, but that would have been more in the lines of a vacation. Because of the different emotions he was feeling, he never could shake the melancholy mood that enveloped him on that first day, until they were back on the same ferry, going in the opposite direction.

They made their way back to France and then it was on to Norway, Sweden, and Finland, which they were all grateful that those countries were visited in the summer months. Their next destination was Moscow and they had a minor issue at the border. Danny had called the Russian ambassador to the U.S., Anton Malakov, who he had hit it off with at the United Nations. He had arranged for Anton to meet them at the border crossing to facilitate their entry, Anton was late and Danny almost had to resort to his talents to keep the guards from shooting all of them. Anton arrived 45 minutes late and only could offer as an apology, uproariously laughing at their predicament.

They ended up staying two weeks in Moscow, not because the government took too much time, but because these people, for having such a reputation for being cold and distant, were the most gregarious they had met so far. Everyone wanted to take them out to dinner and drinks afterward. The president of Russia was more reserved and formal but Anton knew everyone by name and it seemed they all owed him a favor. Danny didn't mind spending the extra time there, he liked Anton to no end and he had something else on his mind. Most nights he would excuse himself after only one or two drinks and retire to his hotel room to be alone. Since they had left Ireland, he called Karen much more frequently, they were getting closer and becoming frustrated at the distance between them. He also was thinking of his traveling partners, there hadn't been one incident where they had to step in and provide the security they were there for. He was starting to think he was wasting their time. Cassandra and Luis had been sharing a hotel room since Spain and might want to start thinking about children, and Carlos had not seen anyone in his family since before Washington. A part of him thought he was ruining any chance they had of leading normal lives. After he had made his decision, the group stayed in Moscow two more days, just to wrap things up, and then their leader, boss, and friend called the three of them into his hotel room for a meeting.

"First off, I want to say that you guys, and gal, have been incredible during this entire trip. I couldn't have done it alone. I had some good times and I hope you all did too. At the least you've seen things and have been to places you probably never would have your entire life. You have all grown so much, taken on responsibilities and matured, it's a long way from Mount Pleasant and I'm not talking about the distance. But you are here tonight because I have come to a decision, I'm calling it. Tomorrow we take the car to Italy, get into Air Force One, and head back to New Britain."

Carlos, always the spokesman for the unit, said, "Whatever you say boss, we will take a break, charge up the batteries, and be ready to go when you say so."

"No Carlos that isn't what I want. Your part in this is over. Not because I don't like you guys, shit, just the opposite, I love you all. This is something I have committed my life to but how long was I going to drag the three of you along, 10 or 15 years, that is not fair. I want you to have a chance at a normal life, get married, have kids if you want, and that simply will not happen if you follow me all over the globe. Besides, pretty soon Cassy will be putting on weight in the form of a baby bump. And then what will we do?" Cassandra smiled and instinctively put a hand over her belly. "And Carlos, how long has you security company been running?"

"Six months."

"Without you, go home and build that business into an empire like I know you can. The traveling will be different for me also. I've been thinking that I will make Bradley Airport my base and only go away for a month at a time. Fly to an area and visit three or four countries, then come back and drive around the states for a month, visiting different cities, then take a few weeks off. After that, I would start the cycle all over again. Give yourselves at least a year, and if you get the urge to come with me on one of the short trips, that could be arranged."

Danny had acquired a bottle of champagne from room service before the meeting. He uncorked it and the four of them shared a drink, then handshakes and hugs as they left his room. In the morning, they began the long drive to Rome, which took two days, and then what seemed like the shortest flight they had been on since they left New York, into Hartford. He didn't want to bother Franti again so he rented a car and drove his security team to their homes, he also wanted this last leg of the longest trip any of them had ever taken, to be just the four of them. It was after midnight when he pulled into his driveway and saw his Santa Fe parked there. He was a little surprised to see it as he had forgotten where he had left it. He told the spotless interior of the rental "Maybe I do need some rest."

He didn't wake up until noon the next day. He was exhausted the night before when he got home, but he still went out to the deck and had two glasses of wine and a cigar. During that time he spoke to Calvin and Hobbes, Carmel, Katherine, Sandra, and Jack, no one spoke back to him, but that was okay, some things he needed to get off his chest.

He needed to take care of some errands and make some phone calls but those would have to wait until after coffee. Danny hadn't told anyone that he was coming home, so his first two calls were to Captain Franti and Karen, who happened to be on assignment in Arizona covering a wildfire. His next call was to a landscaping company, when he left, he didn't think to have someone care for his yard and it was looking a little jungle like these days. He did however think to stop his mail, but he would have to go to the post office today and get what was there, probably a sack or two. So he kept busy with things of that nature for the next four days, and also visited a few people he hadn't seen for a while. When they spoke, Karen told him she had to go to Kansas for another story but then she had a few days off and she would come to Connecticut and they could spend some time together. He picked her up from the airport and they made plans to see each other the next day. Karen no longer had an apartment in Connecticut as Atlanta was her home now, she had gotten a room at a nearby hotel and that was where she was let off.

Danny was at the hotel early so they could grab some breakfast and then make the drive to New Haven where they then took the train into New York City. A cab dropped them off at the Bronx Zoo where they would spend most of the day. The plan was to head back early enough so they could freshen up and go out to dinner, but they didn't make it back to New Haven until 7 pm and they were both a little tired so the plan was altered. They stopped at an Italian deli and bought some fresh meatballs, pasta and sauce, along with a loaf of bread and made dinner at Danny's house. After dinner they cleaned up the kitchen and he poured them a glass of wine, he took two steps toward the back slider and the deck and then thought that he would feel weird out there with Karen so they sat on the couch in the living room and watched the TV. When their glasses were filled for a second time they began to cuddle, and before they were drained they were kissing. Despite the fact that they spoke quite often and told each other things they didn't tell anyone else and therefore felt close, they had not been intimate, and it was slightly awkward. Before it went further, they had gone back to cuddling and a short time later Karen had fallen asleep on Danny's shoulder. He finished his wine and then gently laid her against the couch pillows while he went into his bedroom. He returned a few minutes later and woke her by kissing her cheek.

Karen opened her eyes and tried to focus. When she remembered where she was she sat up quickly. "I'm so sorry, I didn't mean to fall asleep."

"I know, but there is no reason to be sorry. Listen, we have gotten to know each other well but because of the distances between us we have no experience with the intimate side of our relationship. My take on us is that we should go slowly with that part, enjoy each other's company before we enjoy each other's bodies. What do you think?"

"I was getting a little nervous wondering where the night would end up, slow is good for now, but not too slow, ok."

"I understand, and you don't have to wait for me to set the pace, you can put pressure on the gas pedal too."

"I will definitely keep that in mind."

"So for tonight, it's late and we both drank a bit, so why don't you sleep in one of the other bedrooms? Here, you can use these." Danny handed her a pair of summer pajamas he had gotten from his room.

Karen took the pajamas and only made it to the doorway of the living room before she stopped and turned. She held out the clothing and had a sad look on her face. "These are Carmel's aren't they?"

"They were all I could offer you, and they are only pajamas, I wasn't saving them because they were special, I just haven't done anything with the inside of the house yet. It's ok if you wear them."

Karen eased up "Still, it seems a little weird, are you sure these aren't yours?"

"I'm pretty sure mine are in my dresser, but I'll double check in the morning."

They both laughed and Danny walked her to the door of what used to be his daughter's room. After a long, lingering kiss, they parted and he said, "Good night. I had a great time today, it was a good start."

Karen smiled "Yeah, really good start." And then she closed the bedroom door.

They spent the next day together not doing anything particularly special, apple picking at a local orchard and then a late lunch. Karen had to take an early evening flight to her next assignment and Danny drove her to the airport. He told her of his plans to go to China in about a week or so and she said she was going to be out of town for most of that time but there was a day in New York that maybe he could meet her for dinner. They parted with the promise to each other that they would make an effort to meet in the city.

# # #

While Danny was exploring a new relationship, Father Padraig O'Malley was trying to mend one he saw slipping away. Since his return from Minnesota, Paul had kept to himself and answered Padraig's questions with as few words as possible and hadn't sat down at the breakfast table in two weeks. O'Malley had stopped following Warburton via the media, but not so Paul. He made copious notes and recorded what he thought to be the more important news reports and articles on a zip drive. He hid those items in his small suitcase that he kept on the top shelf of the closet in his bedroom, he felt he couldn't trust anyone.

Padraig knew the problem, his mentor was no longer on the stop Satan team and Paul believed he was alone in his mission. Therefore he knew it was up to him to fix this and bring his young charge back into the fold, a confrontation was in order.

O'Malley stood outside the closed door and went over his argument one last time, then he knocked on the door and didn't wait for an answer. He raised his voice and said, "Father Sikora, it's Father O'Malley. I'm coming in." He turned the knob and entered the room.

"This is an invasion of my privacy. Please leave." The voice was quiet but firm.

"Not until I've had my say. This Warburton issue has become an obsession with you, and it has caused you to turn your back on the church and me. I was never sure one way or the other, but you will not even consider any other option. Since I got out of the hospital, I am seeing this thing more clearly. Your theory doesn't add up, and I fear that if you continue, you will be too far for me to help you. All I want is for us to communicate again, so let's talk."

"I have nothing to say to you. Have you not gotten the clue over the last few weeks? Ignoring you has been deliberate, and it will continue to be so. I'll ask you again, please leave."

Padraig stood still for a moment and looked into Paul's eyes. When he saw nothing but hate, he turned and left.

# # #

The day after Karen went to her next story, Danny picked up on his errands where he had left off. Before he went to Europe, he had set up automatic payment of all his bills through the bank account that held all of the donations from when Hope was up and running. He thought he should go to the bank and check on the balance of that account. To his surprise, the donations were still coming in at an alarming rate. He discovered that the account now held over three million dollars and took in more than it paid out each month.

He had to admit the European trip didn't cost him much. He and his companions were given their hotel rooms, dinners, gas for the SUV, and most of the time, fuel for Air Force One was also on the house. He decided that when he returned from Asia and started the first leg of the U.S. cities tour, he would bring some of that money and give it to those he came across that were the most needy. The idea being that when he was all done, he envisioned a Utopian society where money would be obsolete, or he would die before he was done, and he wouldn't need money anyway.

His next mission was to find a couple more guys to take the place of Carlos, Cassandra, and Luis. He had two people in mind but he wasn't sure he could convince them to go, he headed for the New Britain Police Department. He found Tim Grey at his desk in the detective bureau and a bystander would be hard pressed to tell which of the two were gladder to see the other. After some small talk Danny got down to the reason for his visit, Tim was hesitant, he had a wife and young children to think about.

"Four to six weeks max, Tim. You could take a leave of absence from here, and I would pay you for your time."

He wrote a figure down on a Post-It note from Grey's desk and showed it to the detective, which made his eyes go wide.

"That sure is generous, but I still have to discuss this with the wife."

"Understandable, could you get back to me in a few days?"

"I will bring it up tonight and call you either tomorrow or the next day."

At that moment Danny looked up and saw the captain of the Investigations Division enter the room. Franti walked into his office and didn't even get the chance to sit down before his ex-sergeant was fucking with the cigars in the box he kept on the corner of his desk, which Danny now had his feet propped on.

"I knew I should have called out sick today."

"Good to see you too buddy. Say, you got a light for these cigars in any of those drawers?"

"You can't smoke in this building"

He put the cigar in his shirt pocket. "Killjoy, anyway I didn't come here to break your balls, and I know I've asked you this before, but I could use your assistance on a trip I'm taking."

"Damnit Danny, you can't show up and ask me shit like that. You're going to put me between a rock and a hard place with Gina again."

"It's not going to be like before. From now on my trips will only be four to six weeks long. We stick to the air and to business. I've already spoken to Tim, my hope is that the three of us can take off in two weeks. You have enough vacation time, and I pay $10,000 a week."

"Holy shit! But that might make things with Gina a little easier. If we ain't back in six weeks, I jump ship and make it home on my own."

"You won't have to do that," Danny said as he stood and headed for the door. But before he went through it, Michael had one more question.

"Hey, you didn't tell me where we are going."

"China, Korea, Vietnam, and Japan."

"Oh hell, no wonder you want the best at your side."

He left the office laughing and caught Tim's eye as he continued toward the exit of the Bureau. "Detective Grey, if you decide to go, it will be me, you, and the captain. That should be fun."

As it turned out, both Tim Grey's wife and Gina Franti encouraged their husbands to accompany Danny to Asia. The two career police officers were astonished by the size and luxury of Air Force One when they arrived at Bradley Airport with six weeks of clothes packed in two large suitcases each. They were informed by the aircraft's staff that a laundry was on board, so next time they could pack a little lighter. Danny was already there and showed them around the plane and then to their rooms. Not long after the tour they sat in one of the lounges and had a drink while the plane taxied and became airborne.

The trip lasted the full six weeks because it was actually five countries, including two Koreas. They had delays getting the Chinese and North Korean governments to convene on short notice. Back when he addressed the United Nations, the representatives of those two countries did not stick around for a face to face, so he didn't have any contacts to set things up prior to his visit. But to The Healer, those were minor bumps in the road. What he was right about was that the three men had a good time. The people of all the countries they visited were hospitable to down-right friendly. They tasted the local cuisine, beer, and wine, took a side trip to see the Great Wall of China, and caught a baseball game in Japan. And although they had fun, by week five Grey and Franti were anxious to get back to their families. Danny also was eager to return. He and Karen had wanted to see each other in New York, but that didn't come to fruition as she was sent on an emergency assignment. He found that he missed her, which got him thinking about how he felt about her. When Carmel had been alive, he knew that he would never fall in love with another woman, but things were different now. He thought he could love Karen. Before that happened, though, he would have to talk to some people. Tops on the list would be Jessica and Ted McNiff.

Karen was the first person he called upon his arrival home. She told him she only had a few minutes, as she was preparing to interview a movie actress who was about to be released after serving 90 days in prison for her third DWI arrest. She was in New York right then but couldn't stay, three hours from now she was going to be on a plane back to Atlanta. She explained that she was scheduled for several meetings over the next four days that she simply couldn't miss. She promised to call him tomorrow night.

Danny was slightly saddened by the missed opportunities with Karen, but he kept himself busy planning the next endeavor. He would return to the road but stay in the United States for the following two weeks. Driving an RV, he would stay in a city for two or three days and try and make a looping route so he could end at least close to home. First he had to buy what he would eventually call "Rolling Hope" and outfit it with all the supplies he would need. He found the vehicle that suited his needs rather quickly. The dealership he went to was large and must have had 75 models on the lot. Price was not an issue as long as it had what he was looking for; a large bed for himself with room for three more, a shower, toilet, and cooktop. He wanted a full size fridge but had to settle for one that was a bit smaller, but not as small as a dorm sized one. It took most of the next day to get all of the supplies he needed and to pack two weeks of clothes into it. He wanted to just take off and wing it as far as a route, but he knew he would be out there for months if he didn't have an itinerary. So he located the old atlas he had in the house and mapped out the places he would stop. He thought about who he was going to take with him and had some names in mind but by that time it was late in the evening, he would call some people in the morning.

Over a simple breakfast of coffee and toast, he decided that was how he wanted this trip, simple. He cleaned up his dishes, went out to the driveway, got into the RV, and headed for his first destination, Providence Rhode Island.

The road trip took him to nine cities throughout New England and lasted three weeks. He had allotted two days for each stop but stayed an extra day in Providence, Boston, and Portland Maine. He was in phone contact most nights with Karen and he told her that he left on the trip by himself. She was slightly worried for his safety, she knew of his added powers and like himself, couldn't see how anyone would get the opportunity to do him harm. Franti, on the other hand, was a different story. Eight days into the trip, he got a call from his old boss who wanted to know where he was. Michael explained that he had been to Danny's house on several occasions and knew that he had not been home for at least a few days. He told the captain that he was currently in Manchester New Hampshire but would be leaving for Portland in the morning. When Franti discovered he was traveling alone, The Healer took his ass chewing and then told his friend that no one knew his route, he wasn't staying in one place too long, and finally let him in on the mutation that had occurred after the attempt on his life and the resulting additions to his capabilities. Franti was impressed but not convinced that his friend was completely safe because of what he could do, but he lost the argument and the solo journey continued.

His last stop was Hartford, Connecticut, and after two days there he was glad it only took 20 minutes to drive home. He called Karen and Franti and was happy to report that the entire trip was void of any security issues. Since the Vatican, Danny had been noticing the media was slowly waning in its coverage of his activities. What he was doing was still news worthy, hell, he was altering the course of human history, but it was also old news. It had been over a year since that first interview with Karen so people were getting used to what he could do. During his recent road trip, the local media in each city covered his visit, but the national news gave it a couple of minutes two or three times over the course of those three weeks. Danny likened this to NASA's shuttle missions, the first launches were big news with tons of coverage, but after a while, if one wanted to see a launch or touch down, one would have to tune to the Science Channel. The Healer preferred it this way.

He spent the next two weeks mostly at home. Bumming around the house, fixing a few things that needed taking care of, cigars and wine on the back deck, and watching the days get shorter as another summer got ready to make an exit. He was able to make that visit to Carmel's mother and by sheer luck Mel's brother was there also. Ted had just finished making a coffee for himself and poured one for his brother-in-law and brought the cups to the living room.

"I came here not only to visit, but to say something specific to Jessica, it was my good fortune that you are here too Ted because now I only have to say this once and it is going to be difficult for me. You both know that I loved Carmel with all of my heart and a piece of me always will, but I've met another woman. I would never think to disrespect the memory of Mel so I hope you can understand that, even though they messed with my brain out in space, I am still human."

Jessica had always used his formal name. "Daniel, Ted and I both know how you felt about Carmel and you treated my daughter and my grandchildren like they were royalty. I certainly didn't expect you to go through the rest of your life alone. We are happy for you, but I will continue to consider you as my family whether you remarry or not."

"Whoa, we have only been on a few dates and have agreed to take it slow, let's not talk about marriage yet."

Ted laughed, got up and hugged him. "My mother and I are in agreement on this one."

And then the conversation turned to Danny's travels. He got the impression that even if they were ok with him dating, they really didn't want to know any details of the woman, not just yet. They had a great visit and talked through the afternoon and he left with a little less weight on his shoulders.

Speaking of Karen, his travels and her job were keeping their relationship to one of phone calls. She did have one afternoon on the east coast where she was free to see him so he drove to Baltimore for an early dinner after which she had to catch a flight to Vegas. He was standing outside the restaurant when her taxi pulled up. Quick hellos preceded a kiss, which turned into another, and then another longer one. After five minutes they both realized where they were and opened their eyes to see the embarrassed look of an elderly woman who was entering the eatery with her husband and staring at the couple making out. Danny and Karen looked at each other and burst out laughing.

She whispered "Maybe our time would be better spent at a hotel."

"I'm of the mind to say to hell with taking it slow too, but when we finally get into the same bed together, I don't want either of us to get out until morning, and that can't happen tonight, right?"

Karen looked at the ground "I can't blow off this assignment."

"I know, and I understand that." He took her hand, gave her a smile, and said, "Let's go have dinner together and enjoy each other's company."

And so they did. They lingered as long as they could over coffee but eventually had to leave so she would not miss her plane. Once again he found himself driving her to the airport and just before she boarded, he asked her to think about sometime in the near future, quitting her job and going with him on his journeys. Karen opened her mouth to answer and he put a finger up to her lips and told her not to say anything right now, only to think about it. Then she was off to sin city.

The Healer waited until her flight was in the air and still didn't want to leave. He walked around the terminals of BWI airport, touching and talking to as many people as possible. He eventually made it out to the Santa Fe, six hours later, and even though it was late and he was tired, he made the five hour drive home. He watched the sun come up from his deck, snuffed out the cigar, and slept until it was dark out again.

CHAPTER 34

He sat at the dining room table looking through the world atlas and tried to decide which four countries he would travel to next. It had been a couple of days since dinner in Baltimore, and Danny was still riding the high he felt. He remained cautious, but started to think his personal life was coming back into line since the bombing. His revised plans for using his gifts, shorter trips, alternating between plane rides to other countries, and the RV in the United States, he believed, would lend itself to a less stressful situation and leave time for that personal life.

The Healer turned the page of the large map book and saw the countries of the Middle East. "So much for the new plan creating a less stressful life."

He knew he would have to face that challenge sooner or later, and he felt so good about himself and his direction that he decided right then that he would tackle the most volatile four countries of the region, Egypt, Syria, Iraq, and Iran. He briefly thought to bring three of four others as a security team but thought again, his party should be less assuming, they would probably get farther if they didn't look like any type of threat. Which brought him around to thinking of who he would take with him? Keeping with the theme of friendly instead of fierce, two females came to mind, one on the New Britain Police Department, and the other the younger sister of Cassandra, who also happened to be ex-gang. He was about to dial Cassy's number and stopped after six numbers, what was he thinking, he was going to take two women to places that didn't exactly have the best of reputations for treating the fairer sex very nicely. Okay then, unassuming men, Junior, another cop from New Britain and not his real name, he had been on for over eight years but he still had the face he wore in high school, thus the nickname. For the next 15 minutes, he tried to come up with another name but couldn't. He looked up and told the light over the table "Everyone that I know who can handle a weapon either looks like a cop or a gang banger. I guess you can't get much less threatening than two guys, and only one of whom is packing a gun."

The other problem with those four countries was that he had only met the UN ambassador from Egypt, so he didn't have any contacts for the remaining three. His hope was that after he was done in Egypt, the president there could make some calls and smooth the way into Syria and work Iran and Iraq the same way. Danny's thought was that they were all Arab nations and should, at the least, have lines of communication open between them.

So he had called his one contact and was now on his way to an audience with the president of Egypt with Junior, born Larry Hayes, aboard Air Force One. Of course, he and Larry knew each other, being on the same police department for years, but they never had the opportunity to become friends. They had been on opposite shifts when Danny was in patrol, and then he moved to the Detective Bureau and rarely had the occasion to speak with Larry. He wasn't even sure if he minded the nickname Junior, so he decided to stick with his given first name.

He had two bottles of beer in his hand when he found his security team of one in the aft lounge where Junior was reading a book. "Thought you might be thirsty." He said as he handed him one of the bottles. "Listen, Larry, I know you don't have any experience with foreign affairs and all, but stick close to me and do as I do. That way if I insult one of these people, so will you, and then they will shoot us both and you won't have to spend the rest of your life in an Iraqi prison."

"Thank you, that's very reassuring. But really, why did you choose me for this assignment."

"Your baby face, I didn't want to look threatening to those we are going to meet, but I needed someone who could handle themselves in a tense situation. You were the perfect combination of looking like you just graduated high school and a good amount of police experience."

"You expect resistance?"

"There are several different factors that concern me. First, we are American, not the most loved among the Arabs, second, we are arriving in the President of the United States' plane, which may look to them like we represent the government. Also, the countries we will be visiting have been tumultuous in the recent past, governments being toppled, citizens rioting, civil wars and wars between each other. The guy we are going to see first was elected president of Egypt only a few months ago. I'm not sure how this will play out, but I won't let us get killed."

"I have been the recipient of your gifts, so I know that all you have to do is touch the guys guarding the palace and you're in."

"I have tried to be a proponent of free will when it comes to my gifts. In the past I have given most of the people I have touched a choice. But in some instances I have not." Danny thought back to Santini's men in the pool hall. "But those have been few and far between. I will do everything in my power to prevent either one of us from being harmed, but I don't know if I will come in contact with the people of this region if they don't want to. On the flip side, if there was an area of the planet that needed my intervention, this would be it. I know I can bring peace to not only the Middle East but to the entire world, so do I force it down their throats?"

"Well, if you're asking me, I'd say yes. Give it to them even if they don't want it. You and I both know they will be better off for it. Are you saying you haven't made up your mind yet?"

"No, I haven't."

"We are going to be there in another five or six hours, you should step up that decision making process."

"I figured that I would wing it, that's what I've been doing so far."

Larry took a long pull on his beer as he studied Danny. "You're not joking, are you?"

He laughed and said, "No, I'm not joking. But don't worry, I'll get you back in one piece. You just keep your eyes open and let me know right away if you see something you don't like."

Junior nodded and shook his head before getting back to his book. Danny went back to his suite to make a phone call.

Egypt went better than expected. The new president met them with open arms. His new government wasn't completely set up yet, so it didn't take long to take care of everyone. They had time after to visit some of the sights of Cairo and a trip to the pyramids. No one tried to interfere when they spent the next six days on the streets of Cairo.

Before they left, The Healer had asked for an intro to the Syrian president, and what he received was better than he had hoped for. The Egyptian ambassador to Syria went along for the ride.

The Syrian government was not as hospitable as the other countries he had visited, even with the presence of the Egyptian. Most of them looked at Danny and Junior with distrustful eyes and kept their distance. They were losing time, as this was the third day of talking to the Syrian president and the leaders of their parliament, but it was the president who held most of the power here.

The Healer was about to force the issue when the president's wife emerged into the meeting room while pushing a child in a wheel chair. There was a brief, loud discussion with her husband, then she pushed the chair to where Danny was seated. It may have been the only English word this woman knew and it came out soft but with great emotion. "Please."

He looked at the child and could only guess it was the son of this woman and the president of Syria. He looked once at the man at the head of the table who seemed paralyzed with indecision, and then took the boy's hand.

Muscular dystrophy had landed him in the wheel chair but his mind was sharp and there was little else Danny had to do. He let go of his hand and the boy sat up a little straighter, his muscles were still weak and would have to be built up for him to use them as they were intended, but he summoned all of his strength and stood from the chair. He shook Danny's hand and said something in his native tongue that could only be "Thank You" and then he leaned on the table but moved his legs to go to his father and then hugged him. The Syrian president, long known for his autocratic regime and cold as ice exterior, sobbed in his son's embrace. The Syrian government no longer resisted.

For the next two days, he broke from the plan and ventured out to one of the smaller villages where poverty was the norm. These villagers were caught between the government and the rebel forces that occupied these outlying regions. Medicine and qualified doctors were scarce here so Danny was able to mend a variety of ailments and diseases.

When their time in Syria was over, he still wasn't sure of how he wanted to approach Iraq. The president of Syria promised him a convoy of vehicles if he chose to go by land, but he and Larry had discussed that and really wanted to keep their plane with them. The president explained to them that Syria and Iraq were mostly friendly and he could make contact with the president there and almost assure their safe landing. Larry whispered to Danny "almost", to which he received a shoulder shrug in response.

For all their worrying, Iraq went better than Syria. Right from the start the president set up a meeting with the parliament and The Healer took care of business in less than a day. The rest of the week went just as smooth but when it came time to ask for the same kind of help Syria gave when contacting Iraq, there was a snag. Iraq and Iran had a long history of not getting along. They had waged war against each other not so long ago and the distrust lingered into the present. The only semi-bright piece of information they were given was that over the past year or so Iraq and Iran had opened up diplomatic communication in an attempt to mend their differences. Contact was made between the two countries on behalf of their guests but Iran was not very receptive. The president of Iran was the contact point and did agree to allow Air Force One to land at Imam Khomeini International Airport but with an escort of two Irani jet fighters. An hour after Danny accepted the terms he and Larry were airborne once again, but not before being cautioned by the Iraqi officials. They explained that the Irani president does not hold the seat of real power in that country, which was reserved for the Supreme Leader who was a high cleric in the Islamic faith. He may step in and trump the president in which you will be at his mercy as he will take over your visit.

As soon as they entered Irani air space they picked up their escort which brought them to the airport without incident. The crew was to stay with the aircraft, another of the stipulations, so Danny and Junior were the only people exiting the plane. When they exited the ramp that led from the plane to the terminal they were met by at least two dozen Irani military. Six of these were kneeling and had their rifles trained on the two men. Another seven weapons were aimed at them from a second row that was standing behind the kneelers. The travelers were instructed, by use of an interpreter, to leave their carry-on bags where they were and to proceed forward about 20 feet further into the terminal, when they did so five more men flanked them and also aimed their rifles in the direction of the Americans.

They were searched and when nothing was found they saw a tall figure with a long black beard and dressed in a robe come from around a nearby corner and approach them. Danny knew this was the Supreme Leader and what the Iraqis had told them had come true. The man had five of his own bodyguards but none of them walked in front of him, which would be a sign of weakness. The Supreme Leader, Alija Khomeini, came to within five feet of the two unwanted visitors and stared into The Healer's eyes.

When he spoke, it was English. "You are American, you come in the plane of the President of the United States. I do not trust you. It was an error of the man who used to be president of our country to allow you to come here. But since you are here, you will now be treated as trespassers, and after you are both interrogated, you will be put on trial as spies."

Danny didn't say anything, but continued to look into the eyes of this brute. Many thoughts were going through his mind at a rapid pace. Should he make a move on the supreme leader now, or wait until there weren't so many guns pointed in their direction? If he did make his move now, could he stop the bullets from that many guns? He knew if he took hold of Alija and worked the orb he would then have him as an ally, but he would not be able to stop any bullets because of the fugue state when using the gifts, and Junior would die. If he waited until later, perhaps when they had them in a prison, he might lose contact with Junior and again there was the chance he could end up dead. He decided free will wasn't going to work here and if the entire planet wasn't on the same page, his plan was doomed. All these thoughts and his final decision were done in the blink of an eye, and then he reached out as quickly as he could and grabbed the left wrist of Alija. Not to disappoint, the room erupted in gun fire. Danny did not use the gifts on Alija but instead concentrated all of his energy on the projectiles hurtling toward Hayes and himself. His mind circled the room with lightning speed and stopped each bullet individually. He didn't hesitate and sent out another burst of energy around the room again and gave everyone the hardest shove he could. He knew this would give him the few seconds he needed. Danny still had hold of Alija and worked his magic. A second later he let go and the tall cleric sat down hard on the floor. The Healer looked around the room to determine which of the soldiers were recovering and becoming a threat again. What he saw shocked him, those who weren't stopped by walls or columns were about 25 to 30 yards away and none had tried to get up as of yet. Those who were closer were wrapped around columns or in a heap at the base of a wall whose sheetrock had a hole in it the size of a man. Those unfortunate ones were unconscious, some with obvious broken limbs and others bleeding from head wounds.

Danny turned to Junior and in his best Bullwinkle voice said, "Don't know my own strength."

He moved around the room and fixed the damage he had caused. When he was done, Alija had regained his composure and addressed Danny.

"I beg of your forgiveness, I have ruled poorly."

"You don't owe an apology to me, but I think you owe one to the people of this country. You should start by making things right."

"Today starts a new era of peace, prosperity, and equality for all citizens of Iran. And you may stay here as long as you wish and want for nothing."

"We are going to stay for as long as we have in all of the other countries we visited, one week. Today we will make contact with your advisors and others who are part of your government, which includes the guy who used to be president and allowed us to land here. The next six days I will wander around the city and heal as many as I can before we leave."

"As is your wish sir."

On the ride into the city Larry Hayes whispered to Danny "I didn't know you had powers with that capability."

"I haven't been using them, just in practice, but not in a situation like the one we faced. I think I almost killed some of those guys. Keep that part under your hat for a while at least, ok?"

"Sure, I can keep a secret, can we go now?"

He laughed and told Junior that the week would fly by and they would be on their way home before he knew it. That in no way stopped Junior from being on edge for the rest of their time in Iran. Of course the week did end and they returned to the airport and took off as soon as possible. Halfway home Danny emerged from his room and handed Larry a check for $40,000.00.

Larry looked at the amount and whistled. "Very nice, thank you, but next time you pick me for a trip could it be to Hawaii?"

"You've earned an easy trip in the future."

Danny hadn't slept well since the incident in the airport when they arrived in Iran. He knew he had expended a lot of energy but thought he would rest up during the following six days. It seemed to him that he could never get complete rest. Now he went back into his room and meant to call Karen but had laid down on the bed and didn't stir until they landed in Hartford.

Four days home and he found himself bored. Nothing around the house needed fixing, Karen was off on some natural disaster story in the Far East, and every book he tried to start couldn't keep his interest. He had lunch with Franti but that was cut short by a phone call that had the Captain summoned to the prosecutor's office to discuss an upcoming court case. He had talked to Karen on the phone each of those four nights and she told him she was giving his proposal of being his permanent traveling companion a lot of thought but she needed more time to make a decision. He did not want to pressure her so he didn't bring up the subject again.

The plan was to take two weeks off and then take the RV out again, but the news that Karen wasn't going to be back for several weeks, coupled with the fact that he was getting antsier by the day, were the reasons he woke up six days after he had returned home and started to pack Rolling Hope.

Once again The Healer was the only occupant of the big vehicle as it rumbled south on I-95, headed for the Big Apple. This time he planned to hit all major cities so he counted on three days in each, except for New York. Danny decided he would do three days in each of the five boroughs, cross over the bridge to Newark, down to Trenton, onto Philadelphia, and then maybe to Atlantic City on the way back.

New York was a mob scene, everywhere he went he drew large crowds, but they were well behaved and seemed happy to just be part of and a witness to history. Newark and Trenton, it seemed, were cities struggling to keep their heads above water, not unlike many large cities in the Northeast that relied on manufacturing for jobs and taxes in the past and now found those sources dried up. Danny did what he could in the short time he was in both places.

He did receive some good news on his second night in Trenton, during their usual evening phone call, Karen was excited right from hello. She tried to hold it in until the time was right in the conversation but she failed and blurted out that she had four days off and could they meet in New York. The story she would have been working on had fizzled and she wasn't assigned to another. As they talked more her excitement was infectious and Danny was ready to head back that way tonight. She explained to him that she would be on her current story for one more day and then she would fly into JFK. That would work out for him since he had wanted to spend another day in Trenton because he had promised the crowd tonight that he would be back in the morning. Before he hung up he told her that he would pick her up at the airport in Rolling Hope. She was anxious to see it.

The last day in Trenton saw thoughts of Karen creeping across Danny's mind as he tried to concentrate on what he was doing. As the sun went down and the crowd dispersed, he hit the ramp to I-95 but this time north bound, back tracking until he reached NYC again. He parked in the lot of JFK, cooked himself dinner on the stove in the RV and then went inside the terminal for a few drinks and to mingle with the passengers there. He didn't want to spend the night in the RV alone, so he waited until he was good and tired before he returned and fell asleep not long after crawling between the sheets.

The alarm roused him at 10 am. Karen's flight was due in at 1 pm, so he didn't see a reason to get up early. The RV was rigged for satellite TV so over coffee he watched whatever national news he could find. After a shower he headed back into the terminal but didn't make a spectacle of his presence, he discretely touched those he came close to or had interaction with, such as the clerk in the small store where he bought the Post, and the airport employee who was wiping off the table in the cafeteria he was about to sit at with another coffee and the paper. Danny lingered there until 12:30 and then started to head for the gate where Karen's flight would debark. He stopped and thought about his coffee breath and went back to the store to buy breath mints. He killed the last 20 minutes standing at the floor to ceiling windows watching the planes take off and land, then he saw the plane approach the gate and he sat down near the doorway Karen would soon come through.

They saw each other and both of their faces lit up. He stood and went to her, a quick "Hi" from both of them and then a light kiss on the lips. He took her carry-on and they started for the parking lot, thoughts of Carmel crossed Danny's mind and he felt a brief pang of sadness and guilt because, at that moment he knew he was in love with the woman walking at his side. He pushed those feelings aside, he knew that Carmel wouldn't want him to be lonely. They had spoken of this a few times, mostly out on the deck, and they both said that in the event one of them should die young, the surviving spouse had to find love elsewhere, life wasn't meant to experience alone. Remembering those conversations with his wife now brought a smile to his face and in his mind he said to her "I'm going to move on Honey, but you will never be forgotten."

He put his arm around Karen's waist and said, "When was the last time you had something to eat?"

"I was able to finish coffee and a bagel before take-off this morning. Why, you thinking about buying me lunch?"

"We could grab a bite here, in the cafeteria. But I have the RV out in the lot and I was thinking more like cooking you something out there."

"You can cook?"

"I've gotten quite good since I've been driving that beast around and feeding myself."

"That sounds delightful then."

They walked out to the RV, which Danny had to park a distance from the terminal in order to find the two empty spaces he needed. Chicken with rice was on the menu, after which they sat on what passed for a couch and talked for hours. At one point Karen looked out the windshield at the darkened lot and then at her watch and realized how late it had become.

"Do you have anything in that fridge you could make for dinner, because by the time we made it into the city we would be hard pressed to find a restaurant still open."

After checking his own watch, he said, "Damn, I can't believe that much time has gone by. To tell you the truth I'm not that hungry, but I can find something for you if you want."

"Funny, I don't know why I mentioned dinner, I don't feel hungry either."

"But I could go for a glass of wine, how about you?"

"You must have read my mind." Karen shot him a glance. "Wait a minute, you can read minds, did you just…"

Danny interrupted her "NO I didn't, I don't do that very often and I wouldn't do that to those I hold dear."

That brought a smile to her lips as she whispered "Sorry."

Danny brought the two glasses back to the couch and they began to chat again. Halfway through the second glass, he leaned over and gave her a long kiss and when their lips parted he said, "Don't you think we've talked enough for tonight?"

She didn't answer with words, only to press her lips to his. This time there was no awkwardness and after ten minutes, where lips and hands were quite busy, Danny stood, took her hand, and led her to his bed. After they had both reached orgasm for the second time, they were cuddled together and he told her that he loved her. She never hesitated and said the same three words back to him. Thirty minutes later they both had the same thought, each marveled at the fact that they had enough energy for a third time, but neither voiced that to the other.

What Karen did say was "I can't believe I'm not even tired, and now I'm hungry."

Danny laughed and gave her his robe. He put on a pair of lounge pants and a t-shirt. They went back to the couch and snacked on crackers and cheese while they had one more glass of wine. Finally they went back to bed and drifted off as the clock approached 4:30 am.

He woke to the sound of running water, glanced at the clock on the shelf that he used as a night stand, and saw that it was a few minutes after twelve. He sat up in bed and propped some pillows behind his back and waited. He knew that Karen would have to come out of the shower to dry off, there wasn't enough room otherwise. The shower stopped a few minutes later and then she stepped out, her body glistening, and he sat back and took it all in. It took a couple of seconds before the naked newswoman noticed him ogling her, but when she did she didn't cover up, just continued to use the towel.

"Like what you see?"

"I thought I made that pretty clear last night."

His comment elicited a smile form her. "Yes you did."

Karen finished drying dropped the towel and stood for a moment. She then ran the five feet between her and the bed and jumped onto it. She rolled and sat up at the same time coming to rest straddling his legs, facing him. Another long kiss ensued which ended with her softly biting his lower lip. Danny started to put his arms around her and she rolled off the bed as quickly as she got on.

"Later tonight, I want to go into the city today, shop or maybe see a Broadway play and then have a fabulous steak for dinner."

"Sounds like a plan, let me shower and we'll get going."

"Are we taking this thing?" she asked, referring to Rolling Hope.

"I'm getting better maneuvering her, but finding a parking space in Manhattan would be hell. Could you find us a room for the next few nights while I'm in the shower?"

"Sure, with all the traveling I do, I have several downtown hotels in my contacts list."

With the reservations made and Danny dressed and ready to go, they both packed a small bag and walked to the terminal where they found a taxi to the hotel. They then proceeded to spend every moment of the next two days together. There were times they were involved with activities, and other times they just sat in a park, sipping coffee and people watching. That was during the day, at night they picked up where they left off in the RV. It seemed they both felt an urgency because Karen would have to leave shortly, but their lovemaking was not rushed. A cab ride back to the terminal ended their mini-vacation, but neither one was sad. They left each other happy and content, knowing they would see each other soon, and both feeling this was the start of something that could last the rest of their lives, of course, at that point, Danny wasn't aware of how many days he had left.

Karen's flight taxied away from the gate at 9:30 am but didn't leave the ground until 20 minutes later. He found himself at the same windows he was at three days ago, but this time watching the planes as they left. He knew which plane she was on and watched it until it was only a speck in the sky, and then he made his way back to Rolling Hope.

By the time the wheels of the RV hit I-95 again the digital clock readout on the dash read 10:30. The original route would take him to Philadelphia for his next stop. As he drove he figured he wouldn't get there much before 1 pm and he didn't want to short change the city of Brotherly Love, so he wouldn't start his three days there until the next morning.

Rolling Hope entered the city of Philadelphia at about the predicted time and Danny followed the highway signs to a mall, he could always find enough room to park the RV in a mall lot. He made a sandwich for lunch and decided he didn't want to spend the whole afternoon cooped up in the vehicle. As he ate he checked the computer for points of interest in Philly and then he remembered a commercial he once saw about the Cancer Treatment Centers of American and how they had a clinic in this city.

Danny had been thinking about Carmel on the ride down but there was no guilt attached, this was only the never forgetting part now. He also was thinking about his children and when the cancer place popped into his head, started to recall the early days of his powers. The trip to the Hartford Children's Hospital cancer ward and then the Dana Farber place also.

So that was what he decided to do, spend the rest of the afternoon at the treatment center. Before he left the mall lot, he checked an aerial shot of the center on the computer to see if there was room for the RV, there was. Five minutes later he was back behind the wheel, headed for what he thought was going to be a pleasant several hours curing cancer patients.

CHAPTER 35

The relationship between the two priests who were once friends could not be more strained. Father O'Malley continued to try to draw Paul out of his brooding state, but nothing seemed to be working. When the two would happen upon each other in the course of their daily duties, Padraig would always have a pleasant greeting or other comment for him, but his friendliness was greeted with a short "Hello Father," or nothing but a grunt. Recently the younger priest would not even make eye contact and passed by with only silence as his response.

Padraig thought maybe a transfer for Father Sikora would help the struggling young man, but then that would only be sending his problem to another church. O'Malley believed that this was his issue to fix and resigned himself to double his efforts to reach Paul. These thoughts and others were swirling around his head as he ate lunch alone at the kitchen table of the rectory. Katia had made him a sandwich without his consent because she knew he was on his way out and wouldn't stop to feed himself. When he protested that he did not have time, she indicated that he would have trouble finding the car keys if he didn't sit down and eat. He stopped arguing with her because she always got her way in the end.

For years it was the older priest's habit to visit a hospital or clinic once every two weeks just to sit and talk with the patients there. He had a standard rotation of about six different places and today the Cancer Treatment Center of America was next on the list. He'd stopped making these trips a couple of times, like the year or so that he was in his deepest depression, and when he was recovering from his heart attack. After both times, when he returned, he discovered that these visits were better for his recovery than anything else he had done.

Father O'Malley arrived at the clinic only 15 minutes prior to the RV known as Rolling Hope, and was well into his rounds when Daniel Warburton walked through the front door. The receptionist recognized him right away and asked if she could shake his hand, which of course he did. She then called the Director of Administration and paged several of the doctors on duty that day to come to the front desk. He met each of them with the usual hand shake or touch on the shoulder. He explained to them that he wanted to stay the rest of the day and make contact with as many patients as possible if not all of them. One of the doctors asked the receptionist to look up the day's patient list. After several seconds of typing she told the group that there were a total of sixty one patients being accommodated in the facility today. Danny was told that throughout the day patients visited the outpatient clinic, which could up the total by another 20 or 30. It was decided to start at the clinic, then ICU, which were both on the first floor and finish in the patient rooms working from the second floor on up.

Word traveled fast through the building and the news that The Healer, Daniel Warburton, was there to cure everyone found the ear of Father O'Malley before he had visited his tenth patient. At first Padraig became nervous and his pulse quickened, but then he took a deep breath, remembering that he did not subscribe to Paul's theory anymore. He also saw the look on the woman's face whose bed he was sitting next to, she sat up straighter, her eyes became brighter, and a tear spilled down her cheek to her smiling lips, and he thought, this can't be bad. Padraig was looking at the face of revitalized hope from someone who wasn't expected to make another Christmas. He knew that he must meet Warburton for a second time and also thought, if Father Sikora could meet him too, and see what was really going on with this man, then he would have no choice but to abandon the idea that this was some sort of evil plan. He went to the lobby to use the receptionist's phone to call the rectory.

Katia answered on the second ring. "St. Veronica rectory."

"Katia, this is Father O'Malley. It is important that I speak with Father Sikora. Do you know where he is?"

"I believe he went to his room after lunch. Let me go check."

Padraig heard the sound of the old style desk phone being placed on the table in the living room. A few moments later, he heard Paul's voice on the line.

"Father O'Malley, if you could please be brief, I was in the middle of something important to me."

Padraig swallowed the urge to chastise the young priest for his attitude and pressed on. "Paul, I am at the Cancer Treatment Center over on East Wyoming. Daniel Warburton walked in a short time ago. You were looking for a sign, well this might be it. He is here curing people like he has been for over a year. I believe we were meant to meet him again so you would have the opportunity to see that you are misguided about his intentions. Please come here right away, I truly think this is vital to your continuance in the priesthood."

Sikora was stunned, which produced a long silence.

"Paul, are you still there?"

"Yes, I will be there as soon as I can, maybe you are right." Paul hung up the phone before he lost his composure and called the old man something that would have given away his true feelings and jeopardized his plans. He walked back to his room fuming at the aging priest, and muttering under his breath "That idiot, talking to me like I'm retarded. He is the one with the wool pulled over his eyes." He closed the door as he entered and went straight to the bed, reached under the mattress, and retrieved the 9mm. He had purchased a holster with a clip on it and slid the clip over his belt at the small of his back and then checked himself in the mirror to see if the gun was noticeable with his jacket on. It didn't look too bad for the short-term mission he had in mind.

Twenty minutes later, the cab deposited Paul at the front door to the cancer center. He certainly did not want to make contact with Padraig, who would only get in the way. He also did not want to encounter Warburton until he was ready. He had a full clip in the Sig, but figured he only had one shot at sending the devil back to hell.

Padraig was giddy after speaking with Paul. This obsession of his might be finally coming to an end. He wanted to wait by the front door so as not to miss his arrival but was too nervous with anticipation. He thought he should go find Warburton and tell him what had been going on with Father Sikora, in case Paul became irrational, Warburton would be prepared. O'Malley set out in search of The Healer but gave himself only 15 minutes. If he didn't find the man in that time he would return to the front door, he wanted to be with his protégé when he came face to face with Warburton.

Father Sikora entered the lobby whose only occupant was the receptionist. As old men sometimes do, Padraig had lost track of time and was currently on the third floor after not finding Warburton on either of the first two. Paul engaged the young lady behind the lobby desk in conversation and told her he had heard that Daniel Warburton was there today and he had always wanted to meet him as he admired him a great deal. She informed the smiling priest that she was not being updated on his exact whereabouts, but she could make a few calls and find out. Sikora told her that he didn't want to trouble her and he would find him sooner or later, the building wasn't that big. He was about to turn and enter the first floor of the center when he subconsciously moved his right hand to the small of his back and touched the gun to make sure it was still there, a common habit of those who were not used to carrying a weapon. The receptionist didn't notice.

Padraig had just finished checking the third floor for Danny with negative results. He didn't know it, but he had just missed him as he had entered the stairwell that was near this end of the hall and went to the fourth floor. When he left the lobby, The Healer had an entourage of three doctors and the director with him. By the time he reached floor number four, he was on his own. One doctor stayed with the ICU patients after they were healed, just as a precaution, another doctor stayed with a patient of his, also after being cured, the director was paged to his office for a phone call, and the third doctor took a call on his cell and walked away from Danny, still talking. He didn't want to be bogged down, didn't know when any of them were coming back, so he continued on his own.

Father O'Malley looked at the door with the sign over it that read "stairwell" and headed back down the corridor to the elevators. He reached the fourth floor and looked down the hall but saw no one. O'Malley entered the first room he came to and heard the sobbing of a child. He pulled back the curtain to find a boy sitting up in bed, clutching his stomach as the tears flowed.

Out of habit Padraig closed the curtain and approached the bed. "Are you in pain, child?"

The boy groaned. "My stomach hurts"

"Have you called the nurse?"

"I hit the button, but no one came."

Padraig sat on the bed and put a hand on the boy's back. "There, there, this will all be over soon. A man who is here today will take away all of your pain and make you not sick anymore."

"Is he a doctor?"

"No, not a doctor, he's..."

From the other side of the curtain, they both heard, "Hello is anyone here?"

The curtain was pulled aside, and Father Padraig O'Malley looked into the eyes of Daniel Warburton for the second time. He wasn't afraid. In fact, he was relieved that the child would soon be free of the pain.

Danny looked at the face of the priest who sat on the bed, and it didn't take long for him to recall where they had met before. "I'm sorry about the last time we met."

"It is I who should apologize. You did nothing wrong."

"Are you sure about that? I recall trying to read your mind, and I thought I gave you your heart attack."

Padraig's mouth dropped and the boy let out another groan.

Danny said to Padraig, "Excuse me."

And then to the boy on the bed, he said, "I'm sorry, buddy. Here we adults are going down memory lane, and you're not feeling well at all."

The Healer put a hand on top of the boy's head, and several seconds later he rubbed his stomach as if feeling for the pain that no longer existed.

"Feeling better?" asked Danny. The smiling boy nodded.

He turned to address the priest and pointed beyond the curtain. "Why don't you and I talk over there?"

The two men moved to the other side of the room to continue their conversation.

"How did you know I was having a heart attack?"

"You needed help to get into the car. You were as white as a ghost, and you were clutching your left arm. Didn't need any special powers to figure that one out."

"I don't know if you caused my attack or not, but that doesn't matter anymore."

"Ok, how are you feeling now?"

"Except for the usual old man maladies, not too bad. I had by-pass surgery and seemed to be somewhat back to where I was before."

Danny raised a hand and said, "I'm not a doctor. But if you want, I can take a look."

Padraig couldn't remember the last time he laughed so loud and so long. When he finally stopped and wiped the tears from his eyes, he saw Danny's smiling face waiting patiently.

Father O'Malley stuck out his hand and softly said, "It's about damn time." And found that he yearned for this moment. Deep down, he'd wanted this touch from the day he heard what this man could do. He wanted all the aches and pains to go away but most of all he wanted the guilt he had been carrying over the Spellman incident to be lifted from his heart. He opened himself completely to The Healer.

Danny took the elderly man's hand into his own and began the journey through the body like he had done countless times before. The priest's heart needed a little cleaning up and there were several discs in his back that must be causing some pain. Quite a bit of arthritis in both knees, probably from all that praying, but except for tweaking the eyesight and hearing there wasn't much else. Then he went in search of the glowing orb but had a bit of trouble finding it. To his surprise there was no glow at all, only blackness. He wondered what kind of man this priest was. Upon further inspection, he found that it was not the orb that was black but there was a layer or layers of some kind of black material surrounding this man's orb. The Healer had never seen anything like it before. He "touched" the orb and discovered the coating felt hard and it was in many small pieces on top of each other. It came to him a second later, these layers represented months and months of guilt this priest had heaped upon himself and he discovered that the guilt was not from any act of his own but those of another.

Cleansing this orb took longer than any other he had done, it was if he had to chip each piece off and they didn't want to come willingly. He had been at it for minutes now instead of the usual seconds he was used to, and all that time he was in the trance that occurred every time he used the healing gifts. Danny wasn't aware of what was happening outside the priest's body.

Paul Sikora moved from floor to floor, asking any staff he could find if they knew the whereabouts of Warburton or Father O'Malley. Each time he was told they believed The Healer was on the next floor but no one had seen the other priest for at least 15 minutes. When he got off the elevator on the fourth floor and started down the hall, he heard voices from the first room and recognized at least one of the speakers. He stopped outside the door and listened for a moment. From the content of the conversation, he surmised that the other person Padraig was talking to was Warburton. Paul reached his right hand behind his back and under his jacket to retrieve the 9mm clipped to his belt. He held the gun out in front of him and entered the room as the voices went silent.

On the other end of the hall, the husband of the woman who was occupying the last room on the fourth floor had come out in search of another box of tissues. He and his wife had used up all they had in her room from crying at their good luck and her second chance at life, Danny had left that room a short time ago. Officer Jackson Johnson, JJ to his friends, had been on the Pittsburg Police Department for three years when he and his wife of two years were given the life altering news that she had breast cancer, and the prognosis was not good, until today. Even with tears still in his eyes he could have sworn that the man who had just entered the room on the other end of the floor had a gun in his hand. JJ was what the old time cops called a natural, he had a sense when bad shit was afoot, and the brains to follow his instincts, and that was what he did right then. Officer Johnson pulled his off-duty piece from the holster clipped to his right hip and began a cautious jog down the hall.

Paul's hands were shaking and he tried to stop this by gripping the gun with both hands as he moved slowly into the room. He saw the curtain pulled around the bed but it was obscuring the far side of the room. He inched around the curtain and first saw Padraig. His eyes were closed and he appeared stiff. His arms were out in front of him but Paul couldn't yet see his hands. Another two steps and he saw the being who he believed was Satan in disguise. Warburton also had his eyes closed and had a hold of Padraig's hands. Sikora was close to the curtain and gaping at the other two men in the room and did not see the bulge in the curtain inches in front of him. His left foot hit the four wheeled IV pole that was just on the other side of the curtain and the would-be assassin went sprawling. He took one hand off of the gun to put out in front of himself to break his fall. When he did hit the floor, it jarred the 9mm loose from his other hand and it skidded ten feet away. He thought he had lost his chance, glanced at Warburton and saw that he was still focused on Padraig. Paul was on all fours and frantically crawling toward the gun, reaching it seconds later, whirled around while still on his knees and pulled the trigger.

Paul Sikora wanted to go to a range with the gun once he brought it back to Philly, but never did find the time. Being inexperienced, he jerked the trigger, which pulled the barrel to the right, but not enough. Instead of full on to the back of the head, Danny took the bullet behind the right ear. It then went through a portion of his brain, exiting just above his forehead. The impact with the skull sent the projectile in a ricochet slightly right and slightly down. Being a half a foot taller than The Healer, when the bullet exited his head, it was directly in line with Padraig's neck and had enough momentum to find a second target. Father Padraig O'Malley's carotid artery was severed by the same shot that was now sending Danny to the floor. Padraig would soon follow, the only difference was the old priest would die from blood loss before the medical help arrived.

Jackson Johnson heard the crash of the IV pole hit the floor and he sprinted the last ten feet to the door of the room the noise came from. He made it to the doorway before he heard the report of the 9mm. He came around the curtain and saw two men on the floor, both of them bleeding. One he recognized as the man who had minutes ago cured his wife of cancer. He also saw a third man wearing the collar of a priest, kneeling on the floor, with a gun in his hand. JJ yelled for the shooter to drop the gun but the shocked Paul Sikora turned his whole body toward the shouting man who had just entered the room. He wanted to explain that he had saved the world from evil but as his body turned, so did his arm, and the hand that held the gun was now moving in the direction of a trained police officer. Jackson's instincts and training kicked in and he fired three shots at the armed suspect, all three found center mass, one making solid contact with the heart of the idealistic, misguided, young man from St. Cloud Minnesota, killing him instantly.

When the bullet first struck The Healer, the connection between him and Padraig was broken. Danny didn't have time to stop the bullet from entering his brain but he did have one second to think about what was happening to him. A flood of thoughts went through the soon to be damaged brain.

(I failed. I won't be able to fix myself after this one. I did my best, maybe it was enough to turn things around. Maybe that was what Jesus thought also, as he hung from the cross, but it hadn't been. Maybe the human race is too barbaric to become a productive member of the alliance of planets. Twice they killed the person who was trying to save them. I'm sorry Mel, all that for nothing.)

In his mind's eye Danny saw the face of Karen Ayala, then his children, one by one, and finally that of Carmel. He was able to linger for only a moment on the image of his wife before the damage to his brain became too much and it shut down, leaving blackness.

CHAPTER 36

A small part of Danny wanted to die, wanted it to be over, the part that was tired and more than a little bitter that he couldn't be left alone to do his thing. But there was also the part of his brain that controlled the survival instinct, and that part was undamaged and therefore more powerful than the part that was ready to throw in the towel.

Sure there were doctors in the cancer center, but those men hadn't dealt with a trauma patient in some time. An ambulance transported the only survivor of the shooting on the fourth floor, besides JJ, to the same hospital that Padraig had arrived in while in the throes of his heart attack and subsequent surgery for that broken organ. The entire staff at Pennsylvania Hospital in Philadelphia knew who The Healer was including the ER doctor on duty when the ambulance arrived. Working in a Philly ER room, Doctor Samuel Boyd was no stranger to gunshot wounds, but with this patient he was at a loss. He did read the article and interview in Time magazine of the doctor who treated this same man when a bomb also caused head injury, he just couldn't remember his name. Boyd gave instructions to put the patient in an ER room and continue to monitor his vitals as he headed for the nurses' station and a phone.

Boyd barked to the nurse at the desk "Get on the internet and find the names of any hospitals in New Britain Connecticut."

Less than 30 seconds later she responded, "Two, but it seems that the main hospital is New Britain General."

Boyd grabbed the handset of the nearest phone and said, "Give me the phone number."

The connection was made and after several agonizing seconds of listening to a recorded voice tell him to "Please listen, as our menu options have recently changed" he pressed one as that led him to the emergency department. The nurse who answered at the ER desk only had to hear two sentences and she knew who Sam was trying to reach, and he was standing not five feet from her. She handed the phone to Dr. Russell Levesque.

"Dr. Levesque."

"Dr. Levesque, this is Dr. Boyd at Pennsylvania Hospital in Philly, Daniel Warburton came in to my ER with a bullet in his head, there appears to be brain injury. I know..."

"Listen carefully, put him in a dark, quiet room and keep everyone out. Don't do any surgery, give him a standard IV but nothing else. No pain killers of any kind, keep him hydrated and I will be there within a few hours."

Levesque hung up and dialed the office number of Captain Michael Franti who in turn called Governor Martin Acevedo who arranged for Levesque to hop a ride on a Ct Air National Guard helicopter to Philadelphia.

News that Daniel Warburton was once again lying in a hospital room fighting for his life spread faster than wild fire. The City of Brotherly Love was overrun by those who wanted to be close to the fallen Healer. Within 24 hours traffic was a nightmare and a day later there were tent "cities" in every park and open space as far as ten miles outside the borders of Philly.

Russell Levesque took a room next to Danny but only looked in on him once a day, his real reason for being there was to ensure no other physician tried to intervene and screw things up. But this time was different. The bullet from Paul Sikora's gun caused damage deeper inside the brain than the bomb shrapnel did. Recovery was slower, much slower. No communication came from Warburton, which didn't concern Levesque at first, until week ten had come and gone and he was still in a coma.

After three months the cold and the snow forced the tents to come down and the only people left were a few die-hards who had RVs or could afford the hotel rates. Four months after the shooting at the cancer center even the die-hards called it quits, it was past time they had to go on with their lives. Even Dr. Levesque had to return to his family and job. The only person left who was in the city because of Danny was Karen Ayala. She had taken a leave of absence from CNN but recently they were starting to ask when she would be back. Karen put them off for another three weeks but they started playing hard ball and she had no choice but to return to work.

Spring had arrived, like it always does, and there were those who began to believe that he was never going to come out of the coma. Only a few came to visit, Franti drove to Philly once every two weeks and of course Karen came by when she could. They would sit and talk to The Healer, the doctors at the hospital didn't see a reason to keep the patient isolated any longer as they had no idea when he would regain consciousness.

There were two who did know what was going on inside the patient's head. Calvin and Hobbes had the power to reach down with their minds and check on Danny's progress. They could meld their minds to his subconscious and saw that there was healing, at a slower pace than before, but things were moving forward. About 22 weeks after he was shot, the two aliens had reached down once more and then conferred on a report to their home planet on the status of the experiment.

"He is nearing the completion of the healing process."

"And as far as I can tell there hasn't been any new mutation." Hobbes added.

"I have not detected any also. But even in an unconscious state he suffers from depression. I have studied this human disease and have found that, left unchecked, it may cause the subject to become violent with others or, more often to themselves. This must not happen. I acquiesced to your wishes not to intervene when Daniel killed the man who took his family, but a second incident will end this." Calvin said solemnly.

"I do agree with your assessment."

Two weeks later, in a hospital room in the city of Philadelphia, which had been occupied by the same patient for the last six months, Daniel Warburton opened his eyes. The room was dark and he didn't hear any noise or voices coming from the hall. He took the covers off and saw that he had on hospital pajamas, that wouldn't do. Up on his feet now, into the hall and past the nurses' station without being noticed. He did glance at the large clock on the wall at the station and saw it read 2:17. He guessed that it was 2:17 am by the muted lighting and the lack of activity on the floor. He continued through the hospital, not attracting any attention, until he found what he was looking for, the hospital laundry. Slipping through the door, Danny searched for a different type of clothing than what he had on. He found a shelf in the back with dark blue coveralls and another holding scrubs. He opted for the coveralls and found one his size, he stripped off the pajamas and stood there naked for a few seconds. He searched the shelves for a pair of boxers but knew he wasn't going to find any. He started to put on the coveralls and muttered to the darkened laundry "Looks like I go commando for now."

Danny was able to make it to the ground level without anyone seeing him, but didn't head for the front door. He knew a security guard would be on duty, so he looked for an exterior door elsewhere. The emergency exit he found was alarmed, but he used his powers to break the wires that led to the door contacts so when he opened it there would be no noise. Once outside he felt a slight chill in the air and he realized he didn't know what day, month, or even what year it was.

He walked for over an hour before he found a bus terminal that was open all night. He had no shoes or socks, no money, and no ID. He knew he would have to use his powers to get out of this little mess he found himself in but deep down he didn't want to. Danny was still depressed and fed up with humans. He wanted to be left alone and if he had to use the gifts to attain that goal, so be it, but after that he was done, experiment over.

The sun came up, and he went in search of a bank. He needed money and the donations account had plenty, accessing it shouldn't pose a problem. His initial entry into the first financial institution he came to caused a bit of a stir. He hadn't looked into a mirror since he woke up and his appearance was a wreck, long bed head hair, six months of beard growth, and bare feet. Danny walked directly to the manager's office and closed the door behind him. Ten minutes later the manager came out alone, went into the back and returned shortly with a large bank bag that looked heavy. She went back into the office and not long after, Danny came out holding the managers briefcase, shook her hand, and left the building. He didn't bother to look at the balance of the donations account but since he had been in the hospital donations had gone from about $200 a day to over $5,000 a day. The account had grown by nearly one million while he lay in that Philly hospital bed.

Next stop was to find some clothes and shoes. The bank manager told him he could find the Roosevelt Mall about eight miles up I-95 on Cottman Avenue. Danny didn't tell her he would be walking but he kept the highway in sight and soon found the large retail outlet he was looking for. He purchased a good sized backpack and then filled it with what he needed but didn't wear any of the items, not even the socks and shoes. Instead he inquired as to the nearest hotel for a hot shower, only after which did he don his new duds. The Healer was going to keep his long locks, that is until after the shower and he had to dry all that hair. He knew he wasn't staying the night at that hotel so he packed all that he had, including the money, into the backpack and carried the empty briefcase. Stopping at the first hair cut store he came upon, there were very few barbers left in this country and forget about finding a red and white barber's pole, he was back to his crew cut in less than 15 minutes. The beard, on the other hand, stayed, he just had the girl trim it up to look neat. Then it was back the way he came and into the same bank to return the briefcase.

Daniel Warburton stepped out of the bank and realized he didn't have a next step in his plan because he had no plan. What he did know was that he needed some time to himself, to sort things out, and to be anonymous, partly why he kept the facial hair. He wanted to go south so for now he would shadow I-95 because he knew that went all the way to the far tip of Florida, but he would have to buy a map or at least a compass to keep his bearings straight. He wasn't going to be touching everyone he met either, right now he didn't even want the gifts anymore, but he admitted to himself that his attitude might change as time passed. He decided that he would take things day to day and deal with shit as it happened, for the first time in his life he was going to completely wing it. Danny turned to a southerly direction and started walking.

Karen and Franti were understandably upset. They didn't know how a patient could be missing and how no one saw how he left. At first Karen thought someone had taken Danny's body, but the Captain was able to bully his way into the security offices of the hospital and view the camera footage that covered several floors and the exits. They saw Danny deliberately avoiding people as he moved through the hospital and then leave out of an emergency exit. The door was checked as to why the alarm didn't sound and the broken wires were eventually found, more evidence that he left willingly.

Karen was the one who first asked the doctors if it was common for coma patients to have amnesia when the first awoke. She was told that there were such cases but they were rare and many of them regained their memory relatively quickly. But the seed was sown for her, and she surmised that amnesia was the only logical explanation why Danny would leave and not tell anyone (her). This idea would become her obsession in the following months.

Another September came and went, along with Danny's birthday. He didn't notice. He never looked at a calendar and only knew the day of the week or the month if he inadvertently heard it from someone else. Over the summer, he meandered from state to state and slowly made his way south. He only spoke when he absolutely had to, and, true to his word, he hadn't used the gifts at all. He slept in hotels, ate when he was hungry, and kept himself clean and well groomed. He wanted to act like a hobo but not look or smell like one.

As tourists flocked to the northeast to view the foliage paint the landscape in reds and oranges, Daniel Warburton was walking along Route 59 headed into the small Texas town of Livingston on his way to Houston and the Gulf. He was walking up a medium sized hill and heard the crash before he saw it. Rushing to the top of the rise, he saw the mangled metal of the mini-van first. It was off the road near an intersection where the accident had just occurred. He next saw the beat up pick-up truck limping away from the scene. Danny opined to the two yellow lines in the road that the operator of the truck was a son-of-a-bitch and then he ran toward the smoking Caravan. The Healer was still 15 feet from the van when he pulled the door from its hinges and tossed it 50 yards from the scene, he was pissed. What he saw in the passenger compartment broke his heart and brought back memories of Carmel and Kate. The woman's chest had been crushed by the steering wheel and blood smeared her face and clotted her hair. He briefly looked past her at the young girl in the passenger seat. She had her seat belt on at least but a branch from the tree that eventually stopped the forward progress of the van had come through the broken windshield and pierced her neck, again, there was a lot of blood.

Danny had no way of knowing that they were both technically dead and probably past the point where medics could have saved them. He also didn't know that these two were mother and daughter but he could have guessed that. The Healer used his powers to slowly remove the branch from the girl's neck and then reached across her mother and clamped his hand on the gaping hole. Bethany Sinclair was seven years old when she died, which only lasted three minutes before her life was restored and her body put back together. Her mother Tiffany died four minutes before her little girl but would be there to celebrate Beth's eighth birthday.

The Healer stayed until they were both conscious and aware of what had happened, as far as the accident went. He didn't tell them about the post-crash events and left right after Tiffany used her cell phone to call 911. He asked the ladies to keep him out of their versions of the incident to the police and then he continued south and didn't stop until he crossed over into Mexico.

Karen Ayala didn't become a very good reporter by sitting on her hands, or by giving up on a story. The research she was doing wasn't exactly something that would be aired, but she was directly involved, so she used her position to gather information. On most days she was still at her desk late into the evening, pouring over the teletypes from various news services and searching the internet for any article that could remotely have to do with the location of one Daniel Warburton. She also had many of her contacts from around the country looking for her. A couple of thin possibilities turned up over the summer months. She went personally to check them out, but they turned out to be false alarms. Franti knew of her efforts and called her from time to time, but it was more to check on her than on her progress.

"Listen sweetheart, I want you to throttle back a bit. I get reports that you're not taking care of yourself, not eating or sleeping well. Two attempts on a person's life in such a short time take a toll. Danny probably just needs some time, he'll be back."

"What else can I do, Michael? I love him. He could be out there, not knowing who he is, still suffering from brain damage, alone and scared, how could I stop looking?"

"I know, but promise me you will look after Karen as well?"

"I promise."

She hung up and went back to her computer screen.

And then one evening she came across an article from a Houston Texas newspaper about two accident victims that were found in their heavily damaged car with the driver's door fifty yards away and evidence that the door was torn from its hinges. The passengers, a mother and daughter, were covered in blood but didn't have any injuries. A county sheriff who was at the scene and interviewed by the paper said he could not believe that, based on the amount and type of damage to the vehicle, and the presence of that much blood, that neither of the occupants were hurt at all.

Karen's palms were sweating as she scrolled up to find the article was printed five days ago and the accident was seven days in the past. She was on a flight to Houston the next morning, tracking down the two accident victims.

The Sinclairs were being evasive, and Karen picked up on it immediately. She tried to explain to them that if they had received help from someone, she was a friend of that person and was worried about him. She thought she almost had the young girl ready to open up, but her mom abruptly ended the conversation and asked Karen to leave.

Even though she knew something was up with the accident victims, she didn't know where to go from there so she went back to the airport to fly home. At the terminal she was on her laptop and received a phone call from a reporter friend who worked at the *Arizona Republic News* out of Phoenix. The reporter told Karen about a story on the internet that came out of Monterrey, Mexico. The source was from a blog and spoke of an incident in that town where a young boy fell from a third story window of his apartment and suffered from compound fractures to his leg and broken ribs that had punctured one of his lungs. The boy's mother said a gringo angel healed her son in seconds and then disappeared. Karen asked her contact to send her an email with a link to the blog. While she waited for the email, Karen called up a map of Mexico on her computer and found what she already suspected, Monterrey was only 500 miles from Houston, too close to be a coincidence. She rented a car and drove the seven hours to that Mexican town. It took her another day to locate the boy and his mother, who openly wept and thanked God for sending the angel to save her son. The boy, on the other hand, didn't want to say anything and downplayed his injuries. He also tried to keep his mother from saying too much but wasn't having any luck.

Karen decided to fly to Connecticut, and her heart beat double time the entire way there. She landed late that night and got a room at one of the airport hotels but was up early and headed for the New Britain Police Department. Captain Franti came out to meet her in the lobby of the Detective Bureau and showed her to his office. Once she was seated, everything came spilling out faster than she'd intended.

"I spoke to two women in Texas who were healed after a horrible accident. They said they didn't know how it happened but they were lying to me. That was ten days ago. A week after that, a little boy in Mexico falls out of a window and breaks several bones. His mother told me an angel in the form of a white man who was walking by fixed all of her son's injuries. The boy is evasive and hiding the truth, like the accident victims. I know it's him, Michael, I can feel it deep down. I'm quitting my job and going to Mexico to search for Danny."

"And you came all this way just to tell me in person. Weren't you already in Mexico?"

"I came to ask for help."

The Captain put one finger up in a "wait a second" gesture, picked up the desk phone, and dialed a number. Karen only heard one side of the conversation.

"His lady friend has a lead, you in?"

"No, Mexico."

"Ok, I'll let you know when and where."

Franti hung up the phone and looked at Karen. "You go home and pack. Myself and Carlos Cintron will come down to Atlanta, and we will all go down to Mexico and see what we can find."

"I was going to go to Philly and get Danny's RV. I thought that would be easier to travel around in instead of always going to some airport or renting cars."

"That sounds good. We will meet you at your apartment in three days. Karen, we will find him, if he wants to be found."

As she wiped away the tears, she thanked the big man.

The next morning, the sun came up on a lone figure walking on a dusty road outside a small village in central Mexico. In Philadelphia, Pennsylvania, a woman was learning how to drive an RV as she turned onto the ramp for I-95 south. In the darkness of space, two beings from another planet were in their ship that could travel across galaxies, yet they weren't going anywhere, and remained hidden behind the moon. Life went on, not only for those we have met here, but for all creatures on this, and every other world, so can we really say that this is...

THE END?

CPSIA information can be obtained at www.ICGtesting.com
Printed in the USA
BVOW09s1749190715

409451BV00003B/10/P

9 781457 539701